THE TEA LORDS

THE TEA LORDS

Hella S. Haasse

Translated from the Dutch
by Ina Rilke

BOOKS

Published by Portobello Books Ltd 2010

Portobello Books Ltd
12 Addison Avenue
London
W11 4QR

First published in Dutch in 1992 as *Heren van de thee*
by Querido, Amsterdam, Netherlands.

The publication of this work has been made possible by financial support from the Dutch Foundation for Literature.

A CIP catalogue record is available from the British Library

2 4 6 8 9 7 5 3 1

ISBN 978 1 84627 289 9 (trade paperback)
ISBN 978 1 84627 103 8 (hardback)

Text designed and typeset in Sabon by Patty Rennie

Printed in the UK by CPI William Clowes Beccles NR34 7TL

For W. H. J. Haasse, Wim, my brother

You say: those letters have no historical value. Maybe so. But the fact remains that younger generations are often better served by the 'side-lights', which offer a much clearer picture of the conditions prevailing at the time, and especially of the mentality of those days, than for instance lists of figures. The family businesses are no more, but we can bring the people to life again by reading about their thoughts and feelings.

Bertha de Rijck van der Gracht-Kerkhoven
to her brother Karel Kerkhoven, 1959

Un ouvrage de fiction mélange à sa guise le vrai et le faux, le vécu, le retranscrit, l'imaginaire, la biographie.

Philippe Labro

Contents

GAMBOENG, THE FIRST DAY

1 January 1873

'Here!' he cried out loud. His voice sounded thin in the vastness.

He was standing on the edge of a ravine. The nearby peaks were wreathed in afternoon mist. These were the foothills of the Goenoeng Tiloe: deep folds in the earth's crust, a drapery of dense, vivid green covering a gigantic, recumbent body. Between the rugged flanks lay a bowl-shaped valley.

It was there, in the embrace of the jungle, that he would make his home. He had reached the place where the entire, as yet unlived reality of his life awaited him.

'I think I can do it,' he had told his father after their initial excursion to Gamboeng six months previously. His father had listed all the disadvantages of taking a lease on this particular tract of land: the climate would be too wet for a good coffee yield; the old government plantation had run wild; the pathways were overgrown; the terrain was too uneven, with steep slopes and nigh impenetrable swathes of jungle; it was too isolated, so transportation of produce would present enormous difficulties. Besides, would there be sufficient labour to be found on the sparsely populated mountainsides?

But it was at that first moment – the sweeping view! the green lustre of myriad treetops! – that he had set his heart on Gamboeng. There was no alternative, so far as he was concerned. He could see it would be necessary to refurbish the entire plantation, most likely even to uproot all the old stock and plant anew, but he was undaunted. It was a challenge. If things did not work out with coffee, he would switch to tea, of which he had garnered a fair amount of knowledge during his year's apprenticeship.

So his father had put in an application for long-lease tenure. Confirmation from the government was long in coming, as the inspection committee had yet to assess the terrain. He was resigned to this: he knew the wheels of bureaucracy turned slowly. But in the meantime he would go ahead, he would start preparing for planting the land where he had chosen to live and work. Fertile land: the topsoil, two to three feet deep, was soft and crumbly, clay mixed with volcanic grit.

He dismounted, bent down and scooped up a handful of the moist, dark-red earth.

Looking back, he saw a small crowd had gathered around his two servants, Moentajas and Djengot, who were waiting for him with the horses and the coolies he had hired in the plain. He had left his luggage stacked up by the grove of bamboo screening the small kampong of Gamboeng, home to no more than seven or eight families. That was all that remained of the initial band of workers who had exchanged life in the *desa* for the coffee plantations up the mountain. When the villagers realised he was watching, they sank down on their haunches. The headman gave the traditional salutation, calling him *djoeragan*, landlord. He replied in the Soendanese vernacular, in which he had become reasonably fluent. On the way there he had prepared a short speech, appealing for their trust and cooperation. Not one of them met his gaze – that would have been disrespectful – but he took their silence to mean they were compliant.

The people of Gamboeng were of a sturdier build and less finely featured than the workers he had known on the plantations in the Buitenzorg region. They also seemed less forthcoming. He knew their attitude would be of paramount importance. If they proved reluctant to work on his plantation, or unwilling to accept freshly recruited field-hands in their midst, he would be in trouble. Their spokesman made a calm, reasonable impression. That was the man he would look to for help in finding the right tone and approach.

But first the lands. He couldn't wait to explore. Entrusting his dapple mare Odaliske, steaming after the steep bridle-track, to the care of Moentajas, he and Djengot made their way downhill on foot, towards the valley where he envisaged building a house. The rain clouds of the western monsoon burgeoned over the mountain peaks; the air was heavy with moisture. Around the edges of a clearing stood pencil-straight trees with shiny trunks and scarlet blossoms, towering high over the dark jungle beyond.

Having his rifle with him gave him the confidence to venture into the wilderness. Djengot took the lead, slashing a path through the dense undergrowth as he went. There was no sign of wild animals, nor were there any fresh tracks, only the deep, carved grooves signalling regular passage, but the lofty trees were alive with the crackle of twigs and creaking of branches. A shower of fruit pips and scraps of rind came down, and through a break in the trees they spied a swaying progress of grey, white-bellied monkeys, screeching with curiosity as they leaped from one bough to the next.

He peered intently all about him, and at length found what he was looking for: the old water course along the bed of one of the clefts dividing the terrain. They could hear the rush of a waterfall in the depths of the rainforest, and pressed on in the direction of the sound until they came upon a fast-flowing stream, the broadest they had yet encountered. This had to be the Tjisondari; the opposite bank was steep, and looked to him like the natural limit of the territory. But Djengot, who knew the area, said this was not the case. They followed the Tjisondari upstream to a place where they could cross to the other side by wading and jumping from stone to stone. And there he duly discovered several old, neglected gardens whose existence he had not imagined, and several more-or-less open spaces which seemed suitable for reclamation.

He was eager to climb to the top of the Goenoeng Tiloe, to try to see for himself the extent of his lands. He still had no idea how to chart the boundaries of the coffee fields dotted over the mountain. Land surveying would be one of the first tasks he would have to undertake, but he needed expert assistance. It was almost impossible to gauge the total area of the parcels of land between the countless ravines, which were useless for planting.

Djengot was quicker than he to catch the sound of thunder rumbling in the distance. Although it was not yet three in the afternoon, night fell in the jungle. The sky, glimpsed through a parting in the canopy, was pitch-black. They stumbled and slithered downhill through the wilderness – he could hear the fabric of his jacket tearing – and broke into a run when they reached the open fields, but they were overtaken by the lashing rain. Bolts of lightning fractured the sky, striking them deaf and blind.

His father had ordered a *pondok* to be erected for him just outside the kampong – two cubicles and a modest front room with a floor made of planks, walls of woven bamboo, and a roof of palm fibre. Enough to contain the bare essentials: a couch, a table and chairs, a store-cupboard. It was where he intended to make his home while he set up his enterprise.

When the thunderstorm had drifted away, he went outside to sit on the front steps. The sky was now as clear as glass, and in the late-afternoon light the countless flecks of green on the Goenoeng Tiloe seemed to have been daubed with a paintbrush.

He took off his shoes and socks. It was just as he feared: on the last lap of their expedition, leeches had crept under his felt gaiters to gorge themselves on his calves. His elation was undiminished.

'Wretches,' he muttered. He pulled them loose one by one with care, causing thin trickles of blood to run down his legs. He motioned to Djengot, who was unpacking, to pass him the first aid kit. Poultice dressings aplenty.

It occurred to him that he had not eaten all day, except for a slice of bread and some fruit on the way to Gamboeng early that morning. He could hear someone bustling about in the kitchen area; it was Moentajas, who, although not a cook by trade, had offered to prepare him a meal.

'*Sedia*?' he called over his shoulder. 'Is the food ready?'

'*Mangkè*, in a moment,' replied Moentajas in a nasal singsong.

The meal consisted of chicken stew, for which they had brought the ingredients themselves. Spicier aromas wafted towards him from behind the house, telling him that Moentajas and Djengot would be dining on the kind of native dish he still had difficulty getting used to.

Shafts of moonlight pierced the wall of woven bamboo, casting diffuse patterns on the floor and on his coverlet. He lay on his back listening to the sounds of the night, the humming and rustling outside, the distant cries in the jungle. He hoped the horses were safe in their improvised stable. After dark, so he had been told, panthers were on the prowl, even within the fence around the kampong. People kept their dogs, chickens and goats inside at night. He resolved to deal with the predators as soon as his other tasks allowed him the time.

Finding it impossible to sleep, he cast his mind back to what he had to do in the coming days. He had no doubt the adventure he was embarking on would demand the utmost fortitude and perseverance. No planter in the family had ever been faced with restoring a plantation that had fallen into such disarray.

Besides charting the terrain there were other priorities, such as building a bridge across the Tjisondari, as the fordable part was too far up, and restoring the old coffee plantings, as well as laying out a specimen tea garden. He would have to find workmen to clear the weed-infested fields and pathways. He also wanted to have the porous walls of his dwelling plastered and whitewashed, and to set up a daily messenger service between Gamboeng and his parents' estate, some hours away, so that he would be assured of news, tools and food. The latter was not plentiful in the kampong; he had already noticed the locals were not keen to sell their chickens.

At long last he drifted into sleep. He was awakened by a cock crowing. It was daybreak. He took a chair outside and watched in breathless wonder as the sun rose above the horizon and set the distant clouds on fire. The mountain tops seemed to have been drawn in ink on the sky. Sparkling swathes of mist drifted down the valley, curling around the trunks of the towering rasamala trees. The jungle resounded with the cries and whistles of thousands of birds. Clear voices could be heard by the clattering stream at the bathing place. There was a scent of wood fires in the morning air.

Djengot emerged from behind the bamboo thicket with a cloth round his shoulders against the chilly breeze, followed by a seven-year-old boy leading the dapple horse by a rope.

'His name is Djapan,' Djengot said. 'He can be our look-out. He is not afraid. *Djoeragan* can see for himself.'

Astonished, and a trifle disconcerted, he watched as his temperamental mare allowed herself to be patted on the flanks by a complete stranger, a mere child half her height. He thought it premature of Djengot to take on a stable-boy, but, on the other hand, the lad would come in useful. Djengot himself could not be missed during land surveying, and Moentajas had more important things to do than take care of the horses.

'There, there,' he said, running his fingers along Odaliske's cheeks. 'Be a good girl, now. No biting, mind! And don't run away!'

Moentajas brought him coffee, which he drank slowly. The sun was rising fast, but it was still cool. Fringing the ravine were bushes he had never seen before with white, trumpet-shaped flowers like lilies. The scenery confronting him, the fresh day, his sheer existence, all was bathed in the glow of morning.

He was twenty-four years old, and for the first time in his life he was his own man, his own master. Everything he had experienced until then was merely preparation for this moment. He stretched his arms, flung them wide. Eldorado!

SCENES OF PREPARATION

1869–73

Having unpacked his books and ranged them on the shelves, he pushed the table up close to the window. He was beginning to like the look of his new room. The furniture was simple, somewhat the worse for wear due to past contingents of student lodgers, but well kept nonetheless, and it blended quite pleasantly with the various objects he had brought from home. He had slept exceedingly well in the old-fashioned cupboard bed, though he would have preferred a proper bedstead. The landlord and his wife seemed helpful and tidy; his hot water for shaving had been brought punctually to his door.

While he was dressing he looked about him to see what else he could change in the room to make it more his own. Suspended over the chest of drawers was an oval mirror. He lifted it off, and, with the heel of his shoe, hammered the nail into the wall a handbreadth lower down. This way he could see himself in the mirror without going up on his toes. He saw: bright eyes beneath a broad, high forehead; a straight nose; and a mouth with lips that were still boyishly plump. His hair was fine and dark blond, already thinning around the parting. There was a hint of complacency in his expression, which bothered him, because that was not how he felt.

'Rudolf Eduard Kerkhoven!' he intoned to his reflection, as though introducing himself to a stranger. He thought he looked too young for his twenty-one years, a milk-sop. Should he grow a moustache? He passed the black bootlace tie under his collar and tied the ends in a bow.

Standing by the window overlooking the market square, deserted on a Sunday, he re-read the letter he had received from the Indies. It was from his father, informing him of his success, after endless formalities, in securing a twenty-year lease on a tract of land for the establishment of a tea plantation. There were approximately three hundred hectares of wild terrain, traditionally the hunting lands of the local chiefs. Clearance was already well underway, and the plantation had also been given a name: Ardjasari, which in Soendanese meant Fragrant Good Fortune.

In previous letters Rudolf had read about his father's expeditions in search of suitable land in the largely unexplored region south of Bandoeng, the Preanger highlands. He was touched by his father's habit of interspersing his news of the family and business affairs with evocations of the extraordinary diversity and lushness of the landscape. He knew his own future lay there, too. The day he completed his studies in Delft he would pack his bags and go. The prospect of saying goodbye to everyone and spending several months at sea was already making him restless, giving him a sense of detachment, of belonging neither here nor there. This feeling would not go away until he reached his destination.

Java was a constant in the life of his family. His parents had settled there two years previously, in the wake of several of their kinfolk during the past decades. He remembered family gatherings in the old days at Hunderen, the country house his Kerkhoven grandparents owned in Twello, where the 'colonists' were ever in evidence. There were prominently displayed albums with photographs of them all posing before white-columned verandas, or on avenues lined with exotic trees, wearing the blank, staring look of people having to keep very still for a long time. Gifts from overseas – hunting trophies: wild buffalo horns, a panther skin! – graced the walls amid old-world seascapes and plates of Delft blue. There was a sense of unabating concern for their welfare, as though they were there in the flesh, occupying their rightful places in the gatherings at Hunderen, side by side with the bearded and moustached Kerkhoven men, the Van der Huchts, Bosschas, Holles, and with the primly coiffured women and girls in their voluminous skirts: Pauline, Cecilia and Octavia, Ida, Caroline, Albertine, Sophie and Cateau, whose high-necked blouses were adorned with gold brooches containing artfully plaited locks of hair belonging to faraway loved ones. At the table the names of the relations overseas cropped up time and again, and there was always some lengthy epistle to be read out, by the fireside in the salon in winter, or out in the garden under the trees in the summer months. The children of all those families grew up in the awareness that their world extended far beyond the Equator.

From a young age Rudolf, like the others, was conscious of the great family adventure that had taken place in 1843, an undertaking without precedent in the history of relations between Holland and the East Indies. In that year, a party of no fewer than thirty-three members of their family had embarked for the colonies. After a long delay due to bad weather, the three-masters *Anna Paulowna* and *Jacob Roggeveen* had finally, in the month of May, set sail through the Nieuwe Diep and out to the open sea. The pilot ship returned with a final message: the passengers were setting out for the other side of the world full of hope and good spirits. In September of that year they had, thank God, dropped anchor in the roadstead of Batavia, safe and sound.

A fair number of loved ones had since lost their lives overseas. Rudolf, too, had suffered a loss. It was a year since the death of his little sister, the youngest of the children to accompany his parents to the Indies. Pauline, born with deformed hands and feet, had always been a source of worry. In his view her death was caused by congenital defects, and might be seen as a blessing in disguise. He had mentioned this to the grieving relations, meaning to offer words of condolence. To his surprise, they called him insensitive.

'Rudolf is harsh,' was the general opinion. He was informed of this by Julius, his younger brother, who was at boarding school in Deventer and a frequent Sunday afternoon guest at relatives living nearby. Julius had passed on the criticism in a tone that betrayed his endorsement of it. He had promised his parents to accept Rudolf's authority, but often felt his brother was too strict, and resented his interference. At sixteen, Julius was highly impressionable and easily upset. Although by no means unintelligent, he found it hard to concentrate on his schoolwork. Rudolf took it upon himself to correct his brother's presumed laziness or otherwise inept behaviour. He would put on a paternal air and quote a passage from one of their father's letters: 'the prospect of having you join us afterwards, of having a pair of stalwart assistants standing by me . . . *unspoilt*, *good* boys . . . that is a wonderful, heartening thought for me.'

It was on account of such expectations that Rudolf demanded of his brother the degree of discipline he imposed on himself. He was certain he was not harsh. It pained him that his endeavour to act as a responsible adult met with so little appreciation.

There was a knock at the door.

'Sir! Your breakfast.'

Rudolf opened the door. His landlady came in bearing a tray, and with it a whiff of her haberdashery downstairs, a smell of textile and starch that was familiar to him from the linen cupboard at home. Her eyes beneath her mob-cap registered at once that the furniture had been rearranged.

'Oh, sir, Van der Drift could easily have fixed the height of that mirror for you. Our last gentleman was a fair bit taller than you.'

She spread a napkin over the table and set out bread and coffee. Her glance shot from his stockinged feet to the soiled clothes he had thrown into a corner.

'Van der Drift will keep your boots polished, sir, and I will take care of your laundry. We see to everything, except for your hot meals. Can't do that, I'm afraid, not with the shop.'

Rudolf had heard this before from her sallow-faced, coughing husband, when he first rented the room.

'That's all right; I shall be having my meals at a friend's lodging house,' he said tersely. He watched with some dismay as Mistress Van der Drift began to gather up his shirts and underclothes. Two maiden aunts of his in The Hague had promised several months ago to see to his mending, but he had still not taken them up on the offer. He was keenly aware that the state of one's underclothes could ruin one's reputation under these circumstances, and he could tell by his landlady's expression that deficiencies such as missing buttons and frayed hems had not escaped her notice. A subtle change came over her. Briskly deferential at first, her face now took on the expression which Rudolf had heard people praise as the trademark of the ideal landlady, but of which he had no personal experience as yet. He knew what it meant, though: she had adopted him.

'Don't you want to light the stove? It's October, too cold to sit and study without a fire.'

'No need, I shall be away all day.'

'Exam-time coming, is it? May I ask what your line of study is?'

'Civil engineering. I will be finished in June next year,' said Rudolf, trying to impress on her that despite his boyish appearance and slight stature of 1.70 m, he was a man who knew his own mind.

'Sounds good. And then what?'

'Then I shall go out to the Indies.'

She made no comment, merely fixed him with her gaze. This was the cue for him to tell her more about himself and thus build up some kind of familiar rapport. But he was not sure that was what he wanted. From earliest childhood he had regarded the maids and gardeners at home and at Hunderen as fixtures of his parents' and grandparents' lives. They belonged to a feudal world where class differences were self-evident and functional, and by no means detrimental to mutual trust. The ease with which the adults in his family maintained a tone of jovial authority, without sinking to over-familiarity, was an example to him. Only when he had found the right tone would he be ready to take on the tasks awaiting him in Java as right-hand man to his father, among people with whom – so he kept being reminded – a strict division of rank and reciprocal duties was essential. If he gave in now to easy-going placidity, which was his inclination by nature and circumstance, he might not be able to summon the requisite tone of authority later on.

With his previous two landladies, the one dull-witted and coarse and the other annoyingly servile, it had been easy for him to appear self-possessed. To his own surprise he had frequently managed to address them in the curt, commanding tones he deplored in his fellow students; like them, he had berated the 'scum' for any clumsiness or laxity in their ministrations. In short, his treatment of the lower orders had been no different from that of any other young man of his class. Clearly, the short, sharp-eyed woman now standing before him would not stand for such behaviour. She knew better than he did what was appropriate in their relationship and what was not. At this point it was up to him to convey to her in a few friendly words that he had no further questions or instructions, but that he would be stopping to chat with her some other time. His awkwardness did not escape her.

'Now do drink your coffee, sir, before it goes cold.'

She made a bundle of his laundry and left him to himself.

Rudolf was ashamed of his lack of savoir-faire. The brief exchange with Mistress Van der Drift had left him with the same sense of discomfort he had experienced on so many other occasions since he had come of age. It was a problem he could not discuss with anyone. He was eager to be appreciated, indeed, to please, but he often had the impression he was not really well-liked. It was as though he put people off, whereas, deep down, he yearned for human contact. Once his parents had left, he found himself beset by contradictory feelings whenever he was obliged to deal with agencies or individuals in his own right. Being the eldest son, and in a sense also *in loco parentis* to his brother, he counted on recognition for his efforts to behave in a more serious, sensible fashion than was normally expected of a young man. He tried his best to adhere to the codes of propriety instilled in him from the nursery onwards throughout his boyhood in his parents' circle of notables in Deventer. Did that make him appear stiff and provincial? When visiting relations in Amsterdam or The Hague, where etiquette was more relaxed than where he came from, he felt awkward if he was not formally presented to people he had not met before (as if he were a mere child, or an intruder!). Without being introduced he did not feel at liberty to join in the conversation, so he just sat there twiddling his thumbs. Was there any truth in what Julius had said about people thinking him an opinionated prig?

It wasn't his fault that he felt compelled to speak out when he considered other people's opinions and actions to be unfair or simply wrong. He had been confirmed and accepted as a member of the Mennonite community in Deventer, but that did not mean he would keep his counsel when confronted with hypocrisy or arrogance on the part of his brothers in the faith. On days of royal celebration he refused to wear an orange ribbon, much to everyone's disapproval, because he thought King Willem III a worthless bounder. He pinned on a tricolour ribbon instead, in homage to his Patriot forebears, and bore the consequences (disparaging remarks, outright hostility in the street) with stoical resignation.

Having grown up in a family where going to church was a matter of personal choice, he was vehemently opposed to Julius being obliged to attend Sunday service at boarding school. He protested about this to the headmaster, whose response was that any objections of that nature would have to be raised by Julius's father, not his brother. Rudolf argued that Julius, being a slow learner, was taking his schoolbooks to church on the sly, because he knew he wouldn't be allowed out on the Sunday afternoon until his homework was finished, but his effort to intervene on his brother's behalf backfired. Julius was furious about being 'betrayed': 'Tell-tale! Know-it-all! Fuss-pot!' The family thought him meddlesome.

Rudolf regarded women, or rather ladies, as creatures of a superior rank, handmaidens of refinement and good morals, in whose presence the kind of banter students indulged in would be inappropriate. He was frequently smitten, from afar, by a pretty face poring over a piece of sewing, or by a graceful, serene figure at a piano or tea table. What these adored creatures might think of him (they never seemed to show much interest) was a source of harrowing uncertainty. What was he doing wrong? What did he lack? He battled with such feelings from day to day. When people whose company he sought, or whom he esteemed, responded to him with indifference, he would feel mortified for days afterwards. And now he was afraid that Mistress Van der Drift thought him a stuck-up cad, no better than all those other students whom he himself found so objectionable.

He opened the top drawer of his cabinet and took out the photograph he had recently received from his parents. It had been taken when the family were still in Batavia, before travelling to Bandoeng, where they would stay until such time as their new home on the plantation was ready for them.

The photograph showed the family posing together on the veranda, with two female servants in attendance. His mother and sisters, like the servants, were in native dress: a long white blouse worn over a length of striped or floral cotton wrapped round the hips. Bertha and Cateau both had their hair down. Their mother's face was mask-like, strangely blotchy, as if her skin was flaking. His father was not facing the camera, but half-leaning over the balustrade, gazing down at the youngest, August, who stood a little to the side, with a blank look on his small face. Only Cateau's guileless, girlish appearance was unchanged. Poor little Pauline was not in the picture: she must have died before it was taken. There was a touch of drabness and neglect about the look of his family, as there was about the empty depths of the veranda beyond. These were not the same people he had waved goodbye to on the pier. If only he could pluck them from the image, and whisper words of encouragement in their ears!

He reminded himself that the photograph was over six months old, and that by now, in the cooler climate of the Preanger highlands, they would all be in far better form, eagerly preparing for their new life on the plantation and looking rather more like the studio portraits they had handed out as souvenirs on departure. Those portraits now stood in their frames on the table before him. He took them in his hands one by one.

As always, he was struck by the dignified, worthy appearance of his father: the high forehead, the mild frankness of his gaze. Mr R. Kerkhoven senior sat on a carved seat in a relaxed pose, his right arm resting on the table, a pair of kid gloves in his left hand. The full beard and moustache, dark blonde in reality, looked quite black. To Rudolf, it was perfectly understandable why his high-minded father had become disillusioned by his various occupations in Holland – the law practice in Deventer, the peat-cutting works in Dedemsvaart, his stint as inspector of primary schools in Overijssel; even during his time as a member of the States-Provincial he had been thwarted in his ambition to contribute to social progress and popular development. Concern for public service was a family tradition, of which Rudolf was proud. His own great-uncle, Jan Pieter van der Hucht, who had been in charge of the party of kinfolk embarking in 1845, had even published a pamphlet titled 'In Praise of Dutch Colonisation of Java', explaining their motives before setting out, chief among them being to alleviate unemployment at home and to further the material and spiritual well-being of the population overseas. And then there was Engelbertus de Waal, a cousin by marriage, who, after a career in the Indies, was now Minister for the Colonies and a champion of the reform of agrarian legislation in Java.

The 'colonists' had shown they had been right to try their luck overseas. What had once been criticised as wayward and reckless behaviour now harvested praise, given that their venture appeared to be successful. Two Holle cousins and one of the Kerkhoven uncles had taken over the lease of a tea estate from Great-uncle Willem van der Hucht, the last survivor of the pioneer generation of planters, and were doing rather well for themselves in the Buitenzorg region. Not for a moment did Rudolf doubt that his father would likewise succeed in making Ardjasari flourish – all the world drank tea, after all. Nor did he doubt that he and his brothers would carry on their father's work when the time came.

His mother's portrait, on closer inspection, bemused him. He still found her eyes beautiful, but he thought he detected in the cast of her lips the first signs of the sad, almost pinched look she had in the Batavian photograph. His father had mentioned her headaches in his letters, and also that she suffered from 'a nervous condition'. The relatives in Overijssel had the impression that both Bertha and Cateau were as good as engaged – people in the Indies did not seem to set as much store by the conventions pertaining to girls going out in society as they did in Holland. The girls often visited the homes of other families, and Rudolf had been startled to hear of his sisters spending several days with a family living just outside Batavia, where they had gone off with the daughters of the house to roam through the rice fields in their bare feet, and had bathed in a river wrapped in nothing but a native cloth! How did his mother react to that kind of unconventional behaviour? Wouldn't she be concerned about allowing standards to slip?

Eldorado: that was what he had called Hunderen, his Kerkhoven grandparents' country house in Twello, from the time he first learned the meaning of the magical word as a small boy. Eldorado: tall, rustling trees; banks of rhododendron; lawns fringed with dense shrubbery; woods with winding lanes offering glimpses of fields and meadows beyond. An Eldorado indoors, too: the rambling house with entresol rooms, alcoves, secret passages, spiral staircases and deep cupboards, and a vast attic full of nooks to hide in under the rafters. Hunderen spelled freedom to him, a private world of his own in which to lose himself during the long summer holidays spent with his sisters and cousins. When the property had to be sold after the death of his grandparents – he was twelve years old – he was inconsolable. The irremediable loss of Hunderen coincided, for him, with the end of his childhood. Never a playful lad, his entrance into secondary school at Deventer meant that life had begun in earnest.

The way his grandparents had conducted their lives continued to set the standard for the entire family; solid but broad-minded, mild and humorous, but intolerant of bad manners. He recalled his grandmother, invariably in dark, bell-shaped gowns and her grey hair in ringlets beneath a bonnet with long ribbons on either side, as the epitome of calm and restfulness. She rarely left Hunderen, where her favourite quarters were the small sitting room where she kept her sewing table, the scullery with all the paraphernalia for making jam and preserves, and out in the garden an arbour like a green, upturned basket.

Grandmother Kerkhoven's pet name for her husband was 'Kirkie', and the children pealed with laugher each time they heard their dignified grandfather addressed with such apparent irreverence. Although retired, he led a very active life, quite unlike that of his wife, and was frequently away on tours of inspection of his properties in the north of the country or visiting his former associates in the family firm of Kerkhoven & Co., stockbrokers in Amsterdam. When he was at home in Hunderen, occupied at his writing table, he never showed displeasure at the intrusions of frolicsome grandchildren or visitors, of whom there were many. He was always willing to show off his cabinet of curiosities, and would tirelessly pull out drawers and open boxes to display his collections of sea shells and insects on pins. Rudolf had particularly enjoyed being shown the world atlas compiled by Ortelius in the sixteenth century, and the telescope designed by the great German scientist and inventor Fraunhofer. Nothing held more fascination for him than these two heirlooms: the plates showing continents and oceans (not very truthfully, his grandfather emphasised, yet testifying to extraordinary powers of observation), and the metal rings and artfully polished lenses, which enabled one to see the remotest objects, like stars and planets, up close.

His grandmother's forte was story-telling. Rudolf felt that her narrative gift had something to do with the quietness of her daily life, and with her overriding, passionate interest in her kinfolk. He could recall her stories almost verbatim; he had been more enchanted by them than by the magic lantern shows. There was the story about an ancestor in the previous century, an extremely rich man who kept his fortune in gold and precious stones hidden at home, but who died without revealing the hiding place. So the heirs searched high and low, taking up floorboards and seeking out cavities behind bricks in the walls, and in so doing stripped the house bare – all to no avail. In the end they sold the house, only to find that the new owners suddenly became inexplicably rich. The moral of the tale, which grandmother Kerkhoven never failed to supply, was that there was no point in reckoning on future inheritances, or in counting chickens before they hatched. People should be frugal and work hard to build a good life for themselves and their families, and such wealth as they might possess needed to be treated with due care.

Another story revolved around their grandfather's courtship of her, the lovely Antje van der Hucht. He had first seen her in a box at Amsterdam's city theatre, and after the performance had run after her carriage in the hope of finding out where she lived. When the vehicle passed the city limit at Haarlemmerpoort he had, sadly, been obliged to give up. The love-struck young man's desperate attempts to garner information about her led to the discovery that the man he believed to be her father was a manufacturer of lace-working thread in Haarlem. To gain admittance to the man's office, and ultimately to his home, he had started a small business in those goods himself, without success. It was not until much later that they had been brought together by sheer coincidence. She turned out to be the sister of someone he knew at university, whom he had not met earlier at his home because she was boarding with a family in Haarlem at the time.

The story of that courtship had struck a chord with Rudolf. That was how he imagined true love to be: the sure knowledge at first sight of having found the love of one's life – coupled with the determination and willpower to wait for years if necessary. The affinity between husband, wife and children seemed to him to be the only form of commitment worth forfeiting one's personal freedom for; indeed, it might even be a prerequisite for true independence. He could not see why anyone should think him 'too old for his years' simply because he took such matters seriously. It was the natural course of things. One day – he hoped and trusted – he would meet the person who was destined for him, just as he would be destined for her, and until that day arrived he would exercise patience and self-discipline, however hard it might be to resist temptation.

He had gained more self-control since the day he realised that it fell to him to set a good example for Julius in these matters. Using strong language was beneath his dignity, and the idea of visiting a prostitute filled him with dread and disgust, so it was no hardship for him to stay well away from these transgressions. But there was another temptation lying in wait, to which he was no stranger himself and which he knew Julius did not resist with sufficient fortitude. He did not believe that self-gratification was the cause of terrible disease, but there was something shameful about such secret, solitary practices. There was no real freedom to be had from them anyway. He had ceased giving in to the urge, however strong at times, since his discovery, through an incident at Julius' boarding school, that the bad habit was rife in that institution. He thought it was probably the cause of his younger brother's pallor and general indolence. How could he ever persuade Julius of the good of self-discipline if he was unable to control his own instincts?

He knew how embarrassed and angry he made Julius with his admonitions, but he firmly believed he was only doing his duty.

He even tried to let his parents know (in discreet terms, because his sisters would be reading the letter as well). Since neither Bertha nor Cateau would have the slightest idea of the problems confronting a young man, he alluded, as though in passing, to the *profound* and *beneficial* influence girls sometimes had on other people, in the hope of their intuiting his meaning.

Favourite among the stories the children listened to at Hunderen was the one about Great-uncle Guillaume van der Hucht (the forename harked back to the days of French rule). He was a figure of almost mythic proportions. At the age of fourteen he went to sea – to spare his widowed mother, an impoverished gentlewoman, the expense of his upkeep – as a ship's boy on a merchant vessel. Life as the youngest crew member and general dogsbody was harsh, but Willem, as he was now known, was undaunted. On the contrary! He relished the challenge, spending such little spare time as he had in the crow's nest with handbooks on seamanship, thus preparing himself for the examinations for third, second and first mate, which he went on to pass in steady succession. After several years the captain died in mid-voyage. Willem, who had gained the respect of all the crew, took over. In his later years he sailed the seven seas on his own merchant ship, the Sara Johanna, and did well for himself. His last voyage as captain took him to Java.

In those days Dutch colonial policy in the Indies was aimed at the expansion of the cultivation of tea, and new contractors for government-owned plantations were being sought. Willem proved himself an astute entrepreneur. He invested his money in tea plantations already leased by several friends and relatives in Java. Through his mother, née Baroness van Wijnbergen, he descended from a line of great soldiers and keen huntsmen. He would have liked nothing better than to pass those traditions on to his sons, but his only children were daughters, only one of whom survived. After the death of his wife he married an English woman many years his junior, who proved to be neither a friend nor a mentor to his motherless little girl, Mientje. The best he could do for her was to marry her off with a fine dowry. Thenceforward he lavished his fatherly attentions on the sons of his brother and sisters, who had in the meantime also come out to the Indies. He was the undisputed head of the clan: his word was law.

Besides the family sagas about the heroic exploits of Great-uncle Van der Hucht, Rudolf had also heard him being censured for his overbearing attitude towards his relatives upon his return from the Indies in later life, by which time he had amassed a tidy fortune. He had taken up residence on a country estate in the Kennemer dunes. He was a Member of Parliament, where he was regarded as an expert on colonial affairs, and continued to keep a watchful eye on the doings of his long-since grown-up and independent nephews in the Indies, whom he had helped into the saddle when they were young. Rudolf recalled his father going off to consult Great-uncle Van der Hucht in his villa several times in the months preceding his departure, but what they actually talked about he did not know. His father had considered him too young to be involved in planning the family's future. All he knew was that several relatives had declared themselves willing to invest in the new venture. It turned out that his father had not waited for news to come through from Batavia, and that a tract of land had already been marked out and a society founded for its exploitation. These deeds had been done without the blessing of Great-uncle Willem, who, so Rudolf learnt, had been greatly displeased at being ignored, and spoke disdainfully of 'that opinionated fool of a Kerkhoven'.

As the eldest son and a party in the affair, Rudolf had taken the opportunity to put an oar in. He had written to his father in careful terms, informing him of the upset among the relations and of the grudge Great-uncle Van der Hucht, the doyen of the family, bore against him. Although he did not have a clear understanding of the transactions and manipulations involved in setting up the enterprise in Java, nor of the role therein of his cousins Holle and Kerkhoven, he could not help feeling that something had changed. Great-uncle Van der Hucht's insulting remark about his father continued to rankle in his mind, and at length he had written asking to see him. He had received a formal missive in reply, inviting him to Sunday lunch at Duin en Berg. A carriage would be waiting for him at the Haarlem railway station.

The sound of stumbling up the stairs announced a visitor. The door flew open and his student friend Cox bowled into the room.

'What the devil, Kerkhoven! Such steep stairs – I almost broke my neck!'

'Too bad,' said Rudolf, laughing. 'But in that case you won't be distracting me from my work all the time, will you?'

'Why didn't we see you at the club yesterday? It was a lot of fun.'

'I was moving into my new lodgings, remember? Once I finished unpacking, I didn't feel like going out any more.'

'Good boy.' Cox glanced about him. 'Well done – except for the staircase! Oh well, your previous digs were smelly. This room is rather nice. I say, you will be coming next Saturday, won't you? There's a do at the Apollo club for their jubilee celebration.'

'I'm not a member of Apollo.'

'Nor am I. And nor are Ribbius and Berlage. We'll just fork out the introduction fee.'

'That sounds like scrounging to me.'

'Good heavens, man, how principled you are. It's not a pittance, you know, the introduction money. Five guilders.'

'Too expensive for the likes of me.'

'How typical!' Cox threw up his arms in theatrical despair. 'I never knew anyone to be so thrifty!'

'At least you express yourself more kindly than my brother Julius. He says: "Ru is a miser and a skinflint." Yes, I am careful. It's my father's money, after all.'

'Were you swotting over your books again?' Cox went over to the table, giving an exclamation of surprise when he saw the family photograph. 'Why, look at young Cateau! Pretty girl. How old is she now? Eighteen? Nineteen? They say European girls get besieged by suitors out in the Indies.'

'She's only a child,' said Rudolf gruffly, taking the photograph from him. Cateau had always been his favourite. He didn't like Cox pointing out that his little sister had grown up into a young woman of marriageable age.

'We're having a game of billiards later on. Berlage will be there, too. Want to come?'

'No, thanks. I have an appointment.'

'Oh, don't tell me you're going to church,' said Cox, tilting his head towards the window. The church bells were ringing, and across the road they could see a parade of churchgoers in their staid Sunday best.

'I have been invited to my great-uncle's house in Santpoort.'

'Aha! The Nabob, the millionaire uncle in Parliament! And there's your other uncle, too, the Minister for the Colonies. Believe me, if I had your kind of connections you wouldn't find me wanting to join my father on a plantation halfway across the world. You're studying at the Delft Polytechnic, for goodness' sake, you're the elite.'

'But I want to go out to the Indies, I really do.'

'It's not as if you've failed your exams, and you're no fool.'

'That's precisely why I want to go.'

'But what on earth does civil engineering have to do with tea?'

'Walk with me to the train station and I'll tell you,' said Rudolf.

It was not the first time he had tried to explain to his old school friend from Deventer what motivated him and his family to seek their fortune in the Indies. How many discussions they had had when they were at school together in Deventer! Cox was of a decidedly less serious bent, a lad for whom the world seemed to be confined to the frontiers of Holland. In him Rudolf saw the personification of what he had no desire to be: a 'burgher', someone who represented just the kind of bourgeois attitudes that his overseas relatives had shaken off as being too narrow and restrictive. Rudolf, for his part, was well aware that the provincial values of Deventer and Dedemsvaart still clung to him, and that even Delft had its limitations.

'I have been to see Great-uncle Van der Hucht at Duin en Berg. Splendid country seat, several hundred hectares at least. Pine trees aplenty, and oak for felling. Park with ornamental lake, and orangery. Grand indoors, too. Great-aunt Mary looking very smart, but aloof. English reserve, formal manners, just as I always imagined. I can see why Cousin Mientje didn't take to her. All a bit starchy at first, but things loosened up later (Great-uncle became quite jovial). Had a private talk with him after lunch (six courses, manservant in white gloves!) in what his wife calls his study. He chided me for being meddlesome, and then changed his mind, because by coming forward I showed that Papa did care about his opinion after all. Discovered much that I didn't know. Uncle is very down-to-earth, pragmatic. Which has stood him in good stead. I hope one day to be able to retire from my working life like him, in style.'

Rudolf laid down his pen. His mind was still filled with his visit to the villa in the dunes, where he had breathed an atmosphere utterly unlike anything he had known in his home province, even though some of his relatives there were decidedly wealthy, too. He had stared in wonder at the valuable curios collected by his host during his years at sea, which gave the rooms an exotic aspect, and wished he could have spent hours wandering among the profusion of Chinese and Japanese porcelain, the lacquer cabinets, the brightly coloured textiles and masks, and the intricately carved furniture from the days of the East India Company. But after dinner his great-uncle had invited him to smoke a cigar by the fire in another room, which was filled with hunting trophies. The walls bristled with antlers and stuffed heads of wild animals, there was a tiger skin on the floor by the hearth, and a stuffed crocodile doing duty as a footstool.

Once again Rudolf scanned the notes he had jotted down in his pocket book – mainly during the train journey home – in order to give his father a properly detailed account of what had passed between them. He could still hear his great-uncle's deep, somewhat hoarse tones, betraying the heavy smoker and drinker that he was; he could still smell the aroma of that fine cigar, still taste the excellent cognac. In his mind's eye he saw the old man sitting opposite him: the ruddy, weather-beaten face with the impressive moustache, the burly frame encased in the velvet smoking jacket he had donned upon entering his study, so that, he explained, he would not importune his wife with the smell of tobacco when he joined her in the drawing-room later. Thinking of that cheerful fire in the grate, Rudolf was suddenly reminded of the October chill creeping into his room. Upon his return to his lodgings Mistress Van der Drift had brought him a cold supper on a tray, and had asked whether he wanted the stove to be lit. He now regretted having declined the offer – out of a sense of thrift, as usual! He undressed, crawled into the cupboard-bed, and settled down to go over the entire conversation again in his head, from start to finish.

'Young man, you seem to have no compunction about meddling in affairs that are no concern of yours. Not yet, at any rate. I would recommend that you obtain your diploma first.'

'Great-uncle, it has been alleged that you expressed opinions about my father in terms that I, had they been addressed to me, would not have allowed to pass unchallenged. It would have been reason for me to refuse to shake hands with you ever again.'

'Your loyalty is commendable, but your hot temper is not. You are an ignoramus. Indeed, that was what I objected to in your father: he acted without sufficient knowledge of what he was letting himself in for. In the meantime he has learnt that one can only make haste slowly in the East, and that local customs and traditions must be taken into account.'

'Papa was disappointed that he could not set to work at once. He had been looking forward to it for years.'

'Your father went to the Indies out of spite, if you ask me. You look surprised. He never got over the fact that your Grandfather Kerkhoven handed over his position in the stock market to a younger son. The family is well aware that your father has no head for finance. The peat-cutting business and the nursery garden never amounted to much, either, did they?'

'Well, he managed to sell them for a good price.'

'Not bad, I grant you. But he did not make his fortune, not by a long chalk. And he ought to have done, because when your grandfather died there was not much of an inheritance. Your grandfather had too many children.'

'My father didn't go out to the Indies just for the money.'

'I do not doubt his good intentions. He thinks he can realise his humanitarian and philanthropic ideals in the colonies. He was not particularly successful in his efforts to educate his work-force in Overijssel, and yet now he can't wait to implement the new labour relations the colonial government has in mind for Java. Which is all very well, but one should have some background knowledge of the situation before plunging in. I advised him to invest his money in existing enterprises, run by people with more experience, such as your Uncle Eduard Kerkhoven – he wants to expand the area under cultivation at Sinagar – but not to start a plantation himself. Quite apart from his lack of knowledge about growing tea, he is simply too old.'

'But he has succeeded nonetheless. He has Ardjasari now.'

'Well, we can only hope for the best. So long as he listens to the Holle cousins, he will be all right. They know all there is to know about tea, especially Adriaan and Albert, and they have a keen understanding of the workings of the colonial government. What's more, they have connections with the local community, and are on good terms with the native regents – just as I was in my day. We used to go hunting with them, and we respected their *adat*. The Holles go out into the fields wearing a batik *kain*, and keep their heads covered. They know the local manners and customs. Karel Holle takes this a bit too far in my opinion. He has a very close friend, a Mohammedan religious teacher and an aristocrat with a pleasant manner, although you never know with them. Religion and politics are tangled together in the Mohammedan perception; those chaps have a streak of fanaticism about them. This particular *penghoeloe* has a great deal of influence in the Preanger. Karel and he are dedicated to the betterment of the native population, they write books in the Soendanese language, and Karel has already set up a training college for native schoolteachers. A true benefactor. But I'm afraid he is in danger of being carried away by his idealism.'

'My father has great respect for Cousin Karel.'

'As well he might, because it was Karel who helped your papa to secure the lease of that estate, through his connections in the Bandjaran region. Now that it looks as if the whole Cultivation System will be abolished at last, your father can introduce wage labour right away at Ardjasari. Karel has already done so on his own plantation, Waspada. He consults his native overseers about everything, too, and even keeps surgery hours for the workers. The question remains: what will all this lead to in the longer term? He is a dreamer. I can just see Baud raising a quizzical eyebrow.'

'Who is Baud, Great-uncle?'

'Our competitor! Son of the former Governor-General. He had advance knowledge of the changes, and contracted estates left and right, which was easy for him as he knew all the bureaucrats personally. He is currently the leading tea planter in Java. He keeps getting in the way when our people try to lease additional tracts of land. He calls us "veritable vampires", out for our own profit and nothing else. But he's not above seeking our services as administrators – on ridiculous conditions – nor is he above accepting our capital as backing for his own enterprises. I was worried to death that your father, being so ignorant of such things, would fall for Baud's schemes. You know, we of Parakan Salak are the pioneers. We must stand our ground.'

'In his speech at the opening of parliament the King said this would be an important year for the Indies—'

'Cousin De Waal's law for agrarian reform has been as good as passed. I gave him all my support in parliament.'

'Great-uncle, as I understand it, it signifies a step forward for private enterprise. So why is there so still much opposition from the Liberal side? I don't understand.'

'Well, those Liberals have a radical edge. They don't know what they're talking about. They take all their ideas from that man, Douwes Dekker, a cousin of ours by marriage, the one who writes books and calls himself Multatuli nowadays. And his notions are anything but liberal, I'd have you know.'

'But he writes with such passion! I have read his novel, *Max Havelaar*.'

'Pardon me, but Douwes Dekker *stole* that story, characters and plot and all, from Pastor Van Höevell, who drew attention to the whole sorry affair twenty years ago. Now that was a true martyr for the cause – they banished him from the Indies – but he didn't make the kind of fuss over here Douwes Dekker made. Have you ever met him, by the way? When he was in Holland with his wife he used to visit the family quite often.'

'I was too young; I can't remember. But last year I went to hear a lecture by him in The Hague. He is a great speaker. I found myself agreeing with a lot of things he said.'

'Of *course* the native chiefs exact services from the indigenous population, that is the *adat* – and of *course* there is much to be deplored about the methods they use to do so. But it is total madness to think you can do anything about it by lodging a formal complaint with the colonial authorities, who are the root of the problem in the first place. The whole system needs to be changed in such a way that not only the population benefits but also the chiefs retain their prestige, and their revenues as well. Above all, they must not be seen to lose face. Everyone with a few years in the colonial service in Java knows that.'

'At the end of the lecture I went up to Douwes Dekker – Multatuli – to express my admiration. When I introduced myself he said, "Ah, a Kerkhoven!" And when I explained who I was, he told me that the two of you had been friends back in the Indies.'

'Before his marriage to Cousin Tine van Wijnbergen he often came to Parakan Salak, which was where their courtship began. He was angling for a position with us, or else for our help in getting him a position elsewhere, because he was anxious to leave the colonial service. He expected our unconditional support in his change of career, and I believe he felt disappointed by us. You see, we were reluctant to endorse his plans because they were misguided. He had no knowledge of plantations, or of business for that matter. The man was utterly unsuited for the life of a planter. We were deluged with work at the time in Parakan Salak, but it never occurred to him to lend a hand in any way. He just went for walks with the ladies, or sat in a corner reading a book, didn't care a jot about anything to do with the estate. But it's true that we were on pretty good terms for a while, until I began to dislike the way he treated Tine. Oh, he was a smooth talker! It was her money he was after. For years he was gripped by the conviction that she would come into an inheritance. Just ask your uncles and aunts, they'll tell you how he came and scrounged off the family when they were here on their first furlough, in eighteen fifty-three, I believe.'

'My grandmother at Hunderen found him interesting, and amusing, too.'

'He is a fabulist. A charlatan! He stayed at the best hotels, but when it came to paying the bill his wallet had been stolen! Some elderly aunts of ours lent him a considerable sum of money, which they never got back. And look at him now! I presume you know the kind of life he leads. I am no moralist, but his behaviour really is disgraceful. He has abandoned his wife and children, and now travels about with his mistress giving lectures and posing as the hero of the Javanese people. I am not saying he is not a gifted writer, but what has he achieved? Not a fraction of what Karel Holle has accomplished . . . Dear me, this is making me angry, which is bad for my liver.'

'I take it you do respect Cousin Karel, then?'

'Well, his habit of dressing and behaving like a Mohammedan . . . going native . . . that is wrong, in my opinion. In the Preanger they have already taken to calling him Said Mohammed Ben Holle. But I don't deny that he can play an important role as an intermediary. The government will undoubtedly make use of his services. Fortunately he is aware of the advantages private enterprise can offer for the development of the people he cares so deeply about. How are they to learn about cultivation unless we teach them? Rice is a different matter, they have been growing rice since time immemorial, and very good they are at it, too, but they don't know about tea, not about pruning and picking, and they let coffee bushes become overgrown if left to their own devices. Of course, it is a wonderful thing when people work freely for a wage. But what is often overlooked is that the Javanese peasant has a totally different attitude to money than the European. Notions like saving or investing have no meaning for them. The peasant in Java is satisfied so long as he has enough to eat and can keep a few goats or a water buffalo.'

'But Great-uncle, isn't that because those people have been living in a form of slavery until now . . . and because the land is so fertile and the weather so hot? My father says that for anyone with their own small plot of land and a few chickens life can be paradise.'

'You sound like Douwes Dekker! "Go and live in a bamboo house, dress and eat like a native, love one another sincerely, and you shall be happy." Pah! But time doesn't stand still, not even in paradise. The people will have to learn the value of money, and how profits can be used for the good of the community. The mineral resources of the Indies are limitless. For the time being the government does not have the ability to exploit them properly . . . it is beyond the powers of bureaucrats to deal with mining on any scale. I know what I am talking about. I was involved in tin mining on Billiton for a time. The stories I could tell you about that! I envy you, because you are young and going to Java.'

'I intend to work hard, Great-uncle.'

'You must not get discouraged too quickly when things don't go your way. I have known difficult times, too. In eighteen fifty I was unable to pay the dues for Parakan Salak, and I was obliged to take an advance to keep the plantation going. It was only after I married your Aunt Mary that I managed to get over it, thanks to my brother-in-law at Pryce & Co. in Batavia. But believe me, I would give every one of my possessions to have my time in the Indies over again . . . One more thing: make sure you get in touch with Eduard at Sinagar. He's a fine fellow.'

By the time Great-uncle Van der Hucht had finished they were standing on the porch by the entrance, where the carriage was waiting. Looking back, he caught a glimpse of Aunt Mary in a doorway as she greeted some lady visitors.

'Au revoir, my boy,' the old gentleman had said. 'You will let me know how you get on, won't you?'

Rudolf thought about Eduard Kerkhoven, his father's youngest brother. As a child he, like all his cousins, had idolised this handsome, boyish uncle of theirs, who did not seem to belong fully with the grown-ups in the family. Eduard knew everything about horses and dogs; he was a skilled rider, a passionate hunter, an altogether lively, adventurous sort of outdoorsman. That he had difficulty finding a niche for himself in Holland surprised no one. He had followed the 'colonists' overseas and, after a time of apprenticeship at Parakan Salak, had been found a position by Great-uncle Van der Hucht on the Sinagar tea plantation on the western flank of the Gedeh mountain. For many years Eduard sent long letters home recounting his experiences. The most interesting descriptions were copied out and circulated as a family chronicle under the nostalgic title the *Hunderen Courier*.

Eduard generally addressed his letters to Rudolf's father, with whom he had always been close, so it was by him and his immediate family that they were first read and re-read. Rudolf could remember several almost word for word: how Eduard had been so badly injured in an encounter with a wild stag that, as he phrased it, 'yours truly never had a narrower escape from the Grim Reaper.'

Or: how Eduard had ordered his men to clear out one of the hangars at Sinagar, which turned out to be home to scores of rats, several of which 'scuttled up the men's legs and under their clothes all the way up to their necks, where they jumped down again.' Or: how he had scaled the Salak volcano and had wandered about the crater stark naked, amid bubbling pools of sulphur and mud: 'I thought to myself, what a change this makes from taking tea at Mr and Mrs So-and-so's in Twello.' Or: how his favourite hunting dog Vesta, lost in the jungle and thought dead, had found her way back to the plantation after several weeks.

The previous spring one of the aunts had shown Rudolf a letter she had received from his mother. She had made him promise not to tell anyone what was in it: things about Eduard, things no one in the family had ever imagined. The 'inveterate bachelor', as he was reputed to be, turned out to be in possession of a wife and two children. But the woman was Chinese, and their union was not on a par with marriage between Europeans.

Rudolf's mother reported that Eduard had acknowledged paternity of the children, and that they therefore, albeit of mixed race, should be regarded as true Kerkhovens. Surely growing up in an unconventional ménage such as that of Sinagar would not be salutary for them. She and Rudolf's father were of the opinion that it would be a good idea for little Non, whose real name was Pauline, and young Adriaan to be sent to live with relatives in Holland.

The news had greatly disturbed the aunt to whom the letter was addressed – she was at a loss as to what to do with this information. Rudolf didn't know, either. Nor did he feel it would be right to refer to it in his letters to his parents until such time as they saw fit to take him into their confidence.

But now he regretted not having broached the subject when Great-uncle Van der Hucht mentioned Eduard.

The euphoria of graduating with good marks in all subjects but one was of short duration. After celebrating with champagne and a festive run in a open carriage in the company of Cox and friends, as well as having the flag flown in triumph from the attic window at his lodging house (while his landlady proclaimed to all and sundry that the master had passed his exams) and the satisfaction of ordering calling cards printed with 'Technologist', he had been expecting a letter of congratulation to arrive from the Indies by return of post, telling him to book his passage at once on a rapid vessel, and to pack his bags.

At first he attributed the delay to the long-anticipated outbreak of war between France and Germany, but soon began to fear that the reason was his inexplicably poor mark in civil engineering, a subject he liked and for which he had worked hard. The non-committal tone of his parents' letter when it did arrive depressed him. There was no reference to his coming out to join them. Could it be that his father thought he would not be much use to him at Ardjasari, now that he had not excelled at designing bridges and factory hangars?

He felt restless and miserable, and followed the news of the war with impatience, wishing it would end, especially after the humiliating defeat of the French at Sedan.

'It is unfortunate that the labyrinthine twists of diplomacy make it impossible to establish which side is really to blame for this war,' he wrote in his notebook. 'However, on the basis of the information at our disposal, such as it is, my interpretation would be that the French imperial government provoked the hostilities, and that the French population at large backed their government's actions; witness the enthusiasm with which the troops went to war and their stubbornness in pursuing it. Personally I do not agree with all Bismarck's policies, but I do not believe they had anything to do with this particular conflict. It was provoked by the French for the sole purpose of destroying the German alliance. Every French government has preferred to see a fragmented Germany during its mandate. In my view, Bismarck's politics relate exclusively to the *domestic* situation, to the realisation of the German ideal of national unity, using all means at his disposal, good or bad (and that is precisely what I object to, but it is their own affair). I think German unity is a perfectly reasonable aim to strive for, but the way in which it was partially achieved in 1866 was wrong. A mighty German state will do nothing to soften the German character, but I do not believe this represents a direct danger to us. Because we are not German by any means, and have never been under threat from those quarters. On the other hand, Napoleon did annex us, and called us "French".'

Much to Rudolf's bemusement, his father seemed to take the side of France, to the point of condoning French actions undertaken exclusively *pour la gloire*. Reading between the lines it seemed to him that his father did not share his view of the Germans as upright and, on the whole, peace-loving folk, though admittedly unpleasant. He had the impression his father thought him naive.

In their letters his parents lavished attention on their plans to send his youngest brother, August, to secondary school in The Hague, and on his sister Bertha's engagement to Jan Joseph van Santen, who was her senior by eighteen years and in the employ of the Netherlands Indies Trading Bank in Batavia.

All he heard concerning his own future was that his father advised him to seek information about silk-making, and about the extraction of ethereal oils from flowers; Cousin Karel Holle said they offered new opportunities for cultivation in Java, and might be of special interest to someone like Rudolf, since he had done so well in his chemistry exams. The vagueness of these directives tormented Rudolf. Did they really expect him to spend another winter in Holland? How was he supposed to find out about such affairs? He had made enquiries at the Polytechnic and had approached several of his former professors, and the consensus seemed to be that he had a better of chance of learning about ethereal oils and the manufacture of silk in France – but how could he travel to that country while there was a war on?

His father appeared to be receiving considerable support from his prospective son-in-law Van Santen, who had helped him set up the Ardjasari investment fund, which was doing the rounds of the family in Holland. The favourable response from various uncles and aunts reassured Rudolf that there would be plenty of work awaiting him in the Indies. His father had apparently already engaged an overseer in advance of the harvest, but that was understandable. The first harvest had yielded approximately 900 kilos of saleable tea, which was expected to fetch a good price on the Amsterdam market.

His father reported that the planters in Java were obliged to send for even the simplest of utensils and machinery from Europe. Someone with a good knowledge of technical tools would therefore be indispensable. Rudolf decided that he had waited long enough to be told what to do. He rented a room in Amsterdam and volunteered his services to De Atlas, a factory making steam engines and other heavy machinery, with the intention of learning the techniques of welding, forging and filing. He also ordered the components for a small chemical laboratory, which he intended to take with him to Java. He made up his mind to leave in the spring of 1871 at the latest.

'Confound it, Gus, how good it is to see you! You've grown quite a bit taller, I see, but apart from that you haven't changed a bit.'

Rudolf had gone to Den Helder to meet his young brother on arrival from the Indies, and had taken him to Uncle and Aunt Bosscha-Kerkhoven in The Hague, where August would be lodging. After the emotional reunion on the quayside, their excited chatter making neither head nor tail on the train, and the effusive welcome at his new home, the pair of them were now busy unpacking August's trunk in his small bedroom. Though not particularly short for his age, he looked much younger than twelve. Rudolf felt a stab of pity for August, so obviously uncomfortable in the 'Dutch suit' made for him by a Chinese tailor in Bandoeng. From what little the boy said, he gathered that not even a friendly environment such as this, with plenty of cousins to play with, would make up for all that he missed about the Indies. One of the worst things had been saying goodbye to his pony, a birthday gift from Uncle Eduard of Sinagar.

One by one, August placed the carefully wrapped gifts he had brought for the family on the table.

'For Julius I have some sea shells from the south coast. Do you think he will like them? Does he have a collection? And this is for you. Made by a *boedjang* at Ardjasari.'

'What is a *boedjang*?' asked Rudolf, parting the tissue-paper wrapping to reveal a blade made of buffalo horn. 'Splendid! I shall use it to cut my nibs with.'

'That's what it's for. *Boedjangs* are the boys who work on the plantation. The one who made that is called Si Ramiah. He's a carpenter, he can make anything.'

'I can't wait to see Ardjasari.'

'There are loads of wild buffalo there. They trample the young plants. They're a plague. Papa offers a reward for each one they catch.'

'What about the house? Is it finished yet?'

'They are staying on in Bandoeng until Bertha's wedding in October.'

'I hear it is to be a small affair. Why is that?' asked Rudolf. 'Isn't it a bit odd? I mean, surely Papa and Mama have acquaintances in Bandoeng.'

'Well, not very many, actually. Bandoeng is quite small. Anyway, Bertha doesn't want a big party.'

'Is Bertha happy, Gus? That Van Santen seems pretty old.'

August shrugged. The expression on his boyish, slightly sallow face became guarded. 'I wouldn't know. He talks in a very dignified sort of way, like a lawyer, but he's all right.' He paused, fidgeting with the parcels, then added, 'Bertha wants to live in Batavia. Van Santen works in Batavia. He has a house there.'

'What about Cateau? Is she happy?'

'Oh, stop fussing! Why shouldn't she be happy?'

August was more interested in telling his brother all about Ardjasari. He had only visited the estate half a dozen times, on 'excursions', as he called them, which took three hours on horseback from Bandoeng, but his descriptions were so vivid that Rudolf felt he had been there himself. He could just see the open terrain on the high plateau ringed by mountains, the vast wilderness of the former Tegal Mantri, where the district chiefs used to hunt tiger and deer; he could just see the first, newly planted tea gardens and the small settlement of bamboo huts. August told him about the inauguration ceremony two years ago, with the ritual planting of the very first tea bushes at Ardjasari: 'Oh, you should have seen it! There was a procession with musicians and a whole lot of native bigwigs, and Papa and Cousin Karel Holle, and Uncle Eduard of Sinagar, and me, and we had servants holding *pajoengs* over our heads, which was very grand, and all the workers following behind . . . and then each of us, including me, put a plant in the soil . . . and after that there was food, no, first there was a Mohammedan prayer, and Cousin Karel Holle made a speech. I couldn't understand what he said, though, because my Soendanese isn't good enough yet.'

'I shall have to try to learn it, too,' said Rudolf. 'Did you bring those patterns for the clothes I need to have made up here before I go? Mama promised to send some.'

The patterns for the loose cotton pyjama suits were nowhere to be found. His mother had forgotten. The question that was uppermost in his mind – did his parents really want him to come and join them? – was hardly something he could ask August.

He went over to his brother, who was standing by the window peering through the parted curtains (one set of filet lace, the other of heavy plush) at the garden, where the late sun was gilding the backs of the houses across the way.

'Homesick, Gus?'

Rudolf made a habit of going to The Hague once a week to see how August was getting on. If the weather was good the brothers went for walks after supper in the Scheveningen woods. Rudolf was relieved to see that August was bearing up quite well against homesickness, but he was concerned about the boy's unruly behaviour, which often stirred trouble in the Bosscha household. August had a curious, 'un-Dutch' manner of taunting the maids and the family pets, and was often bossy and heartless with the other children, who were several years younger than him. Rudolf concluded that Gus (the baby in the family since little Pauline's demise) had been badly spoiled by his parents and sisters back home. To show how seriously he took his role as proxy father, Rudolf reported to Bandoeng: 'I told Gus he should always make allowances for his young cousins, that it is simply not fair to be so strict about the rules of whatever game they are playing. Once I had told him that, and had set a good example myself, of course, I was glad to notice a significant change in his behaviour: he has become indulgent with the children, and even encourages them to be kinder to each other.'

Rudolf had small-format portraits made of both August and Julius, to send off to Java. He did not have one made of himself: they would be seeing him in the flesh soon enough!

Julius caused him concern for other reasons. He seemed more than a little timid and withdrawn, even in the company of his peers. It troubled Rudolf that his brother – almost eighteen now – had taken to spending his free time with a somewhat backward fourteen-year-old cousin, with whom he seemed to get along rather well. He had also been prevailed upon by a local minister to be confirmed, even though it meant nothing to him. Rudolf remonstrated with him for being insincere, whereupon his brother accused him, not unjustly, of being a hypocrite. It was true; Rudolf himself had been confirmed in the Baptist faith for the sole purpose of appeasing the family in Overijssel. He still felt a twinge of shame when he thought of the declaration of intent he had been obliged to write, a composition running to twenty pages. Re-reading it some time afterwards he had been shocked by the degree to which he was evidently capable of make-believe. Where on earth had he got it all? He had vowed that he would never let anything like that happen to him again.

Like him, Julius would be enrolling at Delft Polytechnic. Although not studious by nature, Julius was quite happy at the prospect. Rudolf believed that it would be better for his brother, being so timid, to side-step the nerve-racking examinations; instead, he could attend the classes as an extramural student, concentrating on subjects that would be useful to him in the Indies. But Julius would not hear of this, suddenly showing himself to have a will of his own. Rudolf resolved to introduce him to the younger members of his own student club, for the sake of some conviviality. He pressed his parents not to be too grudging in their allowance: 'Julius needs to be able to go to a concert now and then, or to an opera, and to become a member of a social club. That is a good thing for someone his age. He might not get the opportunity later on.'

Rudolf himself had foregone such distractions in his student years. His own allowance had been meagre, but that was due to his father's financial troubles overseas, and especially to his own reluctance to ask for more. He would have liked to have gone out from time to time, like his fellow students – to a fancy-dress ball for instance, or to the theatre – but, all in all, he did not feel that he had missed much. Still, a well-considered dose of worldly entertainment might make all the difference to Julius, given his 'quietly philosophical' bent.

'But I'm not interested in any of that stuff!' Julius protested when Rudolf raised the subject.

'So what will you do with yourself? Sleep late in the mornings, take a stroll, attend a few classes, take another stroll before supper, and spend your evenings in your room with a book?' Rudolf had become quite agitated, for who would keep an eye on Julius? Who would be there to offer advice and moral support once he had left? Because he was leaving, that much was certain. He would go as soon as he had mastered those metal-working techniques at De Atlas.

Once he had proved himself proficient at filing, he was seconded to the smithy. There he had to heft a great hammer with both hands and deal accurately aimed blows on a bar of red-hot iron according to the master forger's specifications, backbreaking work through which he became extremely dirty. He was barely able to get his hands properly clean afterwards, and when obliged to remove his gloves in company would repeat the same mumbled apology: 'I am spending half a year as a metal-worker, I'm afraid.' How discomfited the uncles and aunts and their friends would have been if, in addition to that glimpse of a workman's callused hands and chipped fingernails, he had also brought the manners and language of De Atlas into their drawing-rooms!

He felt that the knowledge he was acquiring was by no means restricted to working with metals. At first he had been shocked by the coarse jokes he heard on the factory floor, and by the eruptions of violence among the men he associated with daily, but he had learnt to look beyond that rough exterior. What he saw and heard at De Atlas represented a useful counterbalance to the 'gentlemanly' codes with which he had been brought up, yet at the same time he realised that those codes were integral to his being. He would be bound by them for the rest of his life.

He was likewise aware that the gentry's days of undisputed authority were numbered. The events in Paris, where the common folk seized power after the defeat of the imperial armies, were surely a grave warning to liberal politicians seeking to establish a new Republic in France. Henceforth they would have to reckon with forces that were impossible to contain. He for his part did his best to adapt to life at De Atlas, and was learning more by the day. But the rank and file continued to treat him as an outsider, a toff who could afford to present the foremen with a cigar from time to time.

He had never known a winter as cold as this one. There had been snow on the ground since mid-December, and people went skating on the frozen canals and on the ponds in the newly laid-out Vondel Park. He went there to take a look, and was surprised to see among the skaters a fair number of ladies and young girls, who, unhampered by their long skirts, furs and cloaks, glided most elegantly over the ice. The sight of Amsterdam's beau monde disporting themselves on skates drew crowds of spectators, but Rudolf disliked multitudes and preferred to go the River Amstel instead, where one could leave the city behind and skate all the way to the village of Ouderkerk.

He heard that a good ship had docked in Amsterdam: the clipper-frigate *Telanak*, which plied between Holland and Java on behalf of various reputable shippers and freighters. The preceding autumn he had already visited several ships to enquire about fares, itineraries and duration. His impression had not been favourable. Standards were altogether low, with cramped, musty cabins and little deck space. Prices were high, too. The *Telanak* was not a swift vessel. The captain told him the voyage would take roughly 120 days, as they would be rounding the Cape of Good Hope instead of sailing through the recently opened and not yet entirely trustworthy Suez Canal. The fare would be 500 guilders. That was 50 guilders less than his parents had paid for their passage, and when he was offered an acceptable cabin with plentiful shelving and storage space for his luggage, he signed the agreement. The *Telanak* would not set sail until some weeks after the ice had thawed, and definitely not before 1 March.

'It would have been most inconvenient if I had been obliged to leave by the end of this month,' he wrote to his parents. 'As it is, my *Telanak* is still frozen fast in the dock. I can't even go on board – or rather, I could if I really had to, but it is a perilous undertaking. First you clamber down the side of the quay along a filthy, slippery, ramshackle ladder and jump down the last bit on to the ice, which is beginning to melt on the surface. Then you walk a little way across the frozen harbour, climb over a few peat barges, walk some more, until you reach a channel broken through the ice. There you have to wait for some amenable skipper to position his craft in such a way that you can use it as a bridge to the other side, where you walk across the ice again. Finally, you board a dinghy that noses its way through the ice floes to the ship. Some of the crew go across every day, but I would rather wait until they have broken a proper channel directly from the quay. When I visited the ship the ice was strong enough to walk on all the way, but, with the thaw setting in, that is no longer possible, even though it is still a foot-and-a-half thick in places.'

He went on a round of farewell visits; first to Arnhem, Elst and Velp, followed by Deventer, Zwolle, and Leeuwarden up north – and then back via Putten, Utrecht and Ameide. Seated in those drawing-rooms (heavily furnished in mahogany or oak with plush upholstery in gloomy shades) he repeated over and over to his solicitous uncles and fond aunts all he knew about his father's plantation. Several relations seemed to think – doubtless under the influence of a certain minister in Deventer – that his parents had gone out to the Indies intending to convert the Javanese to Christianity, but he did not dare to deny this as vigorously as he would have wished, for fear of dampening their enthusiasm to invest in Ardjasari. It was only when one of the uncles, referring to Julius's confirmation, mentioned the importance of being baptised 'as an assurance of certain material advantages over the heathen', that Rudolf could not contain himself. He caused even greater consternation when he said, 'I hope the Franco–Prussian war will end up furthering the Republican cause, and that one day all the kings and queens can be put out to pasture.'

He was astonished by his own reactions to the places he had known as a boy, which he had not revisited since 1867, the year he had left to go and study in Delft. Deventer, the town of his secondary school days, was particularly disappointing. He recorded his impressions in his notebook: 'Everything about it seems so small, so backward and old-fashioned that it often feels as if the clock has been turned back half a century. The countrified Deventer pronunciation, even among educated people, came as rather a shock. My own accent has changed, of course, and I felt quite displaced. They stared at me in wonder, almost as if I were some wild animal in a zoo, and all they came up with when they saw me in my hat and gloves was a faltering "My, how tall you've grown!" Well, the Deventers may be good and upright folk, but ye gods, are they *stiff*! They have no ease of manner at all.'

Back in the west of the country he went for a final stroll with his brothers in the dunes at Scheveningen. He trailed after August, who was in boisterous mood, dashing this way and that across the soft sand and stretches of marram grass. Julius, unenergetic as ever, took the footpath, and, despite his plodding pace, was the first to reach the lighthouse.

August wept when they said goodbye, but recovered quickly when Uncle and Aunt Bosscha gave him a watch by way of consolation. Julius accompanied Rudolf to the docks at Nieuwe Diep to see him off.

The *Telanak* set sail on 28 March 1871. Rudolf stood on deck, waving his hat, until he could no longer make out the figure of his brother on the quayside.

Never in his life had Rudolf felt such profound relief as when the *Telanak* dropped anchor in the roadstead of Batavia. The long sea voyage, so eagerly anticipated as a gripping adventure, had turned out to be exceedingly tedious: 107½ days of being confined to the cramped spaces reserved for passengers on deck and in the midship, cheek by jowl with a motley assortment of individuals whom he could not imagine ever consorting with of his own free will. The stuffiness and heat in his cabin, especially after crossing the Equator, prevented him from sleeping at night, and even from spending much time there during the day.

Aside from the crew there were nine adults and fourteen children on board, six of whom were very young. Since the parents seldom emerged from their cabins before noon and the only '*bonne*' among the passengers was a late riser, Rudolf and another bachelor fell into the habit of keeping an eye on the increasingly unruly children as they swarmed over the decks before breakfast. Bitter quarrels had broken out between passengers. There had been a dalliance that led to a hasty betrothal – Rudolf hoped he would never set eyes on the pair again. Frequent storms around the Cape of Good Hope had affected everyone to greater or lesser degrees.

Enormous foaming waves had broken over the ship, a terrifying experience. The reclining chair Rudolf had brought with him to use on deck had been smashed to pieces against the railing. Three hundred live chickens, taken on board in Holland along with a cow to provide milk for the children, had all found their way to the mess table, as well as Rudolf's private store of Deventer cake, biscuits and bottles of wine and beer.

The only good memories he would have of the voyage were the occasional quiet, solitary hours he had passed on deck. He would post himself a little to the side of an awning where some men might be playing cards while two or three ladies wrapped in capes and scarves stood by, braving the wind and flying specks of foam, and he would lose himself in the mighty, billowing sails above the bustle of the crew, and especially in the ocean, heaving masses of water, now indigo blue, now transparent green marbled with foam, with flying fish and leaping dolphins, and swarms of jellyfish in every shade ranging from white to violet. Truly unforgettable had been the nights when he left his airless cabin and stole up on deck to find himself some corner where he could lean back against a crate or a coil of rope and gaze up at the star-studded firmament of the southern hemisphere.

The infinite expanse of the Indian Ocean spelled the tropics. They were becalmed for days at a time in soaring temperatures, with the pitch in the seams melting and the passengers huddling together in sweaty, panting clusters wherever there was any shade to be found. Below deck the heat was insupportable. The ship called at Padang, where they took their first steps on terra firma among the coconut palms, and some days later, sailing through the Soenda Straits, they sighted the Bantam coast and the sensational Krakatau volcano rising up from the sea.

They had arrived in the Indies!

All packed up and ready, he had to wait a long time to disembark, his impatience mounting as he gazed out at the sheds and low buildings and the palm trees beyond, their fronds trembling in the heat. At last the captain announced the departure of the rowing boat to the customs office. He saw several surprisingly Dutch-looking tiled roofs poking out above the spreading tropical trees with huge, elongated leaves, rather like gigantic house plants. There was a smell of fish and rank mud on the quayside. A wave of cloying heat submerged him.

From the crowd gathered on the quay to welcome the passengers, a tall, lean figure stepped forward. He was formally dressed, with hat and cane, and introduced himself as Joseph van Santen, his brother-in-law. Rudolf had expected this initial, rather stilted greeting to be followed by a more personal exchange, or at least some semblance of cordiality, but Van Santen quickly led him away to a waiting carriage. His luggage would be delivered later in the day.

Rudolf was all eyes as they rode through the streets: men with a cloth round the hips and a loose shirt over their bare chests carrying poles over their shoulders with baskets or crates at either end, two-wheeled ox carts, and the throng of likewise two-wheeled vehicles, most of which were drawn by small, piteously thin horses.

'How extraordinary,' he said, leaning forward to peer at the buildings lining the road. 'The houses have such a shuttered look, even a bit run-down. Quite different from what I had imagined.'

'They belong to the Chinese. You can tell by the shape of the roofs.' Van Santen traced a wavy line in the air with his cane. 'And they are only modest on the outside. There is an abundance of finery on show indoors. Very shrewd merchants, the Chinese; they make a fortune out here. I have been invited to several Chinese homes, on business. They keep a coffin waiting on the inner gallery, but apart from that it's all elaborately carved furniture, red silk hangings, vases that come up to your waist, and family altars with porcelain idols . . .'

'I look forward to meeting the Chinese.'

For the first time Van Santen gave a short laugh. 'Oh, you will have plenty of occasion to do so, Kerkhoven. Especially when you get to Sinagar.'

'At Uncle Eduard's, you mean?' asked Rudolf, thinking Van Santen might be hinting at his uncle's domestic arrangements, which were never mentioned in the family.

'Yes, indeed. That is where you will be going. Didn't you know? The Holles thought it best for you to start learning the business with them and with Kerkhoven at Sinagar.'

'But my father is expecting me at Ardjasari! Just before I set out there was a letter from him telling me his assistant was leaving.'

'They have already found a replacement. Good chap, apparently.'

'But what about me?'

'The Holles want you to get a proper grounding in tea first. And it will be for the good of Ardjasari, too.'

Rudolf was stunned into silence, aggrieved by having things decided for him as if he were still a schoolboy. Him, a schoolboy? The Holles thought this, the Holles wanted that . . . Didn't his father have a say in the matter?

They were driving along a canal teeming with bathers and people washing clothes. Women standing in waist-high water shamelessly displayed their naked shoulders, and more of their bodies besides if they happened to be washing their hair. He had heard people on board ship describing this kind of everyday scene of native life in Java as being somewhat embarrassing to the European eye, so he was forewarned, but he was startled nonetheless, and looked away.

He tried to consider the implications of what Van Santen had just told him, but had no time to put order into his thoughts. The leafy crowns of the tall trees on either side of the road met in the centre, providing an agreeable coolness in the shade as they went past deep, green gardens with houses like those Rudolf remembered from the photograph albums at Hunderen. The carriage turned into a driveway, gravel crunching under the wheels. As they drew up at the house, two pale figures came clattering down the steps of the front veranda and ran towards him with open arms: they were Bertha and Cateau, his sisters, wearing long kebayas. To see them in the flesh wearing native dress was even stranger than in the group portrait he had received back in Delft. Bertha had grown rather plump, he thought with mild disappointment, but when he hugged her he understood the reason for her ample girth.

'Yes, indeed, you are to be an uncle!' laughed Cateau, no longer his little sister but a buxom young woman with a pert face. 'We didn't tell you, as we wanted it to be a surprise.'

'You live in a palace – so much space! And so many servants, too, I can barely believe my eyes,' said Rudolf. It was late afternoon; the hours had flown past in eager exchanges of news and shared recollections of the old days. His sisters had not even taken a moment to change their clothes, and there they were, past tea-time, still in sarong and kebaya, with their hair loose. 'I really must go to Ardjasari as soon as possible. I'm dying to see the old folks again, and besides, I need to know what they have planned for me on the estate.'

Bertha and her husband exchanged looks.

'Travel from here to the Preanger requires a fair bit of preparation,' said Van Santen. 'The journey takes two to three days, and messengers have to be sent ahead to arrange for fresh horses at the various staging posts. And everything takes ages in the interior, unless you speak the language. I would advise you to travel with someone who knows how the land lies. Unfortunately, I can't get away at the moment.'

'I will manage. I wasn't born yesterday,' said Rudolf, slightly piqued.

Cateau jumped to her feet. 'But Rudolf hasn't seen anything yet. All he's seen of Batavia is the road between the docks and here. Let's go for a drive! But first we must bathe and get dressed.'

'You can take the calash if you like,' sighed Van Santen, mopping the perspiration from his brow. He looked tired. He had gone without his afternoon siesta. 'You will have to excuse me; I still have some business to attend to.'

Rudolf leaned back in the open carriage, his legs submerged under his sisters' flounced skirts. The sturdy Batak ponies trotted onwards at a steady pace beneath the tamarind trees.

'Batavia looks at its best in the twilight,' said Cateau. 'Look, the moon is rising.'

Rudolf was enchanted. The sultry breeze carried whiffs of unfamiliar scents, of fruits and flowers, burning charcoal fires, exotic herbs and spices from roadside food stalls lit by flickering oil lamps. They were going too fast for him to distinguish what they were selling, but in the ruddy glow he glimpsed moving shadows and streaks of colour.

They went all the way around Koningsplein, the vast main square. On his left white mansions loomed up in the dusk. Many of the verandas were illuminated, in some cases by grand, old-fashioned candelabra, the yellow glow flooding out onto the forecourts and lighting up the undersides of massive trees. Bertha and Cateau rattled off the names of the people living there as they went past; they seemed to know everyone, as in a village, but never had Rudolf been in a place less like a village.

The constant stream and counter-stream of calashes, victorias, gigs and small native drays, the ladies in summery gowns, smiling and nodding to acquaintances, the smell of the horses, the lanterns on the front and back of the vehicles, the torch-bearers running alongside a few luxurious carriages, the moon rising honey-coloured over the trees . . . it all felt to Rudolf like a dream.

They went past the Governor-General's residence ('Look! They're holding a reception!' cried his sisters, pointing to a crowd in full evening dress gathered beneath the chandeliers), then past a round church built like a Greek temple, past the torch-lit gardens of the Concordia society where some similar event was taking place, around another large square, past the government offices and down quiet, dark avenues like tunnels of foliage, towered over here and there by royal palms, their moonlit fronds shimmering against a sky of night-blue glass.

'I just love going for a drive in the evening,' sighed Cateau. 'Now you can see, brother dear, why I prefer being here with Bertha than up in the mountains at Ardjasari! Oh, I like the fresh air in the highlands, of course, but I can't see myself living there. There isn't anything to do! Thank goodness Bertha will be needing me here for the next few months.'

'Well, you might marry a planter one day,' laughed Rudolf.

Cateau rapped him over the knee with her closed fan. 'Never! Never! Never! Out of the question!'

He lay awake for a long time, gazing at his rectangular cage of mosquito netting, but when he dropped off at last he slept soundly. When he opened his eyes again he could tell by the light slanting in through the Venetian blinds that the sun was already high in the sky. Someone was sweeping the yard outside, and he could hear Bertha giving instructions to her servants in Malay. Carrying his towels over his arm, he made his way down the wooden gallery to the washroom. He caught a glimpse of the kitchen maid bearing a tray stacked with bottles and bowls, and saw Bertha emerging from the store-room with her basket of keys on her arm, having just handed out the days' supplies. Feeling a little shy in his nightwear, he did not approach his sister but called out a quick good morning before vanishing into the half-lit space, where a slight dankness emanated from a water-tank. He liked the East Indian habit of scooping up the water and pouring it over the head; it left him feeling wide awake and invigorated.

Bertha was speaking to the servants on the gallery outside. As the previous day, he was struck by the commanding tone used by Europeans to address the natives. He was certain there was no gardener or washerwoman at Hunderen, not even a journeyman at his father's peat-cutting works in Dedemsvaart – people accustomed to deferring to their masters – who would tolerate being ordered about like that. He had been shocked by the way some people had barked out instructions to the luggage coolies on the quay, and had immediately cast them as 'new-style colonials', men of little education and uncouth manners who would never have amounted to anything in Holland.

'My dear sis, you sound like a sergeant major,' he said when he came upon Bertha by the stairs to the back veranda. 'You made a promise to the minister when you were confirmed that you would practise kindness and good neighbourship in Java. Remember?'

Bertha blushed. Her pretty face looked drawn, with dark circles under her eyes. Now that she was wearing a peignoir her advanced pregnancy was painfully evident. She was only a year older than he was, but they were worlds apart in experience.

'Van Santen was a bachelor for so many years . . . the servants were taking advantage. I can't run this household properly unless I am strict with them. The Batavians are an uppity lot and not very hard workers, either, so I have no choice but to keep them to a tight discipline. Where are you off to?'

'To get dressed.'

'Come and have some breakfast first, then Sidin can clear the table when we've finished.'

Van Santen had already left for his office, but Cateau was seated at the breakfast table, in 'Dutch' attire. 'Lazybones!' she said, smiling as she poured him coffee. 'When Bertha's ready we'll be going out.'

'Ah, running errands with my two sisters! I look forward to that, and besides, I will be grateful for your support and advice. Perhaps we could call at that travel office, so I can organise my trip to Ardjasari.'

'We can leave the errands until later. We will be going to Great-aunt Holle's for the traditional *rijsttafel*.'

'Life in the Indies always begins with getting to know the Holle clan,' Bertha said, without a trace of irony, so far as he could make out. She handed him a plate of tropical fruit, carefully peeled and purged of pips.

Rudolf wanted to protest, for he had hoped to get various practicalities out of the way as soon as possible, but his sisters were adamant: the invitation had arrived while he was still at sea. He simply had to meet his Batavian relations first.

'Could we go there on foot?' he asked. 'It would be interesting to see the neighbourhood by day.'

Cateau burst out laughing. 'Did you hear that, Bertha? A real greenhorn! You see, brother dear, no one walks after nine in the morning here. It's much too hot.'

'I'm not supposed to show myself in public any more,' said Bertha dully. 'But going for drives when it's dark is all right, and so is visiting the family.'

*

Great-aunt Alexandrine Holle, née Van der Hucht, reminded Rudolf strongly of her sister, Grandma Kerkhoven, and also of Great-uncle Willem van der Hucht. She resembled the former in appearance as well as in her dedication to family affairs, and her brother in her practical nature and air of authority. She lived in a majestic home on Koningsplein, where she received her offspring on fixed days of the week to discuss family affairs over the copious *rijsttafel*. Being a resident of such long standing, she knew everyone in Batavia, and was in a position to establish contacts and set up negotiations simply by means of an informal note or a private word, thereby avoiding the time-consuming intricacies of normal transactions.

Rudolf began to realise the extent of the Holle family's influence in the Indies. Herman Holle was at the helm of Pryce & Co., the trading firm established by, among others, Great-uncle Willem van der Hucht. Karel, Adriaan and Albert were managing large plantations in the Preanger; one daughter was married to a banker, another to a board member of the main factory-house in Batavia, and a third to a plantation administrator in the Buitenzorg region. To top it all, since Karel Holle's recent appointment by the colonial government as honorary adviser for native affairs, the family's predominantly mercantile and agrarian interests seemed to have the veneer of officialdom.

Great-aunt Holle looked serenely dignified in her old-fashioned crinoline of black silk; her hairstyle was similarly outmoded. Despite her advanced age she struck Rudolf at once as remarkably alert and knowledgeable about affairs in the outside world. From her easy chair among the potted plants and ferns she surveyed her large household with the eye of a strategist.

Carriages rolled up one after the other, bringing the Denninghoff Stellings (Albertine Holle and her husband), the Van den Bergs

(Caroline Holle and her husband), Herman Holle, and finally Van Santen. Rudolf felt himself in the midst of the overseas counterpart of a family gathering at Hunderen. He was impressed by the looks of his middle-aged female cousins, especially Albertine, who was clothed and coiffured like a Parisienne. Cousin Herman was a placid bachelor, fairly stout, with a discoloured, ginger moustache. Denninghoff Stelling made a jovial impression, with side whiskers that were just as fashionable in their way as the expensive gown worn by his wife. Rudolf felt an immediate sympathy for the charming Caroline, whose no less amiable husband, Van den Berg, was of slight build, with intelligent, piercing eyes behind the glasses of his lorgnette.

The guests convened on the veranda at the back of the house. The afternoon light filtered in through the blinds of thinly spliced bamboo, giving the marble floor tiles a muted golden glow. A lavish East Indian meal awaited them there, and Great-aunt Holle was highly amused by Rudolf's hesitation to partake of various dishes whose colour and aroma were new to him.

'You'll get used to the food, Rudolf, never fear. At first your sisters didn't much like it, either, and just look at them now!'

'*Kepiting* pasties, lovely! Ru, this is crab. And that is *dendeng*, beef with spices – oh, you must have a taste,' cried Cateau as she took her pick from the multitude of small dishes offered by two houseboys circulating with trays. Rudolf put up his hand to stop her reaching over the table and piling his plate with tasty confections.

'Your mother makes some very fine *atjar* and jelly,' said Great-aunt Holle. 'But aside from that, she and your father don't like the local food, which is a pity, as it's inexpensive and easy to obtain. On the other hand, they grow vegetables at Ardjasari which we can't get here.'

Van den Berg, having just gnawed at a chicken drumstick,

dipped into the fingerbowl beside his plate. 'Capital *rijsttafel* as per usual, Mama.'

'Well, yours is always first-rate, too,' said Denninghoff Stelling.

'Caroline and Norbert keep open house every Sunday,' Albertine explained. 'They have as many as thirty guests sometimes.'

'You must promise to come this Sunday, Cousin,' said Caroline. 'I'm counting on you.'

'But I shall be at Ardjasari on Sunday, all being well,' said Rudolf. 'I haven't seen my parents for over five years, and I can't wait to get home.'

'It has all been taken care of,' Great-aunt Holle declared in a kind but decisive tone. 'Herman is to take you to Parakan Salak, where you will be staying with Adriaan at first. You will meet Albert there, too, and Eduard Kerkhoven, of course, who will take you to Sinagar and Moendjoel afterwards. And then you can go and visit our Pauline and her husband, Hoogeveen, at Tjisalak, which actually adjoins Parakan Salak to the south.'

'If I am not mistaken,' commented Herman, 'you will be meeting Karel either at Parakan Salak or at Sinagar. Of course, he will want to show you around Waspada. It's only a small detour, and from there you can easily go to Ardjasari.' To which Cateau added, 'That'll save you all the rigmarole of hiring horses and carts and finding lodging on the way. They take care of everything for you.'

'But I would really prefer to go home first,' Rudolf repeated. He noticed Bertha looking at him intently, with a slight toss of her head.

Albertine put her hand on his arm. 'Don't worry; you can leave it all to us. Your parents aren't expecting you yet anyway.'

To Rudolf the meal seemed to go on for ever, with constant offerings of more hot rice and yet more side-dishes. For the men there was good white wine, refreshingly cool – 'we keep our bottles in the *mandi* tank,' explained Great-aunt Holle. The ladies drank cold tea. The conversation was lively, touching on a kaleidoscopic range of topics. There was talk of the *Willem II*, the new steamship that had gone down in flames on its maiden voyage, and Rudolf's remark that he had considered booking his passage on that vessel caused quite a stir. From the dangers of travel the conversation drifted to Cousin Engelbert de Waal, retired Minister for the Colonies, who had been injured during a railway accident on his way to the South of France, when a goods wagon carrying munitions exploded. Thankfully, he was on the mend.

'It's a scandal! Can you imagine the French railway company adding freight wagons with war materials to a passenger train? How dare they!'

'And without even informing the passengers!'

'Cousin de Waal was struck in the face by broken glass. What if he loses his sight?'

'That would be a tragedy, especially in the case of someone like him, a true scholar in his way. He might not even be able to finish writing his book on East Indian finance, for which expectations are running high.'

'Cousin de Waal possesses incredible fortitude,' observed Great-aunt Holle. 'I have witnessed as much with my own eyes. Such an indefatigable worker, poring over papers from dawn till dusk – that was when he was government secretary. He hardly ever went out in society. And then he always suffered from asthma – *kasian*, poor man.'

'All that for a mere pittance,' Denninghoff Stelling remarked dryly.

'If his health hadn't been so poor he could have made it to Governor-General,' said Van den Berg. 'Talking of France, from what we have heard over here, Thiers seems to have taken harsh measures. The Commune is finished.'

'Yesterday, just as we landed, a telegram arrived saying that parts of Paris were in ruins.' Rudolf was glad for the chance to contribute to the conversation. 'They fired into the crowds. I wonder if it was wise of the Thiers government to use such violent means. It strikes me as a reactionary blight on a Republic based on democratic principles.'

All eyes were fixed on him.

'That is the problem,' said Van den Berg. 'How far should one go in suppressing radical elements? How to retain the worthwhile elements of conservatism without hampering progress? Our own contemporary politics will have to reckon with that too. True liberals are thin on the ground.'

'Take Cousin de Waal!' cried Great-aunt Holle, evidently wishing to steer the conversation closer to home. 'An exceptional man. So hard-working and sensible. I trust he will recover. I am eternally grateful to him for the good influence he had on my boys.'

Memories were evoked of the time when she, recently widowed, was living at Parakan Salak with her children. The name cropped up of Douwes Dekker – their notorious cousin-by-marriage. Rudolf took the opportunity to enquire about this distant relative, by whom he had long been intrigued.

'Dekker?' cried Albertine. 'Very humorous, and charming too when he had a mind to it, but a very vain man. He used to flirt with Caro and Paul and me right in front of Cousin Tine. We were only children at the time, but he wanted us all to adore him. All the girls had to adore him.'

'Ah yes, that charm of his,' said Great-aunt Holle, shaking her head. 'I will never forget how Cousin Tine came to the house one evening in a cab – that must have been in fifty-one or thereabouts, because we hadn't been here very long. She had fled from Dekker's bullying. Afterwards he turned up himself, to fetch her. He had such a way with words, that man! I was amazed by how submissive she was, how she flung her arms about his neck. She was at his beck and call. Some people, young people in particular, idolised Dekker. Fortunately, my children never did.'

'Actually, Karel was quite in awe of him for a time,' said Caroline. 'That was when he was working in Tjandjoer at the secretariat. I remember it very clearly, Mama. When Dekker came to Parakan Salak he often mentioned a French novel he greatly admired, about a man who was truly humane, a protector of the poor and the oppressed. Dekker took the hero of that story as his example, he told us. And Karel did the same.'

Albertine chimed in: 'Dekker dreamt of being the Emperor of Insulinde. And Karel dreamt of being the Ratoe Adil. I can still hear them talking on the front veranda, in the moonlight, about how they would free the Javanese people from slavery.'

'Karel has kept his word. He's doing a lot of good.'

'Often at his own expense, too. Money doesn't concern him.'

'He knows where to find us, though, when he needs funding for his projects,' Van Santen observed tartly.

'I am so glad we have such clever financiers in the family now,' said Great-aunt Holle, nodding and smiling at her sons-in-law. 'Times have changed. Oh, it wasn't at all easy in the beginning. And yet we were happy at Parakan Salak, when we were all still together. Such a shame Adriaan pulled the old house down.'

'But their new house is very nice, I'm told. Jans is as proud as anything,' said Albertine.

'Jans is Adriaan's wife, Rudolf. They were married four months ago. She is a Van Motman.'

'Bertha and I went to stay with the Van Motmans on their estate outside Buitenzorg several times,' added Cateau. 'They're quite ordinary people. Very East Indian, but extremely hospitable and kind.'

'They're not that ordinary, you know,' Herman observed. 'The family has been in Java since the beginning of the last century.

They're landed gentry of the traditional type, Eurasian aristocracy, you could say.'

'By the way, Rudolf, did you speak to my dear brother Willem before you left?' asked Great-aunt Holle.

Rudolf replied that he had paid him a farewell visit at his country house, Duin en Berg, which he proceeded to describe. In conclusion he added, 'There was a very strange item in the newspaper about him at the beginning of the year, which said something like, "All we know of Mr Van der Hucht is that he used to sell tea in the Indies and now shoots rabbits in Velzen, and that he votes in Parliament in such a way that it is impossible to make out what his political principles are." It was even suggested that his unpredictability was making him unpopular in his party.'

Herman exploded with laughter. 'That's because his principles come from the Indies! Quite beyond your average members of Parliament!'

That there was more to Batavia than white palatial homes became clear to Rudolf during the days that followed, while he waited for Herman Holle to take time off for travel. He went for long walks, more often than not on his own. Cateau would accompany him early in the morning, provided they kept to the shady avenues west of Koningsplein. They went down Tanah Abang to the cemetery, where they read the names on the tombs and headstones, and stood still for a while at little Pauline's grave.

Kitted out with a hat and a sunshade, he set out on foot (which caused some consternation) for the downtown area, where he imagined himself in China, among the houses with colourful pottery dragons guarding the entrance, signs in undecipherable script on each façade, men wearing their hair in a long pigtail hanging down their backs. He roamed the native markets overflowing with fruits, tobacco, live chickens in bundles tied together by their feet, lengths of printed cotton, and a bewildering array of items he could not identify, observing at close quarters the vibrant, colourful swell of life in the city, so unlike the rarefied atmosphere of noiseless servants at the Van Santens and the Holles. The alleyways separating the gardens of the European houses led him to sprawling kampongs, mazes of dense greenery, bamboo dwellings – some no more than a roof on posts – with fenced-off vegetable plots, or he suddenly found himself on the bank of the river that flowed through the city, where he saw people bathing and doing their business, and huddles of small naked children staring at him in wonder.

It was July, the height of the dry season. In the white heat of the midday sun a paralysing lethargy came over the city. Rudolf longed for a gust of wind. It wasn't until their carriage-ride after sundown that he felt he could breathe again. At Bertha's in the evenings the mosquitoes drove him to seek refuge in his curtained bed, at an earlier hour than he would have wished.

Although each day brought new, absorbing experiences, and he received a letter from his parents at Ardjasari endorsing the Holles' plans for his immediate future, he felt increasingly frustrated by not knowing what would happen afterwards, what would come of the future for which he had spent all those years preparing himself. He felt at ease with his sisters in Bertha's immaculate home, but by the end of the week he had had enough of all the chatter about friends and relations, layettes and the impending arrival of the baby. He did not see much of Van Santen. He had tried on several occasions to gain some information from him about the financial backing of Ardjasari and related matters, but each time his brother-in-law had responded in the vaguest of terms, mumbling something about banking codes of confidentiality.

With Cateau's help, Rudolf set about procuring certain tools and items of clothing which, in the Holles' estimation, were indispensable for life on a plantation.

He was on the point of asking Herman, quite against his sisters' wishes, to make some haste when the news came that everything was ready for their departure.

The four-horse carriage drew up just as day was breaking. The luggage was strapped on to the rear. Bertha and Cateau supplied them with refreshments for the journey.

They set off southwards in the hazy light of dawn as cocks began to crow all over the kampongs of Batavia. Herman leaned back in a corner of the carriage, dozing, but Rudolf was all agog for his first journey into the interior. It was still fairly cool, and as the canvas flaps had not yet been lowered to provide shade he had an excellent view of the rice fields and orchards; amid the greenery he was able to pick out the elongated *pisang* leaf and the hand-shaped leaf of the pawpaw tree, which Bertha had pointed out to him in her garden. He marvelled at the lushness of the countryside and the innumerable shades of green, and could see, now, what his father meant in his letters when he harped on about the impossibility of describing the tropical landscape. In the distance loomed the foothills of the Preanger, their bluish crests paling as the sun climbed higher in the blazing sky.

'Look, there's Mount Salak!' said Herman, rousing himself. 'We'll be in Buitenzorg before long.'

To Rudolf's regret there was not enough time for a visit, however cursory, to the Botanic Gardens, which he had always heard described as one of the great wonders of the world. But Herman wanted to press on immediately after their meal at the Bellevue Hotel, where they were provided with a fresh team of horses better suited to the mountainous terrain.

'Adriaan is expecting us before sundown. The road from here to Parakan Salak is very poor, especially the last part across the mountain. Best to make an early start, in case we run into any difficulties.'

They made a single stop on the way to rest the horses. Herman and Rudolf stretched their legs in a glade, where they could hear water trickling down the thickly overgrown slope. Rudolf stared about him in awe, his senses overwhelmed by the light, the fragrances rising from the sun-warmed bushes, the sweeping views. Flooded *sawahs* glittered on the plains; the hills looked bleached in the afternoon sun. But then, as if by magic, the sky over the mountain peaks beyond darkened into a bank of deep-blue cloud.

Adriaan Holle was waiting for them at the entrance to the Parakan Salak tea estate, astride his Arab thoroughbred. Rudolf was impressed by the handsome stallion, and even more so by his cousin's skill in making his horse describe perfect figures of eight at the gate as they approached.

Adriaan's slight but muscular frame was in contrast to the ailing aspect of his features. The smooth, dark moustache and pointed beard looked as if they had been painted on to his sallow skin.

'Adriaan is not very well,' Herman murmured. 'He suffers from indigestion, and from headaches, too. Pity. He used to be so tough, the toughest of us all. Not afraid of anything, in the old days. When we were living in the old house we used to have a lot of trouble with mad dogs. They would hole up in the *kolong* – that's what they call the space underneath the house – and nobody dared to chase them away, but Adriaan went after them with a long stick, in his bare feet, and if he got bitten he would promptly cauterise the wound with burning charcoal himself. And you should have seen him on tiger hunts! All that's finished now; he no longer hunts. Too tiring.'

Adriaan steered his horse close alongside the carriage, pointing ahead. 'My *gedoeng*!'

In the distance they could make out the much-vaunted new house situated on the brow of a hill, framed by towering trees, against a backdrop of mountains veiled in mist. As far as the eye could see there was undulating terrain scored by straight lines of shrubs. Rudolf's first impression of the tea plantation was that of a thick green carpet shorn into stripes, shaded here and there by the lacy foliage of a tree he had never seen before. Only the palm trees with their huge fronds were familiar to him, as were the tall stalks of bamboo with pointed, down-turned leaves along the wayside.

They approached the house along a drive lined with a double row of tall conifers. It stood on the site formerly occupied by the old, East Indian-style manager's bungalow, the home so fondly recollected by Great-aunt Holle. The new two-storey villa, built by Adriaan prior to his marriage, was huge, and seemed to proclaim the growth and prosperity of his enterprise. Dominating the façade was an upstairs veranda with a rectangular projection rather like the bridge of a ship, from which the estate could be surveyed.

Stable-boys and domestic servants awaited them by the front steps, and once inside they were welcomed by the lady of the house. Rudolf thought her name – Jans – utterly at odds with the stately, exotic vision in sarong and kebaya stepping forward to greet them with great warmth and charm, after which she showed them the guest rooms on the ground floor, brimming with apologies in case she had not got everything right yet, seeing as the house was only just finished.

Rudolf bathed and put on fresh clothes. The sun was just

setting, briefly flooding his room with purple. Through the west-facing window he watched the shadows on the mountain flanks deepen while the cicadas began their shrill chirping in the trees.

The oil lamps were already lit when he climbed the stairs to the living quarters. He found himself in yet another entirely new, doubly foreign world. The drawing-room had a high, domed ceiling, painted dark blue with decorations in paler shades of blue, as one would expect to find in an Italian renaissance villa. The walls were papered in the European fashion, and on the floor lay a large, richly hued carpet.

He came upon Adriaan and Herman seated at the dinner table, drinking their evening bitters. Jans motioned the houseboys waiting by the sideboard to pour Rudolf a glass, too. He had already been served this potent East Indian apéritif at the Van Santens, and was resolved to drink it in moderation.

'Do take a seat!' said Adriaan. 'I am expecting Eduard and Albert tomorrow. They will be bringing Karel, who's at Sinagar at the moment.'

The following morning Adriaan showed Rudolf his stables, where he kept more than fifty horses, several of which had won prizes at the annual races in Buitenzorg. The mildly distracted air Adriaan had possessed during the meal (the conversation had been kept going by a vivacious Jans) vanished completely now that he was in the stable among his horses, talking to them, feeding them tender ears of rice and instructing the stable-boys regarding their care. The horses, noble-headed and moist-eyed, were as distinct from one another as human beings; and each had its own melodious name. They were treated by Adriaan with paternal authority, and by the servants with respect. Rudolf was struck by the sheer variety of breeds: in addition to costly Arabs there were also Batak and

Makassar ponies, sturdy Australian horses, and even some Sandalwoods.

Next they took a tour round the factory. In a hangar consisting of a roof on posts and bamboo walls, they encountered row upon row of circular basketwork trays.

'Those are *tampirs*,' Adriaan explained. 'When the pickers return from the gardens they first have their hods weighed, and then they empty the wet leaf onto the trays.'

'It isn't raining, is it?' said Rudolf, which made Adriaan laugh.

'Wet leaf simply means that it's freshly harvested, in its raw state before treatment. At least half the moisture has to evaporate. We call it "withering", and that's what the *tampirs* are for. It may take only a few hours, depending on the weather, of course, but usually the tea is left to dry overnight, after which the leaf has to be rolled. My people do that by hand, and sometimes by foot, not that I approve of that. Come with me, I'll show you what they're doing with yesterday's withered leaves.'

They entered a second hangar. Here the entire floor was taken up by *tampirs* heaped with drying leaves. Men and women squatted between the rows of flat baskets, taking tufts of leaves and rolling them on a plank with the flat of their hands. A tangy smell of fresh sap wafted towards him, which Rudolf inhaled with relish. The rolled leaves formed a greenish-brown, sticky mush.

'How long does it take to complete the process?'

'About three or four days. Again, that depends on the weather. We get the rolled leaf to ferment by heating it in pans over charcoal fires. We call that "panning". The final stage is drying. What I produce is called Souchon, which is what people like best.'

He led the way to the third hangar. 'This is where the packing is done. Over on the other side is the carpentry workshop, where the tea chests are made. As you can see, I have roughly a hundred people working for me in the factory. The rolling can be done mechanically nowadays, apparently. My assistant is very keen for us to buy one of those machines. It would save time, of course, and labour, too.'

'So it would be more economical?'

'Yes, I suppose it would be. But we believe in providing work for the people. I haven't made up my mind yet. I'll have to discuss it with Karel, see what he thinks.'

When they were outside again Adriaan said, 'I gather you don't ride? Pity, that. It would have been good to have ridden out together around the plantation. But you really must see one of my kampongs. I had them all refurbished a few years ago.'

They went down a deeply shaded lane to the nearest workers' kampong. The contrast with the urban kampongs he had seen in Batavia made him gasp in surprise. Well-maintained, straight lanes and side alleys divided the area into rectangular plots with spruce-looking, whitewashed dwellings and flowering hedges. At that hour there were only a few elderly folk and young children about, all of whom greeted Adriaan with what Rudolf felt was exaggerated reverence: they sank down on their haunches and touched their folded hands to the forehead. Adriaan answered each greeting with a friendly word.

They took a detour on the way back. Adriaan pointed to a small building with a stucco cupola and a slender spire. 'Our mosque! I had it built myself; it was Karel's idea. So now I'm in the imam's good books, and it's the imams who tell the people to work hard and keep their homes in order. There's a fair amount of competition around here as to who has the tidiest home and the smartest fence.'

'This must be what Great-uncle Jan had in mind as the ideal colony!' laughed Rudolf.

Two men came towards them from the big house. There was no need for Adriaan to explain who they were. The one who resembled both Adriaan and Herman had to be Albert Holle. Rudolf recognised the other one at once, even though it was ten years since they had last seen each other. Now that Eduard Kerkhoven had grown a moustache, he looked as if he could have been the son of Great-uncle Van der Hucht. He wore a curious hat, which reminded Rudolf of a picture he had seen of Scotsmen in traditional costume: dented at the top, and with two tartan ribbons down the back. He was quite burly, but still had the same youthful exuberance Rudolf remembered from the old days at Hunderen.

'Welcome!' cried Eduard. 'What's keeping you? Karel is waiting at the *gedoeng*.'

The man rising to greet him looked so familiar that for an instant Rudolf thought his father had come over from Ardjasari to see him.

Karel Holle was slightly younger, and of roughly the same build; he too had a full beard, and his eyes, although paler, had the same friendly gleam as those of Rudolf's father. But in manner and dress he was quite different. Karel wore a Turkish fez with a tassel, and on the little finger of his left hand a large diamond ring, which sparkled with every gesture; his coat was unusually shaped, and on his feet he wore leather mules. He touched his thumbs swiftly to his lips before extending his hand to Rudolf.

'Well now, Cousin, so you have come to join our ranks. *Bismillah*!'

Karel dominated over the gathering, that much was clear. He had an air of natural authority. The others seemed to look up to him as their leader and spokesman, a role he graciously acknowledged. Even more striking was the obsequiousness bordering on veneration displayed towards him by Adriaan's Soendanese servants. Karel Holle settled himself on a low bench with his right knee raised and his right foot curled behind his left knee. He spoke in a soft, measured voice, with a light sing-song to it. He was like a king holding court. Rudolf stared in fascination at this fabled kinsman.

'This is where it all started. Parakan Salak is the cradle of our enterprises. That is why it is fitting that you should visit the tea lands first. You have already seen how extensive the gardens are. I expect Adriaan has also told you about the way this plantation is run – the only correct way, in my opinion. Each household is assigned a particular plot of land, and is responsible for pruning and plucking the tea bushes growing on it. It would be good if your father followed Adriaan's example at Ardjasari.'

'I have not been there yet, Cousin Karel. I don't know the ins and outs of Ardjasari, or which method my father uses.'

'It is not just a question of the best way to treat tea bushes. In my view it is paramount that the people working on the estate should feel some kind of engagement with the product. There has to be close-knit community, such as the peasant population is accustomed to, so they can put down roots. I am glad that Adriaan has taken my advice in providing decent housing for his people. Have you seen where they live? Give people good homes and good tools, and they will be glad to do a good job. What do you say, Adriaan?'

'I am satisfied with the way things are going,' said Adriaan.

Karel Holle turned to Rudolf again. 'You may have heard about the Soendanese being lazy, but don't you believe it. What you need to do is take the trouble to make it plain to them what they stand to gain with the new farming methods. They are not yet aware of the enormous advantages in the longer term. Still, I have made some headway with that, too, I am glad to say. They have learnt how to stop erosion on the upper slopes: by building terraces, just as they have been doing for centuries with their *sawahs*. And I have shown them that planting out the *bibit*, the rice seedlings, further apart yields a better harvest. It's the same with tea. If they care about a crop – I mean, if it is of interest to them on a personal level – they will be prepared to adapt their methods of cultivation. The people here have a preference for so-called green tea for their own consumption, just as they do in China and Japan.'

Rudolf noted the look of understanding exchanged by Eduard and Albert. Karel noted it, too.

'As I have said before, it would be worthwhile switching to green tea. It means little or no fermentation, and as the size of the leaf doesn't matter so much, picking is easier. There's no need for sorting, either.'

'There is no demand for green tea in the European market,' observed Eduard. Karel kept silent for a while. The ferns in their glazed pots stirred in the draught. It was pleasantly cool on the upstairs veranda.

'The government's new agrarian policies are bound to have an effect on our relations with the people,' continued Karel, his tone becoming more familiar. 'Anyone can see that! And we should act accordingly! The people don't only work for us; we work with them, too. Making green tea would mean that we supply the local market. That would stimulate the willingness to work while raising the standard of living, and that is what we have always wanted. There is a huge market for green tea in Asia. That is something European planters ought to realise. Yes, I am quite positive,' he said urgently. 'For goodness' sake, let's not make the same mistakes all over again! Look, Rudolf . . . from the moment I came out here as a boy it has pained me more than I can say to see the contrast between the fertility of this beautiful land and the poverty of the people, the little folk, the peasantry. The Soendalands are a forsaken region, dominated for centuries by the kings of central and eastern Java. They have lost their own culture. It's a wonder they still have their own language. The Soendanese are a case apart. That never occurs to the powers-that-be . . . not in Batavia and not in The Hague, either, needless to say.'

'But Karel,' Adriaan soothed, 'there have been quite a few improvements, thanks to you. You have been appointed as their adviser for Preanger affairs. They have made you a Knight of the Order of the Netherlands Lion. The colonial government listens to you. You even managed to obtain subsidies for those schools of yours.'

'Don't ask me how! There was so much slander. Can you imagine how humiliating it was to have my friends – including the *patih* of Mangoenredja, the *patih* of Galoeh, as well as Radèn Hadji Moesa – summoned for questioning as to the nature of my activities? And there are still preposterous accusations being made against me in the papers, particularly in the *Java-Bode*. The latest one is that, by supporting Islam, I am fomenting a conspiracy against the government. To think that any school of mine, any little grocery shop, any workshop for native crafts could ever be a hotbed of rebellion! Are they blind? Can't they see that everything depends on the kind of attitude we ourselves take?'

He leaned over to Rudolf and patted his knee with the hand wearing the sparkling diamond. 'The people here are highly sensitive to matters of honour. You have to treat them with consideration, and especially with respect for their traditions, their *adat*. Once they accept your authority they are loyal and compliant. Self-control is of the utmost importance. No flying into rages and especially no physical abuse! An unjust punishment or reprimand can have dire consequences. There have been cases of officials and planters paying with their lives for an insult or a blow dealt in anger. But a rightful, properly expressed judgement is always acknowledged in this country. You should try to learn the language as soon as possible. You won't get anywhere without a sound knowledge of Soendanese. It's a pity your father still only knows Malay, and that he needs an interpreter to communicate with his workers.'

'I'll try my best,' said Rudolf, overwhelmed as much by Karel Holle's pronouncements as by his compelling, pale-blue gaze.

'And now for something different. My dear Adriaan, one of the reasons I came over from Waspada was to hear your *gamelan*.'

Adriaan waved his hand dismissively and shook his head. 'We only have the *gamelan* in the afternoon nowadays, when it's weighing time in the factory.'

'There are still some compositions of yours for the *rebab* that I'm waiting to hear.'

'I seldom play my *rebab* nowadays; I don't have the time.'

'Please don't disappoint me, brother,' said Karel, unperturbed. After some prevarication Adriaan relented, making ironical comments about not having enough practice and not feeling up to it, but Rudolf thought he seemed pleased, excited even, at the prospect of making music. Adriaan gave orders for the *gamelan* to be set up on the ground-floor veranda adjoining the guest rooms, after which he excused himself. He reappeared after half an hour in native dress: a high-necked tunic with tight sleeves, and a *kain* that was artfully pleated at the front. His hat was in curious contrast to this costume: like Eduard Kerkhoven, he now wore a Scottish highland cap with two tartan ribbons hanging down the back. He motioned the others to follow him downstairs. He seemed to have distanced himself from them, an impression that became all the stronger when he seated himself cross-legged among the assembled *gamelan* players. Rudolf had never seen percussion instruments of this type before, some of them resembling xylophones, with keys of wood and metal on a low base. There was also a double row of rounded brass chimes in diminishing sizes, as well as a bronze gong in a beautifully carved frame.

'I salute Sari Onèng!' Karel Holle raised his folded hands to his face again. He turned to Rudolf. 'The Javanese think of the *gamelan* as a person, with a name and character of their own. This one here is called Sari Onèng; she is fifty years old and most venerable, and she comes from Soemedang, where they make the best *gamelans* in the country.'

Chairs were placed in a semicircle facing the orchestra at one end of the long veranda. Jans Holle appeared briefly in a doorway, but did not join the audience. Rudolf caught a glimpse of her expression just as she was turning away, which made him think she had reservations about the forthcoming performance, and that her husband's trance-like concentration on his two-stringed fiddle might have something to do with it.

Adriaan held the *rebab* by its long ivory neck, resting the sound box – a coconut shell covered with buffalo gut – on the floor in front of him, and set about tuning the strings by carefully turning the pegs on either side of the neck, testing the sound each time with his bow.

'Watch this,' murmured Karel Holle. 'Adriaan will start off in solo with the introduction, the *gending* – that's the melody of the piece, which he composed himself – and then it will be taken over by the *bonang*, and the *saron*, and the *gendèr* . . . Shush, he's about to begin.'

The tune Adriaan played sounded plaintive to Rudolf, and also outlandish, on account of all the half-tones. After a few bars the other instruments joined in. Rudolf had heard *gamelan* music described as endless rounds of ding-a-ling and clang-a-lang, monotonous and sleep-inducing, but he was quite carried away by the subtle variations in sound and rhythm of the *rebab* in accompaniment with the flute, and the polyphonic percussion punctuated by deep reverberations of the gong. Without thinking, he began to move his head and shoulders in time to the music. When he noticed Karel Holle's sidelong smile, he forced himself to keep perfectly still for the rest of the performance.

After an early breakfast the following morning, Rudolf found his Uncle Eduard waiting for him in the bay of the upper veranda, looking out over the landscape. He stood between two columns with spiral ornaments, which reminded Rudolf of the sugar-stick confections sold at the fairground back home. All over the gardens there were tea pickers at work, wearing large, round sunhats; seen from above, they resembled outsize mushrooms.

'Good morning!' said Eduard Kerkhoven. 'I have heard you do not ride.'

'I did when I was a boy, at Hunderen. But that was a long time ago. No, Uncle, I don't ride.'

'Then we'll have to do something about that. We can start today; you can ride with me to Sinagar. Adriaan has a fine horse for you, as meek as a lamb. Life here is impossible if you don't ride, believe me. For one thing, you can't keep an eye on all the gardens if you have to walk everywhere. I have found your father a pair of first-rate Preangers, a cross between an Arab and the native breed, and I strongly advise you to ride either one of them every day once you get to Ardjasari. Just to make sure you become firm in the saddle. Let's go, then, shall we? Karel and Albert will be following later in the day.'

Rudolf's mount turned out to be anything but as meek as a lamb. On flat stretches he more or less succeeded in controlling the horse, which was called Si Fatima, but on the steep, narrow bridle tracks, sometimes stony, sometimes muddy, with the nervous mare skidding on the brink of a ravine or rearing up in fright from a rock tumbling down the mountainside, his summary riding skills were tested beyond endurance. Now and then Eduard gave a shout of warning or advice, but most of the time Rudolf was too agitated to take notice. He was conscious of the beauty of the surroundings, but could not afford to take it in. After a few hours – an eternity to him – they entered the grounds of Sinagar.

'This is nothing like Parakan Salak,' Eduard remarked. They slowed to a sedate walking pace, to Rudolf's profound relief. The two servants had given their horses free rein, and were galloping ahead to announce the master's imminent arrival. 'My tea gardens, like Albert's at Moendjoel, are too far apart for us to adopt Karel's system. In our situation it would lead to too much variation in quality, what with some of the men pruning far more often than others and some women picking too coarsely and others too selectively, all taking their own time. Too much of it, if you ask me. Until now Albert and I have been getting the best results with organised teams overseen by good *mandoers*. Quite a few of my overseers are Chinese; they're very reliable. Look over there – that's where I live. A bit rambling, admittedly; it dates back to the time of the first government plantations, but it suits me fine.'

'Azaleas!' exclaimed Rudolf. 'I didn't know they grew here.'

The manager's bungalow was partially screened by a flush of azaleas in full flower, scarlet, purple and bright orange in the sunlight.

'They're my pride and joy,' said Eduard. 'Remember the azaleas at Hunderen? I've given cuttings to your mother. Let's hope she'll make herself a good flower garden at Ardjasari; it can be very rewarding in this climate.'

No sooner had they emerged from the shade of the tree-lined drive than a pack of at least fifteen dogs, large and small, came bounding towards them, barking excitedly. Eduard dismounted. 'Down, Mirza! Good boy, Gètok! Down, Courtois! Stop that, Pekoe! Calm down, all of you, calm down, I say!'

*

'You won't find it very cosy inside, not much in the way of knick-knacks,' said Eduard as he led the way into his living quarters with the dogs prancing at his heels. The furniture was sparse, but the walls were covered in antlers and animal hides. 'This house is very practical. No fuss. Adriaan's new *gedoeng* is too fancy for my taste. I want my dogs to have the run of the house, and my pet deer, too, if they feel like it, even my hens. How do you like my mural arrangement over there, on the side of the inside gallery? A fine aid to digestion, wouldn't you say?'

During the midday meal Rudolf was seated in full view of a python skin several metres long, which was mounted on the facing wall alongside the skeleton of a kid devoured by the gigantic serpent moments before death.

'Well, I hope you can handle a gun at least,' said Eduard. 'Your father's a hunter after my own heart.'

'When I was a boy I went shooting snipe with Papa a few times. But he had already come out here by the time I went to university, and they don't hunt in Delft.'

'I advise you to get some practice without delay. You need to be a good shot, living up in the mountains with all that jungle around. Besides, you have the occasional panther or wild boar straying into the gardens, even prowling around the house sometimes. And your prestige depends to a large extent on how you handle a breech-loader. One day, soon after I arrived here, I hit the stem of a huge *nangka* high up in a tree, quite by accident, and the fruit dropped to the ground right in front of me. That did it for me – my people have respected me ever since.'

'You made quite a name for yourself with your marksmanship back in Hunderen, as I remember.'

'You get the best shooting of all in Gelderland, hunting hare and wild fowl! It's not the same over here. I have joined some of Karel's native chiefs on their hunts – if you can call them that, because they're more like organised massacres. Wild boar are let loose in a fenced-off area, then they shoot at them from a grandstand. And when they do go out into the wilds they make a ridiculous spectacle of themselves, with a whole retinue of grooms, boys laden with chairs, tobacco, *sirih*, cigars, rifles and munitions, and at the first sight of game the chase begins without the least plan or strategy. Of course something has to be done to protect the population against predators, but that is not the same as extermination. I still have a dream of leasing or buying a large tract of land somewhere on the south coast, some wilderness with mountains and jungles, to turn it into a game reserve where proper hunting rules would apply. But I doubt my dream will come true. I can't see myself finding either the time or the money.'

The dogs sat in a wide circle around the table, eagerly following every gesture of the two diners. From time to time Eduard held up a bone or piece of gristle, whereupon all the dogs leaped up, but without entering the forbidden circle. Only when he called a dog by its name would it approach the table to catch the tossed morsel. Rudolf praised their discipline.

'I am strict with them. I have to be. We have as many as twenty dogs here sometimes, when we have an influx of lodgers from Moendjoel or Parakan Salak during the absence of their masters. There are some fine hunting hounds among them. You might find this strange, but do you know what else I dream of sometimes? Of hunting in the Mheen near Beekbergen, and in the oak forest of the Orderbos, or the pine woods at Berghuis – you know what I mean.'

'Do you miss Holland much, Uncle?'

'I can't say I do, really. Can't afford to. But with any luck I'll go back at some point in my life. I take a philosophical view of things. Did you know I studied philosophy for a spell in Leiden? Don't laugh! No, I didn't get a degree. I gave up halfway and came out here. I get all the philosophy I need from looking at the mountains.'

The Sinagar tea factory, like that of Parakan Salak, comprised several hangars. The bamboo lattices between the roof posts served not only to admit light and air, Eduard explained, but also to guard against mad dogs, which were still rife in the area.

Rudolf trailed after Eduard as he made his way among the workers. They saluted their *djoeragan* and stared at the stranger with round-eyed curiosity. He did his best to maintain a suitably dignified pose, though he was aching all over from the long ride. Eduard conferred with the Chinese overseers, who wore their pigtails rolled up on the back of the head during work, and showed Rudolf the various stages of production.

'My methods are not quite the same as the ones used at Ardjasari. They follow Karel's advice in everything. I like Karel; in fact, I admire him enormously. He's a good man, and a scholar. He can read classical Soendanese texts written in ancient Javanese script, just as easily as you and I read a Walter Scott novel. But I'm not so sure about his methods as a tea planter. He likes telling me and Albert what to do, and indeed Albert tends to listen to him, but I prefer doing things my own way. I'm a Kerkhoven, not a Holle!'

'When we rode out this morning I had the impression that your tea bushes are more rounded in shape and slightly lower than at Parakan Salak. Or am I mistaken?'

'That is a question of pruning. Our China tea bushes can grow up to three metres, but then harvesting becomes a problem. Naturally I leave some of my bushes to grow and blossom freely, so as to provide seed for fresh planting, but I keep the rest clipped to a manageable size. Look!' Eduard bent down to take a sprig from a tray. 'We never remove more than the top three or four leaves of a young shoot. It takes between a week and ten days for a new leaf to form. It's all about harvesting the leaf in such a way as to strike the best balance between quantity and quality. I have divided my land into as many gardens as there are days between one harvest and the next, and I've kept the size of each garden down to what can be picked in a single day. See what I mean? So that work can go on all the time. Adriaan lets his people prune and pick according to their own insights. That way the leaf is often left on for too long, which makes for a coarser quality of tea. The Souchon he makes doesn't appeal to me very much, neither the look of it, nor the taste. It's Congo tea, really, the cheapest kind. I prefer Pekoe-Souchon, which is made of a younger, smaller leaf. So we pick more frequently here.'

Eduard held forth as they strolled back to the house, where they settled themselves on the front veranda. Eduard offered Rudolf a cigar and lit one himself.

'It is my firm belief that for a tea business to be successful it is no use leaning on idealistic principles, and not on purely commercial ones, either, for that matter – what you need is science. In my opinion the type of China tea we grow out here is not in fact the most suitable for the Indies. And the tea grown in Ceylon is of a different type, apparently. We ought to try to obtain some seed. Albert thinks so, too. I hope he will take the matter in hand once his wedding celebrations are over.'

'I didn't know Albert was getting married.'

'Didn't you? Oh well, the family has known for quite a while. He's getting married in three months' time, to a Van Motman girl. She is Jans' sister. Van Motman is a big name around here; they own more plantations than I can count on two hands. Plenty of marriageable daughters. Adriaan has Jans, his assistant has Suze, and an associate of ours at Pryce & Co. is also engaged to a Van Motman. And now Albert will be married to Wies van Motman, or to Jacoba, I'm not sure which.'

'I enjoyed meeting Cousin Jans of Parakan Salak; she's very charming. Very pretty, too, I thought.'

'Not bad for a *nonna*, I grant you. The same goes for Wies, as it happens. They make fine planters' wives. They know what life up here is like, and can deal with the locals. They are all excellent horsewomen, and they can even swim.'

'Yes, Cateau mentioned that in a letter to me. She said they swam as fast as water-rats.'

'The main thing is that they were born and bred here, so they know what to expect. Jans and her sisters don't object to seeing men lounging about the house in their pyjama suits after work. Ladies in Batavia tend to be so fussy about their husbands being properly dressed at all times. My God! I can't abide those respectable Dutch ladies – although there are exceptions, thankfully, like your mother and Cousin Pauline at Tjisalak.'

Rudolf now expected him to say something on the subject he himself did not dare raise: the Chinese common-law wife and her children, who were surely not far away.

'Let me tell you one thing,' pursued Eduard. 'Europeans must keep up their standards, or they lose prestige. The natives set great store by appearances. The slightest unseemliness can incur ridicule, even contempt. You must always bear that in mind, at the risk of losing your moral authority at a stroke. That's the trouble with all those greenhorns on the plantations, with their drinking and brawling. Their numbers seem to be increasing all the time, more's the pity. It shouldn't be allowed. Anyway, to come back to what Karel was saying yesterday about the Soendanese – you mustn't think of them as a docile lot, submitting tamely to exploitation. There have been quite a few uprisings in the past, against landowners and also against native chiefs. The mentality here is less submissive than in the Princely States, for instance. You'll see.'

*

A flock of doves swooped into the front veranda with so much flapping of wings that Rudolf ducked away. They settled on chairs and tables, and pattered over the floorboards, darting their heads this way and that.

'All right, all right, my friends! I'm a bit late today,' said Eduard. 'They turn up at four to be fed, four o'clock sharp every afternoon. Get out, you rascals, I'll be with you in a minute!'

After feeding the doves and the birds in the aviary beside the house it was evidently time for another daily ritual. Two easy chairs were pushed to the edge of the front veranda.

'Take a seat, Rudolf. You saw Adriaan's horses yesterday. Now I'll show you mine.'

A dozen horses poured from the stables, making the ground tremble under their hooves. The majority were young, both stallions and mares. Snorting and neighing, tails and manes flying, they cavorted around the flower beds in the forecourt. When they had calmed down Eduard had each one brought forward in turn. He told Rudolf their names (Favourite, Bedouin, Gloriosa, Selim, Odaliske . . .) and all the prizes, rosettes and cups they had won at the races in Batavia and Buitenzorg. 'Behold my darlings! But I have also bred first-rate draught horses from native stock. Bimanese, for instance, which are fairly small, but strong and quick. The mountain horses you have here are not large, generally speaking, and their build is not very good, especially the hooves. It always surprises me how little the locals know about horses, and how to break them in. That's why the native horses tend to be such stubborn creatures. I teach my stable-boys how to do things correctly. It's in the interest of the people to keep decent work-horses.'

*

Dusk turned rapidly into night; the mountains were no longer visible.

'What's keeping Karel and Albert?' asked Rudolf. 'Will they be all right on those mountain tracks in the dark?'

Eduard shrugged. 'They will if they have enough men with torches. But I wouldn't be surprised if they ended up staying at Parakan Salak for another night. I bet Adriaan spent all day playing his *rebab* with the *gamelan* orchestra. Last night I could tell from the expression on his face that he's fallen under the spell of that music again – if you can call it music. Personally, I can stand it for a quarter of an hour, but not longer. When I was living with Adriaan at Parakan Salak in sixty-one and sixty-two, he went through phases of practising from morning till night. It drove me mad sometimes. Karel and Albert will turn up, don't you worry, if not by tomorrow, then the day after.'

'Uncle, I do appreciate you and the Holles wanting to show me all the family plantations, but to be honest I would like to go home as soon as possible.'

To Rudolf's surprise, Eduard seemed to have been expecting this. 'Of course,' he replied. 'I quite understand. Perhaps you should leave tomorrow – I'll take responsibility. I can lend you a vehicle and some horses, and a good coachman. I can also spare someone to go with you, in case you need help. You have to hire fresh horses at every sixth post on the way, and one is supposed to arrange that well in advance. Government horses are the preserve of civil servants and other officials, but the native chiefs can also provide horses. Just say you've come from me, the *djoeragan sepoeh* of Sinagar, and you'll get what you need. It will mean getting up at the crack of dawn, though, because it's quite far. On the way from Bandoeng to Ardjasari you have to cross the Tjitaroem by ferryboat, which you can't do after dark. And there are tigers in the foothills of the Malabar. Your best option is to spend the night in Tjandjoer, there's a reasonable lodging house there.'

'I can't tell you how grateful I am to you for this. Cousin Karel was so adamant . . .'

'There's no reason why Karel should get his way in everything. He's the boss at Waspada; here, it's me.'

'I say, Uncle, is it true that I am to spend some time here with you, to learn the ropes? Because that's what they told me in Batavia.'

Eduard stretched his legs over the extended sides of his reclining chair, and stared out at the inky darkness beyond the veranda.

'Yes, that's another of those affairs,' he said after a long pause. 'I don't know, my boy, I honestly don't know yet. I could do with an extra hand, I suppose. We'll have to see about that later. It depends.'

From the corner of his eye Rudolf saw the weather-beaten face, the coarsened, hardened features. But the set to the lips beneath the bushy moustache was anything but hard.

'Listen here,' Eduard said suddenly. 'I presume you know I have children?'

'Yes, Uncle, I do. But that is all I know.'

'Their mother's name is Goey La Nio. Her family is Chinese. Her father owns a rice farm north of Buitenzorg. I do business with him. I have acknowledged paternity, of course. Their names are Pauline and Adriaan, and they are my heirs. You will meet them some time. I am thinking of taking them over to Holland, in which case I will need someone to replace me here. But nothing has been decided yet.'

Rudolf had slept like a log at Parakan Salak, but at Sinagar he had difficulty getting to sleep. He lay on a large square bed, under a mosquito net that smelled of camphor. He could hear Eduard's dogs barking by the servants' quarters behind the house, and further away by the stables. The night thrummed in the tall trees bordering the yard. What lay beyond he did not know. Tea gardens? Jungle, of the kind he had ridden through with Eduard that morning?

He felt himself probing deeper into the utterly foreign world around him, so overwhelmingly green and vivid by day, and so alive with mysterious creaking and rustling by night. Just before he drifted off to sleep at last he thought he heard another sound, the crying of an infant, in or near the guest quarters.

After the generous shade of Parakan Salak, and after Sinagar with its azaleas and lush greenery, Rudolf found Ardjasari – situated on a plateau bordered by hills – disappointingly bare. The peaks of the southern Preanger seemed far away. The forecourt with recently laid-out canna beds and rows of flower pots was open on all sides. Trees had been planted, but they were still too young to provide shade. The tea gardens stretched out in all directions: parallel, undulating rows of three-year-old shrubs.

The house was built in the old style, similar to the *gedoeng* at Sinagar, but on a larger scale. It had a sloping pan-tiled roof supported by six sturdy white columns on the front and back verandas, and four on each side gallery. The views were breathtaking. Rudolf could not have wished for a better room than the one he was given, with an east-facing window, so that he could enjoy the sunrise every morning.

Seeing his parents again made him realise how things had changed over the past five years. Not only did they look older, but his relationship with them had altered. His father's hair and beard had turned grey; his mother's face bore the traces of ill-health and grief.

They did their best to make him feel welcome, but seemed somewhat at a loss as to how to treat him now he was a grown man.

He was touched to see how hard they tried to replicate the atmosphere and habits of their old life in Holland. By day they were in the Indies, their behaviour and activities focused entirely on running the plantation; but as soon as darkness fell they withdrew to the inner gallery and closed the doors. There they would sit beneath the oil lamp surrounded by their floral curtains, their vases with artificial flowers, and their European knick-knacks. They even had a piano. They would sing together of an evening just as they had done back home, songs in descant from Valerius' *Gedenclanck*, or duets, and lieder by Schubert and ballads by Loewe. His father read to his mother while she sewed; as well as classics and books on the history of lands and peoples, their bookcase contained a wide range of novels, mostly by English authors, their favourites being Dickens and Thackeray.

Rudolf was somewhat irked by the constant presence of his father's assistant. His mother did not believe in leaving an unmarried employee of a lower rank to his own devices after the day's work was done – a barbarian custom, in her opinion. At times it seemed as though the assistant was made to feel more at home by his parents than he was. Micola was a middle-aged Eurasian who had gained experience in tea on a plantation owned by Baud. The first tea harvest at Ardjasari, from bushes planted by Micola's predecessor, had yielded a product that had done fairly well at the auctions in Amsterdam. That the next harvest seemed doomed was not Micola's fault, nor that of the workers. An inexplicable plague had descended on the countryside: swarms of cicada-like insects, called *kassirs* by the Soendanese, which stripped the bushes bare. Thousands of the pests were caught each day by the women and children, without this having any noticeable effect.

Rudolf had the impression that work on the plantation was not as well organised as at Parakan Salak and Sinagar. Many of the women sorting tea in the factory carried babies in their *slendangs*, and there were toddlers playing among the assorted trays and racks of drying leaf. Micola complained about slackness in the carpentry workshop, and also among the *boedjangs* doing the digging and hoeing. Almost every day there was some argument between Rudolf's father and his assistant over the treatment of the workers.

'You are too soft, sir. *Ramah-tamah*! They take advantage of you.'

But Rudolf's father believed that, like him, the people needed time to adjust to a new way of working, a more collaborative way, which was not customary in the Indies. He did not hide the fact that his aim, notwithstanding his lack of expertise, was the kind of enlightened landlordship exemplified by Karel Holle. As he didn't speak their language yet – would he ever learn? – he made the rounds of the gardens and the factory more often than was strictly necessary. He would have Djengot, who had been in service at Waspada, interpret for him, and observed the workers with keen, friendly interest, hoping thereby to gain their trust. He agreed with Karel Holle about the 'kindly presence' of the master being of prime importance. That was one of the reasons for his strict observance of the daily tea-tasting ceremony, which amounted to more than simply assessing the quality of the day's produce and trying mixtures of different yields. On a table by the back veranda stood a row of small, glazed jugs, each containing a spoonful of finished tea. One by one they were filled with boiling water, and when the teas were properly infused they were tasted first by him, then by his wife, then Micola, and nowadays by Rudolf as well. They all took a sip in the traditional way (more like a slurp), and went on to assess the aroma of each infusion before a small audience made up of the *mandoers* and a handful of pickers and sorters. The gravity with which his father performed his role surprised Rudolf at first, but he soon came to realise that the tea-tasting ritual, taking place at the same hour every day with the same genial concentration, was a good thing. It created an atmosphere of mutual understanding, a conclusion to the day's work.

It was agreed that Rudolf would temporarily replace his father as manager when his parents went to Batavia for Bertha's confinement. He took care of the daily records and kept the accounts while Micola inspected the gardens and the factory. He made rapid progress in Malay, thanks to Djengot, but was still wary of trying to learn Soendanese as well, in case he got the two languages mixed up. He also went riding every day, and practised his shooting skills. His father's breech-loader no longer held any secrets for him. It was a sixteen-calibre pin-fire with grooved barrels, a model he considered slightly old-fashioned. He couldn't imagine going on a tiger hunt with such a top-heavy weapon. It sometimes failed to go off, either because the firing pin came down off-centre, or, if the weather was wet, because the paper cartridge got stuck, making it impossible to reload quickly. He persevered, and after a time was gratified to find that he become quite deft with 'Si Soempitan', as the formidable firearm was called on the estate.

His father's saddle-horses gave him more trouble, especially Darling, who was by turns lazy and skittish, and altogether lacking in obedience. Since Uncle Eduard had praised the qualities of this mount in particular, he persisted in his efforts to ride her. He succeeded eventually, and this achievement gave him an unprecedented sense of self-esteem.

He explored the outlying reaches of Ardjasari on horseback. Several tracts were still awaiting cultivation, and he decided to draw up a plan for a network of roads, in the hope that his father would let him carry it out. After a prolonged stay in Batavia, his parents returned home to Ardjasari. They were accompanied by Cateau, who declared it was only for her brother's sake that she had torn herself away from Bertha and the baby. Rudolf showed his parents his drawings and calculations. Although they approved of his plan, the roadworks would have to wait. News had come that he was needed at Sinagar, because Eduard Kerkhoven was planning to take his children to Holland. By the time he left, a few months hence, Rudolf would have gained sufficient experience to take over the management of the plantation, under the all-seeing eye of Albert Holle.

How different life was at Sinagar! For one thing, there was a steady stream of visitors, many of whom turned up unannounced: acquaintances of Eduard's from the sweltering coastlands seeking the health-restoring highland climate, as well as planters and civil servants in transit, with or without families and servants. There was always space in the guest quarters.

Rudolf was given his own room, with his own houseboy and laundryman. He loved the bathing pool in the ravine at the bottom of the garden, where he swam every day. The only novelty he had trouble adjusting to, after his mother's 'Holland-style' home cooking at Ardjasari, were the irregular, haphazard meals. When there were lodgers, hunting parties would be organised, and there would be game on the menu – usually fowl, occasionally a deer – but then there would be weeks of the same staple foods, mostly rice with some small fried fish and roasted cobs of maize. Eduard did not seem to mind this at all. Whenever he felt like a hearty meal he simply rode over to Moendjoel to join Albert Holle and his young wife for dinner. He thought it natural that his nephew should accompany him. Rudolf, however, did not yet feel at ease with the informal hospitality of the Indies. He had a sense of being de trop in such situations, and behaved more stiffly than he would have wished.

Albert's wife, whose name was Reiniera-Jacoba, preferred to be called Louise, as she believed her given name to be unlucky for some mysterious reason. She was seldom present; the only words she and Rudolf exchanged were greetings upon arrival and departure. When they had guests she would appear a quarter of an hour before the meal was served, and vanish again as soon as it was over. Eduard and Albert seemed to think this was normal. Eduard explained that it was customary for the women to retire after seeing to the table so that the men could converse 'among themselves'.

Upon his arrival at Sinagar, Rudolf heard that Goey La Nio had died in childbirth a few months previously. Eduard told him briefly that he had acknowledged the infant, as he had done with the other two children, and had named her Caroline, a popular name in the Kerkhoven family. The children were now living with their grandmother and an aunt in a house a little way off, beyond the guest quarters. Rudolf thought of it as the 'Chinese Camp'.

Sinagar was a male household. Women never entered Eduard's rooms, even when he had guests. But four-year-old Adriaan – nicknamed Tattat by all – did have the run of the house, dragging his toys over the tiled floor, climbing onto the furniture and generally creating a liaison of mischief between the 'Chinese Camp' and the main house. He was always teasing the dogs, winding them up and chasing them like a little huntsman in the making, and it was a wonder he had never been bitten. He was utterly fearless. Eduard doted on the boy, and took him everywhere, on his horse when he went out into the gardens, or in a carrying-chair on journeys to neighbouring plantations.

Tattat was a slight but agile little boy, with a matte, pale complexion and unmistakably Asiatic eyes; endearing and obstreperous by turns. He ate and slept whenever it suited him, which was seldom in accordance with the hours kept by the rest of the household. It took a bevy of servants to watch over him and see to his needs. Rudolf thought a good smack from time to time wouldn't do any harm, as the child was becoming badly spoilt by the combination of his father's adoration and the servants' deference. He tyrannised the 'Chinese Camp'. His sister Pauline, nicknamed Non Besar to distinguish her from her baby sister Non Ketjil, was the only one who dared to cross him. Being the first-born, she enjoyed a special status. Whenever Eduard sent for her to come and visit him, the servants dressed her up in striking, colourful ensembles of Chinese silk jackets atop batik trousers. She delighted in her finery, and would strut and preen like a little peacock, much to everyone's amusement.

The 'Chinese Camp' was veiled in mystery. No one referred openly to Goey La Nio, not even her children. Rudolf heard contradictory rumours. The servants whispered that she had committed suicide because the *djoeragan sepoeh* wanted to take her children away – her ghost had been seen about the bathing pool at night. Albert Holle seemed to think she had left of her own free will to marry a rich Chinese associate of her father's. Rudolf's houseboy hinted she was still at Sinagar but was too proud to show herself because Eduard had taken a Soendanese mistress. Rudolf did not know what to think. His own impression was that the sister who was now living in the 'Chinese Camp' was trying to fill the vacancy. Everyone called her Njonja Nèng, which meant something like 'Madam Most Beloved', but Eduard did not appear in the least interested in her. Nèng and Goey La Nio were said to be like two peas in a pod. The sister's fine, round face with high cheekbones and the blue-black hair scraped back in a smooth knot fascinated Rudolf, but there was something about her bearing and her manner that he found unappealing. At times he thought Njonja Nèng and Goey La Nio might actually be one and the same person.

She was there, and yet she wasn't; it was an insoluble puzzle.

The grandmother, Mama Toea, was busy all day in the 'Chinese Camp' with its profusion of potted plants and birdcages, ordering the servants about, fussing over the children, especially Non Ketjil, who was beginning to crawl. Njonja Nèng, on the other hand, kept aloof, seated in an easy chair with her slippered feet up on a footstool, idly fluttering her handkerchief against the flies, or she was to be found in the kitchen, silently preparing dishes of candied tamarind or fruit jelly.

Since Rudolf would be the acting head of the household during Eduard's absence, he had to establish some kind of rapport with these two women. He thought it would be better to put an end to the harem-like isolation of the 'Chinese Camp', which he felt was hardly a suitable environment for little Caroline to grow up in.

With the men he encountered at Sinagar there was little more to talk about than tea, hunting and horses. He was sorry that Eduard had so little conversation, that he did not read books. They played chess from time to time, and Rudolf forced himself to join in the occasional card game when there were guests. The only other social contact he had was with the Hoogeveen-Holles at the neighbouring plantation of Tjisalak. Rudolf liked going there, even though it was a fair distance to travel, especially at night with the road being so poor. Rudolf thought Hoogeveen strong and capable, and Cousin Pauline very friendly, quite the friendliest of all the Holles. With this educated couple he had long, interesting conversations of the kind he remembered from the old days in Holland, animated discussions about a wide range of topics: books, politics, history. The Hoogeveens had one child, Marietje, an intelligent eleven-year-old, whose vivacity and brightness reminded Rudolf of his sister Cateau in the old days. Her features were pretty, too, and in a few years she would undoubtedly be an attractive young woman.

*

'I have been learning a great deal about tea, which is bound to stand me in good stead later on,' he wrote to his parents. He seized every opportunity of sending them letters, fruits, and plant cuttings for their flower garden through the messenger-coolies that were regularly dispatched by Eduard. He wrote in painstaking detail of every aspect of the tea business that he thought worthy of their notice: 'I believe that our tea is not very well sorted. Could you let me have small samples of both the Souchon and the raw tea, by return coolie? I would like to compare them with the produce of Sinagar. Here they package the tea when it's *cold*. If the tea is still warm when it is packed, as at Ardjasari, it gets a soapy taste, according to Eduard. Here they seal off the metalled tea chests as soon as they are full, so no moisture can get in.'

He discovered that there were many ways of producing tea, and that each estate had its own methods of planting, pruning and picking. Albert Holle was, on the whole, a follower of the method prescribed by Karel, but Eduard and Hoogeveen took liberties with it, which they discussed at length during their visits to each other's plantations. Instead of building terraces for the tea gardens – which Karel Holle considered ideal for the mountains – he adopted a system of almost horizontal ditches zigzagging over the slopes. This, in Rudolf's opinion, was a practical solution that saved both time and space. Eduard did not follow Karel's recommendation to concentrate on green tea, as Souchon and Pekoe fetched better prices on the Amsterdam tea market. He did occasionally order some leaf to be prepared for green tea, mainly to investigate the properties of tannic acid.

Karel Holle was ever in the background as the *éminence grise* of the plantation. According to Eduard, he had spies among the *mandoers* at Sinagar, Moendjoel, Tjisalak and Ardjasari, who kept him up to date about everything that happened there. He would turn up from time to time, usually accompanied by his friend, the *wedana* of Tjitjoeroeg (whose business it was to supervise the native contribution to the tea business), and would lodge for a few days at Moendjoel, where meetings were held to discuss urgent matters, such as the leaf-rust fungus that destroyed entire gardens, or the shortage of paddy due to crop failure and the complications of having to buy sufficient rice elsewhere to feed the workforce, or the dwindling supply of labour in the region due to the food shortages.

Karel also exerted a commanding influence on affairs at Ardjasari. To the dismay of Rudolf's parents, who did their best to follow his advice in everything, he raised all manner of objections to the way they conducted their young enterprise: their roads were in a terrible state, their tea chests unattractive, and even the tea they produced left much to be desired. Rudolf responded by sending them a recipe for varnish: 'Here at Sinagar we heat a mixture of oil and red lead until it thickens, then we stir in three bottles of blood, and finally a little resin to promote drying. You might try that on your tea chests.'

Rudolf went on daily inspection tours of the plantation. He relished criss-crossing his lands on Si Odaliske, the proud, dapple mare Eduard had lent him. He felt less enthusiastic making the rounds of the factory, for he was constantly reminded of the insufficiency of his Soendanese. His mistakes in idiom aroused ill-concealed laughter from the women sorting tea, and outright hilarity at the end of the day when the young pickers filed past the weighing table with their harvest of leaves. He did not feel particularly offended by their laughter, but was concerned that it might undermine his authority as *djoeragan*, so he tried not to linger in the factory. In the carpentry workshop he faced other difficulties. The men were often careless when hammering down the lids on the tea chests, perforating the lead lining, but his Soendanese was too erratic for them to take his reprimands seriously. He threw himself into learning the language properly, compiling lists of words and working hard at the correct pronunciation. That kept him occupied during the long evenings. Unlike the market-Malay his parents and sisters spoke with their servants, Soendanese proved to be a rich and complex language. Rudolf began by memorising a number of short, stock phrases to use in his communications with the workers.

He got on quite well with Eduard's Chinese overseers. On the whole they seemed diligent and trustworthy, although he often found their behaviour somewhat arrogant. On the factory premises they represented a separate caste, if only by their dress and hair-styles. They spoke Malay, and the majority were so-called *peranakans*, born and bred in Java. But Rudolf did not believe that their Chinese roots meant they were particularly knowledgeable about the treatment of China tea, and it was not long before he discovered the reason for their condescension towards the native workers: one of the chief *mandoers*, the storekeeper, was the brother of Goey La Nio.

Eduard took Rudolf to Buitenzorg to meet the members of the racecourse committee and introduce him to society at the Governor-General's residence. They went to a ball, which Rudolf had not done since the days of his dancing lessons as a youngster back home. He discovered that he had not lost the ability to enjoy himself in company, although he disliked the rowdiness of certain partygoers at the Buitenzorg Racing Club.

'Drinks were available at discretion, which gave rise to gross indiscretion, especially on the part of several officers,' he wrote in a letter to Ardjasari. 'There was champagne galore, which was even drunk in the morning at the races, also by children (!). At the ball I saw an officer in uniform brandishing two bottles as he wove his way straight through a quadrille, filling people's glasses as he went!'

At last he had the opportunity to visit the famed Botanic Gardens. He found it fascinating and beautiful, and made up his mind to explore the grounds more fully the next time he went to Buitenzorg for the races, when he would be bringing Eduard's horses to run.

At the end of June Eduard departed for the Netherlands with little Pauline and Tattat. The children would be going to stay with two unmarried Kerkhoven sisters. Although he had been warned about the murderous heat in the Red Sea, Eduard had booked their passage on a vessel that would take the new route through the Suez Canal. Sailing around the Cape of Good Hope would take far longer, and on no account could he bear to miss the opening of the hunting season in Gelderland.

Alone at Sinagar, Rudolf felt swamped by his new responsibilities. He poured his heart out in letters:

> A lot of dry tea gets stolen here. Four chief *mandoers*, the bookkeeper and one of the houseboys have been brought before the court in Soekaboemi, where they were sentenced to between one and three months of forced labour. I tried to negotiate with the Resident of Soekaboemi about this, but my letter was too late – he replied that the case had already been closed. But apparently he is even now, two days later, summoning fresh witnesses, so with any luck the verdict will be modified. Uncle Eduard put off bringing charges until a few days before his departure, which leaves me to pull the chestnuts from the fire. It has taught me one thing – that if it was me running the plantation I would try to avoid taking them to court. Because we are the ones suffering the consequences. Now I have only one garden with a head *mandoer*

(a new one), and am therefore obliged to do the overseeing at the other three myself, which is something I had not reckoned with at all. Some of the gardens are quite far apart, and if I am not around to keep an eye on things they do whatever they like. To top it all, Albert Holle has gone behind my back and introduced a different method of treatment, notably for green tea, which the people don't understand yet and which I don't know much about myself. That just adds to the *soesah*.

The people here thought I wouldn't dare to stand up to them. Their work became increasingly shoddy and careless until I started docking their wages. That taught them a lesson, and now they are as good as gold – for as long as it lasts, of course. Another change I have made is that the *mandoers* now get the blame when things go wrong, not the *boedjangs*. And I have also abolished the system of loans and advances.

The price of padi has gone up again. I send our own *boedjangs* to go and buy it. Albert Holle has to pay even more than we do, because he gets the padi delivered to him, but even so he frowns on the solution I have found for Sinagar. That is so typical of the Holles. They always think they know better. Albert seems to forget that he, as co-owner, has a vested interest in the running of Sinagar, and that if I followed his lead and had my padi delivered, he would be the worse for it in the end. He always has some comment to make: either the tea is too coarse, or it's too fine, now this, now that. He thinks he has achieved consistency in production, that his tea is always the same quality, but I know that is not the case. Actually, my people are often astonished to hear Albert complaining about some procedure, when it was his idea in the first place. But there are some instances where

> I do take the liberty of going my own way. Uncle Eduard made me promise before he left *not* to change certain things even if Albert wants me to. Not that he has been giving me a hard time, really. He tends to be critical of affairs at Sinagar and to approve of the way Moendjoel is run, but he is careful and considered in voicing his opinions, so that we can discuss our differences calmly, which in turn makes it easier for me to concede his superior judgement now and then.

Rudolf was aware that his approach to running the Sinagar plantation, and in particular his organisational and disciplinary measures, did not find favour among the Holles. With him at the helm, the relaxed atmosphere that had always characterized Eduard's management evaporated. The number of visitors dwindled. The only houseguest he had during the months of Eduard's absence was the administrator of a plantation owned by Baud. The man had apparently been sent to find out about the process of making green tea, and about the relationship between the Holle brothers. Rudolf did not offer information on either count.

Although he invited Njonja Nèng and Mama Toea to use the rooms in the *gedoeng*, the women continued to treat him with reserve. There had been a falling-out with Nèng when she tried to dismiss a servant behind his back, but he had very quickly made it clear that he was in charge, not her. After that she had given him glass jars of candied fruit for his mother, by way of thanks for some European-style clothing made by the Ardjasari seamstress for little Pauline and Adriaan. Just as he began to think their relations were improving, Nèng suddenly announced that she was going away to marry a Chinese man in Buitenzorg. Rudolf offered her a handsome sarong of Chinese batik from Pekalongan as a wedding gift on behalf of himself and his parents, which she accepted with an inscrutable look, adding, 'I am too old for that floral pattern.' From one day to the next she was gone, without saying goodbye.

After that Rudolf formed an odd little family circle with Mama Toea and Caroline (Non Ketjil). The old woman was wary of addressing him at all, and the child was simply frightened. It was only when Caroline got her head wedged beneath the sideboard (where she was trying to hide during a prolonged sulk) and he succeeded in liberating her that the ice was broken. He wanted her to be in glowing good health when Eduard returned, and did his utmost to rid her of a persistent rash with home-made ointments supplied by his mother.

When he went over to Moendjoel on some errand he did not feel very welcome there. Albert, with whom he got along quite well in the factory, seemed to treat him rather coolly on such occasions, and Louise continued to address him formally as 'Cousin' during their infrequent conversations. It happened several times that discussions were held by the Hoogeveens of Tjisalak and the Holles of Parakan Salak without him being invited to attend. And he felt snubbed one day when he chanced to arrive just as Albert and his wife were sitting down to a meal and did not ask him to join them. He pretended to ignore the slight, but the question of what could be wrong kept gnawing at the back of his mind. Did they suspect him of having taken sides with Baud? Did they think he was amused by the sarcastic references in the *Java-Bode* to the 'omniscient Karel Holle'? He hated the uncertainty, fearing it would affect him in the exercise of his duties.

He had enough on his mind as it was. Heavy rainfall was causing floods all over western Java, including torrents in the mountains which washed away bridges and roads, also within the boundaries of Sinagar. Someone from the kampong had set fire to a grove of bamboo, purportedly by accident, although Albert suspected sabotage in retaliation for Rudolf's punitive measures.

Absenteeism among the pickers and factory workers was on the rise. The Chinese chief *mandoer*, Eduard's brother-in-law so to speak, gave his notice. One of the racehorses had a fatal accident. The newly built drying room with stone walls and a tiled roof proved inadequate, which meant that the huge surplus of leaf after the rains – there were times when 5,000 kilos of raw leaf were brought in daily – had to be dried over charcoal fires, which was not beneficial to the taste.

Then, quite suddenly, the attitude of the Holles changed, as did that of the workers. Once Rudolf had been to the races in Buitenzorg as Eduard's deputy, where he had been introduced to several young ladies, cousins and friends of Jans and Louise, he was given a decidedly heartier welcome at Moendjoel; and when he organised a *selamatan* at Sinagar, complete with music and dancing girls, to celebrate the victory of Eduard's horse Emir (with the garlanded steed being led on a triumphant walkabout and incense being burned in the stable), his prestige seemed to soar. He concluded that he had now shown himself to be 'one of them'.

Eduard's return in the autumn of 1872 was rather sudden. He had not kept in touch at all, not even to acknowledge receipt of the detailed reports Rudolf had sent him. Consequently there was no time to organise festivities for his homecoming. He was the first family member to make use of the brand-new railway linking Batavia and Buitenzorg.

Rudolf went to fetch him from the station at Buitenzorg with an escort of twelve horsemen. Eduard looked well, and was delighted to be back in Java. His stay in Holland had cured him of all nostalgia for the land of his youth. At the first glimpse of his homestead on the horizon, he spurred his horse to a gallop.

Rudolf described Eduard's return in a letter to his parents:

'Before long Uncle and I were way ahead of the rest – I have never ridden so fast. But I had picked one of the best racehorses from the stable for myself, because I had a feeling he would be in a hurry to get home, so I had no trouble keeping up with Uncle on his big Sydneyer. You should have seen how the people came running to greet him! Affairs at Sinagar were in good order, and I don't think there was anything Uncle disapproved of. He said I had done well. I wonder if he will say anything to you about how I coped during his absence. Uncle is writing you a letter at this very moment. You will let me know, won't you?'

Rudolf added a postscript the following day: 'Uncle has been enormously kind. In fact I am quite embarrassed. He has bought me a new shotgun, a central-fire breech-loader, which is on its way here. And when I could barely find words to express my gratitude, he said, "And I think you ought to have the dapple, too – your beloved Odaliske." P.P.S. Why is it that I hear so little about your tea affairs at Ardjasari? Or are you keeping all the news as a surprise for when I get back?'

What did come as a surprise, albeit not a pleasant one, was that his father had taken on a new assistant when Micola's term ended, a young man who, Rudolf was convinced, knew no more about tea than he did. There was also a lodger at Ardjasari, Radèn Karta Winata, a young Soendanese nobleman who had been a student at Karel Holle's teacher training college and whose father was the *penghoeloe* of Garoet. Modest and well-mannered, he spoke fluent Dutch, and was working on the translation of various books for use in the college: he had already produced a Soendanese version of Willem Bontekoe's *Adventurous Travels to the East Indies*, and was now translating *Robinson Crusoe* from the Dutch version of that book owned by Rudolf's father, who offered guidance in exchange for instruction in Soendanese. Rudolf made grateful use of the opportunity to follow these lessons, during which, with great patience and tact, Karta Winata explained the intricacies of the language: the 'high' and 'low' forms of communication between people of the same class, the honorifics, the tokens of respect, the subtle shadings of self-assigned status vis-à-vis one's interlocutor. Never again would Rudolf use the arrogant form '*aing*' when referring to himself in the presence of his subordinates, instead of the milder forms '*oerang*' or '*dèwèk*' – unless, that was, he had strong reasons to express disfavour. By the same token, he would no longer commit the gaffe of referring to himself as '*koering*' instead of the more formal '*abdi*' when meeting members of the Soendanese upper class for the first time.

Karta Winata smiled at Rudolf's astonishment and confusion. 'It would be interesting for you to attend a function at a regent's palace, Mr Kerkhoven. The challenge is to weave old, traditional words and flowery expressions into one's speeches. That is greatly appreciated; it is seen as respect for our culture. Mr Holle is very good at it!'

When asked what he thought of *Robinson Crusoe*, Karta Winata said it gave an excellent description of the gradually evolving relationship between a civilised individual and one whose lack of knowledge reduced him to a lower rank. Rudolf had put the question because he could imagine the students at the Soendanese teacher training college thinking there was some moral intended – and an unflattering comparison – in this story of a European and a savage. In retrospect he was not so sure that Karta Winata's reply had not been sarcastic.

A second surprise, likewise giving cause for mixed feelings, was that Cateau had become engaged while staying with Bertha in

Batavia. Rudolf had not heard anything about his sister having a suitor, and thought it unfair to have been left completely in the dark. Surely it was his concern as much as anyone else's in the family? Cateau's fiancé, scion of a highly respected family in Zutphen, was Government Prosecutor in Batavia. His name was Joan Henny, and he was reputed to be a highly skilled lawyer with a promising future. Rudolf's parents hardly knew the young man, but the information they had obtained concerning his person and character was favourable, while Van Santen, who was a friend of Joan Henny, claimed he was solid and dependable in every respect.

Cateau seemed pleased. She was constantly occupied with her trousseau, and showed great enthusiasm for the formerly maligned 'needlework class' at Ardjasari. Rudolf was surprised to see how quickly she slipped into her new role, given that she and Henny had only known each other for a few weeks. His attempts to gauge her feelings were met with what he felt were all too conventional expressions of delight at the attentions and gifts lavished on her by her fiancé: 'Oh, what a stick-in-the-mud you are! Bertha and Van Santen didn't know each other very well either when they got married, and they're just fine. Besides, Bertha's expecting again. To have a little family of one's own – what a joy that must be!'

The wedding was quite a grand affair, attended by Eduard and the Hoogeveens as well as by the Assistant Resident of Bandoeng, who officiated at the ceremony. However, notwithstanding Cateau's elegant wedding dress, which she had copied from a model in the *Gracieuse*, notwithstanding the banquet, the champagne, the fairy lights in the garden, the Chinese fireworks and the *selamatan* for all the local people, the occasion was not an unqualified success. No one in the family was much taken with the pale-faced, fair-haired groom. Joan Henny seemed to them somewhat foppish, and also a bit of a prig. Besides, not all the invited guests had been able to come: the Van Santens stayed away because the journey was too long and tiring for Bertha in her advanced pregnancy, the Holles of both Parakan Salak and Moendjoel had been indisposed, while Karel Holle had merely sent a gift of fruit from Waspada.

No sooner had the wedding festivities come to an end than the Kerkhovens travelled to Batavia, where Bertha had given birth to her second child, a son. Shortly after their return a few weeks later, Cateau suddenly appeared on their doorstep, having seized the opportunity to join a family travelling in the direction of Ardjasari. She complained bitterly about her husband being more interested in his legal practice than in her. Very soon, however, Henny himself turned up at Ardjasari, brimming with apologies and excuses, to take his young wife home again. There seemed to be no end to the comings and goings at Ardjasari, whether by carriage, carrying-chair, or on horseback. Although the new railway linking Batavia and Buitenzorg was a considerable improvement for the traveller, the most arduous part of the journey came in the Preanger, with the Megamendoeng Pass and the Goenoeng Missigit.

Rudolf's contribution to Cateau's wedding had been to organise a team of workers to improve the road to the plantation, which was steep and often perilously slippery. That project had now come to an end. Having been his own master at Sinagar, he chafed at passing his time at Ardjasari without having a clearly defined task to fulfil alongside his father and the assistant. There was not enough work for three men. He was not needed.

He had been in Java for almost two years, and he still had no prospect of permanent employment. For a while it looked as if an opportunity might arise, as a consequence of the deterioration of Adriaan Holle's health. The doctors in Batavia were unanimous in advising his repatriation. Despite the frowns of the rest of the Holle clan – in whose view 'home' for anyone who had spent the past thirty years in a subtropical upland climate such as that of Parakan

Salak was right there in the Preanger – Adriaan, and, much to everyone's surprise, Jans, too, were seriously considering returning to Holland. They had a young son whom they wished to give a European education. Rudolf heard that the management of Parakan Salak would be taken over for an indeterminate length of time, but his hopes were dashed when the news came that Adriaan was to be replaced by his assistant, who was likewise married to a Van Motman girl.

Karel Holle sent word that there might be a manager's position for him on a new estate he was planning to lease, but Rudolf realised that, given his age and the family relationship, he would always have Karel breathing down his neck. Not a sound basis for collaboration in the long run, he feared.

In the meantime he accompanied his father on several excursions to the Pengalengan plateau and environs to inspect the lands being offered for leasehold. The only location that appealed to him at first sight was an old coffee plantation formerly run by the government. It was named Gamboeng, and lay on the north-western flank of the Goenoeng Tiloe. But it was on tea that he had focused until now; he knew nothing about coffee.

His stint running Sinagar had earned him a reputation of being a stickler for fixed rule in bookkeeping, and for this reason he was asked by Van Santen's Netherlands Indies Trading Bank to travel to eastern Java to put some order into the chaotic accounts of a local tobacco planter. The trip itself, by ship from Batavia to Soerabaya, then in stages to Blitar, was a fascinating experience, but he thanked his lucky stars he was not obliged to live there permanently. The contrast between the lush tea gardens in the Preanger, with their fiefdoms centred on the *gedoeng* and the busy intrigues of those dealing 'in sugar' and 'in tobacco', could not have been greater. He found himself living the kind of life that was considered a nightmare back home, among men whose sole purpose was to make a quick fortune in Java and then get out, men with unhappy wives, or bachelors dispelling their loneliness with liquor.

On his father's advice, he paid a reconnaissance visit to the coffee plantations around Malang on his way back from his mission to eastern Java. He found the plantations interesting, although the work was by no means as inspiring as the far more complex, unpredictable and consequently more challenging business of tea.

'I long for the Preanger,' he wrote to his parents.

CLEARANCE AND PLANTING

1873–6

The sweat trickled down his back; his hair beneath the straw sun-hat was soaked, leaking drops on his face. His vest was wet through, and the sleeves of his calico jacket clung to his arms. He envied the natives for wearing only a loose shirt over their bare chests when working in the fields. He remained fully covered, not only as protection against the sun, which was particularly treacherous in the thin mountain air, but also for reasons of decorum. Seeing the *djoeragan* in person wielding the *patjoel* was sensational enough. He joined in with his men now and then to speed them up, for with Djengot acting as foreman everything took three times as long. It was a mystery to him why the mountain men, so deft with the chopping knife and axe, had so much difficulty getting accustomed to the *patjoel*. He had lost count of the times he had been obliged to warn them with a '*Didijeu koerang djéro matjoelna*!' that they had to loosen the earth to a greater depth.

The reclamation of this field, intended for a specimen tea garden, was the most backbreaking task they had undertaken so far. They had been at it for days. First they had chopped down all the old coffee bushes, then they had burnt the stumps. But there was a tangled network of tough roots spreading underground, and until that had been dug up entirely, there could be no question of new planting.

Each day brought new difficulties, but on the whole he was pleased with how things were going. After a strained start, his relations with the Gamboeng locals improved rapidly. A few days after his arrival he already received offers of help to clear the tracks linking the various gardens, usually from the same half a dozen men. He learnt from Djengot that more workers would come if he paid a better wage. He was aware that his behaviour in this matter would have lasting consequences for his authority at Gamboeng. Although he privately considered their demands quite reasonable, he did not want to be seen to yield too quickly. Instead, he gave the men already working for him less arduous jobs to do than in the previous days, shortened their working hours, offered them tobacco during their break, held target practice sessions and showed them how his gun worked. This softening of his attitude had set tongues wagging. Putting two and two together, he surmised that Djengot was at the back of the locals' reluctance to work for him.

Once again he had occasion to profit from what he had learnt at Sinagar. He realised that it was time for his relationship with Djengot to be consolidated by means of some diplomatic gift. After that things immediately took a turn for the better. More workers were taken on, a slightly higher wage was agreed upon without difficulty, and the Gamboeng folk no longer hurried past his house, but started coming to him now and then with curious finds from the jungle, such as a scaly anteater or a huge black widow spider. The men liked to roll a cigarette with his Dutch tobacco, using the leaf of the ipah palm as paper, and would sit on their haunches in front of his *pondok*, muttering appreciatively as they smoked.

Contact between him and his parents at Ardjasari was maintained almost daily by messenger-coolies. Rudolf's list of requests grew longer: clothes that needed laundering and mending, shoes in need of repair. The latter was complicated by the total absence of shoemakers in the Preanger. In the event, the Chinese cobbler in Batavia sent the boots back with bedbugs in the lining, which Moentajas proceeded to pick off and flick away rather too carelessly, in Rudolf's opinion. He depended on his mother for the most basic stores, such as sugar, eggs and the occasional chicken. After a day in the field he was ravenous.

He laid down the *patjoel* and surveyed the growing heap of unearthed roots and tough sprigs that had already shot up from the felled shrubs. He felt frustrated by his lack of experience in land clearance in this region. He kept coming up against problems he didn't really know how to solve. How on earth was he going to get rid of the mountains of twigs and scrub? He had no carts or draught-cattle as yet. Buying buffalos and making a holding pen would come later. In the meantime he would have to dig trenches for all the loose debris.

A cloud slid across the sun, the first of the steadily rising bank that would break out in a downpour later in the afternoon. He hadn't anticipated how frequent and heavy the rainfall would be at Gamboeng. The only drawback of Eldorado, apart from the sense of loneliness (he had barely heard or spoken a word of Dutch in almost three months), was the rain. He had to smile now and then at the boundless elation he had felt when he first stood on the edge of that ravine overlooking his land. He still experienced such moments of pure joy, on emerging from the dripping jungle after a storm to see the vast panorama unfolding before him, or on stepping out on to his veranda in the morning to gaze at the grandiose mountains of the Pantjoer, the Patoeha and the Tambagroejoeng, with the Gedeh faintly visible beyond in shades of blue and violet, and the triple-peaked Goenoeng Tiloe looming majestically close by. Each time anew he had a sense of the landscape retreating from him, as it were, into an unconscionable existence of its own, for all that he was getting to know it better by the day. He could see why the people inhabiting this landscape believed that each tree, each rock, each mountain stream had a soul, that it was a being with a name and a special power.

Now the sun had gone, he shivered in his damp clothes. He motioned to his men, squatting by the side of the field with their sarongs round their shoulders, that they had done enough for the day. They stamped out the fires and hoisted their hoes over their shoulders. If it hadn't been about to rain, he would have liked to go and take a look at the fields that had already been cleared. The locals had thought up names for the tracts of land newly claimed from the jungle: 'the *badak* field' (after the rhinocerus that had come crashing through the brushwood one day); 'the field of the rasamala with red flowers' (after the dark-red orchid Rudolf had discovered parasiting one of the majestic tree trunks); and 'the field where the *djoeragan* climbed the dadap tree' (after what was clearly a memorable feat on his part).

Going downhill he had difficulty keeping up with the others. He had a painful sore on his leg, a wound that refused to heal. He had tied a handkerchief around his calf, but it kept slipping down.

He had grown accustomed to returning home soaked to the skin and caked in mud. The water in his 'bathing pool' was ice cold, and all the more refreshing for that. Feeling revived and still shivery, wearing a clean pair of loose cotton trousers and a long-sleeved flannel shirt, he sat down to the meal prepared for him by Moentajas: re-heated buffalo stew cooked by his mother and sent to him by coolie earlier in the day.

He thought he would do some reading after supper, so long as it was still light. From the store of books at Ardjasari he had borrowed *The Woman in White* by Wilkie Collins, which he had read before but felt like re-acquainting himself with. He had barely finished the first chapter when someone came running with the news that one of the workmen lay dying in the kampong. His heart sank, for appeals to his medical competence always left him feeling hopelessly inadequate. In his first aid box he had the means to treat superficial cuts and wounds, and he knew how to apply a splint to a broken arm or leg, but he was powerless in the face of illness. On a few occasions he had succeeded in alleviating pain by administering chlorodyne, which had inspired people's confidence, but the powers that were unjustly attributed to him caused him embarrassment.

Using the broad *pisang* leaf Moentajas offered him by way of an umbrella – it was still raining – he made his way to the kampong, where he found a crowd gathered around a man writhing in pain as he lay on a mat in a cooking shelter. From what they told him he gathered that the man was suffering from stomach cramps.

He took the village elder aside. 'What does Pak Erdji think? Has this man had this trouble before?'

After a moment's reflection, Pak Erdji shook his head. No, this was the first time. He did not believe it could have been anything he had eaten. The men had all had the same food when they returned from their day's work in the gardens, and he was the only one to have fallen ill.

'So why did Pak Erdji not call a *doekoen*?'

'The *doekoen* lives in Tjikalong,' replied Pak Erdji. 'A long way away. This man would be dead by the time he got here.'

Rudolf opened his first aid box. All eyes were fixed on him. He thought of that time in Sinagar when he turned out to have cured someone's paralysis of the legs with hair pomade, the only creamy substance he had to hand at that moment. But what could he possibly give the patient in this case? All he had in the way of medicine was the small bottle of chlorodyne. 'Fingers crossed,' he muttered to himself, and tipped out twenty drops into a bowl of water, which he gave the man to drink.

The rain seemed to be coming to an end. He could hear the downpour shifting away across the valley. A hush descended on the crowd as the patient's spasms subsided. Rudolf felt the man's pulse and forehead, then told the bystanders to move him closer to the fireplace, where the embers were still hot. It was not until three-quarters of an hour later, when the man finally scrambled to his feet saying he was feeling better, that Rudolf allowed himself to give a sigh of relief. '*Pourvu que ça dure*!' he said, quoting Napoleon's mother. Being deprived of casual conversation for long stretches of time, he had fallen into the habit of talking to himself, commenting aloud on what was going on around him with sayings or bon mots picked up in the family circle or from books. He noted wryly that his repertory was quite wide-ranging, for he was very rarely at a loss for some apt phrase.

He was glad of the time he had spent with Karta Winata at Sinagar mastering the basics of Soendanese. Since he settled in Gamboeng his vocabulary had increased by leaps and bounds. The only person he still spoke Malay with was Djengot.

By now he knew everybody by name, and had the impression that he was generally liked in Gamboeng. He found the people there more congenial than at Sinagar. They were rougher, in some ways more primitive, but they were generally good-humoured and had a sense of valour about them which he found appealing. They could be exasperating at times, as when they refused to carry out some order for no apparent reason, but he had also known them to render him services entirely off their own bat and in remarkably good spirits. Once they had brought him a surprise load of chopped wood for his kitchen fire – an 'act of servitude' to the *djoeragan*!

The sense of satisfaction he felt as he lay down to sleep that night was rudely disrupted the following day. Returning earlier than usual from the forest – a cloudburst having made work impossible – he was told that Odaliske and the two other horses had made off, and that the boy, Si Djapan, had vanished as well. Moentajas had gone in search of them in the direction of Tjikalong, without success. Rudolf had to take action.

Cursing under his breath, he braved the pouring rain and set out with a small party of men along the steep, slippery pathways down to the village of Babakan and from there to Tjikalong. He was worried about the horses straying into the rice fields and doing damage to the crop, or getting injured by the razor-sharp reeds in the wilderness. Worse still, they might have galloped right back to their old stables at Ardjasari, where their riderless appearance would have caused great distress.

From afar they spotted a crowd by the bridge of Tjikalong, signalling that the horses had been recaptured. They proved to be safe and sound, but covered in mud and trembling with nervous excitement. Sure enough, they had trampled a swathe of rice seedlings on their way.

'Giddy up, you clot!' grumbled Rudolf as he led his grey mare away after paying for the damage to the paddy field.

Returning to his *pondok* later that afternoon he ran into Djengot, who had failed to turn up for work yet again that morning. His excuse this time was that he had been called away to the funeral of a relative who had died suddenly in a village nearby, which Rudolf acknowledged without question. During his time at Sinagar he had learned not to delve too deeply into the reasons people gave for their absences. But he had other, more pressing concerns.

'Has Si Djapan come yet?'

Djengot stared at his feet a long moment before responding: 'I think Si Djapan is shy.'

In other words, thought Rudolf, he's tired of his job. It was possible, although Rudolf found it hard to believe the boy would have let the horses loose deliberately.

'As *djoeragan* I am entitled to ask services of the people at Gamboeng.'

'Yes,' said Djengot, but he sounded doubtful.

'Does Djengot mean to say that Si Odaliske would not have run away if Si Djapan had received a reward for looking after her? Well, I have promised him a new shirt. He will get it in due course.'

'The *djoeragan* knows that people work for wages nowadays, not for gifts.'

Rudolf was piqued; he was inclined to shrug off Djengot's inventive and shrewd efforts to secure payment for services, convinced as he was that the fellow from Ardjasari was regarded as an outsider by the Gamboengers, whose preferred spokesman would be Pak Erdji. He suspected Djengot of secretly being in contact with Karel Holle's people at Waspada, and the idea that he was being spied on annoyed him. He would have liked to send Djengot back to Ardjasari, but, for the time being, his help was indispensable in marking out the boundaries of the terrain. Rudolf had ordered a strip several metres wide to be cleared all around the perimeter of the plantation as a buffer against the jungle, and with Djengot acting as supervisor Rudolf was free to devote himself to land surveying. This was a source of particular enjoyment to him, as it offered the opportunity to explore the full extent of his lands.

Living so close to the kampong made him increasingly aware of the poverty of the local population. Their homes were dilapidated, their clothes threadbare and ragged. The failure of the rice crop, which had brought famine to many parts of Java, had affected life in Gamboeng, too. The diet was now restricted to some locally grown maize and root vegetables supplemented by the occasional catch from the small fishing lake, which was fed by the Tjisondari river. Whenever Rudolf was out in the forest with his men, he would see them scrambling about in the undergrowth for wild berries and the tender shoots of edible plants. Narrow footpaths, undistinguishable to the inexperienced eye, led to secret groves of sap-filled sugar-palms, or to nooks where edible bird's nests could be found. When they were thirsty they chopped off a length of the luxuriant rattan and drank the rainwater that had collected in the hollow stem.

Every day Rudolf woke with a keen appetite, and went to bed feeling peckish. The meagreness of his daily fare was beginning to have an effect. He had no choice but to go out hunting, although he could not really spare the time, and occasionally managed to shoot a wood fowl, which, when prepared by Moentajas, tasted rather like roast game.

Each afternoon it rained for hours at a stretch. He sat in his front room huddled in an old woollen coat, the only warm garment he had brought with him from Holland, poring over the notes and sketches he had made in the jungle. A mist of fine droplets wafted in between the waist-high partition of woven bamboo and the projecting roof, and he could only keep dry by pushing his chair and table up against the inside wall. Sometimes his papers were so soggy that the writing was practically illegible, as were his diagrams of the 'protuberances' (his name for the exploitable parcels of land within the jungle). He drew a map of the area on several sheets of notepaper pasted together.

When the messenger-coolie brought him newspapers from Ardjasari, Rudolf read them from the first page to the last. Dominating the news at that time was the fighting in Atjeh. The sultan's *kraton* had fallen to the Dutch during their second expedition to the region, but that did not signify an end to the unrest by any means. As the *Bataviaans Nieuwsblad* reported, 'the proud people of Atjeh' kept up their constant harassment of the Dutch troops. There was a bizarre contrast between the news of 'victory' and the fact that a quarter of the troops had already lost their lives, and a very large number were wounded. Rudolf agreed with the journalist who had railed against the manoeuvre as 'an undertaking as unwise as it was unjust', and who had been banished from the country for his pains.

How far removed the bloody conflict in Atjeh seemed from the misty, rain-drenched landscape confronting him! The delicate fronds of the tree ferns on the edge of the ravine quivered in the breeze, the pendulous white bells of the *ketjoeboeng* dripped with moisture, and he could hear the rush of the swollen stream by the washing place. On those long, wet afternoons he sometimes longed for a glass of cognac. He abstained from both liquor and pork, out of consideration for the people of Gamboeng. Tobacco was his only indulgence, but he could not afford to smoke more than two or three cigarettes a day or his supply would run out too quickly.

One day the coolie arrived bringing not only the usual foodstuffs, clean laundry and various tools, but also, much to Rudolf's surprise, one of the Ardjasari dogs: an elderly terrier by the name of Tom. Clearly nervous at finding himself in strange surroundings, the dog promptly followed Rudolf everywhere, curled up under his chair as soon as he sat down, and lay down beside the bunk when it was bedtime. But the creature's constant scratching and biting for fleas was so troublesome that Rudolf put him out in the corridor, where he proceeded to keep his nose pressed against the slit beneath the door, whimpering softly but so penetratingly that Rudolf had to force him to be quiet with a few firm slaps. The following morning Moentajas offered an explanation: the dog had caught the scent of the panther that prowled around the *pondok* at night.

Later that day, when news reached him from Babakan that a

villager had been severely mauled by a panther, Rudolf decided it was time to take action against the 'big cat', which the Gamboeng folk identified as a spotted panther, a *matjan toetoel*. At Sinagar he had taken part in tiger hunts organised by Albert Holle and other planters, but he had never taken the lead himself. At Gamboeng he would be expected to do just that.

The least risky way of dealing with the predator would be to poison it. For this to succeed it would be necessary to deposit a sizeable bait, poisoned with the deathly bark of the walikambing tree, in some strategic hollow. The panther would eat its fill then depart, whereupon the hunters would prepare to ambush it when it returned to devour the remainder, which it was bound to do if the bait was large enough. By that time the poison would already have taken effect, so the animal would be easy to finish off. This was not an honourable thing to do, Rudolf thought, and besides, the panther had been wounded by the victim's chopping knife, so it could not be too difficult to track it down.

His appeal for volunteers was answered by half a dozen men, with whom he set out for the steep flanks of the Goenoeng Tiloe, where the attack had taken place. They found paw-prints in the muddy earth, and traces of blood leading upwards in the direction of a precipitous ridge, slitted with gullies and thickly carpeted with vegetation. Slithering down into the gullies, which were filled with fast-flowing streams after the rain, and clambering up the other side past overhanging rocks was bad enough, but battling through the leech-infested undergrowth was a nightmare. The tough, agile Gamboengers climbed ahead, slashing branches out of the way and pointing out secure footholds to Rudolf. He gripped his rifle with his right hand, grabbed hold of lianas and trailing roots with his left. They kept finding fresh tracks, and in some places the ground was scored with scratch marks.

'The *matjan toetoel* is very angry,' said the men, stooping to tread carefully, with their chopping knives at the ready. They halted in front of an impenetrable thicket of brushwood, gesturing mutely. When Rudolf loaded his gun they drew back and flung clods of earth into the bushes, but nothing moved. One of the men tugged at Rudolf's sleeve and nodded towards a patch of darker shade further up the mountain – the mouth of a cave, perhaps, with glints of what might be a ray of sunlight hitting foliage. Rudolf turned without a sound, took aim and fired. Almost instantaneously the panther came crashing down through the undergrowth, unleashing a tumble of rocks in its dying throes. The bullet had hit between the eyes, a fatal shot, which filled Rudolf with grateful astonishment. 'Luck of the devil!' he muttered. He had not had the time to reflect on one of his favourite sayings before pulling the trigger: 'When in doubt, stay out!' The men, who had been standing back with their knives drawn to protect him in case of attack, raised a triumphant shout and poked the cadaver with sticks to make sure it was dead. There were deep gashes about the beast's neck and foreleg, and Rudolf felt respect for the man from Babakan who had fought off his attacker despite being badly wounded himself.

The booty was hung from a bamboo pole with its legs tied, and carried back to Gamboeng along the same tortuous path they had come. Rudolf now learnt at first hand what a difference it made to his status as *djoeragan* to have shown such spectacular marksmanship. In the days that followed several dozen men came to him looking for work. He had the panther conveyed to Ardjasari, which attracted a lot of attention on the way, with the request to prepare the skin for him so that he might display it on the wall in his future home.

Establishing his specimen tea nursery proved to be much harder than anticipated. His plan had been to clear an area of five *bouw*, levelling the ground according to the method used at Sinagar, but that had proved too ambitious: he had only been able to reclaim a plot of thirty by thirty metres. The seeds, which he had obtained from Ardjasari, had been left to soak overnight in his bathing pool prior to planting out in rows four feet apart, and all he could do now was hope for them to germinate.

After weeks of roaming the surrounding jungle, he estimated the size of his lands to be close to 400 *bouw*, but he knew he could easily expand that by another 200. Deep in the jungle there were some old coffee gardens, which were still being maintained, after a fashion, by the local population. But they stripped off the ripe berries too roughly, thereby causing damage to the new buds in the axils. Those coffee bushes would never amount to much, as was the case with nearly all the Arabica grown at Gamboeng. The plants had become too tall, and had sent out suckers, which meant they produced less blossom and consequently fewer berries. Besides, the leaves had suffered damage in the excessive rainfall.

Although Gamboeng was considered to be coffee-growing country, and would be assessed as such by the government inspectors later on, Rudolf's conviction grew that the soil and climate at 1,400 metres above sea level were infinitely better suited to the cultivation of tea. He hoped to find the means of financing an estate of 600 *bouw*. His father had promised to underwrite part of the capital, some of which was money invested in Ardjasari by family members back in Holland. But affairs were not looking good at Ardjasari: the tea bushes had been stricken with a fungal disease, and an outbreak of cholera in the Bandjaran district was driving the workers away. Under the circumstances Rudolf did not feel he could raise the subject of the considerable sum he needed to carry out all his plans for Gamboeng.

Despite repeated invitations to pay him a visit, his parents had never come. He had furnished the other small room in his *pondok* as a guest room, and had the interior carefully whitewashed. Knowing his mother was not keen on travel in the mountain wilderness, he had drawn up elaborate plans for her, explaining exactly which sections of the journey she could make in a carriage, which on horseback, where she would be able to rest on the way for refreshment, and how she would be conveyed up the final, steep track to Gamboeng in a carrying-chair. He sent her messages saying how much he longed to see her and how eager he was to show his father around the gardens and to compare notes. But something always seemed to come up at the last minute; he was surprised how often his parents suffered from headaches and fevers.

He realised his father's mind would be constantly preoccupied by the setbacks at Ardjasari, but surely that was all the more reason for him to have an open-hearted talk about business with his eldest son, the 'second man' in their East Indian venture? During his time at Sinagar he had sent his father weekly reports on the methods employed by Eduard Kerkhoven for harvesting, drying and sorting tea, and had given him useful tips about diverse factory tools as well. He had also taken pains to describe and comment on the way the Holle cousins and their associates treated him, as being relevant to his father's future as much as to his own. How could anyone question his commitment to the family cause? Since his father had shown himself so dedicated in his efforts to help him acquire Gamboeng, he felt ashamed of the doubts that sometimes preyed on his mind. How could he ever have suspected his father of not wanting his son by his side at Ardjasari, of deliberately keeping him at a distance and trying to get him involved in something other than tea? Nonetheless, despite his father's offers of support and his mother's steady stream of food parcels, there were still times when he felt that same niggling sense of rejection which he had found so hurtful as a young man.

He decided to go to Batavia himself in search of investors, and possibly even partners. His hopes were initially pinned on his brother-in-law Van Santen, who, as a father of two (soon three, as Bertha was pregnant again), would have an interest in participating; besides, in his capacity as administrator of the Netherlands Indies Trading Bank (since 1873), he would be able to provide credit, as he had previously done for Ardjasari.

Rudolf's visit to the city was in every sense a disillusion. Given the poor state of the economy and Ardjasari's floundering prospects, neither Van Santen nor Cousin Denninghoff Stelling's trading firm could see any advantage in investing money in a second Kerkhoven enterprise. The atmosphere at the Van Santen home was tense: Bertha, heavy with child, looked pale and drawn, all her time being taken up by their daughter aged three and the little boy who was not yet a year old. Cateau was caught up in a social whirl. The cultural opportunities afforded by the largest city in the Indies did not live up to Rudolf's expectations. He had gone to a concert given by amateur musicians, but that was all. He had also been persuaded to spend money he could not really afford on a much-needed new suit, for which his fashion-conscious sister Cateau sent him to the best tailor in town, Oger Frères, who ran a shop of palatial proportions. A postponed business appointment obliged him to prolong his stay in Batavia by several days, and when he finally departed, his goodbyes were flustered and hasty. A fleeting kiss for Bertha and a final look over his shoulder at the figure waving from the veranda, and he was gone, absorbed in his own cares.

He couldn't bear the thought of having to give up Gamboeng. If the worst came to the worst he could always reduce the acreage he was applying for, although it would be excruciatingly difficult to decide which tracts of the land he had already charted he would exclude.

*

He had only been back at Gamboeng a few weeks when a special messenger arrived from Ardjasari with the news that Bertha had died in childbirth. The infant, a boy, was alive and well. He sped to Ardjasari, but his parents had already left for Batavia to help out in the motherless household. Apparently unmoved, as was expected of the master's eldest son, he took over his father's responsibilities. But that first evening, alone in the silent house, the sight of Bertha's wedding portrait propped up on a ledge in the inside gallery unleashed a flood of tears as the import of her death sank in.

Hard work, that was the only solution. He determined to use the occasion to make some improvements at Ardjasari. Although his parents were liked by the population, there was a lot going on behind their backs which he considered inappropriate. He also made a start with the roadworks he had planned for the tea gardens back in 1872. He was struck by how beautiful Ardjasari had become, now that the trees were standing tall. While he occupied himself plotting a grid of alleys along which the day's leaf harvest could easily be carted away, he wondered what it would be like to work here if he were to lose Gamboeng. Was that what his father had in mind for him?

When his father returned to Ardjasari, sooner than expected, there was no need to pursue the subject. The financial issues appeared to have been resolved. Van Santen had formally agreed at last to underwrite the loan he had applied for; the interest rate was rather high at 8 per cent, but Rudolf thought he would be able to pay off his debt in about ten years. In the meantime Eduard Kerkhoven of Sinagar, in a characteristic flourish of generosity, had offered to contribute, and sent Rudolf word that he should carry on at Gamboeng 'without delay', even though the leasehold was not yet officially finalised. Not only that, Rudolf's father had written on his behalf to Governor-General Loudon (a friend of Karel Holle's!), appending to his respectful but pressing missive a photograph of himself. This Rudolf found somewhat alarming, although it turned out to have been a good move: His Excellency replied almost immediately, saying that he would deal with the Gamboeng application the moment it arrived on his desk, and, as though to emphasise his good intentions, enclosing a studio portrait of himself in return.

'I think I'll grow a beard,' Rudolf said to his father. 'Then I'll look more like you, just as you seem to be looking more and more like Cousin Karel these days. It seems to me that one is better off with a beard when in need of funds!'

Rudolf went to fetch his mother from Batavia, where she was visiting Cateau, who had taken Bertha's children under her wing. Carrying the baby in her arms and with the two toddlers playing at her feet, his sister displayed a new, cheerful energy, notwithstanding all the extra work involved. Rudolf had already guessed that Cateau longed to have children of her own, and that the extraordinary interest she showed in fashion and frivolities, so unlike the Cateau of old, was simply a means of masking the emptiness at the core of her marital life. And now, thanks to her new responsibilities, she seemed to have come into her own.

When Rudolf returned to Gamboeng after several months, he felt as if he had to start again from scratch. His flying visits from Ardjasari – there and back in one day – had not given him time to keep track of everything. The old coffee bushes, which he had pruned down to the stump, did not look bad despite the irregular blossom, and the tea seedlings in the specimen garden were doing quite well. However, many of the paths running between the gardens were badly overgrown.

The most pressing task at hand was the construction of a road to the Tjisondari settlement, situated at the confluence of the Tjisondari and Tjiwidej rivers. From there his produce would have to be transported by cart to Tjikao on the Tjitaroem river, and then by proa downriver to Batavia.

The steep slopes at Gamboeng obliged him to resort to a time-consuming zigzag system, and an additional delay was caused by the rock-hard state of the ground after an unusually long period of drought. In the jungle he faced different complications. On sunless days it was almost impossible to take one's bearings in the wild profusion of tree trunks, lianas and foliage. His spirit-level, which he had ordered from an instrument maker in Batavia after his own design, was some help in measuring the inclination of the ground, but very hard to use on the steeper, densely wooded slopes. It was also necessary to build two or possibly three bamboo bridges in particularly awkward locations. He had repairs made to the roof and floor of his *pondok*, and ordered the adjoining field to be cleared of a wilderness of tall, sharp grasses.

He was sorry to see that the new set of workmen had no desire to move into the dwellings he had had built for them. They preferred to lodge with the Gamboeng folk, which meant that they slept in cramped quarters, like sardines in a tin. There were so many people living in the kampong that some kind of general store was needed. Rudolf offered a local woman a loan so she could buy a stock of supplies, and it was thanks to her busy stall, which attracted buyers from the surrounding area, that Rudolf's new housing eventually found occupants.

An encouragingly large number of men came forward to join the workers felling and burning the trees, but all did not go according to plan. They turned down his offer of 10 guilders per *bouw* of cleared forestland. Lengthy palavers were held followed by whispered consultations among themselves, and each time the men turned and left again. Rudolf had the impression there was only a handful of men stopping the others from accepting his terms. This time he could not blame Djengot, as he had stayed behind at Ardjasari as a night watchman. Rudolf was, in principle, prepared to pay more. He had calculated at 10 guilders per *bouw* he would be getting a very good deal – it even smacked of exploitation – but just as in his early days at Gamboeng, he thought it better not to give in too easily. The end of the affair was that he went back to paying individual wages per day.

There was so much coming and going of workers that he sometimes lost count of how many men he was employing. One day it would be seventy, the next forty, and then suddenly twice that number. He had little confidence in the middlemen, who doubled as overseers, but he could not do without them. His best workers were Moehiam, an 'old faithful' from Ardjasari, and Ramiha the carpenter. The size of his household, too, had grown to include a cook and his family, and a clerk or scribe, who oversaw the payment of wages and kept the books, which, with a daily workforce of several hundred men and women, represented a full-time occupation.

Riding out over his land, seeing the teams of field hands at their various labours, he caught himself thinking what he called 'sanguine thoughts': yes, he was off to a pretty good start! Yes, he would conquer the wilderness!

One day, when a group of Gamboeng men, his elite corps, had spent many backbreaking hours chopping a breach in the jungle on the north-east border of his terrain, Rudolf was actually able to see part of the fence around Ardjasari through his field glasses. How near he was to his parents as the crow flies, and how far – four whole hours on horseback – via the detours of bridle tracks!

*

If the kampong at Gamboeng continued to expand, he would have to find somewhere else to live. He liked picturing the home he would make for himself beneath the rasamalas backing on to the jungle, a low oblong *gedoeng* in the style of his parents' house at Ardjasari but on a smaller scale, with a large clearing in front where he could make a flower garden. He dreamed of the day when the first foundation post would be driven into the ground. But would he have to live there *alone*? He was beginning to feel that bachelorhood was a burden, a somewhat unnatural state of affairs. The unmarried employees he came across at neighbouring plantations found it hard to believe that he did not have a native woman to keep house for him, and deep down he knew he was not the kind of man to remain single all his life.

Among the books in his *pondok* was one he had found lying about, unclaimed, on board the *Telanak*. It was called *Mémoires d'un Compagnon*, and contained the notes made by one Agricol Perdiguier of his time as a carpenter's apprentice in a provincial French town. Young, working for a poor wage and consequently unable to marry, he lived a life of self-imposed abstinence, and his descriptions of his mental states struck a chord with Rudolf: 'I longed for the complete experience, but it was impossible for me to give myself over to prostitutes, women for whom I would not feel any love, or to seduce a young girl, possibly to impregnate her, and then to abandon her to her fate. That was completely counter to my principles, and in conflict with my character. I felt desire, I was ablaze, I suffered, I was at a loss, torn between my lust and my conscience, one voice saying, "Go!" and the other, "Stay!"'

Of course Rudolf had cast his eye over the women and girls in the fields. Among the pickers at Sinagar there had been many pretty girls, who looked especially appealing when they came running to the factory in the rain with their clothes clinging to their bodies;

but he had never felt more than a momentary pang of lust. He had immediately dismissed the possibility of sexual contact in exchange for gifts as being downright insulting to the young women in question. The teasing, brazen looks they gave him sometimes proved that they were perfectly aware of his feelings. There being safety in numbers, they could afford to laugh at him openly.

The upland girls were quite different. Timid and distant, they had none of the coquetry of the cheerful pickers and sorters in the Buitenzorg region, who came to work wearing brightly coloured clothes and flowers in their hair or on their sun hats. In the Preanger it was not customary for women to enter the service of European men as their housekeeper, unlike in Batavia and environs, but quite apart from that he simply could not imagine living with a native woman in a purely opportunistic arrangement, a relationship completely lacking in the very quality that, to him, was essential to marital union.

During his stay in Batavia he had seen Marietje Hoogeveen again, at a friends' house. There was no trace of the sweet-faced, pert eleven-year-old he had seen bustling about her parents' home like a promising little housewife-to-be. Instead, there was a self-important, plump young lady in an overly furbelowed gown, a pretentious chatterbox despite her tender age of fourteen, just the type of European colonial girl he thoroughly disliked. How absurd that he should ever have entertained the idea of proposing to her as soon as she was old enough to marry! Thankfully, he had never mentioned it to anyone.

The southern slopes of the Goenoeng Tiloe were taken up by the government-run plantation of Rioeng Goenoeng. During his excursions to survey his lands he had on several occasions strayed into the quinine fields of that enterprise. As he wished to improve the road from Gamboeng to the Pengalengan plateau, he decided to pay a visit to the manager, Mr Van Honk, whose cooperation he would need. He sent a coolie with a note and promptly received an invitation for the *rijsttafel.* He was not looking forward to all the hot, spicy dishes that would doubtless be served, but he set out for Rioeng Goenoeng in good spirits, armed with a tin of his mother's home-made biscuits as a gift for the hostess.

The Van Honks were Eurasian, and the atmosphere in their home, which was only slightly larger than his *pondok*, reminded him of the 'Chinese Camp' at Sinagar, with birds in cages, hanging plants and rocking chairs, and the scent of spices mingling with that of the roses in the yard.

His discussion with Van Honk about the roadworks was interrupted by the appearance of the eldest daughter of the house, slender and graceful in her sarong and snowy kebaya (he could tell by the sharp creases in the sleeves that she had only just put it on). Introductions were duly made, and he couldn't help thinking how attractive she was, with her dark-complexioned little face blooming, as he thought to himself, with 'European rosiness' thanks to the fresh mountain air, her elegant poise, and the pretty turn of her waist and hips at every movement she made. He also noticed her parents watching him closely during the general patter at lunch later on about what a good cook she was, good with children, too, and how she taught her younger sisters reading writing and arithmetic, 'like a proper school mistress, *betoel*, sir!'

Riding back home to Gamboeng he tried to gauge his feelings. It would be easy for him to fall in love, and to act accordingly. The touch of her fingers as they shook hands, the way she looked at him with her dark eyes said enough. A girl born and bred in the *oedik*, accustomed to life on a plantation, blessed with all manner of domestic talents . . . it seemed an obvious enough choice. What about having children by this pretty *nonna*? Marriage with her would seal his bond with this land for ever. He thought of Eduard and his three small children, and of the shadowy figure of Goey La

Nio; and of Louise, Albert Holle's wife, who made herself scarce if the caller was a '*totok*', someone she suspected of having a bias against mixed marriages. He thought of the elderly Eurasian ladies he had met in Batavia, most of them stout and uncomfortable-looking in their European attire, who were 'accepted in society' simply because they were married to full-blooded Dutchmen in government service. They, too, had been pretty *nonnas* in their day. How would he stand up to the complications that were bound to arise, even within his own family, from his marriage to a Eurasian girl from a modest background and without any intellectual pursuits to speak of?

He decided not to visit the Van Honks more often than strictly necessary.

News came at last from Batavia that His Excellency the Governor-General of the Dutch East Indies had decided in favour of his application for leasehold, whereupon Rudolf sent for the land surveyor from Bandoeng (at considerable expense) to verify the figures. Next came the supervisor, for whom he had to arrange transport by horse and cart, and finally the *wedana* of Tjisondari, whose task was to ensure due observance of the land rights of the population (for him and his suite Rudolf organised carrying-chairs). Rudolf gave a sigh of relief. All he needed now were the official deeds, the formality that would conclude the entire transaction.

On 6 May 1876 he rode over to Ardjasari, where he came upon his father in conversation with Van Santen, who had arrived from Batavia the previous day. A brief, business-like ceremony was held in the inner gallery: for Rudolf, a first milestone on a long road. On the table between them lay the outcome of the lengthy negotiations: a carefully phrased document, using the appropriate legal terms, drawn up by Van Santen. The land called Gamboeng, of which Rudolf E. Kerkhoven could now call himself leaseholder for the duration of seventy-five years, was to be cultivated and exploited in partnership, 'with Mr R. A. Kerkhoven taking one quarter of profits and losses, J. J. van Santen one quarter, and R. E. Kerkhoven half.'

They all read the document through before placing their signatures at the end. Rudolf raised his champagne glass to the happy occasion, his reward after three years of hard toil. But he knew his cares were far from over. The Netherlands Indies Trading Bank had stipulated that all advances would have to be repaid before he was entitled to dividends of any kind. But what matter – Gamboeng was his!

A shadow fell over the festive gathering. Rudolf's mother was worried, as she confided to him in a private moment later that day. A few weeks previously Cateau had turned up at Ardjasari accompanied by the Van Santen children and a retinue of *baboes*, supposedly for the fresh air, but in reality to escape from Joan Henny, who was beginning to find the semi-orphans' constant presence irksome. He had not objected to taking them in at the time, naturally, but had since made it clear that he had no intention of offering them a permanent home. Cateau was deeply shocked. Her stay had caused upheaval in the orderly Ardjasari household: the children, especially the little girl, were a handful, and there had also been disagreements between mother and daughter about the correct way of raising youngsters.

Rudolf had received notes almost daily from Ardjasari telling him of the ups and downs of Cateau's visit, and had also taken a day off from work to go over and see her for himself. He had returned in the conviction that her trouble with Henny was just another storm in a teacup. Henny set much store by 'society'; he relished receiving guests and attending receptions, and expected to have Cateau standing at his side, adding lustre to his presence by her tasteful appearance and charming manners. Rudolf was confident that, with a little give and take, they would come to some satisfactory arrangement.

But now his mother showed him the desperate letter she had just received from Cateau: 'Henny wants to speak to Van Santen. Van Santen! You know what he's like! He will find it all very painful and troublesome, and to avoid all the bother in Batavia he will want to send the children to Holland. But who will take them in? Who do we know in Holland capable of taking three children into their home? Will they be separated? Will they be sent to live with strangers? What about me? Oh, it is so cruel!'

Rudolf promised to see what he could do when he next went to Batavia. He needed to go there on business anyway, as he had heard through Herman Holle that Pryce & Co. might be interested in investing in Gamboeng in a non-executive role. Back in Gamboeng he prepared for his departure at once. He entrusted the administration to his clerk, and put *mandoer* Moehiam in charge of the men clearing tracts of jungle for new tea gardens on the slopes of the Goenoeng Tiloe.

He had the carpenter carve a set of skittles from rasamala wood as a gift for the little Van Santens.

THE COUPLE

1876–9

Rudolf walked down the inner gallery of the Henny residence to the veranda at the rear, where he found Cateau perched on a chair with the three small children gathered around her, their faces pressed to her sarong. She was counting out loud: '. . . three . . . four . . . five . . .'

The garden was bathed in morning sunlight, with clusters of red and orange cannas ablaze in a circular flowerbed and roses in tall pots, like splashes of colour against a deeply shaded backdrop of trees on the far side.

Rudolf held up the box of skittles, winked at Cateau and ducked into the inner gallery to hide. 'You can come now!' he cried.

Cateau led the wide-eyed children to him – 'Look who we've found! What a nice surprise!' – and the next moment there was a cry from the garden, seemingly in echo of his: 'You can come now!'

'Heavens above! I almost forgot: Jenny is hiding somewhere.'

'Jenny who?' asked Rudolf, looking into the garden. He thought he saw something stir in the bushes beyond the cannas.

'It's Jenny Roosegaarde Bisschop, a friend of mine. Oh, would you go and fetch her, please?'

He stepped gingerly across the flowerbed, taking care not to crush the long, dark-brown canna leaves. Peering over the bushes at the back he saw a mass of dark blonde hair tied with a ribbon: the bowed head of a girl crouching down.

'You can come now!' she repeated, her voice muffled by her bunched skirts.

'Here I am!' he said, laughing.

She rose up from her hiding place, staring at him in surprise. The look in her shining grey eyes, grave yet radiant, took his breath away. Before he could say another word, she was striding up the path along the cannas towards the house.

Afterwards she wondered how on earth she could have been so rude as to dash off that like that without giving the young man a chance to introduce himself.

She found Cateau Henny and the children on the back veranda, busy setting out the skittle-pins on the tiled floor.

'Look what Uncle Rudolf has brought us!' said Cateau. 'Where is he, anyway?'

Jenny sank to her knees beside the youngest boy, Rudi, to help him roll the wooden ball. She had no need to reply to the question, for, just then, the gift-bearing uncle started up the steps to the veranda. He put out his hand to her in greeting.

'I am sorry to have startled you. Please think of me as just another planter from the *oedik*, with a habit of stalking wild animals. Do forgive me. My name is Rudolf Kerkhoven.'

Jenny felt herself blushing, much to her own annoyance, as she reached up to shake his extended hand. Rudolf Kerkhoven's straightforward, friendly manner, so unlike the strained politeness of the young men she usually met, gave her confidence, so much so that she replied jokingly, 'Now you're looking down on me all over again!'

'That is easily remedied,' he said, dropping to his knees beside her. 'May I join in your game?'

The children whooped with delight and threw themselves at him, almost making him lose his balance. In mimed terror he clutched at Cateau for support. She tried to keep her composure, but the children tugged at her sarong, chanting, 'We want Auntie Cateau to play, too!' Finally, she sank down gracefully and joined in.

Jenny observed the brother and sister from the corner of her eye. With their heads so close together she could see the likeness between them, especially in the eyes. She was pleased that Rudolf had come, for she knew how fond Cateau was of her brother, and how much she missed him. Besides, he might be able to soothe the trouble that was causing that tearful look she saw in her friend's eyes all too often nowadays.

On his way back from the washroom he came upon Cateau plucking withered sprays from the lush maiden-hair ferns on her back veranda. Inside, the table was being laid for lunch. The bamboo blinds between the pillars had been lowered, thereby tempering the harsh noonday light and keeping out the worst of the heat. The houseboy padded soundlessly to and fro with glassware and cutlery from the sideboard in the passage. While she talked to Rudolf, Cateau kept glancing in the servant's direction, giving the occasional nod or shake of the head to indicate whether he was fetching out the correct tableware.

'He's new, and hasn't got used to us yet. Do have a seat, Ru. You don't mind me staying like this, do you?' she said, patting the front of her kebaya. 'I don't normally dress until after tea. Henny will be home from the office soon. The youngsters are already in bed, so it's nice and quiet. Isn't Jenny Roosegaarde a sweet girl? I don't know what I'd do without her. She's so good with the children.'

'She is not actually in your service, is she?'

'Good heavens, no. Her father is vice-president of the High Court of Justice. The Roosegaardes are old friends of my husband's family, from back home. Jenny likes helping me with the children; it gives her an excuse to go out. She has a hard time of it at home.'

'How so?' Rudolf leant back in the reclining chair.

There had been chairs like that at Sinagar, but not at Ardjasari. His father would never wish to be seen lolling back in an attitude of such nonchalance, let alone to be seen in his pyjama suit during the day. As for Rudolf, he felt agreeably relaxed, as if he had just received a piece of good news, or had finally reached his destination after a long and arduous journey.

'Now then, what shall I tell you about the Roosegaardes?' said Cateau, settling herself opposite him in a rocking chair. Rudolf knew how eager she was to discuss all the people she knew. He enjoyed listening to her airing her opinions, just as he enjoyed her long, rambling letters, even if he had no particular interest in the people themselves. But this time her discursiveness was more than matched by his curiosity. Afterwards, when he was alone, he would mull over every intriguing detail his sister had told him about the grey-eyed girl and her family circumstances, a reservoir of information, which, he could sense, would be of momentous importance in times to come.

There were, so Cateau told him, three girls in the Roosegaarde Bisschop family: Rose, who was nineteen, Jenny, seventeen, and Marie, fifteen. ('Rose is a little slow and stiff, Jenny's the clever one and a darling, and Marie's beautiful but catty.') They clung to their father and cherished their mother as if she were a child or a favourite doll. Mrs Roosegaarde, née Betsy Daendels, granddaughter of the Iron Marshall, was a head shorter than her growing girls, and could even be taken for their sister, thanks to her slight figure and delicate features. She had a nervous temperament that was said to be inherited from her notorious Governor-General grandfather. After giving birth so many times she found herself almost permanently stricken with migraines. ('Eleven confinements! That tiny creature! Some women have eleven children; others have none.') The girls were always able to see her headaches coming, and would put her to bed in a darkened room and try to restrain their unruly brothers (aged between four and twelve and far too spoilt by the servants) while they conducted the housekeeping as best they could. The sprawling house in Gang Scott, a road off Koningsplein, was more like a crowded boarding-house than a home, in Cateau's opinion, what with a nanny for the boys, a governess-cum-companion for the girls, and all those houseboys and maids that no one seemed to keep in any semblance of order. Mr Roosegaarde Bisschop had mentioned to Henny several times how trying he found the disarray in his home, where some member of the family always seemed to be ill and he was constantly being called upon to deal with emergencies, where the children had riding lessons in the garden and dancing lessons on the back veranda, while the front veranda and the rest of the house was overrun by servants preparing for some dinner or reception that he was obliged to host in his capacity as High Court official. He managed to keep his composure under all circumstances, but only at the cost of sleepless nights and shortness of breath, the latter ailment being something that had to be kept from his wife. He adored his three daughters. Cateau had met them a few times before at a friends' house, and had seen their father glowing with pride when surrounded by his charming girls, so close to one another in height and identically dressed in wide skirts with starched pantalettes showing underneath. Such pretty faces! But their hair was cut short against the heat and vermin. Like all girls born in the Indies, they looked older than their years. Roosegaarde was deeply grateful for their devotion to him. As his wife habitually rose late, it was not she but the girls who poured his coffee for him in the morning and saw him off when he mounted his horse to ride to the law court. People going past the house in the early morning were used to seeing him out on the front veranda accompanied by his 'three graces', as he called them.

'An interesting family!' said Rudolf.

'They're coming to dinner tomorrow evening – the girls and their parents, I mean. So you will be meeting them all.'

'Oh, Marie, it's too bad! *Kasian*!' said Jenny as she stepped from the afternoon heat into the shade of the room where her youngest sister stood bent over the sewing table.

'Mmm?' asked Marie, her mouth full of pins.

'Henny insists the children will have to leave. And their father can't have them at home.'

'What about grandparents? Aren't they the Kerkhovens at Ardjasari?'

Jenny felt the blood rush to her cheeks. She glanced in the mirror and quickly turned away.

'Yes they are. But out there in the *oedik* . . . they live so far away, in the mountains . . . hardly the place to bring up small children. Besides, Cateau says her mother will spoil them too much. Her brother thinks so, too.'

Jenny put a chair by the door to the side gallery and sat down. The lowered blind swayed gently in the breeze.

'Is he in Batavia?' asked Marie. 'I think it would be good if I added a ruffle here, don't you? I'll get the seamstress to finish it for me. So, what is Cateau's brother like?'

'Oh,' Jenny hesitated, 'you'll be meeting him tomorrow.'

'Who else is coming? This is what I'm going to wear.'

'Oh, same as usual; just us and Mr van Santen. I wouldn't wear that dress if I were you, Marie. It's too grown-up, and too formal besides.'

'Rubbish! When can I wear it, then? I never go anywhere.'

'And nor do I. Once we're eighteen we'll be able to go out.' As she said this, it crossed Jenny's mind that her youngest sister could easily pass for eighteen. Marie was tall and slim, and there was nothing childish about her, neither in her demeanour nor in the expression on her pretty face.

'There's something else that's too bad, you know. Oh, *kasian*,' Marie said with sudden vehemence. 'Mama's expecting another visit from the stork.'

During his tête-à-tête over tea with Cateau – Henny having gone straight back to the office after his siesta – Rudolf gently steered the conversation to her differences with her husband.

They were sitting on the patio adjoining the back veranda. Little Rudi, astride his wooden horse, was being pulled along by his *baboe*, while Nonnie and Adrie played with their building bricks under the watchful eye of another nursemaid. Cateau's eyes filled with tears, but she fought them back, drawing her handkerchief from her sleeve and waving it about dismissively. 'Well, he's just totally self-centred, that's all there is to it! He has his fixed habits and foibles, and won't have them disturbed for any reason. He wants everything to be punctual and done his way. You have no idea how fussy that man is about food. When we're invited to dinner with new acquaintances he sends our cook over to their house – can you imagine? – to prepare a separate dish for him. I could die of embarrassment sometimes. The children bother him. And yet they're really very good, as you can see. Nonnie does wake up in the night sometimes, crying for her mother, poor lamb, but you can hardly blame her for that. I think he's jealous of the attention I give the children. So silly! And it's not as if he takes much notice of me, you know. He's never at home. I know he has a lot of business to attend to, and that he is expected to appear in public, but he exaggerates. He cares far too much about what people say. For me the children make life worth living; they bring cheer into the house. What is wrong with that?'

'Van Santen might re-marry one day.'

'Well, not in the short term, probably, so soon after Bertha . . . But would a new wife want the children? And would they be happy with a new mother? And what about me? Am I supposed to part with them?' Cateau poured him another cup of tea, in her agitation spilling some onto the saucer. 'It's all quite nerve-racking.'

'Would you like me to have a word with Henny?'

She sighed. 'Oh, I don't know. He's not a bad sort, really. But I don't want you to rub him up the wrong way. He's very touchy, and bears a grudge for ages.'

The dinner party at the Hennys was a small affair, but decidedly elegant thanks to Cateau's best efforts. She had a fine cook, with several European dishes in his repertoire. Whereas Henny set much store by decorum, even for informal occasions, Cateau aimed at creating an intimate atmosphere, and had instructed the servants to place the dishes on the table so that she might serve the food to the guests herself. The wine, much praised by both Van Santen and Roosegaarde Bisschop, had been chosen by Henny, who considered himself a connoisseur. The ladies were full of admiration for the tastefully laid table and the floral centrepiece made up of sokas and coral vine.

Rudolf let his eyes wander about the dinner table. His heart had skipped a beat when Jenny arrived. He hardly knew her, and yet every feature of her face, every line of her figure seemed perfectly familiar to him. He felt a rush of longing and tenderness each time he saw her raising her eyes to whoever was addressing her, in that demure yet eagerly attentive way she had.

The sisters were remarkably alike in appearance, as if they were three variations on a single theme. Jenny's air of natural reserve seemed to be echoed in Rose's timid restraint, while Marie's coquettish beauty took the form of ingenuous charm in Jenny. All three wore plain white frocks made of thin material, without any of the complicated draperies Rudolf disliked so much, even though they were in fashion. Jenny in particular had something pure and airy about her, which he found enchanting.

Mr and Mrs Roosegaarde Bisschop made a remarkable pair: he was quite burly and strong-featured, with silver hair and very dark eyebrows, the contrast giving him the aspect of a bewigged, eighteenth-century gentleman, while his frilled and furbelowed wife was even more diminutive than Rudolf had imagined from Cateau's description, with her small, thin face and ardent eyes looking rather lost beneath the massive crown of plaited hair. These people were on very familiar terms with Henny, as if they were close relations. Roosegaarde had come out to the Indies as a young man after graduating with honours in law and taking a preparatory course for legal practice in the Indies. He seemed likeable enough, although Rudolf was somewhat bemused by his boastful allusions to the fact that he came from a family of tanners for whom obtaining a university degree signified an important step up the social ladder.

Rudolf was also struck by his outspoken criticism of the colonial government, which he accused of wasting millions of guilders on public works without doing anything about corruption and theft in that sector, and further millions on ridiculous perquisites for the benefit of high-ranking colonial officials, while the hard-working, responsible civil servants and lower military personnel were confronted with cuts in their pensions, furloughs and dividends. It was a downright scandal. Why couldn't the government in The Hague see it was essential to raise the budget for the colonies? 'That Holland treats the Indies as if it were just another Dutch province, and in such a niggardly fashion – especially in light of the enormous benefits this "province" brings both directly and indirectly to the mother country – is not in dispute. What we need is a separate economic administration for the Indies. That would only be fair. How else can you expect any major agricultural enterprises to establish themselves here? It's a disgrace that there is no one with any sense to be found to lead the government during the present period of transition! Certainly not a mediocre courtier like Loudon, who will go down in history as the man we have to thank for that horrendous, unjust, indeed insane military campaign in Atjeh.'

Van Santen coughed. The meaning of this signal did not escape Rudolf. Roosegaarde had got so carried away that he had quite forgotten that both the Kerkhovens and the Holles were in the Governor-General's favour.

Rudolf couldn't keep his eyes off Jenny, who was sitting opposite him. He took every opportunity to engage her in conversation, describing the plantation at Gamboeng to her, telling her about his new tea bushes.

'How long will it be before you can harvest the leaves?' asked Jenny.

'From seed to first crop . . . four years, more or less.'

'Such a long time!'

'Good things are worth the wait.'

'So you are sure you will make a success of Gamboeng?'

'It won't be for lack of effort if I don't. I know I am making the right choice,' he said, looking into her eyes.

'Don't you get lonely out there?'

'Yes, I suppose I do. But it's so beautiful, it's like paradise, it's the most beautiful place I have ever seen. And I hope I won't be on my own for ever!'

Mrs Roosegaarde, who had grown increasingly pale and withdrawn as the meal progressed, rose abruptly and hurried out of the room, quickly followed by her eldest daughter. Rudolf saw Roosegaarde whispering something in Cateau's ear, and Jenny and Marie exchanging meaningful looks, after which Jenny dropped her eyes. What was going through her mind? He would have given the world to hold her gaze again, to pursue the dialogue that filled him with the same elation he had felt when exploring his lands for the first time. For the past twenty-four hours he had known he would set out to conquer her, just as he had conquered Gamboeng.

The Roosegaardes took their leave soon after dinner. Van Santen followed suit. No sooner had their carriages rolled off than Cateau dropped into her rocking chair in the back veranda. Henny poured a glass of cognac for himself and for Rudolf, and sat down opposite her.

'What was the matter with Betsy? Did I hear right? In the family way again, is she?'

'Yes, she is,' said Cateau curtly, shaking out her fan.

'Aren't you going to bed yet, Cateau?' asked Rudolf. 'You look tired.'

'Cateau is far too busy these days. Three small children . . . a bit trying, I must say.'

'My God! They're my sister's children! Rudolf, say something, please.'

'It seems to me that Nonnie's behaviour is much improved since I last saw her at Ardjasari. And who better to stand in for Bertha than Cateau? Looking after the children makes her happy.'

'Cateau has all she could wish for,' said Henny coldly. Ignoring his wife's muffled cry of indignation, he turned to Rudolf. 'Look here, Kerkhoven, I appreciate your solicitude for Cateau, but I would rather you kept out of it. It is not your affair.'

'But it *is* my affair. And that of my parents. It concerns the whole family.'

'Ah, the venerable Kerkhoven family! And what of Van Santen, the children's father? What is it with the Kerkhovens and the Holles and the rest of them? You people behave as if you own the whole of western Java. You think everything revolves around you, always expecting people to go out of their way for your convenience!'

'May I ask what you mean by that?'

'Certainly you may. I have grave concerns about all the string-pulling that goes on. It's not just you and your father and your uncle at Sinagar that I am talking about, but also those Holle cousins of yours. Now that old Van der Hucht has died and De Waal is no longer in the Cabinet, you lot get your way in everything – currying favour with that rogue of a Loudon by means of that so-called "friend of the Soendanese peasant"! You know who I mean.'

'Oh, please!' cried Cateau, jumping up from her seat. 'What has any of that got to do with Bertha's children?'

'It has to do with Bertha's children in so far as I have no intention of bending to the will of the Kerkhoven family, not in my business affairs, and certainly not in my own home,' Henny said drily. 'I am glad to receive your brother and your parents, and to visit Ardjasari myself when appropriate, but I warn you: all that will be over if you don't stop complaining behind my back.'

Rudolf too stood up. He put his arm around Cateau, who was trembling with suppressed outrage.

'Let's not have a scene,' said Henny. 'Think of the servants.'

'Leave it be,' whispered Cateau. 'Just let it rest, Ru. I'm going to bed.'

As the sound of her heels on the tiled floor died away, Rudolf turned to his brother-in-law, 'I cannot allow what you said just now to pass, as I am sure you understand. I demand you take it back.'

To his astonishment, Henny smiled amiably. 'Dear me, old chap, it was just the heat of the moment . . . All right, if you insist, I apologise! At times your sister's temperament is enough to make me *bingoeng*, as they say. But having three children here is simply too much. Not that I can think of a better solution for the moment, so they can stay until Van Santen has made arrangements. I expect he will go to Holland eventually.'

Two days later, just before returning to Gamboeng, Rudolf finally contrived to have a private word with Jenny in the garden. Cateau was giving the servants instructions before going out to make some social calls; she had offered to drop her young friend off on her way. After kissing the children goodbye, Jenny strolled through the garden towards the gate, where the landau was waiting with the coachman and groom holding the horses.

She had not yet said goodbye to Rudolf, so he went after her. She lingered in the shade of the myrtle trees, which were in full pink-and-purple bloom.

'I should very much like to write to you,' said Rudolf. 'But I realise I need to ask your father for permission first. Supposing he grants it, would you reply to my letters?'

'Oh, I like writing letters. But I don't have very much to write about, really.'

'I am interested in everything, even the most ordinary things. Everything about you, what you are thinking, what you are up to.'

Jenny rose up on tiptoe to snap off a sprig of blossom, lilac-pink, delicate as tissue paper. She held the stem between her thumb and index finger, rolling it from side to side. Rudolf took it from her and tucked it in his buttonhole. The garden had just been watered, and a scent of moist earth rose from the flowerbeds. Sounds from the kampong beyond drifted over the hedge: the rattle and splash of buckets being filled at the well and, more faintly, the sudden squawk of chickens in flight.

'I'd prefer it if you didn't ask,' she said, but her grey eyes contradicted her. 'Papa won't give his consent, anyway.'

'Well, what then?' asked Rudolf tensely. 'How else can we get to know each other? Because that is what I would like to do. And you? Would you like that, too . . . Jenny?'

'Yes, I would,' she said softly. 'But I don't know how. Look, there's Cateau. Au revoir . . . Rudolf.'

That evening Rudolf and Cateau took a leisurely stroll together in the back garden. The air was heavy with the scent of the sedap malam, the night-blooming tuberose, the cicadas shrilled in the trees, the whitewashed flowerpots lining the garden path shone in the moonlight.

'I want Jenny,' Rudolf said. He had been longing to say those words ever since they left the house.

Cateau chuckled. 'I'm not surprised.'

'Oh, is that what you had in mind? Matchmaker!'

'Jenny is just right for you. Only, she isn't eighteen yet.'

'I can wait. But not too long. Do you think I stand a chance?'

Cateau stood still and placed her hands on his shoulders. 'I've seen the way she looks at you without you taking notice.'

'But I do take notice!'

They both burst out laughing, as the complicity of shared childhood reasserted itself. He kissed her on her hair.

'What I mean is: how will her father react?' he pursued.

'What could he possibly have against you?'

'Things aren't going terribly well at the moment. Not at Gamboeng, and not at Ardjasari, either. Papa has been having a lot of setbacks. The yield from my old coffee gardens was so-so, and my tea isn't exactly flourishing.'

They walked on in silence. From the corner of his eye Rudolf could see Cateau's fan in motion, a pale smudge in the dark.

'I wouldn't rush things if I were you. Just leave the Roosegaardes out of it for the time being.'

'But I couldn't bear to lose her. Someone else might get in the way!'

'Jenny will keep coming to help me with the children. We talk a lot. Just you trust your sister.' She took his arm.

'You must write to me often, do you hear?'

'If you promise me nice long letters in return!'

They saw Joan Henny stepping out on to the veranda at the back of the house, his silhouette starkly defined against the brightly lit interior. They could tell by his movements that he was lighting a cigarette.

'Sshh,' said Cateau. 'I don't want him to interfere.'

'Let's wait a bit.' Rudolf patted her arm. 'Are you all right?'

'You needn't worry about me. I can manage, you know,' she said airily, but her tone did not convince Rudolf.

'Come with me,' she said. Reaching the pavement by the back veranda she let go of the hem of her dress, which she had been holding up with one hand while they walked on the paths. 'Let's have a glass of lemonade. I'm dying of thirst. And our visitors will be arriving in a moment.'

He felt too restless to spend his last evening in Batavia with Henny and Cateau and their guests. They would be playing cards, and he was not needed to make up a foursome. There was to be a concert at Concordia that evening, and it occurred to him that listening to some good music would be just the thing for him in his present state of mind. He instructed Henny's coachman to take the roundabout way to Koningpsplein so that they would drive past Jenny's house in Gang Scott. The front veranda was lit, but deserted. Presumably they were all at the back, in the family circle from which he was banned until such time as he would be granted permission to court Jenny.

The lieder by Schubert and Schumann did nothing to soothe his nerves. On the contrary, the passion and longing of the melodies only increased his turmoil. '*Dein is mein Herz, und soll es ewig, ewig, bleiben*', and then '*Du bist die Ruh, der Frieden mild, die Sehnsucht auch, und was sie stillt*' expressed exactly what he was feeling – that he had found the woman of his dreams. He would have no other. He had been waiting so long already that having to exercise patience for another extended period seemed to him like senseless torture. How could he, out in the wilds of Gamboeng, possibly nurture and cherish that first glow of affection he had seen in her eyes? Cateau's role as a go-between would be invaluable to him, of course, but could she, for all her tact and insight, guarantee a favourable outcome?

From everything Jenny heard about Rudolf – and Cateau was always eager to talk about her elder brother, elaborating her stories as she went – he rose up in her imagination as a strong, protective presence. No one knew him better than Cateau; their relationship had always been close, more so than with Bertha or Julius, even when they were children.

'My parents think he's a bit headstrong, and that he takes himself too seriously. And he does give that impression sometimes,

I suppose. But I think it's just because he has a strong sense of duty, and because he always reasons things out before speaking his mind, which is a good thing. Anyway, he's usually right.

'How shall I describe his character to you? He's not a great talker, but that's not because he doesn't have much to say. He reads a lot, literature mostly. He has an ear for music. He can also be very funny. He has a great sense of fairness, and he's as solid as a rock. A real man! And that, Jenny dear, is worth more than anything. I wish I had a husband like that. You needn't look so shocked! That's just the way life is. Men have to pass an exam to enter the civil service, don't they? To make sure they're suitable. But they don't need to pass an exam to get married! You know what it's like over here, where marriage is concerned. You meet someone at a ball, you dance with him, you talk and laugh with him at dinner parties, but you don't get to know each other properly. It's so superficial. Do you keep a journal, by any chance?'

Jenny shook her head. 'I jot things down sometimes, when the mood takes me, but it's not really a journal. I have an album with a lock. Sometimes I imagine I'm talking to someone I don't know, and who doesn't know me.'

'How interesting! You should let me read it. Then I can write and tell Ru all about you – Henny won't see my letters, I promise. Don't you think that would be a good idea? Not an actual correspondence, since that isn't allowed, but still a way of getting to know each other.'

'You're so clever,' smiled Jenny. 'It reminds me of that fairytale about a girl who had to be dressed and naked at the same time, so she draped herself in a fishing net. All right then, you can take a look at my album if you like, but I'm not sure . . .'

'Trust me!'

FROM JENNY'S ALBUM, 1876

There are some things I can never talk about. When Mama has one of her nervous headaches she becomes a stranger. Sometimes Rose is too frightened to sit with her. But it always passes, thank goodness, and then she is our dear little mother again. Lately her temper has become very uneven – one moment she is bustling about, bright and cheery, the next she is in the depths of despair. Perhaps it's because of the weather, as it's terribly hot, and the rains are late this year. I do so hope things will improve when the new baby arrives. May it be a sweet little girl, strong and healthy, to make up for the loss of our little sister. Boys are so rowdy, such a nuisance! Perhaps it is just as well that Willem and Frits stayed behind in Holland after Papa's furlough. Mama couldn't keep them in order, and Papa's too busy to concern himself with them.

Why did Papa leave Willem and Frits behind and not our Gus? He's the eldest, after all. Frits is only seven. Was it because Papa thought Frits upset Mama too much with his odd behaviour? Frits was ill with brain-fever when he was little, and *baboe* Roesminah says it does lasting damage. Besides, he was born with two of his fingers stuck together. Willem's head was very big when he was a baby, which I thought a bit strange. Now he looks normal, because the rest of him has grown rather big, too. He is not very quick on the uptake, but he tries hard at school. I feel so sorry for the boys, living so far away from us, with a strange family. They cried and cried when we left.

It was especially for us girls – Rose, Marie and me – that Papa went on furlough in 1873. Mama dreaded going. But Papa insisted, because he thought we needed 'finishing', as he put it, before going out into the world. We were supposed to enjoy our stay in Europe, but how much fun did we have? Our family is so numerous that we could not all stay together in the same place all the time, so we were farmed out among different relations. And we had to go to school. Nothing came of all the parties and outings we had been promised. Rose and I ended up being sent to a Belgian boarding school in Liège for several months – so much for a fine holiday abroad.

We learnt French there, and the culinary arts, and the piano lessons there were better than here. How quiet it was in Liège compared to our rented house in Arnhem, with all of us together plus the two nannies, the housemaids, and that peculiar groom who always seemed to be drunk. Mama was rather poorly, she was expecting at the time – our baby sister who died during the voyage back to the Indies. Half a year has passed since we returned, and I am left wondering what good it has done us – all that fuss, all that packing and unpacking and staying in hotels and furnished apartments.

I wouldn't have minded staying on for another year in Holland, or in Liège for that matter. I would have trained as a school teacher, which I think I might be good at. I was actually asked to be an assistant teacher at that boarding school, but Mama needed our help with the little ones on board ship. Rose is a little slow, but Marie is quite useful when she has a mind to it, which is seldom the case. Anyway, I got over my disappointment when I was put in charge of Herman and Philip after our little Betsy died. It's the worst thing that has ever happened in my life. That tiny, stiff body wrapped in canvas! Mama couldn't bear the thought of her being dropped into the sea; she screamed and cried to stop them. In the end they kept Betsy on board and we were able to bury her properly at Padang, right next to the grave of our two little brothers who died when Papa was posted there as a judge. Our little sister's name was Aleida Elisabeth Reiniera, after Mama. She was angry with Papa afterwards for choosing that name. She says it's unlucky to have two people in the family with the same name.

Mama was only fifteen when she met Papa. Grandpapa Daendels was Assistant Resident in Modjokerto in those days, and Papa was at the law court of Soerabaja. Apparently it was love at first sight for Papa. She was a happy girl, and she was sweet-natured, Papa says, and very kind and gentle with her sisters and brother. Their mother died young. Grandpa Daendels fell ill, never to recover. On his deathbed he gave Papa permission to court Mama. Whenever he had to be in Robolinggo, Papa would ride out to the Waroe plantation after work, where she was living in her guardian's house. Papa is twelve years her senior. She agreed to marry him just before she was due to make a trip to Holland, with her stepmother and the other children. The Daendels family in Hattem did not consider Papa to be a very good match on account of his provincial background, whereas Mama's family was upper class. I wonder how Mama felt about him while she was away during those two years. She was so young! But she wore Papa's engagement ring, which he had asked his mother to give her when she paid her first visit to the Roosegaarde family. She still wears the ring today. She was all of eighteen when she came back here, and she and Papa got married in Soerabaja. Papa means the world to her; he is the one who makes all the decisions, and she depends on him for everything. I don't think she could survive without him. Papa adores her, but he treats her as if she were his personal property, always telling her what to think and do. He is so sensible and kind, but he is always the one in command. Mama once read us a letter he wrote to her when they were engaged. It was all about the 'little cage' he was building for her – as if he wanted to keep her locked up! As if that were her destiny! I know it's not my place to question my parents' marriage, but I can feel there is some trouble there, something that never comes to the surface. I wonder what it is.

Mama was born in the Indies, in Semarang, and so was I. We were all born in the Indies, except for poor little Betsy. I noticed in Holland that we were different. We are fair-haired and fair-skinned, but we are not European. I could always tell with people like us, and now I can see it in myself and in Rose and Marie and the boys. Papa doesn't feel like that. He was born in Holland, and he didn't come out here until he was twenty-six years old. He thinks we are just as Dutch as he is, and that it is reasonable to expect us to be strong and sensible like him. But is that a question of willpower? Even the best will in the world doesn't work for some people. There is something inside them preventing it. I don't know what it is, but it is a strange feeling, and I have it often. Sad and rebellious at the same time. With Rose it is the sadness that predominates, with Marie the rebellion. With me they go together. I don't know about the boys, they are just naughty. It's like being pulled in opposite directions. When I feel that way all I want to do is keep perfectly still, like turning to stone. But I know I shouldn't, so I get twice as busy as normal. The houseboys and the *baboes* say, 'There she goes again – *amat rajin, gètol.*' I get into such a state, finding fault with everyone – myself included. Marie hates me when I'm like that.

Marie was terribly spoilt when she was little, which she is paying for now. She has a hot temper, but she is so pretty that no one stays angry with her for long. She starts things then loses interest, so someone else has to finish the job. That someone is usually me. It makes life very difficult at times. The servants are all right, but you have to keep an eye on them. I know all about table linen and dinner settings, and I like things to be just so. Papa does, too, and so does Mama, but she can't keep track of everything; it is too much work and she simply lacks the strength. And it takes ages! It is too much for me, too. Sometimes. I get so annoyed when the house is all confusion and untidiness, but what can I do?

There is something that only Rose and I know about. One day we went to the *pasar* with the governess. An old woman came up to us, a real *nènèk* in filthy rags. She was chewing *sirih*, so her mouth seemed to be dribbling blood. I thought she was a beggar and wanted to give her something, but she launched into a tirade, oh, I shall never forget it as long as I live. She said she knew exactly who we were and where we lived, that we were the descendants of the Master who built the Great Post Road across Java, and that we were surrounded day and night by dead souls who hated us and were out to avenge the suffering of the Javanese at the hands of the Big Master. I said, 'Go away! Go away!' but she just stood there, ranting, and then Rose and I ran away, with the governess at our heels. She didn't know what was going on, luckily, because she doesn't understand more than a few words of Malay.

A few weeks ago, when I was resting, Roesminah came to my room saying there was someone at the back gate with a message for me, someone she didn't dare send away. I went with her, and there stood the same old woman. She began to rant again, as if she was putting a curse on me. I felt numb, unable to move or speak. She came back once more after that, but that time I made the houseboy chase her away. Thank goodness Mama never noticed. But the woman is always lurking about. I catch sight of her by the side of the road when we go out. All she does is stare, but it feels like a shadow falling on my face. I keep thinking of what she said, about our future being full of death and unhappiness, and about all those dead souls waiting to do us evil. Sometimes I try to pray, but would that help? Papa is a freethinker, and we never go to church. I'm not really a believer myself, so I have no reason to be superstitious. So why am I frightened of that woman?

Roesminah says if you don't believe in Allah it means your soul is empty, which leaves it wide open to misfortune.

People need their souls to be orderly. How wonderful that must be. I know for certain that my soul is anything but orderly, but I wish it were. My feelings are all mixed up. One day I feel quite happy being the dutiful daughter and helping Papa and Mama to run our home, but the next I feel it's all very unfair having to be at everyone's beck and call; it makes me cross and miserable, and then I hate myself and end up taking on even more chores, all of which I do with frantic precision, as if my life depended on it. That smacks of superstition, doesn't it?

Such a lot of bad things have been said about our great-grandfather, Governor-General Daendels. It is true that constructing the Great Post Road cost thousands of lives, but, according to Papa, his grandfather was a fine governor, and it was all down to the cruelty of the native chiefs, who didn't care whether their people lived or died. Building a road over the entire length of Java had become a necessity, Papa says, for reasons of trade as well as defence. What I cannot understand is why His Excellency didn't intervene on behalf of the workers. Papa says he couldn't go against the agreements that had been made with the chiefs, and that he had no say in the manner of construction. All he had been charged to do by our Government was to make sure the road was built. He did not keep count of the casualties.

That *nènèk* is very old. Maybe her father and her brothers were forced to work on the Post Road, and that is why she curses us. But it's not our fault! Her eyes are like lumps of charcoal smouldering in deep sockets, with the skin all around looking black and charred. Roesminah is afraid of her, too; she has been burning incense, and she buried something – she won't say what – outside by the gate, to stop the nènèk from coming inside. But she comes anyway, because I dream about her. Rose does too sometimes, but it is me she is after. Roesminah knows that. She is a good, faithful soul. She carried all three of us, Rose, Marie and me, in her *slendang* when we were babies. She wants to protect me, but I still don't feel safe.

Why am I writing all these things down? It would be dishonest of me not to, and I dearly want to be honest. Cateau says I am gentle and balanced. And so I am, when I am at the Hennys. You can't be moody with children. They need clarity and order in a caring environment. You can never be caring enough, as far as children are concerned.

We have had another little addition to our family. His name is Henri. He is tiny and frail, but the doctor says we won't lose him. Papa is pleased, of course, especially because the birth was quite straightforward this time, but this morning, when Rose and Marie and I were having breakfast with him, he said, 'I don't know where we will be if things go on at this rate,' at which Marie laughed so much she almost choked on her coffee. Afterwards I asked her how she could be so insensitive. What she said in reply is impossible to write down.

Mama used to leave us with the servants a lot when we were small. She had no choice, she was too busy, and there was always a baby to look after as well. She had a hard time of it, especially in Padang, where our first little brothers died. The three of us girls spent most of our time at the back of the house with the maids. We didn't have Roesminah to look after us then, because she was Mama's old *baboe* and had to take care of the little ones. Some children see and hear more than others. I think I must have been rather backward for my age, or very dreamy, because I can't remember any of the things Marie says we used to hear about in the kitchen. What I do remember is a gardener who used to rub cockroaches and spiders to a pulp between his finger and thumb, grimacing at our squeamishness. Marie said he wasn't right in the head, and that sometimes he did other disgusting things, too. He once gave Rose a terrible fright, apparently. I asked her what he had done, but she refused to tell me. Marie was the servants' favourite, they all wanted to dandle her on their knee and give her sweets. She says she 'knew everything' by the age of five. I know what she means by that now, of course, because I found out about things, too, but I wasn't nearly as young as she was. I was twelve, and I had become a 'young lady' as they say, which happened to me earlier than to Rose, even though she is a year older than me. I no longer had to wear short skirts with pantalettes underneath, and it was then that Roesminah explained everything to me. But Marie knows a lot of things besides. Sometimes she has a look on her face that annoys me no end – half-smiling, snooty, and also a bit mean. She and I quarrelled terribly the other day. Moenah and Itih had been telling her all sorts of tales about Governor-General Daendels, that he had fifteen children at home and a lot more offspring in the kampong, and then she said something very rude about Papa and Mama. I shook her hard, which made her furious, and then we fought like cats. Rose had to come between us. What do you expect? Marie said afterwards. We have Daendels blood running in our veins. Two sides of the same coin: lust and violence.

RUDOLF TO CATEAU, JANUARY 1877

The tea auction in Amsterdam has been a great disappointment to both Papa and me, but we are bearing up now. I still have good hopes for the future, financially speaking – at least, if Papa does not lose interest in tea altogether. I can quite imagine his concern, though, given the continuing weakness of the market.

As for me, I am in good spirits. My new plantings of Java tea are doing well; the bushes will be ready for the first harvest after the rains. I have planted new coffee on the cleared land, which is a complicated business because I have to set out five or six different varieties, which must be kept separate.

I have bought water-buffalos. Yesterday they were set upon by half a dozen wild dogs. Thank goodness there is one fearless young buffalo among them who charges the dogs when they come too near. Let's hope they don't encircle him to separate him from the others! It rained all afternoon, so I couldn't go there myself to look them over, and today I simply can't face clambering all the way down into that muddy ravine and up the other side to reach them. We are hard at work making them a paddock.

I am also assembling the building materials for my new house.

Julius and August have both passed their exams. Julius a civil engineer! Bully for him, I say. It remains to be seen how much of August's training in Wageningen will be of use to him here. It's the practical side that matters now. Papa's wish has been granted at last: three grown-up sons to stand by him!

The boys are sailing on the *Prins van Oranje*. We are not sure yet when they will arrive. Naturally, I shall be going to Batavia to meet them at the docks.

I need not tell you how much I look forward to seeing them again. And not only them . . . Will you have a nice surprise for me, Cateau? No one knows my heart's desire better than you. My hope of fulfilling that desire is what keeps me going here at Gamboeng. I am counting the days.

The two cannon shots fired by the coastguard announcing the arrival of the Dutch vessel *Prins van Oranje* left Jenny in a state of great excitement, which she had difficulty hiding from her mother and sisters. She had been given permission to accompany the Hennys and Rudolf Kerkhoven to the quayside. All ready and waiting, she posted herself on the front veranda.

The landau drove up, and the two men alighted to greet her. Half a year had gone by since she had last seen Rudolf. She was struck by how lean he was, and how deeply tanned his face. It was very strange to sit opposite him in the carriage making polite conversation, when he had been receiving, for all these months, detailed reports of her doings through Cateau, just as she had been hearing, likewise through Cateau, all about him at Gamboeng. She had been afraid he might show surprise or some sort of displeasure at her confidences – were they something to be ashamed of? She could not decide. It was obvious to her that he was just as nervous as she was, but he was so manifestly delighted to see her (which amused Cateau no end while Henny pretended not to notice) that her fears evaporated. Indeed, she felt so relieved that she was able to keep up a lively patter all the way there, just as if they saw one another daily.

In the crush beneath the shelter on the quayside he clasped her hand, and held it in his, hidden from view between the folds of her skirt. She was very conscious of his firm, warm hand holding hers, and answered the pressure of his fingers, but she dared not look him in the face. They stood close together, wordlessly. The ladies in the gathering gave little cries of laughter and dismay as the fresh sea breeze tugged at their veils while the gentlemen debated the merits of the new-fangled, exclusively steam-powered ships versus those with a complement of sails. The *Prins van Oranje* lay at anchor in the roadstead, and it was not until the dinghy with passengers drew near enough to distinguish their faces that Rudolf let go of Jenny's hand. Then he and Cateau pressed forward, waving their arms and shouting the boys' names.

The brothers' reunion moved Jenny. Her heart went out to Julius, so subdued, and looking most uncomfortable in his tropical kit. August struck her as a mite too big for his boots, good-looking and aware of it; he never stopped talking during the entire drive to the Henny residence, telling them all about the crossing and what an interesting time they had had. She could see how happy Rudolf was, and she could feel it, too, which made her realise how closely bound up his world already was with hers.

'Did you send for me, Papa?'

Jenny found her father in the room everybody referred to as 'the office' because that was where he secluded himself to write letters and read. He was sitting at his secretaire, in his shirtsleeves, as was his habit when at ease. The window was screened by oleanders and other tall shrubs growing in pots on the veranda. At this time of day the slanting sun cast a greenish hue on the plastered walls and tiled floor.

'I have received a letter from Mr Kerkhoven of Ardjasari,' he said. He reached with one finger to lift a corner of the slitted envelope, then let it drop again. Jenny could see the folded edges of the notepaper. 'He wants to pay me a visit, by way of introduction on behalf of his son. You realise that this is about you, don't you? At least, Joan Henny mentioned you being decidedly friendly with that young man at the docks.'

Jenny said nothing. So Henny had noticed after all.

'How well do you know him? I take it there has been no declaration of intent as yet, behind my back?'

A sense of recklessness took possession of Jenny. 'If he had declared himself, I would not have rejected him.'

The dark eyebrows shot up. 'You're not old enough to know what you want. Young people are liable to act impulsively, often to their regret later on. Fortunately, Mr Kerkhoven of Ardjasari sounds like a sensible man. I gather from his letter that he regards his son's plans as somewhat premature, although he would not wish to deny him his support.'

'You met Rudolf Kerkhoven at a dinner party last year. At Cateau Henny's house.'

'I am aware of that. He struck me as an agreeable fellow, intelligent, hard-working, too. But tea is a risky business. I didn't spend all these years raising you for you to go off and bury yourself in the countryside. You don't know what it means to live in some remote outpost as the only European woman. I want you to have at least one year of civilised social life before you commit yourself. I shall write to Mr Kerkhoven and tell him his request will have to wait a while.'

Jenny bowed her head, feeling the tears build up behind her eyes. She was shattered, not with sorrow, but with despair and impotent rage, as if she had been robbed of the chance to shake off her unconscionable fears and become a new person.

'Let him see about turning a profit with his land first,' her father said, in the soft, firm tone he used after giving reprimands, as if to say it was all for her own good. 'We shall review the situation in a year's time. But no letters between you, is that understood? You must give me your word.'

*

Chaos reigned on the back veranda. Philip sat on a chair, bawling, with the nursemaid kneeling by his side to bandage a cut on his shin. Marie was practising scales on the out-of-tune piano, while Rose expostulated with the laundry man. Herman was up a tree in the yard with his catapult, shooting at pigeons in complete disregard of the governess's strident summons for him to come down at once. Mrs Roosegaarde sat in the doorway to her bedroom nursing the crying infant, while the seamstress treadled the sewing machine nearby. If only she could escape, Jenny thought, but her mother was calling: 'Do take the baby for a moment, Jenny! He's got the colic, poor lamb.'

Afterwards, when she was laying the child – asleep at long last – in its crib, she heard her mother stepping into the darkened room and shutting the door to the veranda behind her.

'You do understand, don't you, Jenny? You're such a great help to me, with little Henri. And what would Rose do without you? She's nearly twenty, and it's time she entered society. She won't go by herself. Now that you're eighteen, you could go out together.'

'But Mama, I don't care for balls. All that *soesah*, just to go dancing at the club.'

'You'd only resent it later if we didn't give you the opportunity to look around.'

'When you were my age you were already married.'

'Indeed I was,' her mother said vehemently. 'That's precisely why I'm telling you that you ought to enjoy being young and carefree. Once you're married you'll have no end of cares.'

'Rose will be glad to go out with you, you know. It's no fun being chaperoned by the governess.'

'I couldn't go out when I was expecting Henri, and not now either, not until he's weaned.'

Jenny sat down beside her mother on the edge of the bed,

beneath the canopy of mosquito netting which had been raised onto silver hooks at either end. She put her arm around her mother's frail shoulders and felt her bones through the thin matinée blouse. 'Feeding the baby is wearing you out, Mama. Henri's old enough for porridge now.'

'I suppose he is, but while I'm breastfeeding I can't fall pregnant.'

In the weeks following the disheartening news that he had been refused permission to court Jenny Roosegaarde, Rudolf had great difficulty mustering his energy for his planter's duties at Gamboeng. His expectations had run so high, he felt he had known Jenny for so long already, that it was unbearable having to continue in this state of uncertainty. August lodged with him for a time to familiarise himself with the tea business, while Julius stayed at Ardjasari, accompanying his father on his daily rounds to see if he was suited to that kind of work. For the time being it did not seem likely that the Kerkhovens would be able to expand their interests in such a way as to provide managerial positions for all the sons. Julius was not an outdoors type; August, on the other hand, adapted himself very well to his new surroundings.

Riding through the mountainous countryside with his brother was a boost to Rudolf's morale. The construction of his house by the rasamala trees was advancing with gratifying speed. He had designed the building himself, and with each post driven into the ground and each plank nailed into place he felt the day drawing near that he could show it to his beloved. He wrote letters to Cateau (which he counted on being read by Jenny) describing how the house was progressing, complete with detailed sketches. The front veranda, with steps down to the yard at either end, was to have a wooden balustrade which would eventually be covered in creepers. He had ordered glass for the windows in the four rooms, which was essential in this climate with its spells of chilly dampness. There was a stream down the mountainside at the back, from which he planned to deflect a channel leading straight into the house – a constant supply of running water for the washroom! He laid out a vegetable garden with strawberries, tomatoes and cabbage. The flowerbed at the front had already been planted with rose cuttings.

As soon as the first room was habitable, he moved out of his *pondok* and into his new *gedoeng*. August left again, after which he acquired two young hunting dogs from a litter at Ardjasari to keep him company in lieu of his old dog Tom, who had died. Rudolf enjoyed training the pups, which he named Socks and Stockings after their juvenile habit of lifting their hind legs against his ankles to mark territory. Not a day went by without him catching some inquisitive jungle-monkey snooping about the house and stealing *pisangs* from the back yard. The monkeys were afraid of the puppies initially, but before long they were back in the trees by the house, screeching and shaking the lower branches menacingly. Rudolf thought he had better frighten them off with some gunfire, or they might become a serious nuisance once his orchard was established.

In the evenings he passed the time reading by the light of his paraffin lamp. The loneliness he felt here was worse than when he was living in his *pondok*. As the servants' quarters were not ready yet, his cook and his houseboy were still lodged in the kampong. It was not in his nature to indulge in melancholy ruminations in the moonlight, but it took him a long time to fall asleep at night. 'Need I tell you, <u>Cateau</u>, [the underlining meant that another name was to be substituted here] what is uppermost in my mind? To be honest, I can only think of things I cannot put down on paper. I fervently hope that I am not alone in this!'

From Jenny's Album, 1877

Queen Sophie has died, apparently after much suffering. I overheard Papa and Mama talking about the sadness the Queen had known. How dreadful to have to keep one's composure at all times, to be gracious and smiling even if one's heart is being torn asunder! Mama said that marriage must be hell when there is no love between husband and wife, and Papa said, 'Without the right temperament, love won't get you anywhere!' He laughed in that special way of his, when he wants to show Mama he's in a good mood, and then he kissed her. They didn't know I was in the sewing room, with the door open. I could see them in the big cheval glass. 'Oh no, oh no!' Mama kept saying, but she was clinging to him, and he was ever so passionate, as if he wanted to devour her.

Personally, I do long for love, but there seems to be a sharp edge to what they call love. It frightens me.

There is a waringin tree in our back garden. During the day I think of it as the most beautiful tree in the world, so huge and spreading, so full of leaf and little fruits and leaves, with all those exterior roots trailing down to form yet more woody trunks of the same tree, and the birds and flying foxes and beetles nesting in the boughs, and the figs with wasps swirling around them. It is a tree that reverberates with life. But I don't dare go near it when it's dark because of all the things Roesminah told us when we were small, about it not being the same tree at night, or not even a tree at all but something completely different, something that has no name. It becomes dangerous at night. Nature has that kind of force, while we are powerless. I keep telling myself all this is nonsense, and when I am in the store-room or helping Mama with the baby, or practising the piano, or playing with the children at Cateau's house, it doesn't affect me. That is why I am so determined to be good, and to do my duty, and to take care of those who are dear to me. One night I dreamt I was walking down a path in the middle of the night. I could sense that the ground was dark beneath my feet, and that there was a space above me, without a moon or stars. I could make out the shapes of mountains, solid banks of black against the transparent black of the sky, and darkest of all was the jungle I was entering, as if a wave of terror and blackness was waiting to break over me. I woke up bathed in sweat, then I heard Rose and Marie breathing peacefully in their sleep.

Was that dream an omen? Or was it telling me I must be brave? In one of his letters to Cateau (and me!) Rudolf described his encounter with a panther. What struck me above all was that the only thing he could do, standing there in the jungle, his heart in his throat, face to face with a wild animal poised for attack, was to confront the danger head-on. How brave would I have been? I wonder. To think he knows about my secret fears . . .

*

I have never been in the mountains. How brave must a man be to go and live and work in the wilderness for years, all by himself? He would wish for company, naturally, and he would long for someone he could love and trust and share everything with. I can see that. And if you happen to fall in love with that kind of man, all you want is to be with him for the rest of your life, for better and for worse. Well, that is what I want, too.

RUDOLF TO CATEAU, DECEMBER 1877

When I returned from my rounds this afternoon, my boys were ready to move the furniture and lay the mats on the floor. Mama has promised to run up some curtains and a loose cover for the sofa. She has given me tableware from Ardjasari. My house is beginning to look quite habitable. Papa let me know that he is going to Batavia to see a doctor about the infection in his left eye, which is not getting any better. He will take the opportunity to call on Mr Roosegaarde Bisschop, to whom I have written myself this time. But instead of feeling relieved at having declared my intentions at last, as I had hoped, I am filled with apprehension. All I can do is wait, which has not become any easier since my return from Batavia early this year. *Calme au-dehors, mais agité au-dedans*! I wish I had less trouble sleeping. And I have no appetite at all. I spend quite a lot of time getting the garden into shape, as a way of warding off bad moods, although it doesn't always help. Sometimes I wonder whether I have been handling this situation in the right way. But it's too late now. My letter is already in Buitenzorg, it will be on tomorrow morning's train to Batavia. I sincerely hope it will make a certain person in Gang Scott happy. By the time you read this it will be all over, and I will probably have learnt whether I will be rushing off to Batavia to find happiness – or not.

After receiving Rudolf's letter as well as a visit from Mr Kerkhoven, Mr Roosegaarde sent for Jenny. With a smile and a shake of his head he declared that he would no longer try to stop her from 'retiring from the world' in the Preanger mountains, if that was what she really wanted. Her mother wept as she embraced her, sobbing, 'Oh, I shall miss you so!' Rose reacted with astonishment and some dismay. Marie was outraged: 'How can you go and bury yourself in the *oedik*!' The older boys looked forward to going to stay with her – they had never been upcountry.

Cateau rushed over to see her the very same day, and declared, with an air of triumphant complicity, 'Papa has already sent a message by telegraph. Ru will be here the day after tomorrow.'

Jenny drew her into a corner. 'Did he ever . . . did he ever say anything to you about the things I wrote in my album . . . about when I was a child, and the family?'

'No, angel, I didn't mention all those bad dreams and gloomy thoughts of yours. Far better to leave them out. Let me give you some advice: don't ever talk about them. I want you to be happy. You make such a fine couple!'

'I only did what you asked of me, and what he wanted. I wrote about what I was thinking and feeling,' Jenny whispered. 'Now he knows nothing, nothing at all.'

'All that is just your imagination. So Eurasian of you! And you're not Eurasian, are you, even if you were born here?'

*

During the fortnight that Rudolf was able to remain in Batavia they saw each other daily – strolling arm in arm round the gardens of the Roosegaardes and the Hennys, passing evenings in the family circle, visiting relatives and close friends, going shopping, attending the soirée at the Concordia club, where they waltzed together for the first time – but not once did Jenny feel she could broach any of the subjects she had dared to write about in her album. In retrospect, she could not imagine how she could have let herself go like that. She was grateful to Cateau for having had the discretion not to pass on things that were better left unsaid.

As there was limited time for the engagement rituals – Rudolf had left August in charge of Gamboeng, but wanted to be there for the first harvest of his specimen tea garden – a public announcement was made. This made it possible for Jenny to accompany her future parents-in-law to Ardjasari, where she would get a first taste of the kind of life she would be leading in the future.

How much smaller and more modest the house at Gamboeng was than she had imagined from Rudolf's letters and drawings! It was built of rough-hewn wood, the uprights resting on flat stones, as protection against ants. The roof consisted of native pantiles combined with sections of palm fibre. She hid her misgivings, not wishing to disappoint Rudolf, who was brimming with pride and delight, and who passionately embraced her in the kitchen while his parents and his brother were admiring the view from the front veranda.

The triple-peaked Goenoeng Tiloe reminded her of a great crouching demon, waiting to pounce. Rudolf's bungalow looked so fragile against the backdrop of massed, dark trees. Neither the lush green of the young tea gardens further down the slope, nor the roses in the flowerbed at the front and the potted plants along the veranda, nor even the Dutch tricolour flying in her honour from a towering flagpole carved from the trunk of a rasamala tree, none of those things was able to dispel the sense of gloom reaching out to her from the depths of the jungle beyond. A footpath to the side of the house led straight into the darkness. There was something disturbingly familiar about it, which kept drawing her gaze.

THE FAMILY

1879–1907

Rudolf would always look back on the early months of his marriage as the happiest time of his life, notwithstanding the worst drought in living memory and the consequent failure of his tea harvest. When the rains came at last, they brought unprecedented infestations of tough weeds, which delayed the recovery of his plantings. But he was undaunted; he was walking on air. The state of manhood, for which he had spent all those years preparing himself, had finally been attained. The spectacle of his young wife busying herself about the house, slender and poised in her flannel kebaya and pretty sarong of Solo batik, was a delight to him, and sometimes he could barely resist sweeping her off to the bedroom for renewed intimacy – not in the dark for a change, but in broad daylight, or in the tempered light of overcast skies, or with the rain pattering outside. But there were always servants hovering about. Moreover, as their *djoeragan* and *djoeragan istri*, it was paramount they should observe a certain measure of decorum, and he knew he would incur their derision and contempt by indulging in what was undoubtedly considered to be loose Western behaviour. So he restrained himself from doing as he wished. Jenny and he were not free. They never would be.

Jenny's first pregnancy passed well. She went to Ardjasari for her confinement, and at the end of August 1879 gave birth to a boy, whom they named Rudolf, although they called him 'little Ru' to distinguish him from his father and grandfather. The child was a source of great happiness and delight. Jenny thought him utterly beautiful, a 'bundle of joy' – oh, how pleased the Queen would be with such a darling princeling, she thought, on reading the news that King Willem III's young wife, his second, was expecting a child. Upon Rudolf's return from the gardens, all sweaty and dusty or covered in mud and soaking wet, he would hurry to bathe and change his clothes so as to occupy himself with the bright-eyed little boy while Jenny was in the kitchen, issuing instructions to her new but willing Gamboeng servant.

They lived frugally. Rudolf took pride in keeping his accounts and all the estate affairs in perfect order. He was very busy: there were large quantities of young tea leaf to be processed, coffee crops to be weighed and packed, wagons needing repair, halters to be made. He had also planted quinine by way of a test, because he had the impression it might thrive in the soil and climate of Gamboeng.

His father's eye disease had taken a turn for the worse, which led his parents to decide to return to Holland. Van Santen was to accompany them, taking his two eldest children. (Rudi, the youngest, would stay with Cateau.) Jenny's complaints about their spartan living conditions and the remoteness of Gamboeng induced Rudolf to consider replacing his father at Ardjasari; it might be a good idea for her sake and little Ru's to move into his parents' home, which was far more comfortably furnished and also a fair bit closer to Bandoeng. In that case he would have to leave August in charge. His brother Julius had already been found employment elsewhere. Their father had not wished to see his second son, the qualified engineer, play second fiddle on a plantation, and had used all his connections to secure a position for him on the construction of the new railway line linking Buitenzorg and Bandoeng.

To Rudolf, making his familiar rounds of the plantation or standing on his veranda gazing out over the rolling valley with majestic rasamala trees, it seemed almost like a betrayal of the land he had so laboriously made his own even to think of moving to Ardjasari. Despite his reluctance to leave Gamboeng, however, he felt hurt that his father had not sent for him, the eldest son, to come and discuss what should be done about Ardjasari during his absence, and the news that August was to be the new manager came as a severe blow. He also heard that his brother was to have the support of an assistant – something he himself could not afford. This was the umpteenth time a family decision had been made without anyone bothering to consult him. As usual, he hid his disappointment, so as not to spoil his parents' leave-taking. He did not begrudge August, with his brand-new diploma from the university of Wageningen, this opportunity to show his mettle, and told himself he was lucky to have been spared the ordeal of having to choose between Gamboeng and Ardjasari.

He wrote to his parents each week, to keep them abreast of developments. The first letters they received from him after their arrival in Europe were not encouraging: the cattle plague that had been raging for several months in Western Java had now reached the Preanger.

RUDOLF TO HIS PARENTS, 1880–1

> I am still hopeful that we will be spared the plague, thanks to our isolated location. They have been confiscating buffaloes on the main roads all over the region, six of my own draught-cattle included – government orders. Apparently there are already at least five hundred animals being held by the side of the road, waiting to be destroyed.

Pits have already been dug, in readiness for the soldiers to come and discharge their murderous duty. But I ask myself: can the cattle plague as such ever be worse than an ignorant, stubborn, tyrannical government? Another nonsensical order has been to erect a fence all around the contaminated area, straight across mountains, forests and ravines. The *wedana* of Bandjaran came to stay here for several days, to supervise the construction of just such a fence right through the Tjisondari ravine and up to the top of the Goenoeng Tiloe, where the 'barrier' suddenly comes to an end. The posts are wooden, the transverse sections bamboo. All the work is so-called 'paid forced labour'. Hundreds, no, thousands of men have been conscripted to supply the necessary bamboo over great distances.

In my opinion putting up these fences will be of no help at all, which is also the opinion of all the *wedanas* (as well as of the native population at large), who are much more sensible about these things than all those Batavian bigwigs put together. As if bamboo fences could ever keep out the wild boar, or wild buffalo and rhino – not to mention the locals! In one of the *desa*s near here every single buffalo has been put down, including all the cattle from other villages that were grazing there, which means that I am the only one left with a herd. Strange, isn't it, that my livestock have been spared? I wonder if it has anything to do with the fact that I have not yet received any visits from veterinary surgeons or epidemiologists. The fence-inspector is supposed to be coming tomorrow, so I gave orders for the cattle to be moved far away, where they will be out of sight. And if he insists on taking a look at them, I will take him on such a tortuous walk that his legs will remember it for a fortnight.

*

We are expecting a visit from the vet any day now, a young chap fresh from Holland who does not speak the language and knows nothing about the people, but who seems to think he can make short work of the cattle plague around here. He is extremely particular, insisting that even the most absurd measures be religiously upheld. Confining the cattle to places from which they are not likely to stray, such as a ravine or a steep slope, is not enough for him, oh no. The law says that cattle must only be put to pasture in areas that are *fenced off*, and so he goes out to investigate whether there are any loopholes, and if he finds the least sign of one he sends off a report to Batavia, thereby forcing the government to punish masses of people for committing an offence against the letter, not the spirit, of the law. It is all such a nuisance, and here I am, having to spend a great deal of money and labour on completely unnecessary fencing. That is what comes of calling in a bunch of busybodies who always think they know better than the old-timers. The man will not achieve his goal, obviously, because, as soon as his back is turned, the cattle are let out anyway. Our vet suspects as much, and so whenever he sees a hoof print or a cowpat outside the fence he stops short, demanding to know how it got there. Naturally, no one takes responsibility, with the natives merely exchanging accusing looks. Just as well the vet does not understand Soendanese.

As of yesterday we have our own disinfection station at Gamboeng, which is little more than a roadside trough filled with muddy, foul-smelling water for people to disinfect their hands and feet. They say there are roving patrols of soldiers about, ensuring everyone does this, and that they pose a threat to all the young women. This has caused quite a panic, with fake weddings being held to safeguard the unmarried girls. Should there ever be an uprising in Java, it will be attributable solely and exclusively to the high and mighty pen-pushers in Batavia, with nothing better to do than to think up all sorts of rules and regulations, the effects of which they have no way of knowing. I have written an article on the cattle plague under a pseudonym, which has been honoured with publication as an editorial in the *Bataviaans Nieuwsbad*. But I have no illusions about it having any effect whatsoever.

The cattle plague restrictions are becoming sheer madness. Two thousand natives have been drummed up in Bandoeng for cordon duty in exchange for their keep and a lump sum of twelve guilders, and another three thousand in Buitenzorg to guard the southern border. Not only are the draught-cattle being slaughtered, field hands are also becoming scarce. The fence around us has already cost 120,000 guilders, and cuts *right across* a contaminated area. The same goes for the military cordon!

Splendid weather today, warm and sunny, it is about four p.m., and Jenny, little Ru and I are sitting out on the front veranda, as cosy as can be. Odaliske is grazing near the rosebeds, which are in full bloom. Now and then I can hear the boys in the factory, where they are still at work on account of the day's exceptionally large harvest. Little Ru is beginning to crawl; he likes playing with the dogs, and does his best to persuade his parents to join in. He pulls himself up to his feet by clinging on to our chairs, which he is getting very good at. Quite the picture of domestic bliss, and yet, unfortunately, we have a great deal to worry about. All I have left of my fine herd of twenty-six buffalo is three weak, emaciated creatures that have survived the disease, although I doubt they will ever recover completely. All the others are dead, either from the disease or killed as a precaution. We have burnt down the stable, and all that remains is a miserable expanse of scorched ground with a heap of freshly turned red soil over the burial pit in the middle. It makes me want to weep, and all of this happening within just a fortnight! I had never expected it to be so bad. I have spent the better part of the past fortnight in the stables, keeping watch over the animals, feeding them, taking them outside, burying them. Even worse than the financial losses, though, is that the tea chests have to be carried by porters all the way to Tjisondari, not to mention the fact that I have run out of manure for the gardens. My only consolation is that the leaf crop is exceptionally good. Double the amount of last year.

Ten months after little Ru was born Jenny began to suffer from stomach pains and nausea, which at first she attributed to having caught a cold. She tried to ignore the flickers of suspicion at the back of her mind – she was still breastfeeding, after all. She had plenty of milk, it was just that her periods had not started again. One day a bitch from the kampong gave birth to a litter in the space beneath the house. A small crowd gathered to try and drive the snarling dog away with long sticks, but to no avail. Jenny approached them, feeling as though she were on the deck of a ship in high seas. In a voice cracked with emotion she commanded one of the gardeners to remove the newborn pups at once, by whatever means, and to drown them in the Tjisondari. Afterwards she felt ashamed of her outburst.

*

That night in bed, lying awake after little Ru's crying fit, she found herself unable to banish the thought any longer: she was pregnant. The prospect of feeling 'wobbly', as Rudolf called it, all over again for months on end gave her a sense of being shackled in a small space, with a massive weight pressing down on her chest. Why was she suddenly reminded of the entrance to the jungle, a black hole even in daylight? In an effort to blot out the image of the path vanishing into nothing (she never ventured in that direction of her own accord) she turned over on her side, facing Rudolf, and stared at his serene features in the glow of the night-light. Next time the baby cried it would be his turn to get up. She admired him for the dogged cheeriness with which he performed his self-imposed tasks: changing napkins, sitting by the cot, talking softly or even humming little Ru to sleep. She had never heard of a man being so helpful to his wife. She had a vivid recollection of her mother, dishevelled and pale from exhaustion, with an equally exhausted *baboe* by her side, trying desperately to hush a howling infant while Roosegaarde lay sleeping in a room at the end of the corridor. She was well aware that she had a 'good husband': her respect for him knew no bounds; he was her guardian angel, her rock. But his love for her also felt burdensome at times. Did she love him sufficiently in return? She knew he never doubted her. That certainty of his, so tangible in the way he took her in his arms and made love to her, sometimes roused feelings of defiance in her mind – how could he be so sure that she experienced the same bliss as he did? That she had no unfulfilled desires? She thought of her father's words, overheard long ago: 'Without the right temperament, love won't get you anywhere.'

Running the household presented her with countless problems. She waged a constant battle against all the draughts blowing in through the gaps between floorboards and under doors, as it could get very chilly in the mountains and all three of them kept catching colds. When the rain was heavy the roof began to leak in various places. The damp caused dark stains in their clothes, mosquito nets and bed linen. The table she kept was a source of worry, too. She was determined to put into practice the cookery lessons she had had in Liège, not least because both Cateau Henny and her mother-in-law at Ardjasari seemed to have no difficulty keeping their menus up to European standards. Rudolf was not partial to the local food, so her choice was restricted. She had various types of vegetables in her garden as well as strawberries and pineapples, and rice was always available, but the supply of meat, scarce at the best of times, had ceased completely since the cattle plague. The chickens she tried to raise for their eggs and meat died one by one, or were taken by weasels.

Providing meals for guests presented further complications. One day two lieutenants, posted near Tjikalong and Tjisondari in connection with the cattle plague, turned up at Gamboeng on inspection duty. Their behaviour was civil and congenial, and it was only polite to invite them to stay for a meal. While Rudolf took the two men round the plantation on horseback, Jenny racked her brains in the kitchen as to what she could possibly prepare for them. Then two more visitors arrived: another cattle plague official, this time from the district headquarters, accompanied by his wife: he on horseback, she in a carrying-chair. Jenny was not at all pleased with the casual, typically Eurasian way these people seemed to take her hospitality for granted, barging into her home as if it were a lodging house and ordering her servants around – the very stable-boys and *baboes* she had just promised the afternoon off to attend a wedding in the kampong. The wife went straight to the washroom to bathe, asking Jenny to lend her some clothes to wear at dinner. Later, at the dinner table, she showered Jenny with praise for her culinary skills (all the guests appeared to be enjoying the food – oh, let there be enough of everything, let them not ask for second helpings, thought Jenny, in terror of ruining the reputation of Gamboeng), but the borrowed gown found less favour: both the style and the fabric were judged to be out of fashion. Jenny saw Rudolf biting his lip with annoyance at the woman's bad manners.

Afterwards, the guests installed themselves on the front veranda, first with tea and then with bitters and lemonade, talking animatedly until the light faded, so that Jenny and Rudolf felt obliged to invite them not only to supper but also to spend the night in their home. Later that evening, when Jenny, dizzy with fatigue (little Ru was over-excited by the presence of strangers and refused to go to sleep), stepped into the guest room bearing sheets and nightwear, she came upon the official's wife without any clothes on, brushing her hair.

'Oh, we won't be needing those,' she said, waving at the pyjamas and nightdress, 'we'll just slip under the covers as we are!' Jennny felt faint, and quickly sat down on the edge of the bed.

'You're pregnant again, aren't you? That was quick!' said the official's wife. 'I could tell straight away, I always can. *Kasian*, dear lady, you should be enjoying life! You can buy *djamoe* at every *pasar* to bring on your periods, didn't you know? But it's too late now, you're too far gone.'

The mountain folk were not cut out for domestic service, and, besides, Jenny was not sufficiently fluent in Soendanese to make herself understood at all times. Rudolf thought she got overly upset when things did not go as smoothly as she wished.

Little Ru was being weaned. Since all the cows had succumbed to the cattle plague, Jenny gave him milk from a newly-foaled mare. He did not gain weight, however. He even lost some, and there was talk about mare's milk not being nutritious. Jenny became distraught. What on earth could she feed him if he kept spitting out his porridge? Would she be able to nurse the new baby for as long as nine months, as she had done with Ru? The little boy kept her awake at night with his crying fits, and she worried about giving birth at Gamboeng, with no one to help her but the female *doekoen* who had attended her confinement at Ardjasari under her mother-in-law's guidance. Rudolf thought it might be better for her to have the baby in Batavia.

As it was high time they introduced their young son to his grandparents on his mother's side, and as Jenny needed to see a dentist with some urgency, they decided on a trip to Batavia. At the same time they would look into the maternity care on offer there.

They set out at half past four in the morning, with Jenny, the child and the *baboe* in carrying-chairs, and Rudolf on horseback. In Tjikalong they took dray carts, and after a short delay in Bandoeng they proceeded northwards at eleven. One of the ponies drawing the cart occupied by Jenny and the child turned out to have weak knees, which meant they had to get out and walk up every hill. The child was fretful, so they let him crawl about on all fours at each break. The cart jolted so violently that he was sick all over Jenny's dress, and they had to halt for her to change her clothes behind a tree in the wilderness while Rudolf stood guard – panthers had been sighted in the area. After sixteen hours they reached Tjandjoer, where they spent an uncomfortable night at the only inn. As all the beds were occupied they had to make do with reclining chairs in the inner gallery while little Ru slept on a cushion. They set off again at the crack of dawn.

It was already getting dark when they finally reached their destination: the house where Cateau and Henny were now living with their foster son, Rudi van Santen. It was some distance from Batavia, where the air was reputed to be healthier, but close enough for Henny to commute to the city thanks to the new railway. Cateau's warm welcome, as well as the train ride to Batavia the following day, made Jenny feel much better, notwithstanding her toothache. But she was sure she would not be up to making that horrible journey again in the final weeks of her pregnancy, however alluring the prospect of good maternity care might be.

Upon arrival at her parental home in Gang Scott, she could not help noticing the distance that had come between her and her family. She was afraid that her boisterous, unruly brothers might have a bad influence on little Ru; Constant, the youngest, was only six months older, but he seemed slightly backward, and it worried her to see how Ru imitated Constant's shrieks and tantrums when they were left to play together.

Her father did not look well, and appeared to have buried himself in work. Her mother, outwardly her frail doll-like self of old, behaved exactly as Jenny remembered, weakly reprimanding her sons without any effect, succumbing to sudden migraines, and then having to lie down with a cold compress on her forehead. The house was as crowded as ever, with Rose, Marie, the two nannies and the head *djongos* competing for primacy. Marie was even prettier than before, but still just as sharp-tongued.

'You're getting to be like Mama. A real Daendels!' she said, with an accusing look at Jenny's thickening waist, but quickly offered to make her sister some maternity dresses on the sewing machine.

Rudolf and Jenny slept in the pavilion, the 'outside room'. Being alone there at night after Rudolf's return to Gamboeng, old fears were roused in her mind as she lay in the large bed. Engko, little Ru's *baboe*, slept on a mat by the door, but did that mean she was safe from the *nènèk*, real or imagined? She had never dared to tell Rudolf about her fears, nor had she ever mentioned her horror of the black entrance to the forest at Gamboeng.

*

On his way home Rudolf paid an impromptu visit to Ardjasari. Things were not looking very good there, he thought, although the cattle plague had not been as bad as at Gamboeng. There were half a dozen lodgers, with whom August went hunting every day. The home his mother had cherished made an untidy, neglected impression, and so, more disturbingly, did several of the tea gardens. The assistant was doing his best, but found it impossible to cope with all the work on his own. The new rolling machine, an expensive apparatus purchased by their father before his departure to Holland, and the mechanical sieve bought by August, both served to produce tea that looked good, although Rudolf judged it to have a 'mean flavour', which he attributed to his brother's fermentation method. 'Those layers of wilted leaf are too thick, Gus,' he said. 'You should spread it out more, and those *tampirs* need to be put out in the sun whenever possible; that is infinitely better than drying over charcoal.'

His advice was not appreciated by his brother, who could not resist pointing out, in the presence of his guests, that where tea was concerned, the university of Wageningen was rather more 'up to date' than that of Delft.

Without Jenny and little Ru to keep him company, Rudolf found Gamboeng chilly, wet and bleak. Part of his workforce had taken advantage of his absence to go on strike. As he knew from experience that they were bound to return after a few days, he was not unduly alarmed. He went hunting, and shot two black panthers that had been roaming the countryside killing new-born foals. The workers who had remained loyal to him clipped the tea bushes under his supervision: the most thorough pruning since he had begun planting five years earlier. The processed tea from the latest crop was packed into chests. He escorted the cargo to Tjisondari in person; the carts were not drawn by buffalos, but by horses, some of which were unused to draught work. One of them stumbled and fell on the way, causing the shaft of the cart to snap. The procession came to a halt in the midst of the *sawahs*, in the open countryside. While Rudolf showed the men how to fix the shaft in place using bamboo, it began to rain. It was one of the heaviest downpours he had ever experienced, and he returned home after delivering the chests chilled to the bone and dripping wet.

He made preparations to fetch Jenny from Buitenzorg, where she had gone to stay with Cateau. She had left her parents' house in Batavia on account of little Ru, who was dreadfully spoilt there, constantly being passed from one person's knee to another and given food that did not agree with him. Henny had offered to take her in his carriage as far as Bandoeng, where he was going on business anyway, but she had sent Rudolf a note saying, 'You know what Henny's like, he'll only get annoyed with little Ru for fidgeting and messing his pants, so please, please come and fetch me yourself.'

The streets of Buitenzorg were decked with flags and orange banners: Her Majesty Queen Emma of the Netherlands had given birth to a daughter, Wilhelmina.

The cold Rudolf had caught during the bad weather did not go away. Despite his cough and a general feeling of malaise, he was out in his gardens from dawn to dusk, supervising the pickers harvesting the new flush of excellent leaf: white-point Pekoe, first quality. The hard work proved too much; a high fever forced him to keep to his bed. He treated his illness with powdered quinine, the last word in medication, made from the bark of the type of tree he was seriously thinking of cultivating. The experience taught him that the bitter-tasting substance was indeed effective, although it seemed to him a kill-or-cure remedy.

No sooner had he recovered than Jenny, who had nursed him with unflagging dedication, was stricken with the same fever. Now it was his turn to sit by the sickbed and apply poultices to the patient's burning forehead. He also gave her tincture of quinine, though this caused her to vomit. Suddenly her illness took a completely unexpected turn. She began to have violent contractions, which the native midwife, urgently summoned from Tjikalong, was unable to suppress with herbal medicines, and the result was a premature birth, a seven-month baby girl that only survived a few hours.

Rudolf buried his daughter under a tall tree, just beyond the place where the garden path vanished into the darkness of the jungle.

The first time Uncle Eduard Kerkhoven paid a visit to Gamboeng was in July 1881. He had only just returned from Holland, where he had visited his children (Caroline was now also attending school there), and was staying at Ardjasari with August, with whom he would go to the races. Bandoeng now prided itself on a racecourse that was larger and better laid-out than the one in Buitenzorg. As usual, Eduard would be entering some potential winners, and August would be entering a horse as well.

Eduard clapped his hands in astonishment when he saw Rudolf. 'With that beard you look exactly like your father when he first came out to the Indies. And there's a touch of Karel Holle, too. Such patriarchs, you lot!'

He expressed approval of the way the tea factory was organised, and of the state of the gardens.

'If I were you, though, I'd consider switching to Assam tea,' he told Rudolf, as they rode side by side on the bridle-path alongside the watercourse. 'That is what Albert and I have done.'

'I used the Assam seeds Albert ordered from Ceylon for my specimen tea nursery. But they haven't amounted to much yet. My Java Sinensis is doing far better.'

'Give them time,' advised Eduard. 'The Assam grows much taller and thicker than the Java Sinensis. The leaf is big and tender, a nice fresh green. If you cut out the main stem after one year you get a strong, wide twig system, which yields a good span for picking, provided you prune regularly. We have had a lot of trouble with our China tea – leaf-mould, parasites, and so forth, but you know how disease-prone it is. Assam is decidedly more robust. You can harvest the bushes up to thirty times a year, apparently.'

'I must show you my nursery beds with quinine – *Cinchona succirubra*. Cousin Karel Holle keeps telling me to grow quinine, because I don't fancy making green tea. I am thinking of making quinine my second crop.'

They halted on a rise, from which they surveyed the full extent of the plateau. Rudolf handed Eduard his field glasses. 'You can see Ardjasari from here.'

'Good chap, your brother August. A horseman and a hunter! I have a high regard for him.'

'I just hope he will last at Ardjasari. I thought his gardens were looking a bit straggly. He relies too much on his assistant and on the *mandoers*.' As he spoke, Rudolf was struck by how readily he voiced his criticism. 'Besides, he is away a lot. Unless he has guests to keep him company he can't stick it on the estate for more than a few days at a stretch. That is not a good idea.'

Eduard began to laugh. 'He's lonely! What he needs is a wife. Actually, he's very taken with your sister-in-law, Marie Roosegaarde. Hadn't you heard? And she with him, apparently. He's already asked me about procuring a good riding horse for her.'

Jenny was greatly astonished, even more so than Rudolf, when she heard the news, and she was upset Marie had not confided in her. She knew her sister had met August at the Hennys' in Buitenzorg when he attended the races there. She liked the idea of having her sister living nearby, although she wasn't sure they would get along very well. If Marie became the *djoeragan istri* at Ardjasari, which was an older estate and therefore more important than Gamboeng, she was bound to pull rank whenever it suited her.

Jenny also had misgivings about the influence her sister would have on August's relationship with Rudolf. In the past August had always treated his elder brother with respect, but lately Jenny had noticed them arguing over the Ardjasari accounts, which Rudolf felt was his duty to verify at regular intervals. And Marie would hardly be inclined to be thrifty, either – not that it was necessary to live quite as frugally at Ardjasari as at Gamboeng, thanks to August's privileged arrangements with his father concerning the terms of his replacement.

Marie would be in a position to entertain on a proper scale. She and August would naturally be going to the races, the high point of the year in the Preanger uplands, which Jenny, too, was eager to attend. She and Rudolf had received an invitation for the first time, and Eduard had urged them to accept, saying they ought to go out in society more often, meet new people, make connections. But Rudolf reminded her how much it would cost to stay in a hotel for a week, which they would be obliged to do as they had no friends in Bandoeng with whom they might lodge. Besides, they would have to take servants with them, particularly because little Ru was now walking and could not be left alone for a moment, and she would need a ball gown, and dresses to wear to the races. It was all far too expensive, and too much *soesah*.

In the end they had a good excuse to decline the invitation. She was expecting again, and by the time she was six months pregnant she would be in no state to show herself in public, let alone to attend formal celebrations.

*

When it became clear that his parents would be remaining in Holland for good, Rudolf thought it incumbent upon him to make an inventory of the furniture and household goods they had left behind at Ardjasari, and decide what to send over to Holland and what to dispose of.

August insisted there was no hurry. Both Rudolf and Jenny took this to mean he had no desire to part with the items that lent a certain allure to his living quarters.

'He wants people to think everything belongs to him,' said Rudolf, in whose opinion August was getting off too lightly, being spared the laborious accumulation of personal property over years of toil. Things Rudolf himself had worked very hard for were apparently being handed to August on a plate: land that was already cleared and planted, productive tea gardens, a fully equipped factory, a fine stable of horses.

'He simply wants to have a nice, comfortable home for Marie,' Jenny said, remembering how disappointed she had been when she first arrived in Gamboeng. She had secretly reckoned on acquiring some furniture and bibelots from the house at Ardjasari. The rigour with which she set about helping Rudolf to clear out cupboards and pack silverware and household linen into boxes for dispatch to Holland was inspired, as she herself was well aware, by her belief that Marie was quite spoilt enough as it was, and that it would do her no good to get everything for nothing.

August received them warmly when they came over from Gamboeng, but did not concern himself with clearing out cupboards and making lists. Although there was no question as yet of an official engagement between him and Marie, he behaved as if the wedding day had already been fixed. He had written to his parents of his plan, and they referred to Marie as a 'dear daughter' in their reply, which he read out to his brother and sister-in-law.

The suggestion to store supposedly superfluous furniture in a shed prior to their sale at auction grated on him, and Rudolf and Jenny's idea of having a value placed on certain items which they wished to acquire for Gamboeng – so that they might reimburse his parents for them – was dismissed by him as utterly absurd. Old toys! A suitcase full of skeins of wool and sewing patterns!

Jenny was determined to keep herself busy and active, to avoid having to think about her pregnancy. But a playmate for little Ru would be very welcome; the child longed for company. When the *mandoers* presented themselves in the afternoon to report on the field-work and collect money to pay the workers, Ru crawled across the veranda to where they were squatting and scrabbled among the coins with both hands. The *mandoers* indulged him, gathering up the coins and piling them into towers for '*Agan*', the little master, to scatter all over again. He was beginning to talk, and as Engko, his *baboe*, patiently told him the names of everything he pointed to, he was picking up more Soendanese than Dutch. He was interested in animals, rolling over the floor with the dogs, wanting to stroke the horses in the stable, imitating the cock's crow and the cries of birds. His favourite place was the carpentry shed, watching the men saw planks and assemble tea chests.

With the intention of obscuring the dark fringe of forest where the tiny grave had been dug, Jenny lavished attention on her flower garden, creating banks of blossoming shrubs with cuttings from Ardjasari, spreading colour wherever she could. She invited two of her brothers, Gus and Herman, to spend their holidays at Gamboeng. Gus had grown into a lanky, shy, fifteen-year-old, quite unlike his former unruly self, but Herman, aged twelve, was twice as troublesome as before, constantly getting into scrapes and behaving so irresponsibly that she did not dare to leave him alone with little Ru, even for a moment. He reminded her of Frits, who had been just as difficult in the old days, and she wrote to her parents-in-law about her brothers in Holland, whom no one seemed to talk about in Gang Scott: 'I would like to ask something of you, if I may. Could you let my brothers know where you will be staying during your holiday in Arnhem, so that they may come and visit you? I would dearly love to hear what they look like nowadays, and what sort of impression they make on you.'

When the races were over it was the Hennys' turn to pay a visit to Gamboeng. Joan Henny, Cateau and young Rudi van Santen travelled in a handsome carriage, followed by a dray-cart with servants, as far as Tjikalong, where Rudolf came to fetch them with saddle-horses and carrying-chairs. Jenny had gone to great lengths to make the guest rooms – they had two extra ones now – as comfortable as possible, and was initially somewhat annoyed that Henny had thought it necessary to bring their cook along, too, as if her table was not to be trusted, but she soon came to appreciate having an extra pair of hands in the kitchen.

Rudolf took his guests on excursions in the surrounding area, either on horseback or on foot. Jenny stayed behind with the children, wistfully waving goodbye from the veranda, for she could no longer ride in her condition, let alone clamber up steep paths. Rudi van Santen was almost seven years old, a precocious lad, very fond of Cateau and amusingly candid with Henny. Rudolf and Jenny were pleasantly surprised by their brother-in-law's amicable treatment of the Van Santen boy. 'I can understand why, I suppose,' said Rudolf. 'The worst is over, as far as Henny is concerned: they'll be going to Holland in six months, then the boy will go and live with his father and the other children, and Henny will have discharged his duty.'

There was much to be discussed. First of all, there was August's courtship of Marie, which was not going smoothly, to say the least. During a stay at the Hennys' in Buitenzorg the young pair had behaved strangely. They had slipped away, just the two of them, from a house-party, and upon rejoining the company after a lengthy absence had suddenly announced their engagement, but had quarrelled so bitterly the following day that Marie returned posthaste to Batavia, and August was about to leave Buitenzorg as well.

'But why? What on earth can have happened?' Jenny cried in alarm.

'We don't know,' said Cateau. 'We weren't there. Henny was at the office, and I was at the back of the house with Rudi. I could hear Marie shouting inside; the servants were quite shocked. I felt so embarrassed!'

'They aren't right for each other,' Henny remarked. 'She has already started nagging. She has no respect for him whatsoever.'

Rudolf nodded. 'August is rather young to start a family, anyway. He still has to get to grips with Ardjasari.'

'I have a feeling life in the *oedik* is not Marie's cup of tea,' offered Jenny.

'That's the trouble,' said Henny. 'She wants to live in Buitenzorg, or even in Batavia. In that case August would be better off appointing a manager. Marie seems to think the Kerkhovens have a great deal of money.'

'As you did, when you married me,' murmured Cateau, whereupon Jenny quickly interposed, 'They are both so impatient, and so demanding.'

'The pair of them ought to be seeing each other every day for a month or so, just to see how they get along,' declared Rudolf.

'I have asked Marie to come back to us at Buitenzorg,' said Cateau. 'I could invite August to come, too. But she won't. So now August thinks she doesn't care.'

'I think the best thing would be to do nothing at all, just let the whole thing rest,' said Henny. 'Just do nothing! Engagements get broken all the time, no news there.'

'But it's much worse for Marie. A girl has her reputation to think of.'

'I shall write and tell my parents,' said Rudolf. 'They meant well, of course, but giving their blessing to the marriage was a bit premature, to say the least.'

'I have already written to them,' said Cateau.

'Well, I will have a word with August in that case,' resolved Rudolf. 'He needs to realise they just had a crush on each other. They fell for each other's looks.'

Henny stood up and drew his cigar case from his pocket. 'That's that, then. We all agree. The sooner the engagement is over the better.'

While the men strolled back and forth outside, smoking their cigars, Jenny and Cateau withdrew to the bedroom and sat down.

'Such a nuisance we don't have an inner gallery. Whenever we have visitors and it's too cold and damp to sit out on the veranda, I have to receive them here. If they're ladies, that is, because Rudolf takes gentlemen to his office.'

Through the window they could see the children scampering on the lawn.

'Look at Rudi playing with little Ru – how endearing! He's a funny lad. When you were out I called him over to have a chat, and he sank down on his haunches at my feet, all respectful, just like the servants. I couldn't help laughing!'

'I shall miss him terribly. He has been my little boy for seven years.'

'And I shall miss you, dear Cateau.'

'I'd like to visit a spa in Germany, to take the waters. They have all sorts of healing waters for women's troubles there. You never know . . . Look, Jenny, I didn't want to say anything in front of Rudolf and Henny, but I received a letter from my parents saying that your brothers, Frits and Willem, paid them a visit. That was your idea, wasn't it? Mama was rather shocked by Frits, apparently, who behaved in a very peculiar way. Actually, Marie says Herman's quite mad . . . And as for Marie herself . . . she's a bit strange, too, sometimes, so capricious . . . Perhaps it's just as well she and August have fallen out.'

Tears welled up in Jenny's eyes. 'Poor Marie. *Kasian*!'

'I will be frank with you, Kerkhoven: your land is rather a disappointment to me. I was in Soekawana recently, where Hoogeveen is the manager. I think his tea looks better than yours. And his quinine is doing spectacularly well. You have reservations about quinine, I gather.'

Over the past few days Rudolf had been surprised at the mildness of his brother in-law's opinions, but now the old irritation returned. Why did Henny have to be so critical of Gamboeng? During their recent tour of the grounds he had made endless remarks about the condition of the roads, the layout of the factory, and so on and so forth.

'What makes you think I have anything against quinine? Let me show you my seedlings.'

He expected Henny to be impressed by the sight of thousands of plants thriving in his nursery beds, but that was not the case.

'Too dry. They water the seedlings every evening at Soekawana.'

'What? I can just see myself going about with a watering can! The beds are far too big for that, and besides, there is plenty of moisture in the air around here.'

'At Soekawana they say you are against cultivating quinine, and that you have advised August against it, too.'

Rudolf felt his anger rising. 'Who did you talk to at Soekawana? Not once have I mentioned quinine to Hoogeveen.'

'Actually, Karel Holle was there, too, and he said the same. They can't see why you planted *succirubra* – that species has a low quinine content. You ought to take *ledgeriana*, that's the best.'

'I am aware of that, and if I can get hold of any seeds I shall certainly plant them. But they are hard to come by. Anyway, I think I am the best judge of what I plant on my estate!'

'Pardon me, Kerkhoven, but you only own half of Gamboeng; the other half belongs to your father and Van Santen. I am only saying this on account of Cateau and Bertha's children, now that Van Santen is away in Europe. And the same goes for Ardjasari. It seems there is a possibility of your father becoming director of a quinine factory in Amsterdam, and my youngest sister's husband, who is an estate agent, would be prepared to act as intermediary at the auction.'

That Joan Henny, who knew nothing about either tea or quinine, was pretending not only to be an expert but also the guardian of the family interests, was less of an affront to Rudolf than the fact that his father had neglected to inform him of these new developments. But he could not deny that his brother-in-law was formally entitled to have a say in the running of Gamboeng.

'I will show you the books tomorrow,' he said gruffly. They turned away from the quinine beds and slowly made their way back to the house. At the factory the day's harvest was still being sorted, but another team of workers was lined up waiting for their wages and the *mandoers* were already sitting in a row on the front veranda.

*

August paid another visit to Gamboeng before the Hennys' departure. To everyone's surprise he seemed to be in high spirits, full of enthusiasm for the races in Bandoeng and all the parties he had been to. When Rudolf found himself alone with him he carefully steered the conversation towards the engagement. August said he hadn't heard from Marie for weeks. It didn't sound as if he cared very much, and Rudolf said no more on the subject.

August spent the night at Gamboeng, on a bunk in Rudolf's office. The evening was passed in the atmosphere of a cheerful family reunion, and breakfast the following morning was similarly amicable.

'What a shame Julius isn't here with us!' sighed Cateau. 'How is he, anyway? Such a dear, but we never hear from him.'

Rudolf reached into his pocket and drew out a note he had received from Julius. 'He is doing quite well, over in Krawang. I think that job with the railway is just right for him. Let's hope he gains promotion! Because he still has a tendency to stay in the background, just as he did in Holland. He keeps to himself a lot.'

Henny had risen from the table, and was pacing to and fro with his watch in his hand. The horses were brought out by the stable-boys, after which the porters came forward with the carrying-chairs and squatted down beside them.

'He's always in such a hurry,' whispered Cateau, raising her eyes to the ceiling.

'Behold my presence of mind!' cried August. 'I am helping myself to another sandwich even as our locomotive gathers up steam.'

Rudi van Santen almost fell off his chair laughing, and began to make chuffing noises like a train, much to little Ru's delight.

When they took their leave, Henny's parting words to Rudolf were: 'You just go on planting tea, then. Your books have convinced me; nobody makes tea as cheaply as you do. It will make you rich one day.'

'Only yesterday you were saying I should switch to quinine,' retorted Rudolf. He turned to his brother. 'Did you hear that, August? About us Kerkhovens not wanting to plant quinine? Even Cousin Karel Holle said so, apparently.'

August, who was to ride with the Hennys as far as Bandjaran, leaned over in his saddle to address Rudolf: 'I have received a packet of *ledgeriana*.'

'How did you manage that?' asked Rudolf. 'I have been badgering the government quinine plantation for months to supply me with *ledgeriana*, without success.'

'Well, that's where I got it from, as it happens.'

Rudolf was perturbed. 'I don't understand. They must have sent you my order by mistake.'

Jenny hugged Cateau. 'Will I see you again before you leave for Holland in April? I'll be nursing another baby by then, so I won't be able to travel.'

'Happy Jenny! Lucky Jenny!' exclaimed Cateau, then whispered, 'Did you notice how calmly August seems to be taking it all? Everything's going to be all right.'

Everything will be all right for the Kerkhovens, Jenny thought, as she waved goodbye from the veranda. But will it be all right for Marie? And for Herman and Frits? And for me?

On 7 December 1881, after a protracted, difficult labour, without assistance from either a doctor or a midwife, Rudolf and Jenny's second son was born at Gamboeng. They named him Eduard Silvester.

The sun was setting; the fan of fiery streaks in the western sky was paling by degrees. Rudolf and Jenny, arm in arm, strolled among the nursery beds planted with *ledgeriana*. There had been endless delays, but it was now three months since they had obtained the seeds, and Rudolf had arranged for awnings of woven bamboo to be put up to provide partial shade.

They walked barefoot; it had rained long and hard in the afternoon, and the paths were spongy with mud. Rudolf felt content; he inhaled the fragrance of the jungle, that mixture of bitter, tangy and musky aromas. He squeezed Jenny's arm. She had never looked more radiant than she did now, four months after Edu's birth. At her bedside during those long hours of torment he had vowed that this would be the last time, and she, exhausted, weak from loss of blood, had agreed that from then on they would sleep in separate beds. Besides, with a cot on either side of the marital bed and Engko unrolling her sleeping mat for the night, the master bedroom was getting crowded. Rudolf moved a couch into a corner of his office, behind a screen, where his sleeping quarters were completed with an improvised mosquito net draped over the coat-hanger, and a small wash-stand. That was where he would sleep, like a

Spartan soldier on the march or a hermit in his cell.

But now, looking at Jenny in the glow of the sinking sun, his vow seemed impossible to keep. Her formerly girlish prettiness had ceded to a new kind of beauty, softer and more mature, which he found deeply attractive. He had overcome so many seemingly insurmountable barriers over the years that he would doubtless succeed again now. He gave her a kiss; her almost imperceptible, instinctive recoil reminded him of the early days of their lovemaking, and roused the same tenderness in him as then. It was as if everything was beginning anew.

Myriad droplets glistened in the treetops and in the brushwood. Beneath the blazing sky, the vivid green of the forest and the tea gardens dazzled their eyes, yet the mountains to the west and north were already darkening into silhouettes. From the kampong came the familiar sounds of evening: muffled drumbeats, cries of '*Tah! Eh! Paman kadijeuh!*' And the hiss of '*Sijeuh! Sijeuh!*' as the chickens were driven in to roost.

The houseboy and the stable-boys were sitting on the steps of the servants' quarters, talking in low voices. The lamp in the clerk's house was already lit. But at the front of their *gedoeng*, facing south-west, it was still light. They could hear little Ru calling Engko, then saw him emerging from the house with her. He toddled forwards to meet his father. '*Ama*!' he cried, wanting a piggy-back ride. His mother lifted him up by his arms and dangled him over a deep puddle while Engko washed the mud off his feet.

They lingered a while in the vegetable garden, Rudolf with his son on his shoulders, Jenny stooping to inspect the plants. Darkness was falling rapidly.

'It's time we went back,' said Jenny. 'Edu needs his feed.'

*

Rudolf thought he had every reason to be satisfied. The yield had exceeded that of the previous year by far, and although he had been obliged to improvise on treatment methods, the finished tea produced at Gamboeng looked good, and, when infused, proved to have not the slightest hint of the earthy taste he had noticed in the tea of Ardjasari, which he believed was due to careless sorting. He had received visits from the Resident of Bandoeng and *wedanas* of Bandjaran and Tjisondari. All three had expressed admiration for the progress being made at Gamboeng, which was particularly gratifying to him after Henny's critical remarks. He conceded that his gardens were not quite as lush as August's at Ardjasari – but then those were more mature. He had high hopes for his own bushes, still modest in size but thriving. For the following year he was reckoning on a potential yield of over 500 kilos per *bouw*.

Jenny had planted cypresses in the front garden, and fruit trees in the kampong. She asked Rudolf to have the expanse of wild *pisang* between the house and the jungle cleared and levelled, so that they would have an unobstructed view of the magnificent tree trunks overgrown with creepers and orchids. No longer could a panther prowl about the house unseen.

The plantation flourished; each month brought a closer resemblance to Rudolf's dream. When he rode out in the morning and surveyed his lands from the spot where he had first set eyes on Gamboeng, he could scarcely believe how much he had already achieved: his very own *gedoeng*, with outbuildings and stables and proud rasamala trees, the factory emplacement and the nursery beds lower down, and then, as far as the eye could see, his tea gardens, divided from one another by paths and clumps of trees.

His two young sons were strong and healthy. The baby was still largely a blank to him, aside from the little smile of recognition when he looked in the cradle, but his devotion to Ru grew stronger by the day. His firstborn was a sturdy little boy, already able to walk some way with him in the gardens, wanting to know the names of all the plants and the trees. He loved to ride on the horse seated in front of his father, and had submitted to being vaccinated against smallpox without flinching, along with fourteen other children from the kampong.

Rudolf was thankful to see Jenny looking so serene. After tending her garden, she would sit with her sewing on the front veranda with Ru playing at her feet and little Edu snug and safe in Engko's *slendang*. Day after day the weather continued to be fine with glorious sunshine until three or four in the afternoon, followed by showers to slake the parched soil.

Things appeared to be going smoothly in the extended family, too. August seemed completely wrapped up in the affairs of his plantation, and particularly in his plans to establish his own racing stables. He was not heard to mention Marie, but all the more eager to tell everyone about his new Sandlewood stallion. Marie wrote to them rarely, and did not mention August, either. Rudolf and Jenny avoided alluding to the engagement in their correspondence, and it was soon as if there had never been word of it. There was one unpleasant reminder, though, in a letter from Rudolf's parents, who seemed to think his critical attitude at the time was to blame for the estrangement between his brother and Marie.

He replied, 'You refer to the "disparity" between August and me with respect to our positions as administrators of Ardjasari and Gamboeng. Indeed, that disparity exists. I am reminded of it daily, and I cannot say it is always agreeable. But I take a philosophical view of things, so I do not feel bitter. It cannot be helped now, and it has no effect on our happiness.'

Jealous? Perish the thought. He was thirty-four years old, middle age was beckoning. He had no time for such petty sentiments; he was a husband and father, he was his own master, and besides, being the eldest member of his generation in the Indies gave him a certain natural authority within the Kerkhoven family. He also enjoyed authority on his estate, and received tokens of loyalty and trust from his subordinates. To distance himself from the 'fashionable' and 'modern' habits of August and Henny and Cateau, which he did not think favourable to the development of colonial relations, he made a conscious effort to emulate his father's standards of dignity, both in appearance and in manner. In addition to the long beard he had grown, he took to going about with his head covered at all times, even indoors. He abstained from pork and alcohol, in keeping with the customs of the people at Gamboeng. Riding homeward at dusk after a long day's work, his heart lifted at the sight of the lamp-lit veranda in the distance. As he drew near he could distinguish Jenny sitting by the tea table while a small head peeped up from behind the balustrade – Ru would be standing on tiptoe on a stool to look out for his '*Ama*' – and he was overwhelmed by a sense of being the luckiest man in the world. '*Où peut-on être mieux*?' he murmured to himself, with his habit of resorting to his fund of bon mots. He was happy.

Jenny believed, like Rudolf, that they had entered a time of peace and harmony in their lives. When she was out gardening, with Ru playing on the steps of the front veranda and Edu cradled in Engko's *slendang*, she delighted in the tranquillity of her surroundings, and felt safe at last in the lee of the triple-peaked Goenoeng Tiloe. One beautiful day, with insects buzzing about the flowers and the voices of the tea pickers beyond rising up in the clear sky, she and Rudolf went for a stroll. She halted in the nursery garden, gripped his hand, and in an unprecedented surge of confidence, said, 'We ought to stay here for ever. It would never be as good anywhere else.'

Just then a messenger from Bandoeng arrived with a telegram that had been received from Batavia early that morning: Mr Roosegaarde Bisschop had suffered a stroke, and had died without regaining consciousness in his residence in Gang Scott.

Jenny packed a travelling bag for Rudolf in great haste. Horses were rapidly saddled for him and one of the servants, to ride to the train station at Soekaboemi. She wished she could have gone in his place, but she could not leave the children. Not until the horsemen had vanished from sight round the mountain did the full import of the tidings sink in.

Towards evening, August, having heard the news by courier from Rudolf, came over from Ardjasari. They sat together in the office until the early hours. Jenny wept for her father; August poured his heart out about Marie.

'What am I to do, Jenny? I don't want to leave her in the lurch. When we're together I'm always smitten by her, but it isn't love. I can't see myself living with her.'

Rudolf remained in Batavia longer than anticipated. Roosegaarde had left a chaos of paperwork; his widow had sunk into apathy, without any notion of how to deal with the inheritance and other practical matters, unable to decide whether or not she should go to Holland with her seven children (which was generally expected of her as the 'proper' thing to do). Or should she send the older boys there for their education while she rented a house in the salubrious climate of Buitenzorg, to live there with Rose and Marie? Should she sell the house in Gang Scott? Roosegaarde had died intestate. One half of the assets therefore fell to her, the other half to the children, while the underage siblings' inheritance would have to be held in trust by the Orphans Chamber.

Rudolf was amazed by his father-in-law's erratic financial

administration, but set to work at once, sorting out papers, writing letters to relatives in Holland, and establishing some sort of order in the fatherless household. In the end, the Hennys' departure to Holland moved Mrs Roosegaarde to follow their example, at least for the duration of the boys' schooling, after which they would, in all likelihood, return to the Indies. Rudolf advised her to rent out the house in Gang Scott to the government. Marie, whose animosity towards him was unmistakable, although she avoided him as much as possible, was vehemently opposed to this.

Finding himself alone with her on the inner gallery, he overcame his reluctance to broach the subject of her engagement.

'I have received a letter from August. He wants to know where he stands. He is not backing out; he says the decision is up to you.'

Marie was about to brush past without speaking, but stopped to confront him. White-faced, with her hair smoothed back into a knot, dressed all in black, she looked dramatically beautiful.

'He knows where he stands. I told him in Buitenzorg. I don't want the kind of life Jenny leads. I couldn't bear it, I'd kill myself. I am not a brood hen, nor am I a white *njai*, for that matter.'

Rudolf stared at her, aghast. He was seized by an impulse to slap her in the face for her rudeness, but mastered himself.

'You should not insult Jenny. And you are being unfair to August. The pair of you should have taken the time to get to know each other first.'

'We didn't get a chance! And whose fault is that?' cried Marie, stamping her feet. 'Why does everyone have to stick their nose in, anyway? You especially. Now you know why I've been avoiding you. You think you can just sweep in here and lord it over us all. Oh, I can't stand it!'

'But who else is there to take responsibility?'

'Me, me, me! I can take responsibility for myself!' shrieked Marie, and rushed away.

RUDOLF TO HIS PARENTS, APRIL 1882

Settling the inheritance preoccupies me, as it is a complicated affair, and you would not believe how little the notary knows about the value of coupons and so on; he can barely tell the difference between stocks and shares. I caught him committing some awful blunders, so now I keep a close eye on everything he does. Jenny is to inherit a sum of 15,000 guilders, which she wants to keep in a savings account, and I think that is a sensible idea. She is to have some shares in the Java Bank, too.

The Roosegaarde family is in a very difficult situation. Marie seems to get her way in everything. I will spare you the details. Her mother does not stand up to her; she will do anything to avoid argument. If anything should happen to Jenny and me, then *under no circumstances* do I wish our children to be taken in by them. You must promise me that.

The explosions that were heard at Gamboeng during the first week of May 1883 were attributed at first to excavation work in connection with the new railway line linking Buitenzorg and Bandoeng, and Rudolf imagined his brother Julius out in the mountains dynamiting rocks. Then they read in the newspaper that the Krakatau volcano in the Soenda Straits had erupted; news of this had taken several days to reach Batavia, where pleasure boats were being organised to ferry the curious to the site so that they might see the spectacle for themselves.

There were active volcanoes all over Java, and once the initial excitement had passed, life at Gamboeng continued as usual. There was a drought and consequently a drop in the harvest, but the prices fetched by Rudolf's tea were no lower than those of other estates, while the yield per garden was still within the range of what could be expected at an altitude of 4,000 feet. Rudolf had been able to add ten *bouw* of young bushes to his acreage, and he was out in the gardens before breakfast every morning.

He had more concerns about his new quinine nursery beds, which he took to watering daily, just to be sure. At intervals, he walked over to the government quinine plantations at Rioeng Goenoeng, often accompanied by Jenny, to see how the crop was progressing there, and to acquaint himself with pruning methods and the ways of stripping and drying the bark. As soon as his trees matured he would be applying the same treatment. His determination grew to use more of his land for quinine. A total of 120 *bouw* was now under cultivation at Gamboeng, so there was still plenty of forestland that could be cleared to establish new plantings. How else could he keep his head above water, with tea being such an unpredictable, unreliable crop? Sancta Cinchona, Saint Quinine, help us in our hour of need, he prayed under his breath.

When the weather turned warm and sunny again, Ru and Edu were out of doors all the daylight hours. They particularly relished splashing about naked in the shallow pond that had been dug near the vegetable patch to provide water for the gardeners, or making mud pies with the aid of flower-pots. Four-year-old Ru was already learning to ride the new pony Rudolf had bought for the children, and sat with great confidence in the saddle. An agile child for his age, he would climb into the spreading tree in the forecourt and, hiding among the foliage, imitate the monkeys' shrill chatter while shaking the branches, at which Rudolf or Jenny would go up on tiptoe to hand him a *pisang*. Little Edu mimicked everything his brother did, albeit on terra firma, by hiding among the root-stems of the tree and making animal noises.

The children were usually quiet during the night, especially after Rudolf had taught them some discipline by banishing the one who cried longest to his office, cot and all. Jenny was thankful for the good night's rest she had been getting lately, the more so since she was, yet again, 'in a sorry state', as she put it. 'Mama has asked the stork to come again,' Rudolf explained to his young sons.

RUDOLF TO HIS PARENTS, 27 AUGUST 1883

. . . Yesterday afternoon there was a thundery look to the sky. It was drizzling slightly, and we heard a rumbling sound far away, we even thought we could feel it reverberate in the ground beneath our feet. At first we thought it was thunder in the distance, but there was no lightning, and the booms grew louder, with loud thuds in between. From about 7 p.m. onwards we heard a succession of big explosions. It turned out to be the Krakatau erupting again, which is 270 kilometres away from here. The last time that happened was three months ago, but on a much smaller scale. The children, though frightened, fell asleep eventually. At midnight I was woken up by the commotion. Doors, windows, cupboards, everything rattled. Then came a very loud bang, like a cannon being fired beneath the window. It was not an earthquake as such, but there were plenty of tremors. When things quietened down I looked at my watch: it was a few minutes before 1 a.m.

Outside, it was pitch-dark, balmy weather and not a breath of wind. The booming sound returned, rising and falling in volume. The following morning we discovered that a crowd of natives had sought refuge at the clerk's house. Some people thought the Goenoeng Tiloe was falling down, others that it was our house or the factory collapsing. They were all ready to flee, the women with their babies in the *slendang*, the men clutching an armful of their most valued possessions. But no one knew where to go.

This morning the explosions alternated with spells of

quiet. At half past ten a dingy, leaden bank of mist rose up in the west. The haze thickened, blocking out the sun altogether, and it grew darker and darker. At noon it was too dark to read in my office. The workers left the gardens to go home, the chickens went to roost, and the crickets began to chirp. After several violent blasts of wind from the south, complete calm ensued. There was a sudden drop in temperature, it became disagreeably chilly. After half an hour the sky in the east became streaked with light, as if dawn was breaking. The cocks began to crow and the birds to sing. Nature was all topsy-turvy.

The fog lifted slowly, and at some time between three and four o'clock we were able to distinguish where the sun stood in the sky. I cannot stop thinking about what was making the air so thick and grey; my idea is that it must have been a cloud of ash, at a high altitude. But we did not see any ash falling around here, nor did we smell sulphur.

3 SEPTEMBER (A POSTCARD)

Just a note to say we are all right. Since my last letter we saw great flames from Krakatau lighting up the sky at night. What a disaster for Bantam! You must have read about it in the papers. We can think of nothing else. Little did we know, when I last wrote on 27 August (Ru's birthday!), that it would be so catastrophic.

11 SEPTEMBER

. . . We have been spending a fair amount of money on having the newspapers sent to us by messenger from Bandoeng, as we are very anxious about the news. The Bantam coast has suffered terrible flooding as a result of the undersea disturbance. Huge waves washed inland for miles, destroying everything in their path; entire buildings and many people were swept out to sea. Then the ash rain began to fall. Tèlok Betoeng is in ruins, and the bay is no longer navigable due to the huge accretions of lava. There are tens of thousands of corpses floating by the entrance to the Soenda Straits . . .

Whereas Jenny's previous confinements had been marked by pain and fear, her fourth, at the beginning of October 1883, was blighted by the presence of an imperious '*accoucheuse*' from Batavia, engaged at considerable expense, who was a qualified midwife but had no practical experience whatsoever. Jenny found it harder to cope with all the fuss and commotion, the premature filling of pails and jugs of water, the setting out of piles of towels and sheets, the constant gabbling of 'that woman', than with going into labour. That she cried out for Rudolf with each contraction, wanting to hold his hand, and that he remained at her bedside throughout, was taken as a personal affront by the midwife, who proceeded to react in the most hostile fashion to everything Rudolf said or did. When he suggested it would be better to wait a while before breaking the waters she made a show of her authority by doing the opposite. Never would Jenny forget that spiteful face looming over her, with the blue bead earrings swinging from side to side, nor the huge hands and the arms, greased up to the elbows with salad oil (there goes half a bottle! Jenny fumed), groping inside her.

Feeling herself, and her newborn baby – another boy, to be named Emile – at the mercy of this virago made Jenny so nervous that Rudolf decided to send the woman back to Batavia before completing her term of service, even if it meant paying her the full fee and making arrangements for her journey.

'Never again!' he said to Jenny. 'Far better to have Ma Endoet come over from Tjikalong, or Ma Mina from Bandjaran, or some other *doekoen* if need be.'

Jenny sighed. 'I do hope that won't be necessary. Not for the next ten years anyway.'

Three sons! Rudolf wanted to toughen them from the start. Baby Emile still needed his mother most of the time, but he wanted Ru and Edu to be responsible and independent from an early age, so that they could play outside without endangering themselves. They had to promise to stay within at least thirty metres of the forest, a boundary Rudolf had indicated to them by means of landmarks: trees, a clump of bushes, rocks. Young Ru never went out riding on his pony without two stable-boys to accompany him, and the children only set foot in the jungle if Rudolf was with them, carrying a rifle. Ru loved wading in the foaming Tjisondari, although he had to cling to his father with all his might not to be swept away by the current.

One of the boxes of presents sent by the children's grandparents in Holland contained a toy gun and a box of caps. Ru was enchanted by them, and Edu, too, was soon intrigued. They had no fear of the *petasan*, the small firecrackers that were sold in strips at the *waroeng*. Most of all they liked helping Irta, the houseboy, to polish Rudolf's gun. They each had a small chopping knife, and were often to be found slashing away at logs of *pisang* wood, preferably among the workers in the carpentry shed. The *mandoer* would give them a straw cigarette, without tobacco or fire, for them to puff on with a lordly air.

Kind-hearted Ru was always protective of Edu, and Rudolf encouraged his sense of responsibility. When Edu started biting his brother during rough games, Ru was told by his father to give him a firm smack. The ensuing tantrum usually petered out of its own accord after a time, although one day Rudolf resorted to locking the irate toddler in his office, where he stood and screamed from two in the afternoon until half past six. Jenny couldn't help admiring the child's tenacity, but *baboe* Engko squatted beneath the office window looking distraught, and the *mandoers* scowled at Rudolf when they came to collect the men's wages.

From behind the door Edu wailed, 'I'll be good! I'll be good!' but when Rudolf unlocked the door and told him to repeat his promise, he refused. Jenny chewed her lip; it was not up to her to intervene in this exercise of paternal authority, and besides, Ru, who was shedding tears of sympathy, had had tantrums too when little, albeit less protracted ones. When Edu finally looked his father in the eye and said in a hoarse little voice, 'I'll be good', he was treated like the prodigal son, hugged, comforted, given a bath and dressed in clean clothes. He was allowed to drink his milk out of young Ru's silver birth mug for a treat.

The influence of the rearguard in Holland – his father, Van Santen and Henny – was becoming increasingly irksome to Rudolf. He felt constrained in his actions as plantation manager by the often contradictory recommendations they sent him from afar. As soon as he had the money he would take over their share in Gamboeng, that he knew for certain.

Meanwhile it had transpired that the tea he had planted some years earlier on the express advice of Eduard Kerkhoven and Albert

Holle was not 'Assam', as they had claimed, but a hybrid. He had only recently acquired seed of the pure strain, which he had sown immediately. He wanted to buy a great deal more of it, but it was very expensive, so he needed to gain permission from his partners first. And even if they gave it, he was afraid they would not be sufficiently aware of the risk he was taking: the new tea would have to fetch a very good price on the market for it to justify the cost of outlay.

His plantings of quinine were another matter. Quinine cultivation was on the rise all over the region, which he feared might well lead to over-production, even in the short-term. That would leave the planters with no choice but to lower their prices to rock-bottom, while the quinine factories and chemist shops overseas sat back and made a fortune. The only way profits could be made with quinine was to manufacture the end-product on the estate itself, or on behalf of the estate in a local factory. The cost of growing quinine was minimal compared to that of maintaining tea gardens. Furthermore, the cost of treating bark was infinitely lower than that of manufacturing tea. Rudolf's first harvest of quinine, six crates of branch-bark, had already raised enough money to cover the initial investment, thereby exceeding his expectations by far.

As the sulphate content of quinine differed greatly from one tree to the next, he sent his father some shavings of a tree he had grown from a *ledgeriana* cutting acquired from the government-run plantation nearby. If the quality was shown to be superior during laboratory tests, he would reserve that particular tree for seed.

From time to time, August, who was facing similar problems, came over from Ardjasari. Tall and well-dressed, the country gentleman to a tee, with humour and a cheerful disposition (the little boys doted on him), he brought a breath of worldliness to Gamboeng. Rudolf felt himself decidedly rustic by comparison.

Jenny on the other hand could not help feeling envious as she listened to his enthusiastic accounts of betting on the races, the parties he had been to, the dresses worn by the wives of senior civil servants and army officers, the buggies and victorias and other elegant conveyances drawn by handsome horses and driven by these ladies in person, the flower pageants and fancy fairs, the resplendent dinner parties hosted by Eduard Kerkhoven of Sinagar in the house he always rented in Bandoeng for the duration of the races. Rudolf's remarks about all the money being squandered on fashionable goings-on which held no attraction for him whatsoever – indeed, which were a complete waste of time – frustrated and disappointed her. Why was her opinion never asked? Why did he take it for granted that she, like him, had no interest in anything fun and amusing? It was time she took her life in her own hands. After much soul-searching, she took her young house *baboe*, Nati, into her confidence, and sent her to the *pasar* in Tjikalong to buy some *djamoe* of the type recommended to her by that rude official's wife years ago. From now on she would use those herbs to keep the stork at bay.

She badly needed to see the dentist again, which signified a trip to Batavia. Thanks to the new railway connection at Bandoeng she was able to make the journey without Rudolf. Accompanied by Emile and his *baboe*, she sat in the train for eight hours, which was sheer luxury compared to the old means of transport. She had little opportunity to admire the magnificent views across the mountains that could be seen from successive viaducts, because the child was fractious and ill from the heat. He cried incessantly, and they had to alight at each station on the way to wash him and change his napkin.

Life in the city seemed to her like heaven on earth. She lodged with a girlhood friend in a fine house on Koningsplein, round the corner from Gang Scott, and feasted her eyes on the furniture, the gardens, the shops, the new neighbourhoods south of the city. She laid flowers on her father's grave, and visited various families of her acquaintance, mostly relations of Rudolf's, such as the Denninghoff Stellings and the Van den Bergs. She bought herself a parasol and a pair of plaited leather shoes, fancy goods she had no use for at home. The dentist introduced her to one of the latest blessings of science: laughing gas.

But when she was back in Gamboeng the evocation of all the impressive, modern sights she had seen in the city made her despondent. How shabby her house was, how different her life from that of her friend! She began to lose her temper with the servants, and grew impatient with the children. When the rain kept them indoors and they ran and jumped up and down on the floor making the whole house shake, she wanted to scream with exasperation.

Rudolf was pleased: a spell of good luck for a change! The yield of his coffee bushes, which he had come to regard as a minor concern, suddenly turned out to be huge: no less than 2,500 kilos was being brought in daily. The entire population of Gamboeng was picking coffee, the men carrying the heavy loads to the shed where the peeling mill stood, while the women and children remained in the fields, gathering berries until sunset. The mill was powered by the waterwheel, which Rudolf had fabricated out of rasamala wood, and which was originally intended to provide energy for the mechanical saw in the carpentry workshop. Within a single fortnight he had already harvested over 300 kilos in excess of his initial estimates, and since the produce could now be sent by rail directly from Bandoeng, transport was far less of a problem than in the old days.

*

It riled Rudolf that his father always took such a bleak view of Gamboeng. He hoped his parents would make one last voyage to the Indies, so that they would see with their own eyes how the plantation was flourishing, how much everything had changed for the better in the past four years. He was also frustrated by the fact that nobody seemed to realise how hard he had worked at refining and innovating his methods of tea manufacture, and of quinine, too, for instance by grafting *ledgeriana* quinine onto stems of an inferior species and conducting various other experiments.

He had also designed an up-to-date version of the *tampir*, and special clamps for the tea chests – both improvements had gained him the respect of his fellow planters in the Preanger. The recently founded Bandoeng Agricultural Society offered him their chairmanship, and, although he felt honoured, he declined. He did not think he could spare the time for all the travelling he would be required to do, and the cost, too, was a consideration; the Society's meetings tended to coincide with the horse-racing events, which were the most expensive days of the year.

On several occasions Henny and Van Santen gave him to understand that, in their opinion, he was behind the times with his ideas, which was all the more wounding in light of the objections they always seemed to raise against his proposals to buy much-needed new machines for the factory, which were admittedly costly, but which August already possessed. He was also reminded that it was time he started paying the 8 per cent interest on the working capital originally advanced by Van Santen. It was only thanks to the excellent coffee harvest that he was able to comply without teetering on the brink of bankruptcy. This time Sancta Arabica was his patron saint.

In November 1885 Marie Roosegaarde came over from Holland unexpectedly, the reason given being that she wanted to visit old friends in Batavia and Buitenzorg, and especially her sister Jenny. Rudolf had a feeling there might be another reason, given Marie's wilful temperament, and it was with some trepidation that he went to fetch her from Bandoeng station. The moment she stepped onto the platform he knew 'something was up'. He still thought her beautiful, but she seemed highly agitated. Riding in the carriage to Tjikalong, the luggage cart following, she never stopped talking, jumping from one subject to the next without rhyme or reason. He could not get a word in edgeways, and kept his eyes on the landscape so as not to encourage her. At Tjikalong they were met by grooms with saddle-horses for the final steep climb to Gamboeng. As they rode through the tea gardens, past the factory sheds and the kampong, he was struck by how interested she seemed in everything she saw on the way. He took this to mean she was on some kind of mission to find out how the estate was faring, and his suspicions grew once she told him she had seen the Hennys and Van Santen just before she left.

He noticed her startled look of concern when she set eyes on Jenny. In tears, the sisters fell into each other's arms. The rest of the afternoon was spent unwrapping and admiring the gifts 'Auntie Malie' had brought, amid whoops of excitements from the three little boys.

'My God, Jenny, you don't look at all well! And so thin, too!'

'I'm having a lot of tummy trouble. Hardly any food agrees with me.'

'Why don't you go and see a doctor in Batavia?'

'I don't think that's necessary. We have enough to worry about as it is.'

'Well, the plantation seems to be doing very well, from what I've seen. But this house you live in is rather dismal, don't you think? Those cheap rattan chairs! Those bare floorboards! I can feel the cold draughts coming straight through the mats.'

'Once Rudolf's salary goes up and we start getting a share of the profits we'll be able to buy new furniture. I can't wait. Anyway, Ru ought to have an assistant. And I want a good governess for the children, someone who can teach them. But none of those things are feasible yet.'

'Cateau mentioned you have ordered a piano. So that is something you obviously *can* afford.'

'It's my money, Marie. The interest on my inheritance. I want the children to be able to hear music and to sing songs. It will be good for them; there's so much they go without already.'

Jenny and Marie had settled themselves in the *succirubra* grove, as though in a bower. The smooth trunks bore crowns of broad, shiny foliage, green on the upper side and deep crimson underneath. The sisters had spread *pisang* leaves on the ground to protect their sarongs from the mud. The children ran about among the trees.

'Marie, tell me honestly, why did you come? Was it because of August?'

'They told me to . . . Mama, and your parents-in-law as well. Is it true that people round here still think August is engaged? In Holland they all think I am, so I don't get many invitations.'

'What I don't understand is why you treated August the way you did four years ago.'

'I wanted to teach him a lesson. He was so cocksure. Everyone thought he was wonderful, and he knew it. It was only because I was the belle of the ball – well, I *was* the belle at the time – that he wanted me. He wanted to have the best estate, the handsomest horse and the prettiest girl, in that order, you understand. He pretended to be madly in love, he even went down on his knees in that garden at Buitenzorg: Marie, Marie, I beg you, I can't wait, I'll do anything you ask! All right, I said, but I'm not going to live in the wilderness, I want to see the world first . . . Paris . . . Venice. Which he promised me. That's when we announced our engagement. But the next day, at Cateau's, he just laughed about his promise. He had only said that so he could kiss me. I was livid. I thought if he really wanted me, he'd have said yes.'

'Oh, Marie, how childish of you! How could you believe . . . how could he possibly have taken you abroad?'

'If only he'd said yes . . . then I'd have felt different, I'd even have considered living at Ardjasari. I just wanted him to prove that I was more important to him than his estate and his horses, that I meant the world to him. And he wouldn't. So I refused to see him after that.'

'Do you still have feelings for him?'

'Oh, I don't know. I wish I knew. I think of him a lot. But it's all such a long time ago.'

'Rudolf thinks it would not be right for the two of you to meet while you're here with us.'

'People are already gossiping. In Batavia they're saying I came back with my tail between my legs – isn't that awful? Oh, Jenny, I wish you could help me!'

Rudolf ordered a large, deep trench to be dug at the back of the house, into which the water from the mountain stream was channelled. Ru learnt to swim in the space of a few days, Edu and Emile splashed about like buffalo calves in the shallow part of the muddy pool, which was the colour of chocolate. Jenny and Marie sat on tree stumps, watching them.

'Don't you think Ru is a bit too old to go around naked like that?' said Marie. 'It doesn't seem right to me.'

'Come, come, Marie, you just told me that you're the one who always gives Henri and Constant their baths. Both of them are older that Ru. Such big boys! That doesn't seem right to me, either.'

Marie blushed. 'They're still babies as far as I am concerned. They like being cuddled. Your Ru is a little *man*. He talks in such a grown-up way. Our little brothers are different.'

'How do you mean?' Jenny asked gently. Their eyes met. Marie shrugged.

'Constant is angelic . . . but Herman . . . you know . . . he's very difficult, which is sad for Mama. And Frits, oh, I needn't tell you. He's the same as ever. It's the Daendels blood. We just have to live with it. You can thank your lucky stars your children have turned out so well.'

The sisters were busy in the front veranda making a kebaya for Jenny from a length of red silk that Marie had brought her.

'Do you realise that the only women I spoke to during the whole year were Engko, Nati and the clerk's wife?'

Marie reached out to touch Jenny's hand. 'I might be staying on . . .'

'What was that?' said Rudolf emerging from the office. 'Of course, taking holidays to the other side of the world is an expensive business.'

'I paid for my passage out of my own pocket, with money from my inheritance. At least I get some enjoyment out of it.'

'If you invested that money properly, the way I did for Jenny, you would be getting interest. Your capital would grow.'

'Tea grows, quinine grows, capital grows. That's all you're interested in,' Marie burst out. 'Just look at Jenny, look at the state she's in! And the rain, that awful rain day in day out! No wonder you all keep suffering from colds. And fevers, too, so Jenny tells me.'

Jenny tossed her head; she could tell that Marie wanted to pursue the subject, so she stood up and made her way to the narrow back veranda, where the children were blowing bubbles.

Marie left for Buitenzorg and Batavia, where she would be staying with friends from the old days.

'It's far too quiet for me around here! Besides, I must get a chance to wear the evening gowns I brought with me,' she cried with exaggerated coquetry, waving goodbye to Rudolf as the train departed. But before the month was out he was back at the station in Bandoeng to fetch her. He was bemused when she said that August had been to see her in Buitenzorg, and that they had sat next to each other at a dinner party. They had even danced together.

'And now he seems to want to come over from Ardjasari and see her here.' Rudolf told Jenny. 'What do you think? I'm not sure August knows what he's doing.'

Jenny remembered with secret satisfaction the note she had sent to Ardjasari a few weeks before.

August took some time to respond, however. They were still at breakfast one morning when he finally made his appearance, mounted on his Sandlewood. He drank a cup of coffee and suggested going for a long walk with Marie. Jenny followed them with her eyes as they vanished down the alley lined with tree ferns bordering the forest. They stayed away a long time.

That a decision had been reached was clear when they re-emerged from the leafy tunnel: August's expression was stony; Marie was as white as a sheet. Jenny thanked the Lord Rudolf was out in the gardens and the children were paddling in their pool with Engko to watch over them. Because no sooner had August turned his back on the house than Marie began to scream and sob, throwing herself down on the veranda and beating the floor with her fists. Nati came running, alarmed by the commotion, then she and Jenny pulled Marie to her feet and led her to the bedroom.

'Why should I go on living? What's the point?'

'Shame on you!' said Jenny, dabbing Marie's forehead with a wet cloth. 'Don't say such things.'

'Don't you ever feel like that? We're all unhappy, all of us are. Rose wanted to jump in the water once. Am I supposed to spend the rest of my days looking after my dotty younger brothers? He says he came to Buitenzorg out of *politeness*, would you believe! But we danced the waltz, we had tête-à-têtes. Everyone will know he won't have me. Who will ever want me now?'

'Marie, I am sure—'

'Oh, of course, of course,' scoffed Marie. 'There is someone in Holland who will have me . . . the son of a friend of Mama's, nothing wrong with him. He wants to go into tobacco. But my God, am I to live with someone like him year in year out, in the back of beyond? Just so as not to end up an old maid! I'd rather die.'

'You'll find happiness one day, I'm sure. You deserve to.'

Marie began to laugh, but the sound of it frightened Jenny even more than the scene on the veranda an hour before.

She was too worried to sleep that night. She drew aside the mosquito net and lit the candle on her bedside table. Emile was curled up under his blanket in his cot, breathing regularly. She peered into the adjacent nursery: Ru and Edu were fast asleep; she could smell the coconut oil Engko used on her hair.

She made her way to the guest room, where she found Marie

sitting on the edge of the bed in the soft glow of the night-light, holding a glass of water. On the table lay sheets of paper covered in writing.

'What are you doing?' whispered Jenny.

'Oh, just leave me alone. Please go away.'

'What have you got there?' Jenny snatched the sachet of powder Marie was hiding under the pillow. 'Are you mad?' She slapped Marie on the face, left and right, then knelt on the bed and took her in her arms. Marie began to weep.

'It's my punishment. Everything that happens to me is punishment.'

'Punishment? What on earth for?'

'When Constant was born . . . Mama was so afraid of having another baby . . . The maids said there was a *nènèk* at the *pasar* selling *obat* . . . against lust . . . you know? So then, each morning, while Rose and I had coffee with Papa, I slipped a teaspoonful into his cup . . . I wanted to help Mama, and I thought, if Papa felt less . . . the woman at the *pasar* said it had a calming effect. But now I know it makes the heart stop beating.'

When visiting the quinine plantations on the Pengalengan plateau, Rudolf discovered, to his surprise, that the administrators and their European overseers carried arms during working hours. There was talk of an uprising among the native population of the Preanger.

Rudolf was convinced that any planter who treated his people justly and fairly had nothing to worry about. Bearing arms was a cowardly thing to do, in his opinion, utterly uncalled for.

When rioting broke out on a plantation near Buitenzorg, during which forty people were killed and seventy wounded, he blamed the disaster on the irresponsible behaviour of the owner of that extensive property, who, according to hearsay, had over the past few years brought charges against no fewer than 700 of his people for being absent from work and various other minor offences.

In the planter community it was said that a fanatical Muslim sect was inciting hatred of the white infidel rulers, and that there was a connection between these disturbances and the ongoing conflict in Atjeh.

Rudolf recalled that there had been an assistant *wedana* in Tjikalog back in 1874, who had told him something which he had thought wildly unlikely at the time, and which no one had been able to confirm: that Karel Holle was on a secret mission, touring the archipelago to gauge the mood of the Muslim leaders. Later Rudolf learnt that Karel Holle had indeed been absent from his Waspada plantation for several months, but no one, not even Rudolf's father or Eduard Kerkhoven, could say where he had been.

Although he did not harbour particular fears for disturbances at Gamboeng, he decided that he owed it to his wife and children and their safe-keeping to gather what information he could about the circumstances from someone with expert knowledge of the Muslim community in Java.

It was years since he had last visited Waspada. He was just as impressed this time by the splendour of the location, with Karel Holle's house high up on the slope of the Tjikoeraj mountain overlooking a vast expanse of terraced tea gardens, as lush as paddy fields and totalling approximately 200 *bouw*.

Rudolf was received in the office-cum-study, a cluttered space with overflowing bookshelves, tables piled high with papers, and on the floor a row of stones deriving from what had once been some form of pillar. His eye was caught by the traces of ancient Javanese script on one of the stones. Karel Holle sat on a low bench, holding a magnifying glass in his hand. Rudolf was surprised by how old he looked, and how little was still discernible of his former air of command and authority. The numerous Soendanese servants (or were they students?) bringing tea and refreshments, or searching among the papers or books, treated him with respect, but more as an elderly patriarch than as their master. Knowing that visitors were expected to observe the native *adat* in their dealings with Karel Holle, Rudolf listened patiently to a lengthy discourse on the inscription his host was deciphering: in all probability a laudation of a warrior-king from the days of Airlangga. Not until Karel Holle enquired after the purpose of his visit could the conversation begin. Karel conceded that there was indeed a degree of unrest in the region, but that it only concerned Muslims belonging to a certain sect, not those led by his friend, the *penghoeloe* Radèn Hadji Mohammed Moesa. In fact, Moesa was vehemently opposed to the ideas of the agitators. According to him, the latter were associated with a number of native chiefs who were incensed by the government reforms. Moesa had many personal enemies in those circles, because he had supported the new agrarian laws introduced by the colonial government in 1871.

'What makes the situation tragi-comic is that they have no reason to hate Moesa nowadays, considering how little has come of the reforms. The government assured me at the time that the native population would be permitted to raise the prices of their products, which they have counted on being able to do, and which is in fact necessary for their livelihood. And now the prices are not to be raised after all, and my recommendations for setting up schools have likewise been ignored. A step backwards! It is as though we are back in the old days when the East Indies were there to be exploited, with a population prepared to work on the plantations on terms that amounted to forced labour. It was out of shame towards my people at Waspada that I gave them the extra money that is denied to them by the colonial government.'

Karel Holle took the view that the bloodshed on the plantation near Buitenzorg was an unfortunate excess resulting from the people's protest against the restrictions, not a case of collective frenzy on religious grounds, although he did not rule out the possibility that the Muslim sect had deliberately been stirring trouble.

'The administrator of that plantation is no worse as *djoeragan* than the majority of private entrepreneurs. He is not directly involved, he resides elsewhere most of the time, leaving his employees, and particularly the native and Chinese overseers, to do as they see fit. His chief mistake is that he takes no notice of the *adat* pertaining to rice, according to which the paddy must be harvested by local families. He employed outside labour to do the job, which meant insufficient rice for the locals. A most unfortunate business, and a sign of things to come. I wonder what the reaction of the government will be.'

'Cousin Karel, is it true that you went all over the Indies on a secret mission, even to Borneo and Singapore?'

Karel Holle sighed. 'That, too, appears to have been a waste of time and effort. My good friend James Loudon, the then Governor-General, asked me to investigate the opinions held in religious Muslim circles regarding the Atjeh expedition. In those days it was claimed the Muslims were seizing every opportunity to start a holy war against us, all over the archipelago. I was able to inform Loudon that, notwithstanding Atjeh, we still had the people on our side. I was given repeated assurances that we would be able to maintain our position so long as we treated the people with justice and humanity. And don't forget, I was dealing with educated, forward-looking Muslims, not with fanatics or puppets of native chiefs seeking to regain their former power over the population. But let us talk of other things. It makes me sick to think of that "Dutch Line" in Atjeh, that senseless enclave, which serves no other purpose than to demoralise the troops and spread disease.'

Karel Holle began to question Rudolf about Gamboeng, his family, and the prospects of his tea and quinine plantings. He nodded approvingly as he listened to Rudolf explain his efforts to obtain superior quinine seeds by means of a special pollination technique.

'You work hard on your land. It can't be easy for a man on his own. At Sinagar Eduard has an apprentice at the moment – your cousin, Ru Bosscha, whose father is a professor at Delft.'

'Yes, so I have heard. I met him when he was a boy back in

Holland. I felt sorry for him, because he was lame, and had to wear special shoes.'

'You would do well to take him on. A promising young man, not one of your well-bred softies from the old country.'

'He failed his civil engineering exams, I gather, and being lame is not exactly a recommendation for our line of work.'

Karel Holle eyed him pensively a moment before replying. 'He and I had a conversation when I was in Buitenzorg recently. A fine chap, made of the right stuff. I would want him for Waspada myself if I were staying on here.'

'Are you thinking of leaving?' asked Rudolf, startled.

'I have to sell Waspada. I can't stay. I no longer have the means to run this place properly. And I am worn out. My time is over. My good friend Hadji Moesa is ill, and unlikely to recover. We have planted the *bibit*, but the harvest will pass us by. There will be others to continue our struggle. There were times when I had hopes of you, Rudolf, being among them. You have a sense of justice, you provide decent housing for your people, but what else do you do for them?'

'I have three sons to raise. And Jenny is expecting again. I can't afford philanthropy just yet.'

'It is not a question of philanthropy, but of honour and duty,' concluded Karel Holle with a sigh. 'So be it.'

A fourth son was born to Jenny and Rudolf in April 1887: Karel Felix, a frail, wizened baby. His brothers compared him to a lizard: 'Just like a *tjitjak*!'

Before he was six months old his successor announced itself. Jenny wrote to her mother-in-law:

> No, dear Mama, I have not yet come to terms with the impending arrival of our fifth child. It is not the extra work that I am concerned about, because I am so busy anyway with *baboes* and babies that one more won't make much difference. But my dearest wish – to keep my boys at home – looks ever less likely to come true. If only I were able to teach the three eldest myself, with Rudolf's help, then we could manage for a few years on our own. Even if we needed a tutor for them later on, to prepare them for admission to secondary school, it would cost us a lot of money. But with so many mouths to feed, we probably won't be able to afford the expense. I cannot bear the thought of sending them to Holland, either, unless we could take them there ourselves to get them settled, and visit them after a few years. But I

cannot see that happening. No, hectic as things may be with all the children, sending the boys away is too high a price to pay for a little more ease and freedom of movement. Besides, I would still be tied to the house by the little ones. I don't seem to have half the energy and strength I used to have. If only we had a bigger house, then things would be a lot easier. Can you imagine what it is like when it rains, with everyone crowding into our tiny front veranda and front room! It is beyond endurance at times. The ceilings are so low, and I hate the cold, and then I wish I was far, far away, in the middle of the forest, surrounded by peace and quiet. I used to be frightened of the forest, but now I sometimes wish I could lie down there and go to sleep.

RUDOLF TO HIS FATHER, JANUARY 1888

Henny and Cateau have suggested we send our Ru to go and live with them, for the sake of his education, and we will be glad to take them up on the offer in due course. We could hardly find a better home for Ru, but for the moment he is doing fine being taught by Jenny and me, so we are in no hurry.

Postscript from Jenny: Ru and Edu must never be parted!

That the joylessly expected addition to the family turned out to be a girl was of slight comfort. When Bertha was displayed to her brothers, they responded with even less enthusiasm than when Karel was born. Ru and Edu stared in silence. Emile clambered onto the big bed to inspect the baby occupying his mother's arms. 'God, God, another *orok*!' he said in Soendanese, in his markedly deep voice for a four-year-old.

Rudolf bent over Jenny. She saw something she had not noticed before: his hair and beard were streaked with grey.

In January 1890 Rudolf's father died. His estate took a long time to be settled, and it was revealed during the valuation of the assets that Ardjasari was worth a lot more than Rudolf had inferred from his meetings with August, which had become infrequent. The plantation had recently become solvent, and August turned out to have ambitious plans for expansion, including the establishment of additional quinine plantings in the near future.

Rudolf was surprised to learn that his father had given August credit for virtually all the progress that had been made in Javanese quinine cultivation, completely ignoring the fact that he, Rudolf, was raising a superior quality of trees, not by the unreliable grafting technique still being used at Ardjasari, but from seed procured from the very best *ledgeriana*, according to a method he had devised and perfected himself.

Several codicils in the last will and testament reflected the disproportionate expectations his father had entertained with respect to August. Rudolf could see why August did nothing to rectify this, given that he wished to marry; he had his eye on the daughter of the Resident of Bandoeng, which meant that he needed all the prestige he could muster. Nonetheless, it pained Rudolf to see his brother acknowledging praise and preferential treatment as though it was his due.

RUDOLF TO HIS MOTHER, AUGUST 1890

> My tea crop is still doing well, and prices are satisfactory. To hear both Van Santen and Henny complimenting August on his good prices makes me feel hard done by, because our Gamboeng tea fetched far higher rates, and was even specially recommended by the brokers. It is fair to say that, on average, we have been getting the best rates at auction. Please be so kind as to show Henny and Van Santen the enclosed auction results, just to prove to them that Gamboeng is doing at least as well as Ardjasari, if not better!

He felt assuaged when the opportunity arose to open the eyes of his mother, Julius, Cateau, Henny and Van Santen to his gains. The quinine market, public opinion, facts and figures – that would show them!

RUDOLF TO HIS MOTHER, 20 MARCH 1891

> Just a note to tell you of our splendid success at the quinine auction last February. It is a remarkable and unequalled achievement in the annals of quinine cultivation, as several newspapers have pointed out. The best bark ever to come on the market! We scored no less than 200 per cent higher than the maximum ever attained by a plantation. And that is entirely in accordance with what I wrote to you a while ago, namely that Gamboeng would find itself at the top of the list eventually. Besides, it was only the harvest of about twenty *bouw*, and I already have between 170 and 180 *bouw* planted with the same species – i.e. the best!

Naturally, we cannot expect to maintain our leading position indefinitely. I have no illusions about besting the competition in the long run. Other planters have started taking over my methods. And it is not unlikely they will achieve even better results by introducing further refinements. It was ever thus. People profit from other people's experiences. But considering the excellence of my current results, I feel justified in saying that I have been the pioneer in this affair. I have led the way.

JENNY TO HER MOTHER-IN-LAW, AUGUST 1892

. . . I am writing this to you on the reclining chair, because I have miscarried. It happened the day before yesterday. I had no idea these things could be so painful.

I am not really sorry. On the contrary, I was feeling very low about having to cope with raising yet another baby, and especially because I hope to take Ru and Edu to Holland myself.

I am anxious whether Cateau will be able to have both our darling boys to stay with her and Henny. I dread having to part with them. I wouldn't want them to stay with anyone but Cateau, who is so conscientious and kind-hearted and caring and sensible.

RUDOLF TO HIS MOTHER, SEPTEMBER 1892

. . . We are hopeful that Henny and Cateau will decide to take both Ru and Edu into their home. We are well aware that it is quite an undertaking for them, but I believe having Ru and Edu together would be almost easier than having just one child to look after.

RUDOLF TO HIS MOTHER, NOVEMBER 1892

. . . I am so glad you and Cateau found your visit to the spa beneficial. We were very worried for a time about Henny and Cateau deciding not to take in Ru and Edu after all, on account of Cateau's health. So we were greatly relieved to hear that they have reiterated their kind offer.

I have reserved a cabin with three bunks on the *Bromo*, the Rotterdamsche Lloyd's best ship.

JENNY TO HER MOTHER-IN-LAW, DECEMBER 1892

. . . We have been fortunate in finding just the right person to take my place. Her father is the minister in Soekaboemi who has nineteen children. Several of the girls have become teachers.

All being well, the *Bromo* will sail on 1 March, with Ru, Edu and me on board.

For the children at Gamboeng the years flowed together in a sea of time. All their games were attuned to their natural surroundings and the activities taking place on the plantation.

The youngest ones, too small to ride a pony, cavorted about on the lawn in front of the house with the harness and a whip, taking turns to be the pony and the rider; later on they were taught the rudiments of horsemanship in the yard by the stable, and once firm in the saddle refined their skills in the quinine groves and in the forest, until they were able to jump over felled trees and across ditches without effort. They all had their favourite horses: Falco the handsome, Amina the mild-tempered, Hector the proud, Badjing the frisky. For the boys, as for everyone else at Gamboeng, it was a day of mourning when their father's old dapple mare, Odaliske, lay down and refused to get up again.

As toddlers they had been kept safely away from the circular saw, but as they grew older they pretended to be carpenters working an imaginary machine, while imitating the familiar whine: *nè- nè-è-èng*! They fashioned a miniature saw out of a cigar box, a piece of string and a serrated disc cut out of zinc or tin, which they used to cut mildewy wood, slices of papaya, or paper. An upturned wheelbarrow served as their mill for imaginary quinine bark. They made toy waterwheels complete with scoops out of large, green citrus fruits. Ru and Edu, aged twelve and ten, built a proper waterwheel out of wood on the rear veranda.

They spent endless hours hunting. The row of tall shrubs outside their father's office was their jungle, where spears were thrown to tigers lurking behind the leafy boughs. Edu carried a (blunt) knife around at the age of three, and Ru, when he reached six, wielded a real *golok*, of the kind used by the men in the jungle. They chased wasps with a fly swatter, and used straws dipped in syrup to extract fat wood-bees from the holes they bored into pillars and beams. They handled sticks, pea-shooters, and pop-guns with equal facility, and before they were ten had been allowed to fire their father's small Flobert rifle. They were never without matches, empty gunpowder tins or spent cartridges. They roamed the quinine groves, shot at spiders in their lofty webs reaching from one tree to the next. By the age of seven Ru was able to hit a shooting target several times in a row, including reloading the gun properly after firing. At twelve years old the boys were allowed to take part in the clay pigeon event their father organised from time to time for the *boedjangs*. When their father came home with a panther he had shot, which happened fairly often, they scrutinised the beast at length, knowing its hide would be cured and then sent over to Holland as a gift for the family. Together with the dogs (they lost count of how many they had over the years, large and small, special breeds and mongrels alike) they went chasing after weasels and rats.

They kept a pet rooster, which was buried in a box when it died, and a hen they called Queenie and which they insisted had to be saluted with a curtsey or bow when encountered in the yard.

They went fishing in the lake downstream the Tjisondari with Martasan the gardener to keep an eye on them and show them how it was done. They went kiting with Sasatra, the chief *mandoer*, who taught them how to make their own kites with Chinese tissue paper pasted on a cross made of thin bamboo: the vertical rod being a man, the horizontal a woman. They listened with rapt attention to the stories of Moehiam, who had worked at Gamboeng longer than anyone else. He told them about the snakes on the islet within wading distance from the lakeside, and how he had killed one once with his bare hands before it could strike, which was something a child could never do, so they had better stay away from there. Besides, there was a huge kind of leech in the lake waiting for you to dangle your legs in the water – yet another danger the children should avoid when they went out on their raft.

They felt at home with the clerk and his wife. A regular treat for them was to sit on their heels among the charcoal burners in the kitchen being offered goodies that weren't to be found in Mama's sweet jars: *asam* cookies and coconut pudding, and especially sticks of sugar-cane to suck. The clerk had an endless reserve of Soendanese riddles, such as: What runs and stands still at the same time? Answer: the *pantjoeran*, the hollow bamboo water conduit. Or: Which mother goes naked while her children wear shirts? Answer: the shaft of bamboo with her green shoots.

They were devoted to Engko, who had carried them all in her *slendang* when they were small, and it was from her that they had learnt their first words of Soendanese, which they spoke before they knew any Dutch. They ran to Engko for help with their buttons and laces, or to be comforted after a fall, and she would always be the first to be shown the gifts that came out of parcels from overseas.

Engko slept on a mat in the room with the youngest children, and got up to light a candle for the others when they needed to go outside to the bamboo privy. They marvelled at her ability to extinguish her straw cigarette on her tongue. She knew all sorts of mysterious sayings, and could make pain vanish by the touch of her fingertips or by blowing on the place where it hurt.

They loved their mother with her soft, pale-grey eyes. She watched over everything indoors, taught them reading, writing and geography (arithmetic was taught by their father). Lessons took place in the schoolroom, which was really the guest room, and which had to be cleared when they had people staying. When she was teaching she wore a skirt and a white blouse with a bow at the collar; at such times she would wear a stern expression, meting out reprimands and punishments, and being an altogether different person. When Edu waved a fistful of pebbles saying, 'Whoever makes me do lessons today will get these pebbles in their face,' he was kept in for a fortnight after lessons to write lines.

Whenever their mother sat down at the piano they came running; they couldn't get enough of the familiar tunes, and at bedtime she played the piano until they fell asleep. They called her 'Little Mama', and 'Catty' when she lost her patience and spoke sharply to them and to the servants, even to Engko, who was quite slow and forgetful, although she had a heart of gold. But when they saw their mother sitting on the low bench in her bedroom, staring into space as if she were asleep with her eyes open, the children kept their distance.

They worshipped their father. He was the strongest, cleverest man on earth. With his rifle Si Matjan, 'The Tiger', he made short work of the most perilous of predators. He knew how to make machines and tools, and how to repair things that were broken. He knew the answer to everything. People came from miles around to consult him when they were ill, seeking medicines and treatment. Ru and Edu were present when he helped a man whose hand had got caught in the circular saw; everyone thought the man would bleed to death, but a few weeks later he was back at work. If there was an outbreak of fever, all the people had to take quinine under their father's eagle eye, because if he gave it to them to take home, it would only be thrown away due to the bitter taste.

The children's trust in him was boundless, whether it was a splinter or thorn that had to be removed from their feet or a particle of grit from their eyes. Loose milk molars were gently drawn using his finest pliers, and later on, when their teeth were permanent, there were times when he extracted molars that were causing pain, but only if daubing with cotton wool soaked in chloroform did not help and the annual visit to the dentist in Batavia was far away. If the first attempt had failed, their father's steady gaze and the touch of his warm hands was enough to make them go back to him of their own accord, holding their bleeding mouths wide open for him to try again.

He was strict with them, too, and would not tolerate any sign of unfairness among them, or of cowardice, deception and disobedience. One day, when they tormented a *baboe* who was *latah* and consequently aping every gesture she saw around her (to the point of dropping whatever she was holding, be it a tea cup or a pail of water), they received the worst beating they had ever had.

From 1887 they came into regular contact with people outside the family: not only employees of their father's but also a string of 'Misses' who came to help their mother with the teaching. Some stayed for such a short time that the memory of them soon faded. Others made an unforgettable impression: the dim-witted assistant who never remembered to tether his horse so that he was obliged to go everywhere on foot; the man who was dismissed for drunkenness, but not before he had taught them a dirty rhyme; the German who spoke with a hilariously funny accent; the Miss whose favourite expression was 'shoddy work', which provoked gales of laughter every time, and the cheerful lady who taught them English and who plunged into the swimming hole wearing a frilly bathing costume.

There were mysteries, too, such as the abrupt dismissal of the employee who was jeered at by the field hands for making eyes at the tea pickers. They had to make themselves scarce when they saw the employee's walking stick propped against a bush with his sun-hat on top; the workman who told them this had made a gesture which Ru and Edu knew to be obscene but little else, and which they did not dare ask their parents to explain. Equally mysterious were the snatches of conversation they overheard, and the leaden atmosphere that sometimes pervaded the house, which was especially tiresome when the rain kept them indoors for days on end. As they grew older they minded less about the rain; it became part of their lives, and they thought nothing of hanging their clothes to dry by the charcoal fire in the kitchen when they came home at suppertime.

They were happiest at home, in the familiar setting of Gamboeng. On the rare occasions that they went to stay with another family, either in Bandoeng or at one of the neighbouring plantations, they ended up with indigestion or a severe chill. Even at their Uncle August's at Ardjasari, where they liked going chiefly on account of Kees, the tame monkey, it would only be a few days before they started pining for their own back yard with trees to climb and a water hole to plunge into, and for Engko, and for the rasamalas, which were bigger and leafier at Gamboeng than anywhere else, and which had names: Si Toembak, Si Sroetoet, Si Pièn, Si Bangboem, Si Sentèg, and, the tallest of them all, Si Doekoen, the Wizard.

To Ru the trees were giant friends. One day, all alone in the yard, he was talking to Si Doekoen while pressing his forehead to the trunk, when he suddenly noticed his father standing behind him. He was not so much startled as shy. But he saw at once that his father didn't mind him talking to a 'mala'.

'They're the best trees in the whole world.'

'I totally agree. That is why we have to protect them. They are all being chopped down on account of their fine, hard wood. That means they will die out unless they are replaced by new ones.'

'Doesn't that happen, then? How stupid!'

'Well, it does happen, but not in the right way. Those forestry commission chaps take mala saplings from the jungle and plant them out in nursery beds. That doesn't work, because the roots can't tolerate being out of the earth for so long. Thanks to my experience with quinine, I think I know how to go about growing new malas. Come with me, I want to show you something.'

They went to the office, where his father took a small box from the cupboard. It contained a round, slightly scaly berry.

'You know what this is, don't you?'

'A mala berry. I've seen them through the field glasses, high up in the trees.'

His father sliced the berry in half with his knife. 'Look, the inside is divided into four compartments. Now let's take one and open it . . .'

'Seeds,' cried Ru, pointing to the pale, minuscule grains.

'That's what I thought, too. But I never succeeded in getting them to germinate. Now look through the magnifying glass. Can you see those flakes, thinner than the thinnest tissue paper, among the grains? Here, I'll pick one up with my tweezers. It's thicker in the middle. *That*'s the mala seed.'

'How can anything that tiny turn into such a huge tree?' Ru wet his fingertip with his tongue and picked up the flake.

'Let's go and look at my quinine seedlings. I have raised a rasamala bed there too. Some of them are nearly a metre high. I shall soon be planting them out in the yard.'

'You know everything, just everything, don't you, Father?'

*

Edu, too, held private conversations, but not with rasamalas, and he did not like being disturbed. As soon as he noticed someone was watching, he fell silent and ran off. One time he was so engrossed in his game he did not hear his father come up behind him.

'What are you doing? Who are you talking to?'

Edu did not want to reply, but his father persisted.

'To my *mentjèks*,' Edu said gruffly.

'Really? Do you keep deer?'

'Dozens. A hundred, maybe.'

'So where are they?'

'They only come when I call them. They do everything I say.'

'Such as?'

'They pick apples from the trees.'

'Apples? But you know perfectly well apples don't grow here.'

After that Edu clammed up, because he could sense his father's displeasure. He didn't dare to say anything about seeing ghosts, or about other scary things that had happened; he didn't even dare to confide in Ru. He did tell Engko, though; she understood, and so did the kampong boys he sought out from time to time, despite being forbidden to do so by his mother. They had even creepier stories to tell, which was why he was so afraid of the dark.

One day, when Emile was playing with some puppies in the space beneath the house, he saw a scorpion emerging from an old flower-pot with its tail poised for attack. His immediate reaction was to bundle the pups into an empty crate before running for help. That he should be so afraid of thunderstorms, when he was such a brave child, puzzled his father. At the least sign of lightning or distant thunder he would crouch under the table on the front veranda, or lie down on the bunk in the office with a rug pulled over his head.

The storm over, he would race around the house like a maniac, or demonstrate how long he could stand on his head.

Their life was filled with experiences no city child would ever know. When they visited Bandoeng or Batavia they would kick their shoes off whenever they could, and didn't mind when people gave them strange looks. At home in Gamboeng the children, including little Bertha, were only obliged to wear prickly 'Dutch' clothes when they had visitors. They went into the jungle with their father, where they once encountered a whole herd of wild boar, which their father sent dashing in all directions simply by imitating the growl of panther. On one occasion, while they were playing a game that entailed tugging at the veranda posts with all their might, an earthquake made itself felt and the whole house rattled and shook. On another, they saw the entire landscape become thickly carpeted with grey ash after the Galoenggoeng volcano erupted, and they saw the same landscape turn white during a hailstorm. They knew how to pick tea and how to graft quinine; they were allowed to help peel the bark. They could take their daily bath outside in the rain if they wanted, stark naked on the lawn, or stand under the torrent of water spouting from the roof-gutter on the east side of the house. At twelve years of age each boy was presented with his own single-barrelled Paderborn shotgun. Their father had killed dozens of panthers, and even a royal tiger once, a huge striped beast, which, when stiff, had been set upright and tied to a post in the sorting hangar by Martasan and Artaredja, their father's huntsmen, just to scare the wits out of the sorters when they came to work the following day. After that, every time Ru and Edu rode through Tjikalong with their father, he would be hailed by the old crones on the *pasar* with: '*Djoeragan*! Going after tigers again?'

*

They had many uncles. There was jovial Uncle August at Ardjasari, who brought them wonderful Chinese fireworks, although they saw less of him since his marriage to the not-very-nice aunt who was the Bandoeng Resident's daughter, and there was Uncle Julius, whom they called Uncle Bandjar because he had worked on the railway there – he sent them parcels of sweets for St Nicholas' eve. There was Great-uncle Eduard, who figured prominently in conversations between his parents, although Ru was the only one who had been allowed to accompany his father to Sinagar, where he had ridden on a tame elephant. That was their famous uncle, who received visits from the great and the good, including a prince and an archbishop, and whose horses won prizes at all the races. Then there was Aunt Marie's husband, Uncle Udo de Haes, who lodged with them at Gamboeng for just a few days but whose ability to wiggle his ear like a hare made a lasting impression, and Uncle Frits, their mother's brother, who moved in with them at Gamboeng to help in the factory, but who suddenly left because, their father said, he was 'cracked', and took to locking himself in his room for days. They had another uncle, who was really a second cousin, and whom they called Bisa – he was lame and walked with a stick, but his arms were incredibly strong, even stronger than their father's. All these uncles they saw little of, as opposed to the man they called 'Uncle' although he was no relation: Mr van Honk, who often came over from Rioeng Goenoeng to discuss quinine or roadworks with their father. The whole family visited him at home sometimes, where his wife plied them with delicious *kwee-kwee* sweets. Mrs van Honk only spoke Malay, which they had some difficulty understanding.

Their childhood at Gamboeng fell into three distinct stages. The first was defined by Ru's and Edu's experiences (Emile was allowed to join in, provided he obeyed his elder brothers). Then there was the brief stage during which Emile took the lead over Karel and Bertha, when the eldest were at school in Holland (Emile had heard them ride off with their parents at the crack of dawn amid cries of 'Godspeed' from the country folk, but Karel and Bertha had slept through it all). The three youngsters sadly missed their mother at first, but were soon absorbed in their games once more, and were much taken by the new Miss, a tiny, cheerful woman. The last stage began with Emile's departure, which left only Karel and Bertha, who were so close in age as to behave almost like twins: they were inseparable, they liked the same games, they spun their tops on the hard factory floor when the *tampirs* were put outside, or played *bèngkat*, a kind of skittles using stones or fruits. Their play was not as wild as when all the brothers were still together, in the days when they staged battles between the English and the Boers, or re-enacted the siege of a fortress in Atjeh, or launched attacks on the big aubergines in the vegetable garden, which then had to be operated on in the field hospital. On the other hand, Karel and Bertha were the only ones to witness memorable events such as the installation of the telephone (dear old Engko couldn't comprehend how voices could be transmitted through a tube that wasn't hollow), and in 1899 the construction of the new, much larger family home just behind the old one. Their parents had taken them to Holland two years previously to see their brothers, but the time they spent there became lodged in their memories as an unpleasant experience, due to their parents' sombre mood, the mysterious goings-on in the family, the half-understood allusions to things that went over their heads. And when they returned to Gamboeng after eight months' absence, the plantation had turned into a wilderness and half the workers had left the kampong.

RUDOLF TO HIS MOTHER, SEPTEMBER 1894

. . . I must tell you about my plan, which I have mentioned to you before, and which will naturally involve Van Santen, namely to acquire ownership, preferably by purchase, of the remaining quarter-share of Gamboeng that is currently still held as part of the undistributed assets.

I realise full well that it will mean having to work much longer to pay off my debts, which is no small matter given the circumstances of age and health and so on. But it is something I hold very dear. Just as Father wished to become the sole owner of Ardjasari, so it is now my aim to become sole owner (in so far as this is possible) of Gamboeng.

I sincerely hope you will take a favourable view of my plan, and that you will lend me your support. I would be very grateful for that. I shall write to Julius and ask him the same.

RUDOLF TO HIS BROTHER JULIUS, 9 JANUARY 1895

. . . The government is trying desperately to find ways of curbing the overproduction of quinine in Java. With such huge quantities of bark, the prices will remain low for another ten years at least. This is what I have foreseen, as everyone knows, but it has no relation to my wish to take over the remaining quarter-share in Gamboeng.

I suppose Henny's provisional estimate of the value of that share at 100,000 guilders has been adjusted accordingly. I would rather not comment on that until I know what you have in mind.

I cannot help pointing out that all of you have referred to this matter in your letters – Mama, you, and Henny – and yet none of you has ever mentioned a specific sum.

RUDOLF TO VAN SANTEN, 10 JANUARY 1895

. . . I am still awaiting further news regarding the transfer of one quarter-share in Gamboeng. Henny's report on the valuation is presumably with August at present. I am very eager to see it.

RUDOLF TO VAN SANTEN, 15 JANUARY 1895

. . . I am unable to give you a definite answer as to the transfer of one quarter-share in Gamboeng, because August is still holding on to that report of Henny's. Until I have read it I would rather abstain from all comment, in case I seem to be drawing the wrong conclusions.

RUDOLF TO HIS MOTHER, 23 JANUARY 1895

Dear Mama, I am afraid that I cannot accept the proposal the executors have made to me with regard to the sale of one quarter-share in Gamboeng, because it is simply too much money. I sincerely hope that my salary will be adjusted according to the extremely high estimate of that quarter-share in Gamboeng – almost 100,000 guilders! It is also my wish that Jenny should be entitled to a widow's pension. She has done just as much as I have to make Gamboeng what it is today. With the undivided assets benefiting from an immediate added value to the tune of 100,000 guilders, it is only fair that I should receive some form of compensation, don't you think?

RUDOLF TO HIS BROTHER JULIUS, 24 JANUARY 1895

. . . The mistake at the bottom of all this is that the valuation was made on the basis of Gamboeng's most profitable year to date, i.e. that of 1891. No wonder the final estimate is inflated. Nor do any of you take into account that prices on the quinine market are falling. Your estimate (described as 'moderate' by you and the others) is so at odds with mine that I will say no more. It is obvious that we will never agree. I have abandoned my illusion. But I do think the person responsible for adding to the undivided assets the 'moderate' sum of 100,000 guilders deserves better pay, the more so because no one else has lifted a finger for Gamboeng. I also believe Jenny ought to be assured of a widow's pension, should I break my neck or fall ill and be unable to work. I have already notified Van Santen and Henny of this, so I expect the matter will be discussed between you at some point. I hope you will back me up.

RUDOLF TO HIS SISTER CATEAU, 9 FEBRUARY 1895

. . . I cannot be as outspoken in my letters to Mama as I am to you, because I will probably end up drawing a comparison between me and August, which would put Mama in an awkward position. But I dare say you understand that I often wonder why he should be privileged. As it is, he enjoys all sorts of advantages at Ardjasari which I do not have, while I have been working much harder and longer than him, not to mention the fact that the value of Gamboeng is now considered to exceed that of Ardjasari. Lying before me is August's letter telling me of his ratification of the estimated value.

RUDOLF TO HIS MOTHER, 27 APRIL 1895

. . . Aside from the news that both Van Santen and you have conceded my request for a salary increase, I have heard nothing. If Father were still alive, I would have had my way by now, because he actually offered me the possibility himself, and things were not looking nearly as good then as now. I declined the offer at the time out of consideration for the others. If Henny breathes a word about favouritism in connection with the raise in my salary, I hope you will tell him that I have never received preferential treatment. Everything I own is the fruit of my own labours. Van Santen has been generously repaid for his sponsorship by the interest he receives and the increased value of his share in Gamboeng. By keeping a tight rein on our purse, and by forgoing almost every form of entertainment or luxury, Jenny and I have actually managed to save some money, which few people with an income of 500 guilders a month can claim. Not until the last few years have I been getting a decent share in the profits.

RUDOLF TO HIS BROTHER-IN-LAW J. E. HENNY, MAY 1895

. . . Your words of appreciation regarding loyalty, commitment, honesty, great satisfaction, diligence, good work, high honours, flourishing trade, and so on and so forth, are certainly gratifying, but it seems to me that they should be accompanied by some tangible proof of their sincerity, if they are to mean anything more to me than the sweetening of the proverbial bitter pill. Because it is indeed a bitter pill that you have given me to swallow, and here I am, oppressed by a feeling of injustice, which hampers me in my work.

Throughout the period when Gamboeng was not faring particularly well I did not complain, and contented myself with a salary that was lower, significantly lower, than that of any of my peers.

In later years I accepted a share in the profits, but my expenses had risen considerably in the interim, and even today the situation is such that my salary is simply insufficient. For all our parsimony, and for all your willingness to look after Ru and Edu free of charge, we are still unable to live on 500 guilders a month.

If only you had granted my wish for a decent widow's pension for Jenny, I would feel less constrained, freer to go my own way. But even that is asking too much, it seems. So we have no choice but to continue living as modestly as before, so that I will at least be able to leave something to provide for Jenny and for the children's education.

The only person who might have any reason to oppose an increase in my salary is Van Santen, because of my outstanding debt to him. And yet Van Santen considers my request to be reasonable, to the extent that he is in favour of raising my salary by 200 guilders a month, as of 1 January 1895. That any of the other parties concerned – Mama, Julius, or August – should have any objection to that is something I find impossible to believe. In other words, your opposition, as a minority vested with the power of veto, will be costing me 2,400 guilders a year. Has that ever crossed your mind?

I still maintain that there is not a single manager of a 'thriving plantation' whose salary is as meagre as mine – after twenty years of hard work. Father started out with 420 guilders. Sinagar and Parakan Salak pay a good salary as well. And do you really think their revenues are so much better than Gamboeng's? Then you are wrong! August started out earning 470 guilders, and then 500, plus 10 per cent of the profits, plus perks, and other people have more than I do either in salary, or in perks, and moreover they get a share of the profits.

I can assure you that I have never, even when things could not have been worse at Gamboeng, felt so little enthusiasm for my daily work and so much desire to have done with it all, as I feel now, since receiving your letter.

JENNY TO HER MOTHER-IN-LAW, JUNE 1895

. . . It is very sweet of you to compliment me on the good behaviour of our Ru and Edu. They are by nature kind-hearted, that is the main thing, and for the rest they have had their father's example to follow.

My contribution has been the physical sacrifice, and the privations I have had to endure. All that has taken its toll on my health, and I feel tired, very tired.

To know that all those years of hardship have been to no purpose makes me bitter and sad. A great deal more has been demanded of me than of other women in my position, and what did I gain? Years went by with literally nothing in the way of ease and comfort for me; I was unwell, and had to summon the last of my energy to look after the family, and all that time there was not a single thing I had just for myself, except the bed I slept in – which is rather shocking, given the size and importance of Gamboeng.

If only I could believe in heaven as my reward, I would at least be able to dream of a prettily furnished boudoir. But I don't believe in that, more's the pity. So much for the good Lord's beneficence . . .

Oh, I wish I had not started on the subject of this palatial residence (!) of ours, in which I made all those needless sacrifices. Those lost years will never return.

RUDOLF TO HIS MOTHER, SEPTEMBER 1895

. . . I was not aware that Jenny had written you such a despondent letter. But she is right. We are both saddened by the want of appreciation and consideration for my – no, for *our* work.

A new house. Yes, we could certainly do with more space, but what about furnishings? What we own is practically nothing.

A trip to Holland? Yes, that is an old dream of ours, but it would make a huge dent in the small sum we have scraped together as a nest-egg for Jenny and the children after my death.

In the event of my falling ill, which is a permanent worry of mine, the heirs to Father's estate will have the satisfaction of seeing me 'go under', and of having me beg them for money on behalf of my wife and children.

RUDOLF TO HIS BROTHER JULIUS, JANUARY 1896

. . . I am left with Henny's *parti pris*. None of you can do anything to change it, I gather. And my hands are tied by the fact that Ru and Edu are living in his house, not to mention that Cateau is my sister.

I do not doubt Mama's and your good intentions, but you are mistaken in your view of the affair, and I seem to be incapable of convincing you of the injustice that is being done to me. It is kind of you to offer me the consolation of paying for half my travelling expenses for a furlough in Holland. When August went on furlough it was at the expense of Ardjasari.

You all seem to be in favour of my coming to Holland, and, by the same token, to think Jenny and the children should go and stay somewhere in Bandoeng for the duration. Do you really believe that going on furlough under those conditions would have a calming effect on my frayed nerves?

And have you forgotten that time when you asked stingy old Henny if he could spare you another glass of wine in exchange for ten cents?

RUDOLF TO HIS SISTER CATEAU, 24 JUNE 1896

. . . I have reached the end of my tether. I am sure you must have seen this coming for ages: you know I am not the kind of man to go on forever accepting favours from someone who does not care for me. I waited a full year; I still hoped that Henny would see sense eventually – but it has all come to nothing. I do not want to risk incurring the contempt of my boys by allowing them to profit from someone who makes it clear (through you and other people) that he is against me, without even bothering to tell me why, let alone to reply to my letters.

I have had enough. I have asked Julius to find another home for Ru and Edu.

All this is so depressing that I feel little inclination to write about other things. I cannot believe that you hold me in the same low esteem as Henny appears to do, for whatever reason that may be, but it is only natural that you should side with your husband, which leaves me wondering what will become of the bond of friendship you and I have shared since we were children.

The sudden demise of Van Santen in January 1896 marked a critical turning point in Rudolf's life. From the moment Henny had taken against him, the only one who had shown confidence in his worth had been his sister Bertha's husband. In his capacity as director of the Nederlands Indies Trading Bank in Amsterdam, Van Santen had even offered to act as intermediary for a new loan, should Rudolf wish to lease further lands with a view to establishing a new plantation to secure the future of his sons.

In his bitter bewilderment with regard to Henny's animosity, his mother's bias towards August, and the failure of his brothers and sisters to side with him, Rudolf had taken a momentous decision. On the high plateau of Pengalengan, south-west of the Malabar mountain ridge, there were several tracts of land available, totalling over 1,100 *bouw*, mostly given over to jungle and wilderness but with the right kind of soil for planting tea. With quinine proving to be far less profitable than the planters in the region had anticipated and the English tea trade being hampered by the war against the Boers in South Africa, Uncle Eduard was sure that the Assam tea grown in Java would soon be 'the rage'. There were several plantations – including Hoogeveen's Soekawana! – already making the switch back to tea. Rudolf did not wish to give up his extensive qinine plantings at Gamboeng. A new enterprise, with all the land already cleared and planted before the rest, would be a huge gain. Moreover, this would not be the first time he took a risk, and the odds were more in his favour than before.

His Uncle Bosscha, the professor, had two grown-up sons already working in the Indies. Rudolf thought it would be a good idea to appoint the youngest, 'lame Rudolf', who had been so warmly recommended to him by Karel Holle, as manager of the enterprise until such time as his own Ru could assume full responsibility. That would not be for another ten years at least.

Van Santen's death, so soon after Rudolf had laid claim to the five tracts of land making up the Malabar estate, threatened to scupper his financial arrangements. Without Van Santen's backing, the terms which the Batavian Netherlands Indies Trading Bank saw fit to propose were unacceptable to Rudolf. Under no circumstances did he wish to abandon his plans. With the aid of other investors he founded a joint-stock company, and sent out a prospectus for the purpose of attracting potential investors.

He had thrown himself into these preparations with unshakeable resolve. He went to Bandoeng to parlay for the necessary licences, and to Batavia for financial negotiations. As his plan advanced, with an encouraging take-up of the Malabar share issue, he felt a growing sense of triumph, although he realised that he was driven by the desire to show his relatives that he could do without the kind of income they granted him, as if it were a gratuity to an underling. Henceforward he would use his natural thriftiness, and what even Henny had to admit was his 'talent for reckoning', to achieve an aim which he had previously not regarded as the be-all and end-all of existence: to get rich! To provide Jenny and the children with such wealth as to throw that of the Dutch fusspots in the shade.

RUDOLF TO HIS MOTHER, AUGUST 1896

K.A.R. (Ru) Bosscha is to be the manager of Malabar, and I will have a supervisory role. I will be the owner of one-quarter of the enterprise. Land clearance will probably begin in the near future. It takes under three hours on horseback to reach Malabar from Gamboeng.

The telephone has been an enormous help in this affair. Praise be the day when the thin cord linked us up with 'the world at large'!

Malabar, as well as my good quinine prices, appears to have made me enemies, even among my own kinsfolk. Regrettable, but it cannot be helped.

August Kerkhoven's annual report for the year 1895 contained the following statement: 'I flatter myself that Ardjasari will boast, in addition to prime gardens, one of the best, if not *the* best, tea factory in Java.'

He proposed reserving 10 per cent of the year's revenue at Ardjasari for a fund destined for the construction of a model factory. Rudolf's reaction was to claim his right of veto in the matter (why should August be favoured yet again at the expense of himself and the other heirs?). August took this as a deliberate act of revenge.

RUDOLF TO HIS BROTHER JULIUS, DECEMBER 1896

. . . Malabar is proceeding well. Of the 400 shares issued, 380 have already been taken up, and there is a steadily increasing interest in the remainder. I have very high hopes. Now that the forests are being felled, we will probably be selling the sawn timber wholesale.

August greatly resents the fact that I was not in favour of

his model factory costing 100,000 guilders. Although all the others, including yourself, went along with me on that score, it is I who gets the blame, as usual. This new unpleasantness could have been avoided had you given less prominence to my name in the family's rejection of August's proposal.

MR JOAN E. HENNY TO RUDOF KERKHOVEN, FEBRUARY 1897

For the past year and three-quarters I have not written to you. It was for the sake of your boys, Ru and Edu, during the three and a half years that they were with us. Had I written, I would have had to tell you bluntly what I thought of your attitude, in which case you would have felt morally obliged to find another home for your boys as paying guests. I wished to put off that moment for as long as possible, in the belief that they were better off with us, being treated with far more affection and care than they would ever get from strangers, and I did not think it fair that they should suffer the consequences of your behaviour, or rather, of a new and entirely unexpected side of your character. So I kept silent. Unfortunately, my silence only served as further provocation, as often happens when a man's conscience is not completely clear. My wife, Cateau, pleaded with me not to aggravate our differences. Now that you have decided to send Ru and Edu to live with strangers, the main cause of my silence no longer applies. Personally I would have been only too happy for them to remain with us, but it is not in my hands. In view of your impending trip to Europe, I will now clarify to you my reasons for not replying to your letters.

In 1894 you stated your wish to purchase the quarter-share in Gamboeng which forms part of your late father's estate. I discussed your intention with Mama, Cateau, Van Santen and Julius. We all thought it reasonable, and were inclined to give you our support. Purely for the purpose of expediency, I made a provisional estimate (which has since been shown to be too low rather than too high, given the market forecasts for the produce of Gamboeng).

However, you considered my estimate too high. In addition, it transpired that you wished to become the owner of that quarter-share in Gamboeng not at a reasonable price, but at a very cheap price. You did not take the trouble to explain why you considered my estimate too high. Then came your request for your manager's salary to be increased, in addition to the assurance of a widow's pension for your wife, which you motivated by drawing the most far-fetched comparisons with your brother August's situation at Ardjasari. You make mountains out of molehills!

Given that you already own half of Gamboeng, it seems to me that you are among the best paid managers of comparable plantations. When I wrote to you saying: never mind about Ardjasari, just go ahead and build yourself a bigger and better house, you replied that you had desisted from the idea because you did not have the money to furnish a new home. When you complained about August being allowed to go on a short furlough to Europe while he was still single (whereas you yourself never asked to go on furlough before you were married), I immediately advised you to take a year's furlough as soon as possible, and likewise that I was minded to propose to the executors that your travel expenses be reimbursed in addition to the expenses incurred by your absence from Gamboeng. Your answer was that a trip to Europe was beyond your means.

You resent the fact that I could not take seriously your wish to acquire such a major portion of your father's assets for a risible sum of money, which would be to the disadvantage of your mother, your brothers and your sister. You resent the fact that I did not support you in your bid for an increase in your salary, which would, in all honesty, amount to your receiving an annuity in excess of those of your mother, your brothers and sister, and your sister Bertha's children. You also resent my continued support of my brother-in-law Van Dusseldorp, the trader, who oversaw the sale of Gamboeng's quinine bark at the Amsterdam auction year after year, to your full satisfaction, until one day you were disappointed by the price and so went behind his back to have your bark traded by another firm under a different name.

I have not taken your part in these matters, and that makes you angry. You feel hard done by. Stamping your feet like a spoilt child is not going to help.

In a recent letter to Cateau you stated that you preferred not to give Ru and Edu the full reasons for their removal from our home. Cateau and I agree. Ru and Edu have not heard a single word said against you in our home. Nor have they asked for an explanation for their departure.

We have grown fond of your boys, and have tried to shield them from the consequences of your unreasonable behaviour and the tone of your letters. Our hearts and home will always be open to them. They can come to see us whenever they like, so that we may at least offer them a day's conviviality from time to time.

As to your reproach against Julius, about him being manipulated into acting as my spokesman vis-à-vis yourself – all I can say is that Julius will be writing to you himself on this matter.

*

(Rudolf filled the margins of this scrawled letter with pencilled notes: 'Wrong!' 'Perfidy!' 'The opposite is true!' 'Lies!')

RUDOLF TO HIS UNCLE EDUARD KERKHOVEN

. . . Julius has, out of weakness, repeatedly gone along with Henny's attacks on me. Henny is therefore bound to think Julius agrees with him.

Julius has now written to me saying that he does not agree with Henny, but Henny does not know this. I want Julius to make it clear to Henny once and for all that he is on my side, not his. I think it is wrong of him not to disabuse Henny in this matter. It is not fair towards me.

Julius will not comply with my request. Hence the tension between us.

EDUARD KERKHOVEN TO HIS NEPHEW RUDOLF

. . . I am sorry to hear that relations between you and Julius are strained, seeing as he is really too good-natured a chap to fall out with. But I can see your point. He is very much under the sway of Henny, who has a natural preponderance over someone as gentle as your brother Julius.

He mentioned in a letter to me that the reason he has not been in touch with you is your insistence that he take sides between you and Henny, and he does not wish to be told what to do by anyone, not by you, either.

Actually, he did not speak ill of you at all, except to say that you had expressed yourself in unnecessarily harsh terms.

Rudolf interpreted Julius' refusal to declare his support not so much as a mark of his independence, but rather as a gesture of spite in connection with an entirely different issue. Some years previously, Julius had taken an orphan child under his wing, out of the goodness of his heart, as usual. She was the daughter of a European soldier and a native woman, and he wished to give Truitje a good education, and seriously considered adopting her as his own.

Rudolf had pointed out the problems that might arise from such an arrangement, to which Julius had responded by accusing him of being prejudiced and cold-hearted: 'You have no idea how harsh you lot are! You dare to refer to the natives as "monkeys", even if it is only in jest. You believe that people of mixed race are inferior. I remember hearing Jenny say "thank goodness!" when young Ru's *baboe* had a child that died soon after birth – it saved both her and the *baboe* a lot of bother! And are you sure you are not against my adopting Truitje just because you are afraid of what it might do to OUR INHERITANCE? No point in expecting that poor, dark-skinned little girl ever to be welcomed as a member of the FAMILY, is there?'

When Karel was sent to secondary school in Batavia in 1900, only returning to Gamboeng for the holidays, Bertha's world shrank to the confines of the family home and immediate surroundings. They had a new house, handsome and spacious, where she had her own room filled with the 'girls' toys' she had barely touched when her older brothers were still at home. Henceforth she had to wear dresses and proper shoes, and was taught on her own in the schoolroom either by her mother or, more often, by a governess. There was a succession of governesses, none of whom stayed longer than three or four months, and their departure tended to be sudden. Her mother never seemed to be satisfied with them: one was too slow-witted, the other too lazy, and a third couldn't teach, and the rest were found to be too coquettish, too forward, or simply not good company.

A particularly fearful memory of Bertha's childhood was associated with one of those governesses, Miss Nora Verwey, who had studied music in Zurich and played the piano even better than Jenny. She had only been at Gamboeng for a few weeks when she fell seriously ill. Bertha had listened at her door, quaking with fright, and had heard her cry out in pain. The doctor was summoned from Bandoeng, but could do little; she was said to be suffering from an intestinal infection. One morning Miss Nora was dead. Bertha was told to keep to her room, but through a crack in the window-blind she had seen the factory carpenters bringing a coffin to the house, and, after a while, that same coffin being carried up the alley with the tree ferns, with her father following behind. Later that day she had been allowed to lay flowers on a patch of freshly turned earth, beside the small grave of the baby sister who had died before they could name her Bertha.

Without her brothers, life didn't seem worth living. Why wasn't she a boy? Only boys counted at Gamboeng. Her father laughed at her when she asked to go hunting with him: 'No, Kitten, far too dangerous!' But surely she could learn to shoot? She had so often shouldered Si Soempitan or Si Matjan – unloaded, of course! – in the old days. She was still permitted to ride, but only when accompanied by her father and no longer astride the horse, as she did when she was small, but side-saddle.

After the midday meal she kicked off her shoes, climbed up a tree in the yard and settled herself on a branch to read a book. At teatime she was a young lady again, poring over her embroidery. She liked sitting with Engko, who was getting on in years and who, without small children to look after, was generally to be found on the back veranda, happy to receive Bertha's offerings of goodies or tobacco from the storeroom.

When Karel 'came up' for the holidays, they discovered they had outgrown the games they used to play together. The brand-new tennis court in full view of the house had not been laid out for her sake, but as a gift from her father to her mother, who had expressed a wish to practise that modern sport (she had seen pictures of ladies playing tennis in ankle-length skirts in *The Ladies Home Journal*). Once the grass had the required thickness and the net was put up, tennis was played every day – by Bertha and her mother and the Miss of the moment, by Karel when he was there, by visitors and by the employee. Her father did not care for tennis. He had enough physical exercise as it was, he said.

PORTRAIT OF A FAMILY REUNION, 1901

The time is midsummer, the place a back garden in the Dutch provincial town of Apeldoorn, where Jenny's mother is living with her sons Herman and Frits. Luncheon has been copious, and now the guests are standing in formation with Mama Roosegaarde at the centre, against a backdrop of tall shrubbery. Still as dainty as a porcelain doll, wearing a flowered hat on her snowy hair, she smiles sweetly at the photographer. This group portrait commemorates an exceptional family reunion of the Roosegaardes and the Kerkhovens of Gamboeng, who are on furlough in Europe to visit their three sons.

The Kerkhovens are ranged behind Mama Roosegaarde: seventeen-year-old Emile, looking self-important in his high collar and tie; thirteen-year-old Bertha, all in white; Rudolf senior, bearded and moustached in long-outmoded fashion; nineteen-year-old Edu; Jenny, elegantly dressed (her hat was purchased in Paris); Rudolf junior, a young man of twenty-two. Missing from the picture is Karel, who has had to stay behind for his annual exams at school in Batavia.

To the right of Emile stands Frits Roosegaarde, looking just as unsure of himself as during his ill-fated stay at Gamboeng ten years before. Beside Ru stands Jenny's youngest brother, Constant, an idler and a dandy; on the other side is Gus Roosegaarde (tall, thin, and withdrawn, he has come over from South Africa where he runs a business), and in front of him, a little to the side, his English wife and one of their children.

The chairs on either side of Mama are occupied by: Marie's husband Udo de Haes, retired planter in Deli; Marie herself, a stout, matronly figure (no trace of her former beauty on her chubby cheeks); a brother and a cousin of Mama Roosegaarde's, and her two unmarried sisters. On the grass, at the feet of the adults, sit four children: three belonging to Marie, and one to August.

Absent from the picture are five of the Roosegaardes: Herman (severely disturbed, leading a shuttered existence in his mother's house); Rose (who has broken with her family); Philip (working in Hong Kong as chief agent of the Java–China–Japan shipping line); Willem (practising law in London); and finally, Henri (who is behind the camera).

Jenny looks happy and proud, linking arms with Ru on one side and holding hands with Edu on the other. She enjoys being in Europe, and would love to stay on. When she escorted her two eldest to Holland, back in 1893, she took them to Paris and Brussels, to the Rijksmuseum in Amsterdam, the Sint Bavo cathedral in Haarlem, the castle at Muiden, to Delft and to The Hague, but the boys had been too young to relish these excursions, and that in turn had marred her own pleasure. She would love to do it all over again, at a leisurely pace.

To Rudolf, their furlough has lasted long enough. He was delighted to see his sons again, especially Ru, who should obtain his degree in electrotechnical engineering at the Zurich Polytechnic next year. Edu, with his learning difficulties, has long been a source of worry, but now that the lad is following a practical course in machine technology, with the prospect of undemanding but respectable employment at the end of it, he feels assuaged. Emile will be going to Zurich, of course. The expensive dark suit from Oger Frères feels stiff and uncomfortable; he longs for the time when he will be able to change into his twill trousers and calico jacket, clap his old straw hat on his head (the modern 'sun-helmet' is not his style) and go out into his groves and gardens. This time, when he returns to Gamboeng, he will not find the plantation neglected and overgrown, as after his previous furlough in 1897: he now has a reliable assistant to replace him.

The way he poses here, surrounded by Jenny's kinsfolk, is not feasible with his own relatives. His mother has been dead these past six months; the opportunity to make up for the impersonal, conventional tone of his letters with a heartfelt tête-à-tête is lost for ever. His refusal to meet Henny has also caused him to become distanced from Cateau. Fleeting encounters with Julius have made him realise that they have little in common: his younger brother is married to a 'scholar' (a doctor of science and mathematics!), he belongs to a circle of intellectuals with highly advanced ideas, he reads books by a Russian anarchist, Kropotkin, which he warmly recommends to Rudolf. But *Memoirs of a Revolutionist* and *The Conquest of Bread* hold little attraction for Rudolf: after a cursory perusal, the books are returned to their owner with the comment: 'It all strikes me as rather tendentious and one-sided.'

The only kinsman in Holland who is congenial to him is his elderly Uncle Bosscha, emeritus professor of science, whose sons are now among the new generation of planters in the Indies. Rudolf Bosscha, commonly known by his initials, K.A.R., has been the manager of Malabar for some years now, with considerable success. Rudolf's own function remains supervisory. Kar has promised to hand over his job to young Ru in due course, as agreed at the outset. Kar's older brother Jan, until recently working in

Borneo, has also been found a position, notably as manager of the Tahoen tea plantation newly leased by Rudolf on the Pengalengan plateau, not far from Malabar and Gamboeng.

Life in Holland does not appeal to Rudolf: he finds the mentality utterly and incomprehensibly altered. The liberal and aristocratic world view typical of the men who set the tone when he was young seems to have vanished without trace. The social-democratic movement, voting rights for women, the new developments in the arts, none of these novelties strike a chord with him, and Jenny's eagerness to acquaint herself with the wider world is putting a strain on their relationship. Fortunately their sons have a soothing influence, especially Ru, who is markedly self-posessed and already a 'man of the world'.

The objections raised against him by his relatives are utterly absurd, in his opinion, and he holds Henny responsible for their antagonism. He has been accused of unfairness towards Julius and August, of trying to gain advantage over them by giving his parents misleading reports on their doings, of cheating his way to the top in the quinine trade and acquiring Malabar by underhand means, of trying to get everything on the cheap while taking the moral high ground, of pretending to be the benevolent patriarch at Gamboeng while exploiting his workers; in short, of being selfish, hypocritical and tight-fisted. They will have to drop the latter charge now, though, given the lavish style in which he is passing his furlough. With Gamboeng being fully solvent at last and the dividends amounting to a small fortune, he can afford to rent a smart country house near Apeldoorn and, moreover, to stay in Hotel de l'Europe with the whole family when visiting Amsterdam.

But the other accusations continue to rankle with him. Had there been the slightest grounds for them, it would be too much to bear; he would rather kill himself. Neither Henny and Cateau nor Julius and August seem to realise the devastating effect of such indictments on a man whose guiding principles have always been honesty and good faith. Most wounding of all was the remark made by Henny in one of his letters, which he cannot get out of his mind: 'Unfortunately, my silence only served as further provocation, as often happens when a man's conscience is not completely clear!'

It is a consolation to him that his sons have not been exposed to spiteful gossip in Europe. There is no danger of that happening in Zurich, where they have a fatherly friend in Professor Schröter, the botanist who visited Gamboeng on his field trip to Java and proceeded to publish scientific articles on Rudolf's quinine plantings, thereby making it known to all the world that the laurels won by 'Java's leading *Cinchona* planter' were well-deserved.

It will not be long now before he can resume his life with Jenny and Bertha in the world he has made his own: the world of Gamboeng, the Goenoeng Tiloe, the rasamalas.

FROM THE MEMOIRS OF CARMEN ERDBRINK-BOSSCHA, DAUGHTER OF J. BOSSCHA, MANAGER OF TALOEN

On 20 December my sister Connie and I paid our first visit to Gamboeng. Cousin Rudolf Kerkhoven had promised to send horses to meet us on the way. We started out (from Malabar, where we were lodging with Uncle Kar) on foot. Mama saw us off at the gate, and my father accompanied us for a good part of the way, first through the old government coffee gardens, which was like being in a wood, following narrow footpaths like long tunnels of green, sometimes with a splash of golden sunlight at the end. The ground was covered with moss, and there were thick clumps of maidenhair ferns, which grew like weeds in the area. After a while we reached a more open space and went down into a wide valley, past potato patches belonging to the country folk, where the flowering *ketjoeboeng* hedges filled the air with their intoxicating scent, then past the pretty little lake of Tjileunta until we reached the fork in the track leading to Rioeng Goenoeng. There we were met by the groom with the saddle-horses. Papa rode with us until we came upon Cousin Rudolf Kerkhoven sitting by a stream farther into the quinine groves. He was accompanied by his four chocolate-brown German hounds, each with a white tip to the tail.

My father took leave of us there and turned back, while we rode on with Cousin Rudolf through the old plantings of quinine, the decorative *succirubra* which has tall white stems and large leaves that turn crimson part of the year. The more recent plantings consisted primarily of the narrow-leaved *ledgeriana*, which is economically more advantageous but far less impressive as a tree, though the flowers of both species have a similar fragrance.

After crossing the pass of Rioeng Goenoeng we went down a very steep slope, on a track through the jungle that was so gouged out by the rain that the rocks underneath were laid bare, and we had to dismount for the safety of the horses. Once we arrived at the foot of the mountain we soon found ourselves in the grounds of Gamboeng. A grassy lane through a lovely stretch of parkland made of thinned-out jungle led up to the main house, which was situated on the slope of the Goenoeng Tiloe, with a fine view to the west.

Cousin Rudolf was in his fifties at the time, and rather striking in appearance. He was quite burly, not very tall; not stout, either, but strongly built. His beard had turned white, and on his bald head he wore a black cap, a Scottish model, with a dent in the middle and two short ribbons hanging down the back. Both my Uncle Eduard of Sinagar and my father used to wear the same kind of cap, which I do not recall being worn by anyone else.

The ambience at Gamboeng was quite special, decidedly conservative. The plantation was fairly isolated, and the population still kept to their old ways. My cousin epitomised the traditional lord and master. In the afternoon, when we were having tea on the spacious front veranda, two *mandoers* came to report on the day's work. Sitting on the steps, cross-legged, they waited to be addressed before intoning their responses with the requisite recitation of honorifics. Notwithstanding this formality, however, relations between the family and the locals were amicable.

Cousin Rudolf came out to the Indies as an adult, and although he had adapted himself very well, being fluent in Soendanese and also knowledgeable about the manners and customs of the population, there was still something of the old 'Dutch gent' about him. He was an impressive figure, upstanding and well-read, generous and dependable, but conventional in character. His word went, and his children accepted this in a way that other people sometimes found surprising, or even disturbing. He was a man of taste and good judgement in art, music and literature, provided they were not modern. He dismissed anything 'new-fangled' out of hand, which was when his notorious stubbornness came to the fore.

Cousin Jenny was also a cultured person, but she was far more open-minded than her husband. In fact, she was remarkably unprejudiced, and took things as they came, without feelings of resentment when things did not go quite as she had wished. She had a keen understanding of human nature, and displayed a remarkable soundness of judgement in many respects. Her only weakness was her nervous disposition, which worsened over the years, and which was not helped by the fact that her marriage was under strain. It had not always been thus: when she first arrived in the uplands as a young woman she had been happy with her husband, but later, as her personality matured, and especially after she took her two eldest boys to Holland without him in 1893, she found it increasingly difficult to assume the clinging-ivy sort of role, which, when it came down to it, was what Cousin Rudolf expected of a wife. He did share his plans with her, and she was fully informed about his business affairs, but his autocratic nature ruled out the possibility of anyone in the house venturing to disagree with his opinions. This became a source of mounting conflicts between them. His response was to clam up completely and proceed to do whatever he wanted, which only increased her resentment. It was a great shame, because they were both such wonderful people.

1903–4

In the meantime my father was very busy at Taloen. Before my mother and Connie and I went to live there, we paid another visit to Gamboeng. Cousin Rudolf and Jenny were celebrating the homecoming of their eldest son. Ru had completed his engineering studies in Zurich, and had toured the United States, Japan and China prior to his return.

RU KERKHOVEN TO HIS BROTHERS EDU AND EMILE,
6 FEBRUARY 1904

Mother has probably sent a postcard telling you of my return, but I expect you would like to hear about it in more detail, so I will try to give you a proper account of my '*Joyeuse Entrée*'.

On 25 January, at the crack of dawn, we steamed into the harbour of Tandjong Priok, and just as we reached the quay the first train arrived from Weltevreden, with Father, Mother and Bertha on board. Karel was not with them, because he did not want to miss school before taking a few days' holiday in Gamboeng with the rest of us.

The train journey to Bandoeng was still just the same, except that we arrived at noon instead of at three o'clock. Bandoeng has changed beyond recognition. While we were there I couldn't help noticing that something was being planned up the mountain, because there was a constant coming and going of messengers and delivery men, while Mother had interminable conversations on the telephone with Malabar, Taloen, Ardjasari and so on and so forth.

At last the Big Day arrived. Our own carriage took us first to Koppo, where a fresh team of horses was waiting for us, and then over the Tjisondari. There was nothing unusual to be seen until we struck left at the settlement, where we came upon crowds of natives in their best clothes making their way to Gamboeng. We were met at the assistant chief's house by an escort of village horsemen, who rode ahead of us and were joined by other horsemen along the way, so that by the time we reached the entrance to Gamboeng there was a long procession of us. The kampong folk had erected a splendid festive gateway, and there were bamboo arches decorated with young maize leaves along the road, all the way from where it rises from the Tji Enggang ravine up to the tea garden overlooked by the house.

I first laid eyes on the new *gedoeng* when we halted by the waringin tree in front of the clerk's dwelling. The lane was overflowing with people, but there was no jostling or shouting; it was all quite dignified, which was just as well, as it meant that we could hear the festive tones of the *gamelan* very clearly. It was most impressive. I will never forget how moved I was as our grand parade drew near to the big house – there stood the family home before me, even if it had replaced the old one, in its uniquely beautiful setting, with the crowd in celebratory mood on the forecourt, the music, the glorious weather – all those things together suddenly effaced the sadness I had felt at parting, eleven years ago, and filled me instead with a sense of gratitude that will remain with me for the rest of my life.

The moment I stepped out of the carriage, a little old woman rushed towards me and clung to me so tightly that I had difficulty climbing the steps to the front veranda. It was Engko; she was weeping with emotion and would not let me go, so I had to wait until she calmed down a little before I was able to greet anyone else. The *wedanas* of Bandaran and Tjisondari arrived after half an hour; then we were all given a tour of the house and immediate surroundings. There were flags and bunting everywhere, and directly in front of the entrance stood an imposing triumphal archway on four pillars, for which Mother had provided the design.

The new factory building was likewise decked out with greenery and bunting, and a stage had been set up for the wayang performance, as well as *gamelans* for the musical accompaniment. All this was for the popular celebration, which was to take place the following day.

We took a siesta in the afternoon, after which I renewed my acquaintance with several much-loved attributes of my boyhood, such as the old rifles called Soempitan and Matjan, and the Flobert shotgun, and my old story books. Many old-timers came forward to greet me, some of them from so long ago that I didn't even remember their names. I couldn't say very much to them because I had forgotten almost all my Soendanese, so Father and Karel did most of my talking for me.

It was extraordinary how each sound I recognised unleashed a flood of memories, and the birdsong in particular transported me back to my old environment. Actually, not very much of that environment remains. Only the stables near to the house are still standing, and the shell of the first factory. The flower garden is not very changed, but the vegetable patch has vanished entirely. The tea gardens and the plantings of quinine looked the least altered to me, but then I have not yet seen them all. I had thought everything would appear smaller than I remembered, but that was not always the case. The Goenoeng Tiloe looms much closer than it did in my memory. What struck me most of all was the beauty of nature at Gamboeng. I am a better judge of that nowadays – when I was a boy I took it all for granted. But I know of no place on earth where Nature possesses such awesome beauty combined with such sweetness and solace. The location of the house, too, is superb.

The next morning I was startled awake at half past six by the sound of a polyphone. I got up at once, and found everyone bustling about in readiness for all the guests that were expected in the course of the morning. A native fanfare from Bandoeng was ranged beside the house to announce each new arrival. The first came at about ten o'clock, and an hour later there were twenty-three people seated on the front veranda. At noon a typical native ceremony was held: the burial of a buffalo-head beneath the floor of the new factory, by way of dedicating the building. First the head was carried around on a handsome palanquin, to the tones of the *gamelan*. In the forecourt we, the Europeans, took our positions at the head of the procession, and made our way slowly to the new factory, where a hole had already been dug at the main entrance. The head was wrapped in cloths and lowered into the ground along with floral tributes, after which the *lebè* intoned a long, solemn prayer, and finally the hole was covered up. Father was also required to add a spade of earth, after which it was my turn, and those of the other men present. Then the ceremony was over, and the feast could begin. There were about eighty guests, all of whom had contributed in some way to the construction of the new house or the new factory, or else had known me as a boy.

When everyone was seated, on the floor as is the custom, Father gave a very fine speech. Afterwards he let me have the following translation of what he had said, in the grandest Soendanese he could muster:

'Dear sisters, brothers, friends, Radèn Wedana of Bandjaran, Radèn Tjamat of Tjisondari, village chiefs, *mandoers*, carpenters, factory *boedjangs*, people of Gamboeng, and all those who are present today: the reasons why we are gathered together in celebration today are threefold.

'Firstly, we have built a new *gedoeng*, which has been achieved without accident.

'Secondly, we have recently established this new factory, likewise without accident. From the felling of timber in the forest to the placement of the metal sheeting that constitutes our roof overhead, not a single accident has come to pass, thanks be to Allah. No one was struck by a falling tree; no one fell off the scaffolding.

'The third reason is that, ten years and eleven months since I sent my two eldest sons to school in Holland, my first-born has been restored to us.

'That is why it is my wish for you all to share in my joy and gratitude, and in extending our humble thanks to Allah for his grace.

'And now, may I request the honourable priest to conduct the customary prayer to Allah: that he may grant you all a life of health and prosperity.'

This was followed by a lengthy oration by the *lebè*, after which the festive meal took its course.

Our 'own' dinner party began at 8 p.m. It was a great success, thanks to Mother's best efforts. Speeches were given by Uncle August, Cousin Jan Bosscha, Father and myself. Among those present were, besides the *wedana* of Bandjaran, the employees, some neighbours, Bertha's governess, and quite a number of relatives:

Kar Bosscha, the Bosscha girls, Rudi van Santen, and Lien (the youngest daughter of our late Uncle Eduard of Sinagar) accompanied by her husband and Cousin Adriaan ('Tattat') Kerkhoven. And our own immediate family, of course – the two of you were sorely missed!

I have gone hunting with Father and Karel several times already.

In other words, it is time I started doing some work. For now I will be acting as Father's apprentice, helping to draw up plans for the new electrical installation and the necessary water conduits. I am going to catch up on my Soendanese, too.

GROUP PORTRAIT: A WEDDING, 1905

The back garden of a country villa in Hilversum, owned by Mr Lambrechtsen, director of Public Works in Amsterdam. A warm September day (the sash windows on the first floor are open). The trees are still thick with summer foliage, except for one leafless specimen.

The family members pose on the lawn by the conservatory. The bridegroom, Eduard Silvester Kerkhoven, in his long morning coat with a rose in his buttonhole, and the bride, in a white wedding dress complete with veil and a large bouquet, seem less prominent than the bride's parents, stout and dignified, arm-in-arm at the centre of the group. Also the sprightly Mrs Roosegaarde, grandmother of the groom, and two strapping bridesmaids draw attention. Rudolf is to be seen in the background, his eyes shaded by the rim of his silk top hat, and sporting a long, flowing grey beard. The face peeping out from behind the shoulders of two burly gentlemen must belong to Emile, who has come over from Zurich for his brother's wedding. Missing from the group is Jenny, the groom's mother, unless she is the lady whose lavishly furbelowed gown is partially visible at the edge of the picture. Bertha, too, is absent.

The wedding ceremony between Eduard Kerkhoven and Madeleine Lambrechtsen has just taken place. Financial assistance from Rudolf has made this marriage possible. Edu did not quite complete his course, but he has gained practical experience in machine technology in a factory in Pittsburgh, Pennsylvania, and, through his father-in-law's mediation, has found a position with the paraffin works in the port of Amsterdam, where he will hopefully make a career and a reasonable income. His marriage to this daughter of a worthy, well-to-do official is a great relief to Rudolf. Edu is not cut out to be a planter, nor would Madeleine, whose constitution is delicate, be up to living on a plantation in the Indies. However, she is steady and sensible and knows her own mind; in that respect she is the ideal wife for Edu with his quick temper and lack of ambition.

Now that Emile, too, is on the point of gaining his degree in Zurich, that Karel is finishing school in Batavia (he is confident of passing his exams), and that Ru is replacing his father at Gamboeng (besides monitoring the construction of an electrical power station similar to the one August has at Ardjasari), Rudolf feels the travails of the past have not been in vain. His sons can stand on their own two feet, and, if need be, he can facilitate their plans for the future: money is no longer an issue, what with Malabar flourishing as never before (over 500 kilos of tea harvested in 1903! A dividend of 30 per cent!), and Taloen – currently headed by Jan Bosscha, but hopefully by Emile or Karel eventually – holding ever more promise, not to mention the prospect of clearing a third tract of wilderness, Negla, in the foreseeable future.

It is time for Bertha to come out in society. When all the receptions, dinner parties and other social engagements are over and Rudolf is finally at liberty to embark at Genoa or Marseille for his return voyage, Jenny and Bertha will stay behind for the 'finishing touches', which will tranform the girl from overseas into a young lady of European stature.

Rudolf's top hat presses tightly on his forehead. He is a trifle preoccupied, for a disagreement has arisen between him and the bride's parents: it concerns the promise exacted from his sons to refuse to shake hands with Henny should they ever come across him in company. This dates back to Henny's offensive letter to Rudolf regarding their differences, since which time Ru, Edu and Emile have kept their word. Lambrechtsen takes the view that it is not in the interest of the young couple, nor in that of the two families – indeed, that it is prejudicial to all parties concerned – to allow a mere 'tiff' to assume the proportions of a family feud, and that Rudolf would do well to consider that Henny (a Member of Parliament as well as State Councillor!) took Ru and Edu into his home for three and a half years, and that Cateau was like a second mother to them.

Rudolf, for his part, insists that if his sons are civil to Henny, for whatever reasons of social convention or diplomacy, it would be tantamount to failing their father in public. He will not hear of any kind of reconciliation. Not long ago Cateau sent him a note suggesting they should 'forgive and forget', but he took that to mean that they were offering forgiveness rather than the other way round. His response was to let her know that he could not take her words seriously unless her husband retracted the allegations against him and offered an apology. He did not hear from his sister again.

DOUBLE PORTRAIT, MOTHER AND DAUGHTER, 1906

The picture was taken in a well-known photographic studio in Amsterdam. Jenny and Bertha pose side by side, their half-length figures looming up from a blurry background, in accordance with the modern artistic style. Bertha is seventeen and already a little taller than her mother, whose clear, grey gaze she has inherited.

There is a story attached to this portrait. A few months earlier, Bertha sends a picture of herself with her hair up to her father in Gamboeng as a surprise, to show him what a year in Europe has done for the barefoot tomboy who used to love climbing trees, the little daughter whom he thought intelligent but, alas, somewhat ungainly – that she has blossomed, not into the belle of the ball perhaps, but into an energetic, radiant young woman.

Rudolf writes back to Holland with profound gratitude: '. . . Do you know who is looking at me this very minute? It is you! And it is time for me to say: my darling Kitten, how pretty you have grown! I have your picture before me on my desk, propped up against the inkwell. I was overjoyed to receive it! The only twinge of disappointment was not seeing your mother at your side.'

She takes the hint, and sets about persuading her mother to

accompany her to the studio to have their photograph taken together; this is no easy task, for Jenny has been feeling increasingly despondent lately, and is liable to fly into rages over the pettiest things. But Bertha succeeds in the end, and today Jenny has agreed to pose for the photographer's double portrait in style, elaborately coiffed and wearing one of the expensive gowns they purchased in Paris or Vienna during Bertha's Grand Tour (Bertha marvels at the ease, indeed the indifference, with which her mother spends large sums of money). At the last moment Bertha turns to her mother with a whispered: 'Please, Mama, don't look so severe!' whereupon Jenny's expression softens, not quite into a smile, but into a serene gaze that betrays nothing of her recent moroseness and inner tormoil. Bertha beams at the camera: How do you like this double portrait, Father? Mother won't pose by herself; she says she's too 'staid'. Have you ever heard such nonsense? Don't you think she looks lovely?

Bertha knows her father longs for them to join him at Gamboeng, but that he also understands their wish to remain in Holland for the birth of Edu and Madeleine's baby, which is due in August. Besides, they would like to be there when Karel comes over after his school exams in July, as he is not at all looking forward to leaving the Indies.

RUDOLF KERKHOVEN TO AN ASPIRING TEA PLANTER, 1906

. . . In the course of my career in the East Indies, spanning thirty-five years, I have gained much experience, and I am still convinced that the opportunities for a young chap with spirit and determination are better in the Indies than in Europe.

A qualified mechanical engineer who is self-possessed, even-tempered, strong and healthy, a good 'worker', in possession of a well-reputed surname and some capital to boot – well, I can hardly think of a man more likely to succeed. I say 'likely', because such things cannot be guaranteed.

However, it seems to me that you might exercise a little more patience. You want your plan to be 'definite' beforehand, and to enter into a partnership likewise beforehand. Are you considering my son Rudolf as a potential associate? We expect to begin clearance of Negla next year, for which I will be providing the capital. We will begin on a small scale, with a view to covering the cost of gradual expansion of our plantings with the profits we hope to be making. In that way we can remain in full control of the enterprise. I have always regretted the moment, ten years ago now, that it became impossible for me to retain full ownership of the Malabar estate, which I had bought cheaply. Instead, I turned it into a joint-stock company with me as the principal shareholder. My Cousin Rudolf, better known as Kar Bosscha, has a fine position there as manager. It is our aim to ensure that Negla remains exclusive to the family – even if it means waiting a while to begin reaping the rewards.

So as far as Negla is concerned, there is no partnership on offer.

SNAPSHOT, FOUR GENERATIONS, 1906

A corner of the room where Madeleine Kerkhoven gave birth to a son three days ago. A flower-patterned screen obscures part of the washstand with basin and ewer.

Old Mrs Roosegaarde is seated in an armchair holding an infant swaddled in a crochet blanket: her great-grandchild. Edu, standing behind her, looks down at his son.

The fourth person present is the brand-new grandmother, Jenny. The lady in the double portrait with Bertha has changed (in barely six months!) from a plump, still attractive woman of middle age into a bloated, grim-faced matron. Her hair has turned grey, and she stands there as stiffly as a wooden doll. She is past caring what anyone thinks of her appearance.

She has a grandchild, but she feels neither pride nor joy. She will not live to see the child grow up and to take pleasure in his existence. She is feeling her years. The next generation is taking over. Her children will leave her, one by one. She will return to Gamboeng and stay there for the rest of her days with Rudolf, surrounded by memories of their years of hardship, failed harvests, plagues, setbacks, illnesses, cramped housing, anxiety and the rain, the never-ending rain. They have become rich. The new house is more spacious and more comfortable than the shambling wooden bungalow she had to live in for twenty long years. They have a telephone, electric lighting and lamps of Venetian glass on the front veranda. The steep road rising from Babakan to Gamboeng has been much improved, and when Bertha and she return they will find a new carriage, in which she may ride to Bandoeng whenever she pleases to call on a friend or do some shopping. But it will be too late.

She has seen Cateau only once during her stay in Holland. Not at her home, because Jenny, like her sons, is not permitted to meet her brother-in-law. The encounter did not go well. The last thing Jenny expected was that her sister-in-law would blame her for Rudolf's real or imagined shortcomings, but she found herself being accused of resenting his mother, Cateau and Marie, and of driving August's wife, the Resident's daughter, to distraction. It was for her sake, in his efforts to make more and more money for her to spend, that Rudolf had resorted to half-truths. She was oversensitive, typically 'East Indian', and it was her fault that Rudolf had fallen out with the rest of his family. And it was only because she was afraid her boys might love Cateau more than their mother that she had schemed to take Ru and Edu away: 'No one knows better than you, Jenny, how much it pains me to be parted from children I have grown to love, children I have cared for like a mother. They came here as half-savages, undernourished, badly dressed – we made Dutch boys of them. Is this the thanks I get for acting as your discreet go-between in the old days, when Rudolf wanted to be friends with you? Well, so much for getting to know the Roosegaardes! I even noticed a trace of your fears and phantasms in Edu. You are Rudolf's downfall!'

The grim-looking woman standing stiffly to one side, as if she does not belong there, is so utterly unlike the Jenny he left behind almost a year ago – not to mention the old Jenny, his sweetheart and comrade, the young mother of his children, the centre of his life – that Rudolf cannot take his eyes off the photograph Edu has sent him. That strange personage is now sailing on the *Rembrandt*, on her way to the Indies, to him.

The change in her mother's personality had been too gradual for Bertha to notice at first, and it was mainly through other people's reactions that it began to dawn on her. Her mother's agitation during the final weeks in Holland could still be attributed to the fatigue of packing for the voyage and the emotional strain of leave-taking, as Karel suggested, but her nervous behaviour assumed a fixed pattern once they were on board ship: irritable during the day, with incessant complaints about the service, the accommodation and Bertha's lack of sympathy, but vociferously sociable in the evening, after a few glasses of wine during dinner. Bertha was ashamed of her mother's loud chatter and unseemly eagerness and excitement during board games in the lounge. The raised eyebrows and visible embarrassment of the other passengers mortified her, yet social convention required that she, being a 'debutante', should remain in her mother's company regardless of her pursuits or the hours she kept.

After Suez, Bertha fell ill. Recurrent fevers obliged her to keep to her cabin, where she had to bear the full brunt of her mother's nervous attention-seeking. Until Batavia they passed their days in two adjoining cabins.

Catching sight of her father waiting on the Tadjong Priok quay for their ship to come in, Bertha burst into tears. All her pent-up emotion poured out. There he stood, in one of the 'good suits' he so disliked wearing; he had even exchanged his old sun hat for one made in Panama. Beneath his moustache his lower lip was swollen and scarred as a result of an infection that had required surgery. His mouth was disfigured, but his voice was the same. Bertha rushed into his arms, sobbing. His dismay at seeing his daughter looking so pale and drawn somewhat mitigated the shock of his wife's altered appearance.

It was not until they were back in Gamboeng that the full import of the alteration began to sink in. But because there was a constant stream of visitors from practically the first day of their return – never fewer than three or four guests at a time – and the reception and accommodation and entertainment of all these people kept them too occupied to pay much heed to Jenny's troubled state, on the surface things seemed back to normal. The house in its lovely park-like setting with rasamalas and flower beds, bordered by the jungle on one side and the tea gardens on the other, the scores of people working in the hangars and gardens, the familiar faces of Engko and of Irta and Nati, the elderly clerk and his wife, the fragrances and sounds of the hill country, the light, the breeze, the afternoon showers, the dogs and the horses – all of life at Gamboeng, the way Bertha had known it since early childhood, clamoured for her attention. All she needed to do was to lapse into her old habits, pick up the old rhythm, and she would be truly at home again, where strange, bewildering occurrences were simply the way of nature.

But she had changed. Something at the core of her being, something which she experienced as 'self', held her back. That 'self' was aware that action was called for, that help and care were needed for their mother, whose mood swings (euphemistically termed 'nerves' by her kin) were becoming more disturbing by the day. The first time Bertha found herself alone with her brother Ru, during a walk to his electric power station, water-driven by the Tjisondari, she tried to broach the subject. But her brother had other things on his mind. She was flustered, groped for words (they were sitting on a boulder upstream, the same one that had served as a citadel in their childhood war games), and before she had spoken half a sentence he broke in with: 'Did you know they're building a big power station in Bandoeng? But this one here is the very first of its kind in Java, and far better than the one at Ardjasari,' and quickly launched into an explanation of cables, dynamos and turbines. His tone left her in no doubt: she was not to speak of the unspeakable.

Bertha could well understand his need to shut himself off from the plight of their mother; it was the same need that drove her to engage his attention, and arose from the desire for self-possession. Ru was almost twenty-eight, and as soon as Emile came out in a few months' time to take over at Gamboeng, he would be going to Malabar as Cousin Kar Bosscha's assistant, or rather as the second man. With that future in mind he had become engaged to the daughter of a retired colonial official in Bandoeng. A house for the young couple was already under construction at Malabar. He and Jo, his fiancée, who spent a day or two at Gamboeng each week, seemed determined to defuse any crisis before it happened, and thanks to Jo's charming way of smoothing over difficult exchanges and tense moments by quickly coming up with something entertaining, they often succeeded. One day, after several weeks of having visitors to stay – the Kerkhovens (including Jo, who was already considered part of the family) were left to themselves at last – a violent altercation erupted between the lady of the house and the housekeeper, and Jo rescued the situation by proposing a bonfire on the freshly cleared tract of woodland, thereby managing to persuade Jenny to go outside with Ru. The unfortunate housekeeper, who had tried her utmost to please her mistress, fled to her room in tears, knowing her days at Gamboeng were numbered. Bertha linked arms with her father, who was still visibly shaken by his wife's hysterical outburst, and led him to the garden. In the distance they could see the smoke of Jo's bonfire rising up over the trees. The light was fading.

As they made their way along the roses, Bertha could almost feel her father's anguish weighing down on her arm. That he kept silent about what was going through his mind was simply his character; she had not expected anything else. But this time it was impossible for her to respect his reserve.

'Father, it can't go on like this.'

He paused, loosening his arm from hers.

'I have spoken with the doctor at Bandoeng,' he said gruffly. 'Her condition leaves us little hope.'

There had been a time when Bertha was her mother's darling girl, her 'little woman'. None of the old intimacy remained. Day after day she was assailed by remarks, often made in anger, about her resemblance to the young Jenny, as a consequence of which her mother saw her one moment as a rival and adversary, and the next as a victim, a copy of herself. But when Bertha looked in the mirror she could see she did not resemble her mother at all, except for the colour of her eyes. She did her best to respond to her mother's muddled statements with patience and loving care, but was left feeling that whatever she did or said was lost in a void. Her mother had retreated into a world of her own, where only her grievances counted. Neither the news of Grandma Roosegaarde's demise nor Emile's homecoming seemed to affect her very much.

By contrast, she was singularly preoccupied by the appearance of the motor car in Java, and notably by the fact that Adriaan

'Tattat' Kerkhoven of Sinagar already possessed an automobile (with licence plate number 1!), and that Kar Bosscha had also ordered one. The arrival of the telephone had already made it possible for her to keep in vocal contact with people in Bandoeng and the neighbouring estates, and now she longed for a motor car so that she could go and see them face to face whenever the fancy took her. She had never been allowed to drive the four-horse carriage, and their new barouche needed a coachman to ride on the box. The idea of driving her own motor car loomed in her mind as the epitome of earthly pleasure.

Bertha dreaded the recurrent debates on that subject. Her father was not in favour of automobiles, and would go against his wife's declarations that they badly needed one, giving a variety of reasons that Ru and Emile would then proceed to gainsay, citing expert knowledge. Often this would result in Jenny making a scene, during which she would vent her temper about all manner of other things besides whether or not a Dion-Bouton motor car was preferable to a Voisin.

There were dark hints about financial affairs and hostilities within the extended family, culminating in a recent *perkara*, or feud, which Ru and Emile apparently knew all about. Bertha only knew that her mother blamed everything on her father's domineering and meddlesome nature; he was infuriatingly opinionated, and grasping, too. Hadn't he taken charge of all her money, her very own Roosegaarde inheritance, right from the start? Her father's reaction to these diatribes was to say nothing and escape to his office.

With Ru being so occupied by the preparations for his impending marriage, Bertha and Emile fell into the habit of taking a walk with the dogs after tea, while their father conferred with the *mandoers*.

Emile had taken up his boyhood pursuit of bird-watching again.

'Look, Bertha! *Manoek seupah*. Can you see them?'

'Those red ones?'

'Have you forgotten what *seupah* means? It's what they call the spurt of red *sirih* juice!'

'But there's also a *manoek* that's yellowish.'

'Have you noticed how the birds in the jungle around here sing in chorus, all those different species together?'

'I listen to them, but I don't know all their names. I can remember some of them, though, from the old days, like *berkesèset* and silver-heads.'

'In Soendanese most of the birds are named after their calls. *Doedoet troktrok*, for instance, is their name for the swamp pheasant.'

'Oh, yes, and there's the *djokdjok*, too!'

'Sometimes it's just as if they're having a long palaver, with everyone shouting at once.'

Bertha stood still, picked up a stick and flung it away. The dogs bounded after it.

'Emile, what's behind that *perkara* Mother keeps going on about? It's obviously bothering Father very much. Am I right in thinking it has something to do with Ardjasari, not with Gamboeng? I wish you'd tell me.'

'In a nutshell, then,' replied Emile with a sigh. 'You know Uncle August went back to Europe for good last year. Well, he didn't pick a successor for the estate. He just appointed two deputies and kept the functions of director and administrator for himself, which is a ridiculous thing to do if you're on the other side of the world! Besides, he's taken all the Ardjasari archives and accounts with him. Father and Cousin 'Tattat' of Sinagar are supposed to be dealing with the shareholders here on his behalf, and Father has been given power of attorney. It turns out that Uncle August wants to change the statutes in a way that is much to his personal advantage. It's all highly irregular, and so Father isn't having any of it. The trouble is, as Uncle's deputy, he's obliged to carry out his wishes, while, as his agent, he would protest.'

'How tiresome,' sighed Bertha.

'Father let him know that it was impossible to keep Ardjasari going properly under such conditions. This made Uncle August angry, and now Father has been dismissed as his legal representative. By his younger brother! It's very painful for him. You know what he's like, about which the least said the better, if you ask me.'

'Do you think Father autocratic?'

'Oh, *betoel*! The King of the Preanger.'

'What was that book you and Father were talking about yesterday? Had you been reading Nietzsche again?'

'No, something by Couperus. Father says his novels are decadent, in bad taste. He can't stand them. From now on I think I'll read Couperus and Streuvels in my room, and stick to Father's favourites, like Stevenson's *Treasure Island*, or some book by Van Lennep, when he's around.'

Ru departed to Malabar. Emile was out in the gardens every day. At her mother's insistence, Bertha accepted invitations to go and stay with friends. She was to 'come out' during the races in the first week of August, and her mother thought she would do well to make some connections beforehand, to avoid being a wallflower at the balls. At the age of thirteen or fourteen she had been envious of her Bosscha cousins, and also of Pauline and Caroline, her grown-up cousins at Sinagar, for the social whirl they enjoyed, but now she was bored by the interminable discussions about hats and fans and what to wear to the fancy dress ball, and she felt stiff and awkward during her stays in the various homes. Upon her return to Gamboeng she discovered that her mother's feverish energy was focused entirely on the debutante Miss Bertha Elisabeth Kerkhoven, a personage with whom Bertha found it impossible to identify.

Although they possessed seven guest rooms at Gamboeng, kept an excellent table and dozens of good saddle-horses, and had a lawn tennis court to boot, her mother deemed it necessary – and only fair to the debutante – for them to have a house in Bandoeng as well; besides, it was unclear whether they were still welcome at Cousin Adriaan Kerkhoven's '*pondok* Sinagar', given the recent troubles in the family. Bertha's father had complied with his wife's wish by renting a furnished house belonging to an acquaintance, but it was not to her taste. Instead, suites were reserved in Hotel Wilhelmina in Bandoeng, which, though less favourably located than the traditional Homan, had better service.

So Bertha went to the races, to make her entrance in the world. People came from far and wide, including the smaller towns of Garoet, Tjandjoer and Soekaboemi, and, if they were race-horse owners, also from Buitenzorg and Batavia. To accommodate the influx of visitors, the mansions bordering the Post Road, Keboen Djati and Soeniaradja temporarily became like private hotels, with the low boundary walls on the street side, the pillars flanking the entrance, and the garden flowerpots all freshly whitewashed for the occasion. Braga shopping street and the avenues shaded by kenari trees and flamboyants were choked with traffic, from victorias and gigs to dog carts and other small conveyances, all of which veered away at the first sign of a motor car, of which there were three or four in Bandoeng. The roads to the racecourse were lined with *waroengs* selling fruit, goodies, savouries wrapped in *pisang* leaf, flags, firecrackers, flowers to wear in the hair-knot, sweet syrup and straw cigarettes. The local population appeared to have swollen to ten times its usual size. From early morning on the streets were thronged with people in their best finery, and all was aflutter with paper parasols in all the colours of the rainbow, ephemeral sun-shades for use at the racecourse. The music of *gamelans* and *angkloen* orchestras flowed together into a cacophony, over and above which the brassy tones of a military band rang out.

Bertha rode to the Tegallega racecourse in the carriage with Ru and Jo and her parents. They had reserved seats in the shaded part of the grandstand. Bertha looked strikingly pretty in a European summer dress of spotted voile with a sweet-smelling nosegay (the debutante's emblem) pinned to the shoulder, and a hat of fine straw decorated with bows of starched gauze. She watched the races with interest (Buccanneer and Jason of Sinagar were among the winners, as usual), and had the distinction of presenting the Gamboeng Cup, which her father had instituted in honour of her eighteenth birthday. She stayed to watch the comical finale of the dog cart race, after which she went home to change into her evening dress for the dinner party and, finally, to the grand ball. It was not until the early hours that she tumbled into bed at last, half fainting from exhaustion and champagne.

The following morning she and her father became anxious about her mother, who had stayed behind at the hotel in a dark mood. A message sent round by Adriaan Kerkhoven inviting her to join them for the midday *rijsttafel* at the '*pondok* Sinagar' went unanswered, because, so they were informed, Madame Kerkhoven had gone touring in a motor car with some other hotel guests.

EMILE KERKHOVEN TO HIS BROTHER EDU AND HIS WIFE,
14 AUGUST 1907

Dear Edu and Madeleine,

At Father's request, I am writing to you in haste, before

the mail closes, to tell you of the great sadness that has befallen us. Oh, I am still reeling from the shock. We brought our dear Mother to her final resting place this afternoon. An end has come to the distress that Mother had to endure these last years. Her condition was worsening lately, and her unhappiness increasing, until last night, between midnight and 1 a.m., she suffered a nervous stroke. The doctor was called at once, but by the time he arrived, at about two, her heart had stopped beating. And now it is all over, and our dearly beloved Mother is buried in the forest. You can imagine where: in the old specimen tea garden, near the graves of our little sister and Miss Verwey. Aside from Ru and Jo, only the Bosscha cousins attended the funeral; other people could not make the journey in time.

And now we are just sitting here together, and we can't get over how quickly all this has happened. We try to console ourselves with the idea that Mother is at peace. Life had become such a burden for her, and the doctors had no hope of her recovery. But what a loss for us! What will become of us all without her? Because Mother was the heart and soul of this place.

I must say I can't help admiring Father for his tolerant attitude towards Mother these last years. And oh, you can't imagine how grief-stricken he is!

Bertha promised her father that she would notify Karel on his behalf, but she could barely hold her pen. The events of the past twenty-four hours had been a reprise – even more horrifying – of an experience she had had in this house before, when, on just such a night, she had woken to hear urgent, low voices and muffled footsteps in the corridor and had been told to stay in her room. Just as then, she had not been allowed to know what was going on, nor would they let her see her mother. She had tried to push her way past Emile, but shrank back at the sight of Father shaking his head from side to side, wordlessly, his face contorted with anguish. She had been permitted to enter the darkened room for a brief moment before the coffin was closed and borne away.

Later, she went to sit on the back veranda, numbed with grief. Seeing Engko, Bertha instinctively reverted to a childhood habit: she sank down on her haunches and leaned her head against her old *baboe*'s familiar shoulder. Engko put out her hand and stroked her back softly, with the absent-minded, mechanical gesture of an old woman.

It was Engko who told her what her father and Emile were keeping from her, and which had to remain a secret: her mother had taken poison.

RUDOLF TO HIS SON EDU AND HIS WIFE, 18 AUGUST 1907

. . . It was Mother's extreme nervousness that caused her sudden death. Her mind was all agog with Emile's homecoming and the plans for Ru and Jo's wedding, as well as various other less salubrious affairs, which did not leave her a moment's peace. At the same time, Mother was ever in search of distraction and entertainment, but to me it was clear that all those so-called distractions often did her more harm than good.

It was her wish that we should all go to the races in Bandoeng. On the second day, Mother went touring in a motor car with some acquaintances, to Malabar and back, and apparently it was too much for her. She was never quite right again after that. Automobiles became her all-consuming passion. Visitors motoring over to see us made her over-excited, and even the mere mention of automobile trips in your letters was enough to set her off, and there were other things, too, of course.

On the night of the thirteenth, Mother went to bed fairly peacefully. I still had some business to attend to, and when I retired eventually I noticed to my surprise that she had been up, and that she had lit a candle, for which there was no apparent reason. I went to the bedroom and drew aside the mosquito net to find her barely conscious, murmuring something about Bertha, and about a bunch of keys. And then it all went very quickly. Thank God she was spared prolonged agony.

We kept Bertha at a distance. Only Emile and I were with Mother during her final moments. The doctor came, but it was too late, of course. There was nothing he could have done anyway. Heart failure, as a result of over-agitation of the nerves, was his verdict. I had consulted him (as well as other specialists) regarding Mother's condition on several occasions, but I was never given hope of improvement; in fact, I have now been told that her sudden demise has probably saved her from a worse fate.

Mother was laid to rest by Ru, Emile and me. We could not bear the thought of her being touched by strangers. In the afternoon of the fourteenth, we buried her at the edge of the forest – you know the place, Edu. May she find the peace there that was denied to her in life.

Her restlessness during the late stages worried me exceedingly. She could not remain seated on a chair for more than a few minutes, and kept jumping up to see what the servants were doing, or to fuss over some trivial housekeeping detail. She had also become uncharacteristically voluble, and would get very carried away in conversations. But her opinions were always worth listening to, unless she was airing her grievances. Latterly that had only too often been the case and was so noticeable that other people were beginning to comment on the state of her mind.

Her loss is irreparable. We are left with a gaping void in our lives, because we all know how good and kind she was at heart, a true helpmate, indeed she personified almost every womanly virtue. We can only lament that her nervous illness robbed her of the ability to grasp the happiness that lay before her. It was beyond her powers. What is to become of us now, I cannot say.

GAMBOENG, THE LAST DAY

1 February 1918

He stood in the deep cool shade at the edge of the forest. Flecks of sunlight quivered at his feet. Raising his eyes, he gazed past the shifting masses of foliage at the glaring afternoon sky. The ground was still damp from the last shower. He inhaled the green fragrance of Gamboeng. He heard the breeze whispering in the treetops, the soft rustle and creak of twigs within the tangled undergrowth.

He looked at the tablet engraved with her name and dates, set in the masonry before him. The headstone to the right was nameless. A little further on there was another grave, without a stone. It was forty-five years since he had planted his first tea on this mountainside.

He leaned on his stick, without which he had been unable to walk for some time. The dull ache in his lower body was not pain – not yet. He knew that it would never leave him, that something (he did not know the name of his disease) was eating away at him, hollowing him out. The limit of his existence was in sight. This would be his last visit to Gamboeng.

For the past year he had lived in Bandoeng with his daughter Bertha, in the house he had bought in 1907 but had never occupied. Not far from there rose the third *gedoeng* of his life, a splendid home where Jenny would have been happy, with spacious galleries, high-ceilinged rooms, marble floors. Despite his failing health, he had accompanied Bertha to Batavia to order the furniture and lamps that Jenny would have chosen. The location of the house was magnificent, on a site that was considered almost sacred by the native population on account of the ancient waringin trees growing there. That white house, built in a harmonious modern style, would be left to his children, a place in town where they could come together from Gamboeng, Malabar or Negla. It would be a Kerkhoven family seat, an East Indian counterpart of Hunderen.

He had come to Gamboeng to say goodbye. He had made the rounds of the factory hangars, had seen the new machines for withering, drying and sorting. Among the workers there he had recognised several who were born and bred in the kampong, the sons and daughters of Martasan and Moehiam and Kaidan and Moentajas and Sastra.

Since he had difficulty walking and could no longer ride, he had to abandon hope of going out into the gardens. Emile and his wife, who now ran Gamboeng, had placed an easy chair on the front veranda for him to sit and enjoy the view in peace. But even with his eyes closed he could see that landscape, for it was etched on his soul: the wide, downward sweep to the valley of the Tji Enggang, the array of rasamalas, Jenny's tjemaras and damars and cypresses, raised by her from seed and now grown into majestic trees, the green, blue and violet of the mountains close by and in the distance. It was the backdrop to his entire existence. Sitting there, he was reminded of a remark Julius had once made: 'A man ought to try to create something of lasting value.' At the time it had made him smile, and from his vantage point on the veranda he had let his eyes wander in all directions. Of lasting value? There it is, for all to see!

But he no longer possessed that proud certitude. Since losing

Jenny he had begun to ask himself whether there was any truth in the accusations she had hurled at him in her furious rages: that he had sacrificed everything, his own life as well as hers and the youth of their children, for the all-consuming ambition that made him work himself to the bone and dig in his heels, stubbornly refusing to forgive and forget the slightest imputation against his judgement, real or imagined. Vanity had never been his weakness. Nor was it in his nature to regard others with mistrust. His commitment to his family was unconditional. In long nights, when he could not sleep, he had 'tested his kidneys' in the biblical sense. It had been wrong of Henny to think he, Rudolf, did not dare look himself in the eye.

He gazed at the tablet inscribed with her name. Beneath it, in the ground of Gamboeng, her beloved body had turned to dust. The plants and bushes surrounding the grave were rooted in soil containing minute particles of her flesh and blood.

From his correspondence with her sister Marie he had learned, to his shock and dismay, that Jenny had known bitter disappointment in the early years of their marriage, long before he had the least suspicion that all was not well. Marie had sent him a page from an old letter written in 1890, in Jenny's familiar, flowing script: '. . . I don't want to deceive myself. I am not happy; it is not in my power to be so. I tell myself that there are other forms of happiness besides the luxury of passion. I have not known such luxury. And yet, my life has a purpose. There is also satisfaction to be found in doing one's duty and caring for others. My children are my happiness.'

'Luxury of passion.' Where had he failed? She had been the love of his life. He had given her all the passion he possessed. And she had meant so much more to him than a lover. To Marie's intimations that he might be lacking in understanding of the workings of a woman's mind he had replied, 'Not a day goes by without me feeling a sudden urge to tell Jenny about something I have heard or read about or thought. We used to talk about everything that interested us, in minute detail – at any rate in her good times, but also in later years, during spells of respite from the nerves and delusions. Losing Jenny has meant losing the purpose of my life. I always enjoyed my work, just as I enjoyed the successes it brought us. But it was all about her, really. That was what kept me going, ever since we were married, and now I am bereft of that aim. How I yearn sometimes for the old days, when we were living in our small wooden bungalow with our five children, when we were poor and often had to struggle. I would give anything to have my dear, sweet Jenny by my side again.'

The memory of her bad years still washed over him from time to time. He had been deeply hurt by her delusional claims that he had appropriated her inheritance – whereas he had on the contrary, by shrewd investment, made it grow into a considerable capital. For a time he had believed that her aberrant suspicions arose from her fear of finding herself without a widow's pension and dependent on strangers or grudging relatives, of having to 'eat humble pie'. But even when the profits of Gamboeng, Malabar and Taloen were such as to guarantee her financial security, she had continued to complain about her legal inability to dispose of her money without his mediation.

Things he had never stopped to think about appeared to him in a new light. When Jenny took Ru and Edu to Holland in 1893, she had postponed her return several times, for what reason he did not know. She had also left his weekly letters unanswered for some time. He had not even known her whereabouts prior to her embarkation in Genoa. The explanation she gave upon arrival – that she had seized the opportunity to visit Florence and Verona, see a little of Italy – had evaporated in his great joy over her homecoming. The Jenny who rode beside him all the way from Tjikalong to Gamboeng, sitting proud in her saddle and wearing a smart black riding habit he had never seen before, had enchanted him as never before. The familiarity of her presence had been tinged with something novel, which he attributed to the stimulating effect of the European climate and the sea air. Since the revelation in that letter she had sent Marie, however, he wondered whether there might have been another reason for her new look. Had she considered leaving him?

He had come to realise that she had never been the same after 1893. She had wanted to earn herself some 'pin money', as she put it sarcastically: she could do translation work, or write travel reports, or submit topical reviews of modern French and English authors to the leading newspapers in the Indies, and she had greatly resented the fact that he had phrased his letter of recommendation to the *Java-Bode* in such a roundabout way, as if he barely knew her, with reference to 'a Mrs X, who wishes to remain anonymous, and who wishes to know the fee she can expect for her work prior to submission.' The editor had replied they were not looking for contributions from amateurs. She had also resented his lack of interest in what was happening in the rest of the civilised world. But his attention had always been focused on the immediate needs and problems of the plantation, on discharging the duties he had taken upon himself. It was the same pragmatic principle that shaped his attitude towards world events. He followed the news in the papers in as much as it affected Holland and the East Indies, particularly with regard to economic developments. That was the case throughout the Great War raging in Europe, and it had been no different in the days of the Boer War or the Russo–Japanese conflict.

He had not obstructed Jenny's fierce engagement in political and social affairs, which found expression primarily in the endless telephone conversations she held with a small number of like-minded souls, nor had he opposed her contributing financially to a good cause, at least when circumstances allowed. It was largely thanks to Jenny's efforts that signatures in support of Captain Dreyfus were collected on the grandstands of the Bandoeng racecourse in 1899, six months after the publication of Emile Zola's famous open letter, *J'accuse*.

In his student years he had believed that his mind was by nature attuned to horizons wider than those of most people, but that had been self-delusion. In reality, his world had always been comprised of his parents, brothers and sisters, with a periphery of members of the wide-ranging family descending from his great-grandparents Van der Hucht. With Jenny and his children he had formed a new shoot on the family tree. In practice, he had experienced every phase of concord and war, of conflict and truce, within the limited circle of his kindred. He was prepared to admit in all humility that it had been his life's ambition to occupy a place of honour within that circle, to be respected, admired and loved by the only people he regarded as truly his equals. The horizon he had, of necessity, defined for himself was not on a human scale. His horizon was Gamboeng.

For ten years not a day had gone by at Gamboeng without him standing still for a while, sunk in thought, on this spot beneath the rasamalas, preferably at dawn, when the leaves were pearly with dew and the jungle roused itself, while the birds launched into their thousand-voiced chorus to greet the sun.

He believed he was acting in Jenny's spirit by devoting all his care and protective attention to Bertha, his daughter. She helped him to bear his loneliness, she was the hostess in his home (in charge of Jenny's keys), she accompanied him to Bandoeng or Batavia on business, she filled him with pride when she rode her black

Sandalwood over the mountain roads at his side. He allowed her to order dresses and fripperies from Paris whenever she wished, and books, music and knick-knacks from all over the world, she was free to have friends to stay at Gamboeng, and to go and stay with other people herself (but not for too long!). It was for Bertha's sake, and also to see Edu and Madeleine's three little boys, his only grandchildren, that he had travelled to Holland on extended leave in 1912. Money was not an issue. They had lodged in grand style at the Amstel Hotel in Amsterdam, and at the Kurhaus in Scheveningen. Bertha had led a busy social life. He believed she had enjoyed herself. For her sake he had made an effort to refrain from criticising people or showing his annoyance at certain aspects of life in Holland.

Upon their return to the Indies they had resumed their previous way of life. Karel settled at Negla with his new wife. Emile became engaged; he would remain at Gamboeng after his marriage. Ru was still the second man at Malabar, and Rudolf was mildly concerned about Kar Bosscha's reluctance to hand over his position as chief administrator to him, as initially agreed. On the other hand, Kar did an excellent job; he was popular among the workers on the plantation, and appeared to be following in Karel Holle's footsteps. Ru and his young wife seemed content to remain in the shadow of this second cousin, whose ambitions to be a friend and benefactor to the people of the Preanger went even further than those of Karel Holle. Kar invested a large share of his revenues in the advancement of social and cultural affairs in the region, particularly in Bandoeng.

Bertha's presence was Rudolf's comfort and consolation. To him, housekeepers, however competent and well-mannered, were too intrusive. Experience had taught him that it was best to let Bertha take charge of the regiment of servants: three houseboys, three *baboes*, two cooks, two laundrymen, one seamstress, and various gardeners, grooms and errand boys. He observed her with respect and satisfaction as she went about her daily tasks, giving instructions in the morning, bargaining with vendors of rice, fruit, vegetables, chickens and ducks, keeping count of laundry items, and in the afternoon and evening, especially when they had guests, which was very often, pouring tea, seeing to the table, and making sure that any people staying overnight were as comfortable as possible. When she was not needed in the house she would go into the garden with the dogs. Seeing her in the panorama unfolding from his office window gave him a sense of tranquillity and fulfilment. He was not looking for change. He had all he wished for. But one day Bertha announced: 'Father, I will be thirty next year.'

And Jo, Edu's open-hearted wife, had in a private moment told him quite bluntly that keeping Bertha at Gamboeng was tantamount to 'moral murder'.

He had tried to see his 'Kitten' through the eyes of an outsider. For the first time he noticed the advent of middle age in his daughter's appearance. Her figure was more rounded, and her jawline less taut, but most of all he was struck by her air of resignation. He had ordered his Chinese builders to make haste with the construction of Gedoeng Karet in Bandoeng.

In the distance he could hear Ru's motor car crunching over the gravel road leading up from the Tji Enggang valley. He knew what to expect: as soon as they halted by the front veranda, Ru and Jo would step out of the vehicle, he in a spotless tropical suit, linen cap and motor-goggles, and she likewise in white, with a scarf tied round her head, the long ends of which she would let fly in the wind as they drove along – at great peril, in Rudolf's opinion.

He did not enjoy riding in a motor car, but had to admit that the speed was an advantage. It was hard to imagine that the distance it took him half a day to travel forty years ago, now took little more than an hour.

He leaned on his stick; standing for any length of time fatigued him. He thought of Cateau and Henny, both dead now, whose graves he would never visit. When tidying his papers in preparation for the move to Bandoeng, he had come across Henny's letter, which he had considered perfidious at the time, a deliberate twisting of his own meaning in an earlier missive relating to Gamboeng, the need for a bigger house, going on furlough to Europe, financial security for Jenny and the children. Now, after all those years, Henny's letter seemed to him tragic. Re-reading those lines, he could taste the sadness felt by the childless couple at having to part with the boys, his boys. He understood why Henny, against his better judgement, had rejected his appeal for better compensation. The spartan living conditions, the hard toil in the gardens and the jungle, the deprivation – they would have been a small price to pay for the privilege of having a family. He realised that both Cateau and Henny had truly loved the boys, who had lived with them for three and a half years, and he felt ashamed that he had allowed his own grievances to blind him to their anguish and pain at losing them.

In a flash, like the flitting shadow of a bird winging from one treetop to the next, he saw himself as a small child in the park at Hunderen with his sister Bertha, who had just given him a firm smack for having left muddy fingerprints on her best dress of checked taffeta silk. He burst into tears, not because of the smack, but out of rage that she was a year older than him, the first-born child, whom everyone said was sweet and kind and clever, while he was always thought a nuisance, however hard he tried to be a good boy. Cateau was a babe in arms at the time; Julius, August and little Pauline had not yet been born. Old hurt, buried for a lifetime, suddenly became conscionable. Could it be that the estrangement between him and Cateau, August and Julius had something to do with his young self's sense of hurt and indignation at having to accept that he was no longer his mother's only darling and his father's sole pride and joy?

Back in 1880, when his father was gravely ill and they all feared for his life, Rudolf had gone over to Ardjasari from Gamboeng to help nurse him. He had kept vigil at his father's bedside in the narrow, high-ceilinged space with bare walls, the so-called dressing room which had been converted into a sickroom for the invalid. Most of the time his father lay stretched out, motionless, in a state of semi-consciousness. There was too little light to read by. Rudolf sat very still beside the bed, staring through the mosquito net at the face on the pillow, or watching the *tjitjaks* streaking across the whitewashed wall, snapping at insects.

One night his father began to talk to him. Rudolf slipped under the netting to sit on the edge of the bed, and clasped his father's extended hand. 'You are the eldest,' his father whispered, and proceeded to tell him where certain documents relating to Ardjasari were kept and where he wished to be buried: 'in the garden at the back of the *gedoeng*, in my soil.' Despite the gravity of the moment, those whispered words and the weak pressure of his father's fingers gave Rudolf a sense of happiness. He had been married for almost two years, he was a father himself, but at that moment he was a son first and foremost, profoundly aware of the bond between them. His father, believing he was dying, had turned to *him*, not to August or Julius, both of whom were staying in the same house; he had not even asked for his wife, asleep in the next room. But later, when he had recovered, his father had never alluded to this rapprochement in extremis.

Footsteps approached over the path behind him; he could hear the swish of a skirt.

'Bertha?'

'Are you coming, Father? Ru and Jo are waiting in the car to drive us to Bandoeng. And you need to take your siesta. Why are you laughing?'

'I was just thinking of Marnix van Sint-Aldegonde's motto, "Repos ailleurs". That is what Cousin Karel Holle wanted on his headstone. What epitaph shall I have?'

She came to stand beside him and slipped her arm through his, out of habit. 'There's no need to think about that yet.'

'My father would have liked to be laid to rest at Ardjasari. But now he is buried in Amsterdam. I have no wish to be buried in Bandoeng.'

'Please, Father!' Bertha said soothingly.

He looked at the ground at his feet.

'Here!' he said, half aloud. 'Here.'

Acknowledgements

The Tea Lords is a novel, but it is not 'fiction'. The interpretation of personalities and events is based on private correspondence and other documents kindly placed at my disposal by The Indies Tea and Family Archive, a foundation established by descendants and kindred of the characters in my book. I am especially grateful to Dr K. A. van der Hucht for his stimulating interest and willingness to provide me with additional material in the course of my writing.

Many thanks are also due to J. Ph. Roosegaarde Bisschop, for the use of his family archives.

The material is therefore not invented; rather, it has been chosen and arranged to meet the demands of a novel. This means that all manner of factual details pertaining to a properly historical account have been omitted, and that the emphasis is on the lives of a select group of individuals.

H. S. H.

Glossary

Note: the old Dutch spelling of vernacular words has been retained. As there was no standard spelling of the strain of Malay spoken in the East Indies at the time, the Dutch devised their own spelling. One of the main differences is 'oe' – pronounced 'oo' in Dutch – which has been replaced in modern Indonesian by 'u'.

adat – indigenous law, custom, ritual
amat rajin, *gètol* – fussy, over-diligent
asam – tamarind
atjar – pickle
baboe – female domestic servant
badak – rhinoceros
besar – big
betoel – really, truly!
bibit – rice seedling
bingoeng – confused, mad
Bismillah – commonly rendered as 'in the name of Allah'
boedjang – unmarried plantation worker
boengoer – *Lagerstroemia loudoni*, deciduous tree with pinkish purple blossom
bonang, *saron*, *gendèr* – percussion instruments of diverse shapes and materials

bouw – a unit of land measurement which varied from one part of Java to another, but which was standardised in the colonial period to approximately 71m².

Cultivation System – compulsory cultivation of certain crops on behalf of the colonial government

dendeng – spicy dried meat

desa – independent hamlet

djamoe – medicinal herbs, whole or powdered

djoeragan – landlord, master

djongos – houseboy

doekoen – herbalist, medicine man

gamelan – Javanese orchestra, mainly percussion

gedoeng – large house made of stone or brick

golok – chopping knife

istri – wife

kain – a length of batiked cloth similar to the sarong, but with the short ends sewn together.

kampong – generally: native settlement within a city, but also: the collection of worker's dwellings on an estate

kasian – sorry, sad

kepiting – crab

ketjil – small

ketjoeboeng – *Datura arborea*, shrub with white bell-shaped flowers

kolong – space beneath a house

kraton – palace of a Javanese prince

kwee-kwee – biscuits

latah – agitated, hysterical

lebè – priest

mandoer – overseer, foreman

mangkè – presently, shortly

manoek – bird

matjan – tiger

matjan toetoel – panther

mentjèk – deer

nènèk – grandmother

njai – concubine to a European
nonna – young (mixed race) woman
obat – medicine
oedik – wilderness
pajoeng – the parasol used exclusively by persons of high rank or birth
pantjoeran – water conduit of hollow bamboo
pasar – market
patih – adviser to a regent
patjoel – hoe
penghoeloe – Mohammedan teacher of religion
peranakan – Chinese born in Java
perkara – dispute, feud
petasan – small firecrackers
pisang – banana
pondok – simple (guest) house of wood and bamboo
ramah-tamah – very kind
Ratoe Adil – the Just King, a messianic figure
rebab – Javanese string instrument
rijsttafel – 'rice-table', elaborate meal served in a multitude of dishes
sarong and kebaya – Javanese women's clothing: a batiked cloth around the hips, and a long-sleeved tunic; commonly worn in the morning by European women until about 1930
sawah – an irrigated rice field
sedia – ready
selamatan – ceremonial feast
sepoeh – old, senior
sirih – leaf of the piper betel, chewed like a wad of tobacco
slendang – long shoulder scarf, carrying-cloth
soesah – trouble, bother
tampir – circular tray of woven bamboo
totok – full-blood European
waringin – *Ficus*, banyan tree, venerated in Java
waroeng – small shop, stall
wedana – district chief

Tea Estates in the Preanger Highlands

Estate	*Hectares (approx.)*	*Altitude (metres)*	*Crops*	
Parakan Salak	1,500	625–950	tea, also rubber in later years	1844: G. L. J. van der Hucht buys one half of contract
Sinagar and Moendjoel	1,400	400–500	tea, also rubber	1865: G. L. J. in later years van der Hucht buys contract on behalf of A. Holle and E. J. Kerkhoven
Waspada	200	1,250	tea, quinine, some coffee	1865: K. F. Holle becomes contractor
Ardjasari	620	950–1,250	tea, quinine	1869: R. A. Kerkhoven becomes contractor
Gamboeng	620	1,250–1,400	tea, quinine, some coffee	1873: R. E. Kerkhoven becomes contractor
Soekawana	455	1,500	quinine, also tea in later years	1877: W. F. Hoogeveen acquires leasehold
Malabar	1,710	1,500	tea, quinine	1890: first leasehold R. E. Kerkhoven
Negla	1,120	1,800	tea, quinine	1899: first leasehold R. E. Kerkhoven
Taloen	930	1,600	tea, quinine	1902: first leasehold R. E. Kerkhoven

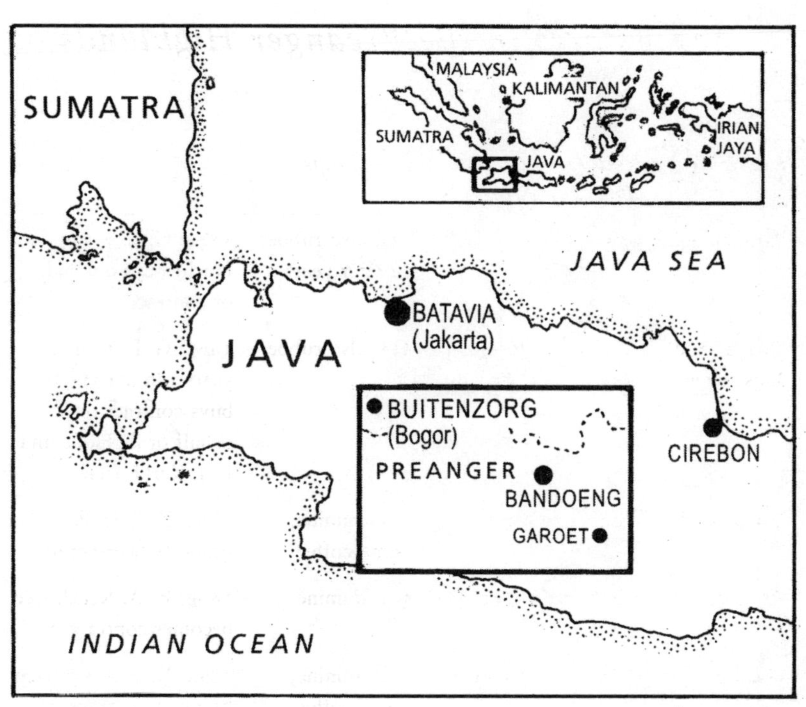
SUMATRA
MALAYSIA
KALIMANTAN
SUMATRA
JAVA
IRIAN
JAYA
JAVA SEA
BATAVIA
(Jakarta)
JAVA
BUITENZORG
(Bogor)
PREANGER
BANDOENG
GAROET
CIREBON
INDIAN OCEAN

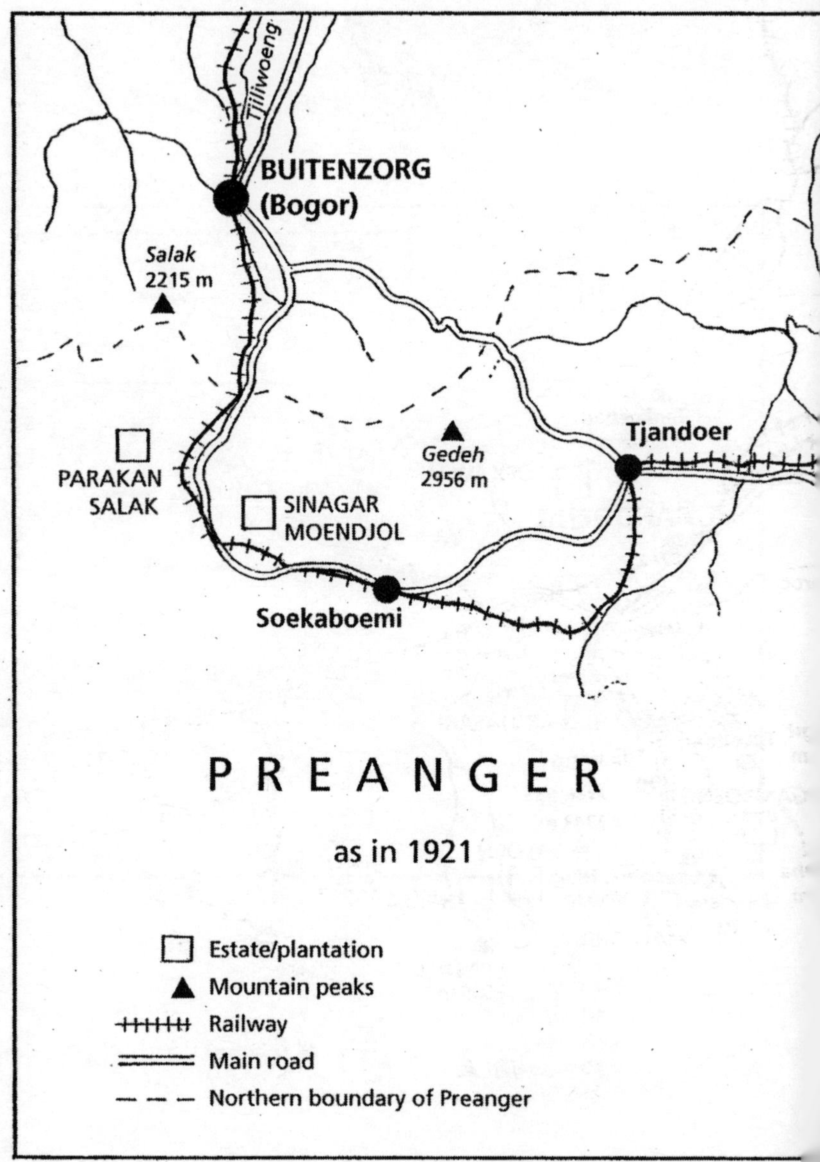
Tjiliwoeng
BUITENZORG
(Bogor)
Salak
2215 m
Gedeh
2956 m
Tjandoer
PARAKAN
SALAK
SINAGAR
MOENDJOL
Soekaboemi
PREANGER
as in 1921
Estate/plantation
Mountain peaks
Railway
Main road
Northern boundary of Preanger

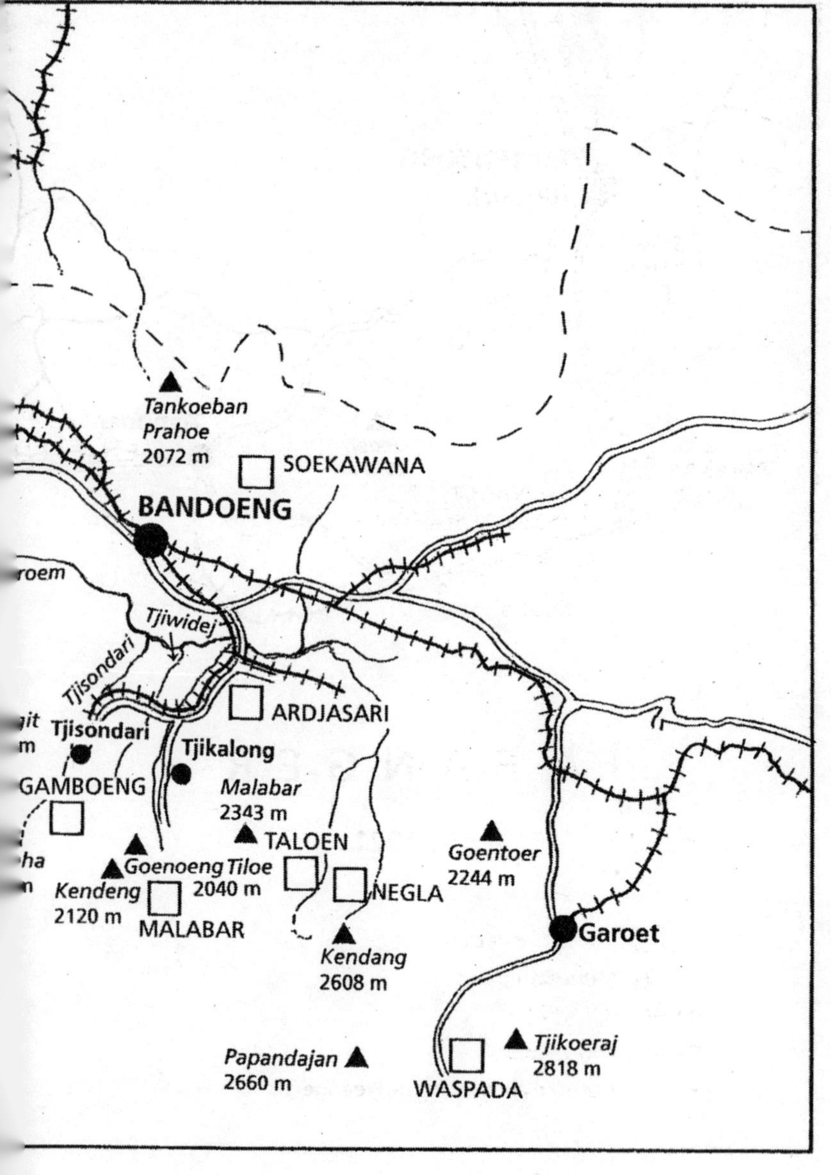
Tankoeban
Prahoe
2072 m
SOEKAWANA
BANDOENG
Tjiwidej
Tjisondari
ARDJASARI
Tjisondari
Tjikalong
GAMBOENG
Malabar
2343 m
TALOEN
Goentoer
2244 m
Goenoeng Tiloe
2040 m
Kendeng
2120 m
MALABAR
NEGLA
Garoet
Kendang
2608 m
Papandajan
2660 m
WASPADA
Tjikoeraj
2818 m